THE RIVER RUNS DEEP

MICHAEL BRADY BOOK 2

MARK RICHARDS

AUTHOR'S NOTE

The River Runs Deep is set in Whitby, on the North East coast of England. As I'm British and the book's set in the UK, I've used British English. The dialogue is realistic for the characters, which means they occasionally swear.

This is a novel. I've taken some slight liberties with the number of police officers there would be in Whitby. Other than that I have tried to stay faithful to the town and the surrounding countryside.

As it's a work of fiction names, characters, organisations, some places, events and incidents are either products of the author's imagination or used fictionally. All the characters in this book are fictitious. Any resemblance to actual persons, living or dead, is purely coincidental.

www.markrichards.co.uk

SEPTEMBER 2015: THE RIVER ESK

"Daddy."

Maisie Hopkins was four. Red hair, brown eyes, a mischievous face. A little girl that liked to ask questions. She tugged her father's sleeve.

"Give me a minute, sweetheart. I'm paying for our rowing boat."

"Daddy!" She tugged her father's sleeve harder. "Daddy, why is that lady swimming?"

"What? I don't know. People do swim in rivers. Even in September. Wild swimming, they call it."

"Yes, Daddy. But why is she swimming with all her clothes on?"

Nine minutes later PC Dan Keillor was standing at the side of the River Esk in Ruswarp.

It wasn't just Maisie. No-one would be going on the rowing boats today.

The lady with all her clothes on was face down in the water. Her blonde hair streaming out behind her as if it was trying to float down the river and out to sea. Another hundred yards and she'd have been over the weir.

A dark blue bodywarmer, faded blue jeans, green wellingtons. Dressed for an early morning walk. Not the cold, dark water of a North Yorkshire river.

Dan Keillor thought he could reach her. Maybe. "You haven't got a longer boathook in there have you?"

They hadn't.

"Jake, give me a hand will you? Hold on to me. I don't want to go in. 'Dozy copper falls in the river.' I can live without being on YouTube."

And with PC Cartwright hanging onto him Dan Keillor managed to hook the dark blue bodywarmer. 'Like that game at the fair when I was a kid,' he thought – ashamed of himself for thinking it.

Six or seven ducks watched from the middle of the river. Slowly, carefully, he pulled her into the bank.

Keillor knelt down on the concrete. Turned round and spoke to the middle-aged man who'd opened for business ten minutes ago. Who definitely wouldn't be taking £5 for an hour on the rowing boats any time today – but who was already thinking the *Mirror* might be interested in the pictures on his phone...

"Keep everyone back, will you? And make sure they don't get in the way when the paramedics arrive."

Keillor leaned forward. The second body he'd pulled out of the water in four months. A lot easier than the last one. No stripping down to his boxers. No wading into the North Sea.

But just as dead.

He started to pull her out. He'd need some help. She was heavy, her clothes saturated with water.

He turned and called Jake back. Saw that the paramedics had arrived. Louise? Was that her name? She'd been at his first RTA. Experienced, no nonsense, not fazed by anything. Good.

He hauled the woman up and saw her face for the first time. Her eyes were closed, her mouth half open. She looked resigned, Keillor thought. Resigned to her fate. But somehow... defiant at the same time.

"Come on then, Jake. Let's get her out."

It was hard work. Lifting the dead weight out of the water. But finally she was lying on the bank. Back on dry land. Exactly where Maisie should have been holding her daddy's hand as she stepped nervously into the rowing boat. But where – if she ever came back to Whitby – she'd remember the lady who went swimming with all her clothes on.

"No," Louise said to Dan Keillor. "No pulse. And looking at her I'd say there's not been a pulse for two or three hours."

"You don't recognise her, I suppose?"

Louise shook her head. "No. Not at all."

"Let's hope someone reports her. There's no ID in her pockets. No cards, nothing. Not even a phone. A dog lead. Some very soggy dog biscuits. Nothing else."

1

Detective Chief Inspector Michael Brady was cold. He was several degrees beyond cold.

And there was still a lap of the cross-country to go.

Here she came. "Come on, Ash!" he shouted. "*Come on*, you can catch her."

Ash was fourth. The girl in third was 20, maybe 30 yards in front of her. The first two were away and gone. And if the leader –

Yellow and black. Is that York? I need to learn the local schools.

– didn't run for England there was no justice in the world. The girl in second was well clear. But Ash could get third. "Come on, Ash!" he yelled.

His 13 year old daughter – pain and determination etched on her face – ran past him and chased a black and red vest up a hill and into the fog.

"She'll catch her." Fiona Gilroy was next to him, waiting for her daughter, Bean, to appear.

"Maybe," Brady said. "I'm not sure Ash has run this far before. Look, here's Bean. Jessica, sorry."

Fiona laughed. "I'm going to wave the white flag. I'm the only one who still calls her Jess."

Bean didn't look like she was enjoying the cross-country. No wonder. Richmond Moor was cold, bleak and damp. They were so high up Brady wasn't sure whether it was fog or low cloud. And it was only late September. Welcome to the school cross-country league. North Yorkshire promised to be very different to Manchester...

"There's Ash!" Fiona said.

Brady strained his eyes. Was that Ash on the far side? Was that a blue and white vest? And where was the girl in front of her?

"Come on, Ash!" he yelled into the fog, deciding to take Fiona's word for it. "You can catch her!"

His phone rang.

North Yorkshire. Eight hundred feet up, the top of a moor, in the fog and there's still a signal? I'd been counting on a quiet afternoon...

Brady glanced down. Geoff Oldroyd. The pathologist. A bluff, no-nonsense Yorkshireman not given to political correctness or to holding back on his opinions.

Brady liked him. But a pathologist wasn't as important as his daughter. He pressed the red button and stared hopefully into the fog.

He'd Googled it that morning. Richmond Moor had once been a racecourse.

They must be in the home straight by now.

The leader flowed effortlessly past him. Waved nonchalantly as she broke the finishing tape. The girl in second looked resigned to a winter chasing the yellow and black vest.

Brady stared into the fog. The seconds passed. There. The girl in the red and black vest came out of the gloom. And Ash. Four, five yards behind her. A hundred yards to go.

"Go, Ash! Come on, Ash!"

She was gaining. Two yards behind. One. Barely any distance to go. Ash was level. Brady saw his daughter glance across at the other girl. Dig deep inside herself. One last effort. She surged across the line. Snatched third place.

Fiona put her hand gently on his arm. "I'm not sure parents are supposed to get that excited, Mike..."

"GEOFF, I'M SORRY." The congratulations were done, the Lucozade Sport had been handed out. He'd even had a hug from a very wet daughter. "I'm on top of Richmond Moor, I lost the signal. What can I do for you?"

"Nothing. But I've a young woman on the table in front of me. And... I don't know, Mike. She drowned. Yesterday morning. But I was away all day. Something doesn't look right. And it doesn't feel right. Are you busy?"

"I'm freezing to death watching my daughter in a cross-country. But she's just finished. With you in an hour and a half?"

"That'll do. Di's out tonight. So there's no rush. Not like there's anything on TV on a Wednesday night."

"Can I bring a plus one?" Brady said.

"Bring as many as you like, Mike. Last orders is at ten, though."

BRADY WALKED ACROSS TO ASH. She was standing with Bean and Fiona. "Brilliant, Bean," he said. "Rather you than me in that fog."

"I hate it," Bean said. "Cross-country is definitely child abuse. We should sue."

Brady and Fiona laughed. "What's happened to photography?" her mother said. "I thought I'd put you off law?"

"Are you both going back on the school bus?" Brady asked.

Ash and Bean rolled their eyes. "Yes. We've been lucky," Ash said. "We've come in the school bus that smells of stale vomit."

"Not the one that smells of stale pee," Bean finished for her.

Brady turned to Fiona. "Could I..."

"Could I collect Ash from school for you?" she said. "Of course I can. And I'll give her something to eat."

"Thank you. I seem to be forever in your debt."

"So what is it now?"

He smiled at her. "You know me. I was talking to the pathologist. He's made me an offer I can't refuse. I've been invited to look at a dead body."

HE PARKED outside her mother's house. Detective Sergeant Frankie Thomson – grey eyes, dark brown hair tied back, jeans, favourite leather jacket and still reminding Brady of a warrior princess from *Lord of the Rings* – was waiting for him.

But a warrior princess who looks vulnerable today. Who knows she's fighting a battle she can't win.

"How's she doing?" Brady asked as Frankie climbed into the Tiguan.

"The same," she sighed. "Just the bloody same." Frankie leaned forward. Put her head in her hands. Breathed in deeply. Shook her head as though she was trying to shake the futility away.

"Just the bloody same," she said again. "I was Louise today. But at least she still knows she has a daughter. She called me Katie yesterday. 'How's my little girl?' she said. That's when it breaks my heart."

"You don't..."

"Tell her that Katie's dead? No. Supposing she grasps it? What's the point of causing her pain?"

Brady didn't know what to say. But felt he had to say something. "Yeah, I can see that."

"She's in this bloody awful place," Frankie said. "She has moments of clarity – some insight – and you can see she knows what's happening. It's beyond cruel."

Brady started the car. "I'm really sorry," he said. "It must take a toll."

"What can you do?" Frankie shrugged. "It hacks away at you. Day after day. Anyway, you're clearly here to cheer me up, boss. Give me some good news. Who have we fished out of the harbour?"

"No-one. Well, not this afternoon. Geoff Oldroyd's been on the phone. He's doing an autopsy. Correction, done an autopsy. But thinks we might be interested."

"Sounds good to me. Alex is at some staff meeting at school until late. Looking at a dead body and fish and chips on the way home. The best night out a girl can get in Whitby. I'm all yours..."

A TEN MINUTE CAR JOURNEY. He'd left Frankie alone with her thoughts. Her mother, memories of her sister. He'd stayed silent.

"You ready for this?" Brady said. "However many of these I see I still can't get used to them."

"Dead bodies or autopsies?"

"Both. Everything. The body on the table. The smell. The complete absence of life. All of it."

"I'm guessing it's Gina Foster?" Frankie said as she got out of the car.

"Geoff didn't say. But yeah, you'd think so."

"I thought she drowned?"

"She did. Dan Keillor fished her out. Seems to be his role in life. But there's clearly something Geoff doesn't like."

The body was laid on the table. A young woman, mid-30s, blonde hair fanned out behind her. Her skin pale, but Brady knew that was the effect of the water.

He shook hands with Geoff Oldroyd. "Geoff, how are you doing? You know Frankie, obviously."

"I do. I do. In both of her incarnations. Miss Thomson used to teach my youngest. When she had a proper job. Before she ran away to join the circus."

"How's he doing?" Frankie asked. "Robbie wasn't it? He was a bright boy."

"Second year at Imperial. Not that paying his rent in London is doing his dad's bank balance any good."

"What have you got for us, Geoff?" Brady asked.

"Gina Foster, as you no doubt guessed."

"I thought it was straightforward?"

"She drowned, Mike. Pure and simple. Her lungs were full of the Esk and that's what killed her."

Brady didn't reply. He walked round the table and looked down at the body.

"So what set the alarm bells ringing, Geoff?"

"Look."

Geoff walked over to the body. "There are marks on her face. The Esk has done its best to wash them away. But there are abrasions. For want of a better word, scuff marks."

"Like when you're a kid?" Frankie said. "When you fall over and scuff your knees?"

"Exactly." Geoff took a pencil out of his top pocket. Used it to point without touching the body. "Here, on her left cheek."

Brady bent over and looked. Squinted. Had to admit it to himself. He couldn't quite see what Geoff was pointing at.

I'm 43 next month. None of the detectives on TV have reading glasses...

"Frankie, what do you think?" he said.

He moved out of the way so Frankie could look. "If she was in the river she could have bumped along the side of a bridge, couldn't she? The stone could have done that. The old bridges over the Esk must have some rough edges. Or branches hanging over the water?"

Geoff shook his head. "Not if she's floating face down. And the angle's all wrong. Try it yourself. Walk over to that wall and scrape your cheek along it. Bloody difficult, even for someone young and fit. There's something else," Geoff added.

"What's that?"

"There are some bruises on her left arm. Just below her shoulder. They look relatively new. This week. But not the last two days."

"So what are you saying, Geoff? Domestic violence?"

"Maybe. But she lived on a farm. Must have helped her husband. Bruises would have been an occupational hazard. But they're consistent with someone doing this."

He reached out to Frankie. Took hold of her left arm with his right hand.

"So there might have been a struggle?" Brady said.

"Might. That's the best I can say."

"Rough sex?" Frankie offered. "Could the marks on her face be carpet burns?"

Brady raised his eyebrows. "Careful, Frankie. Geoff will be needing one of his blood pressure tablets..."

"She definitely drowned?" Brady said again.

"No question. That's what killed her. Like I said, lungs full of water. Particles of mud – but you'd expect that in a river."

"Nothing that would make our life easier? Brain haemorrhage? Heart attack?"

Geoff shook his head. "No. Not a natural blonde, but not many people are. But she was in good health. Five-three, nine stone. A touch over 57 kilos if you want it in new money. Good muscle tone. Working on the farm, walking the dog." Geoff pointed at faintly visible tan lines. "Wore shorts and a t-shirt most of the summer. Exactly what you'd expect."

"Alcohol?"

"A trace. Maybe a glass of wine the night before. A slice of toast before she went out in the morning."

"So the simple explanation is that she went out for a walk, slipped and fell in the river?"

"Yes, that's the *very* simple explanation. But it doesn't feel right. That's why I'm talking to you, Mike. Public sector paperwork doesn't have a box marked 'hunch' – but right now I think it needs one."

"Something in your water?"

Geoff laughed. "Bloody incontinence at my age, Mike."

"It doesn't happen though, does it?" Frankie said. "Statistically, it doesn't happen. Where do we walk? Where we walk every day. Where we know the path. If there's a bit where we might fall in the river we walk round it."

"There you are, Mike. Miss Thomson the maths teacher strikes again."

"What do we know about the husband?" Brady said.

"Ian Foster," Frankie answered. "I checked yesterday. When the report came in. He's got a farm out at Grosmont. Nine years older than her. No record. Ploughs the fields and scatters and keeps himself to himself."

"He's the one that reported her missing?"

"Yes. Said he came in at lunchtime. The dog was there, but no wife. Thought she'd gone shopping. Said Tuesday was her day for going to Sainsbury's. Then he saw the car was still there. Thought she might have gone to see a friend."

Brady walked over to the table again, looked down at Gina's face. Scuff marks on her face, indeterminate bruises on her arm, her lungs full of the River Esk.

Is this a murder? Do I think it's murder? Or do I want it to be murder?

2

"What do you think?" Brady said. They'd left Geoff to go home to his empty house and 'nothing much on TV.' Now he was giving Frankie the promised lift home.

"We're just talking? Speculating?"

"Yes, obviously. You know me well enough by now. Nothing's off limits. No idea is too stupid."

"OK," Frankie said. "She drowned, clearly. If Geoff says she drowned, she drowned."

"You want something to eat?" Brady said.

Frankie looked at her watch. "Seven-thirty. The best time to eat fish n' chips. Sure."

"Alex won't mind you being late back?"

"Alex is acting head of department. You think the police is bad. You should try teaching. He's drowning in paperwork. I can't remember the last time we had a night out."

Brady parked behind the Co-Op. Sent Ash a text.

Just finished with the pathologist. Back for 9. Hope you're not aching too much.

No later, Dad. Remember it's a school night.

"Trenchers?" he said. "Magpie?"

"No, not for a takeaway. The little shop through the alley. Turn left at the end."

Brady came back with the fish and chips. They walked down the steps by the swing bridge and sat on one of the benches.

"Not sure I've seen the water this high," he said.

"Spring tide," Frankie replied.

Brady looked at the lights from the pubs and shops on Church Street, sparkling and reflecting off the water.

"I need Carl to do it justice," he said.

"How's he doing?" Frankie asked.

"Yeah, good. He's part of an exhibition next week. Work by new students."

Will I ever forget? Watching Jimmy Gorse throw Carl off the end of the pier? No, I won't.

"It's one of the fundamental questions of life, isn't it?" Brady said five minutes later.

"What is?"

"Why fish and chips tastes better with your fingers. It's just an inescapable fact. Outside. By the sea. With your fingers. Whoever invented those wooden chip forks needs to be on a spit, revolving in hell."

"Next to the bloke that came up with 'paperless office,'" Frankie said.

"Right. He wasn't in the police, that's for sure."

Brady looked across Whitby harbour again. The tall ship in front of him. The swing bridge to his left. And behind the swing bridge, the alley. New Way Ghaut.

Where his best friend had been murdered. Five months ago...

"It can't be long now," Frankie said.

"What are you, some sort of mind reader?"

"It's not hard to see where you're looking. When did you last hear from her?"

"Kara? A couple of weeks ago. Says she's fine. But they've pushed her date back a few days. Some time around the 20th, she said."

"And the baby's definitely..."

"Definitely Patrick's? Yeah. She had the blood test. Anyway, that's for next month. What did you make of the late Mrs Foster?"

Frankie finished off the last of her haddock. Rummaged in her pocket and fished out a well-used tissue. "Drowned, obviously," she said. "And judging by what was in her pockets very clearly drowned while she was walking the dog."

"I'd like to think Archie would jump in and pull me out. Clearly not. The dog must have gone back to the farm. Sat by the back door barking until her husband came in."

"By which time she'd floated down the river into the arms of PC Keillor."

"What time did he phone?"

"Without checking I'm not sure, boss. Mid-afternoon, I think. I'll check the log in the morning."

"You can see a gap, can't you?" Brady said. "She says, 'I'm going to walk the dog.' He says, 'OK, I'm going to plough a field.' I don't know, what *do* farmers do at this time of the year?"

"That. Plough fields. Worry about money."

"So he goes off to plough a field. They might not have seen each other until lunchtime."

"So he doesn't have an alibi..."

"We're getting ahead of ourselves, Frankie. You don't need an alibi for accidental death. And right now that's what Geoff will say it was."

"With a caveat."

"Right. He said he had a 'hunch.' I thought you were the maths teacher, the analytical one?"

"I was," Frankie said. "I am. But my mother used to do that. Give us breakfast. Make sure we were ready for school. Give my dad a flask and a sandwich if he was going to be out all morning. Then she took Bess for a walk."

"So what are you saying?"

"I'm saying what I said yesterday. Mum went on the same walk every day. Across the fields, down to the river. Along the river bank. Back up the hill to our farm. And she never once piped up at teatime and said, 'Whoops, nearly fell in the river this morning.'"

"So you're ruling out an accident?"

"I'm saying it's unlikely. And I'm saying you don't get bruises like that on your arm by falling over in the barn."

"So we're left with suicide. Or murder."

"And we both know why it wasn't suicide."

"Exactly," Brady said. "No-one commits suicide in front of their dog. If I was going to do it, I wouldn't do it in front of Archie."

"So we're only left with one option, boss."

"No 'boss,' OK? We're off duty."

"Sorry. I'm trying to train myself to say it. For all he was a prick it came naturally with Bill – "

"But I haven't earned it yet?"

"No. It's not that. It's knowing you before. When you were a civilian."

"Not quite a civilian..."

"Yeah. But it's still different."

"What do you make of the marks on her face?" Brady said.

"Definitely not a bridge," Frankie said.

"You sound very certain all of a sudden?"

"I tried it while you were buying the fish and chips. I stood in the alley next to the shop and tried to scrape my face on the wall."

"That must have attracted a few odd glances."

Frankie shrugged. "It's Whitby. Once you've lived through a Goth weekend you're not going to be fazed by a policewoman trying to scrape her face down a wall."

"OK. So I'm in the shop wondering if you want mushy peas and you're in the alley trying to scrape your face on a wall..."

"Yeah. And thank you for the peas. You can do it – scrape your face – but it didn't happen by accident."

"So you think carpet burns are more likely?"

"*More* likely, yes. Likely? After they'd been together ten years? No. Besides, they have a teenage daughter. You don't have sex in the lounge if your daughter's upstairs doing her homework."

Frankie stood up and reached her hand out. "Thank you," Brady said, passing her his empty fish and chip box. She walked across to the bin, put the boxes in it. Turned and faced him. "Suppose you wanted to drown me," she said from six feet away. "How would you do it?"

Brady stood up and walked over to the railings. Stood next to her at the side of the harbour. Still couldn't believe how high the water was. Like someone had left the tap on. Filled the harbour too full.

"I'd hold you under," he said. "The middle of the sea and I can throw you off the boat. But a river's different. You're young, you're fit. I'd have to hold you under."

"Right," Frankie said. "That's what I thought."

"So there's doubt. A lot of doubt. Maybe we should go and talk to Ian Foster. And first thing tomorrow I'll have a word with Dan Keillor. I like him. He's bright. Let's see what he's got to tell us."

Brady closed Dan Keillor's file.

The son of a Scottish deep-sea fisherman and an English mother. His father's boat had gone down when Dan was 16. Last reported position 50 nautical miles south east of Iceland. His mother had come back to Yorkshire.

Lose someone you love. Come back home. Sounds familiar...

Dan had joined the police at 18, excelled at police college, translated the theory into practice. And waded into the North Sea to retrieve Jimmy Gorse...

He knocked on Brady's door. "You wanted to see me, boss?"

Just over six foot. Dark haired. Better looking than any copper in North Yorkshire Police had a right to look.

"Morning, Dan. Sit down. Gina Foster. You pulled her out of the Esk. Tell me all about it."

"There's not really that much to tell, boss. We got the

call, drove down there. Nine, maybe ten minutes tops.
Jake was on crowd control, I fished her out."

"Describe her."

"She's floating. Face down. Body warmer, jeans,
wellingtons."

"Dog lead in her pocket?"

Keillor nodded. "Nothing else though, boss. No
wallet, no cards."

"No phone?"

Keillor shook his head.

"Why not?" Brady asked.

"Maybe she forgot it?"

"Come on, Dan. I read your file this morning – some
of the reports from police college. You can do better than
make a guess. When was the last time you went out and
forgot your phone?"

Dan nodded. "OK, boss. Never."

"Right. Money, cards, car keys, phone. Just the same if
I'm walking my dog. Lead, biscuits, ball if we're going on
the beach. Black bags for the inevitable."

"You're saying she left it behind on purpose?"

Brady nodded. "Why would she do that?"

"No signal?" Keillor said. "No point taking it?"

"Supposing she sees a kingfisher? Supposing the
mist's rising off the river, the sunlight reflecting through
it? We all take our phones."

"You're saying she made a conscious decision to leave
it behind?"

Brady nodded again. "That would be my guess.
Another question: when do you turn your phone off,
Dan?"

"When... When I'm with my girlfriend. You know, when..."

Wait until you're a DCI, Dan. You won't even turn your phone off when you're... You know...

"Right. And that's the only time. So we assume that Gina Foster didn't want disturbing on her walk. And that she wasn't into photography. But if that's the reason, why not just turn it off? Why take a conscious decision to leave your phone behind? Especially a woman. A lonely walk by the river. No telling who she might meet."

"I don't know then," Dan said.

"No, right now neither do I. But it's a question we need to answer. Let's backtrack. You pull the body out. No marks, nothing you can see?"

Keillor shook his head. "Nothing. Just the clothes she was wearing. Nothing in her pockets except the dog lead. Tissues, some very soggy dog biscuits."

"No bumps, bruises, scratches?"

"Nothing I could see, boss."

"Which more or less tallies with what Geoff Oldroyd said." Brady paused. Looked out of the window. The hospital entrance: the car park. Maybe he should have joined counter-terrorism instead. The Thames and the London Eye out of his office window...

"You said Jake Cartwright was on crowd control. Nothing unusual in the people watching?"

Keillor shook his head again. "No. A father and his daughter. They were the ones that spotted the body. I've got their details if you want them. Two other people waiting for the boats. Husband and wife walking past who stopped to look. Exactly what you'd expect at that time in the morning."

"No-one on their own? No-one with 'suspicious' tattooed on their forehead?"

"No, boss. Definitely not."

"One more question, Dan. How did she look?"

Dan looked confused. "Gina Foster? Dead, boss."

"No, think past that, Dan. Some people die looking surprised. Some – if you believe the stories – die looking terrified. What about Gina? What was the expression on her face?"

Dan Keillor looked past his boss. Saw the face again as he pulled her out of the river. "She looked resigned, boss. Like she accepted it. But – this sounds stupid – "

"No, Dan. One thing you'll learn working with me. Nothing ever 'sounds stupid.'"

Dan nodded. "In that case, boss, she looked defiant as well. I don't know, the two sound contradictory. But that's how she looked. 'I'm not going down without a fight.'"

Brady smiled. Tapped his finger on the desk. Looked out of the window again. Made a decision. "This case might develop, Dan. If that happens DS Thomson and I will need some help. I'd like you to do that. Probably just for a few days. Sorry, it's all 'might' and 'maybe' right now. But if it happens I'll square it with whoever I need to square it with."

Dan smiled. "I'd love to, boss. Sorry, I mean 'yes, sir.'"

Brady laughed out loud. "Don't apologise to me, Dan. Nothing wrong with ambition. It's a long time ago, but we were all young once."

. . .

BRADY WALKED through into the main office. "You busy today, Frankie?" he said. "Fancy a ride out into the country?"

Frankie put her pen down and looked up. "I assume we're not taking a picnic, boss?"

Brady shook his head. "Ian Foster. I thought we'd pay him a visit. I've just talked to Dan Keillor. Five minutes alright for you?"

"Five minutes is fine, boss."

"Good. I'll see you at the car."

"Mike?" Brady turned. His superior officer. Detective Superintendent Alan Kershaw. Silver haired, silver-tongued, and sliding steadily up the promotion ladder. "Spare me a minute will you?"

Brady followed Kershaw into his office. The office without the view of the hospital car park. The harbour instead. Whitby Abbey on the hill above it.

...And the office with the ego wall.

What is it some people call it? The 'Me Wall.'

The Vanity Wall.

Certificates, commendations. And photographs.

There wasn't one of Kershaw with Barack Obama or Nelson Mandela but he'd managed to be photographed with just about everyone else.

David Cameron. Alan Shearer. Ant and Dec.

Even Nicola Sturgeon.

Just in case Scotland invades. Whitby's only 130 miles from the border. Best be on the safe side...

"You got anything important on today?" Kershaw said.

"I was going out to interview Ian Foster."

"The one whose wife was floating down the Esk?"

Brady nodded. "It looks accidental. But Geoff Oldroyd has some doubts. There's a few inconsistencies."

Kershaw shook his head. "You'll be wasting your time. Accidental death. All the rain we've had lately. The path would be slippery. I've got something more important for you. But if you insist on someone going out there send DS Thomson. Tell her to make sure she takes Sally Brown. Got to tick the Family Liaison box, remember."

"Is she around?"

"She should be. But Thomson can sort that out."

Kershaw looked up at him. "There's something I need your help with."

Brady stifled his surprise. Kershaw wasn't a man given to admitting he needed help.

"What's the problem?"

"No problem," Kershaw said. "Opportunity." He held a sheaf of A4 paper out to Brady. "I'm giving a speech tomorrow. 'Initiatives in Modern Policing.' I remembered that presentation you gave in Birmingham. You made a couple of decent points. So I thought you might like to look through this for me."

This time Brady made no attempt to hide his surprise. "Yes... I'd be happy to. I'm just not sure it's the best use of my time, sir."

"Let me be the judge of that. Policing is changing. It's not all about crime now. Burglars don't have a bag of swag over their shoulder. We're part of society, Mike. A building block. An integral part of the foundations."

He pushed the papers even further forward. Brady had no choice other than to take them.

"Steve Jobs, Mike. 'People don't know what they want

until you show it to them.' A modern police service can do so much more than simply catch criminals."

Looking at Kershaw's speech seemed an easier option than listening to any more management clichés. "Early afternoon alright for you, sir? I expect you'd like some time to rehearse?"

"Perfect. I'm on the train at three. It's in Edinburgh. And there'll be some big hitters in the audience. Politicians. Media people. Important I make a good impression."

BRADY WALKED across to Frankie's desk. "I'm sorry," he said. "You'll need to do Foster on your own. I've got something far more important to do."

She turned her head. Gave him a quizzical glance. "Sounds exciting, boss."

"I'm Kershaw's new speechwriter. 'Initiatives in Modern Policing.' Forget nicking villains and all that old-fashioned crap. We're a building block in society."

"I knew that was my role. A building block with a shitload of paperwork. I'll give Foster a ring," she added. "Try and get out there this afternoon. You alright with that? If I finish this paperwork?"

"Sure. We need to get our priorities right. And you need to take Sally Brown with you. We're not just a building block. We're part of the foundations as well. Kershaw says we need to 'tick the Family Liaison box.'"

"No need," Frankie said. "I'm FLO trained."

Brady shook his head. "Just humour him will you?"

"If you say so. How do you want me to play it?"

"As low-key as you can. Whatever happened to his wife Foster's going to be in a mess. Just get some background. How he met her. What she did before they married. But most of all your general impressions. That goes without saying."

"Report back on Monday?"

"Any chance I could buy you breakfast? I'm impatient. I trust Geoff's instincts. And I haven't seen Dave for a while."

"Sunday morning?"

"If you can square it with Alex."

"Don't worry. That won't be a problem."

"Thank you," Brady said. And went back to his office to look at a speech.

4

_____

7:30 Saturday morning.

A pale, early-autumn sun was shining as Brady drove through Grosmont, went under the railway bridge and parked the car by the trees. He needed to be back for ten. Ash was playing hockey and wanted a lift to school. But 2½ hours must be enough...

He reached for his coat and the directions. He'd printed them off: the Esk Valley walk from Grosmont to Sleights. Three-and-a-half miles. And somewhere in that 3½ miles was the place where Gina Foster went into the River Esk.

He followed the instructions. Crossed the bridge, the trees at the side of it turning golden, and turned left.

What am I looking for? I don't even know if I am looking for anything. I just want to feel the walk. Take it in. Walk where Gina walked. See what she saw. And let the fresh air wash away Kershaw's bullshit.

'People don't know what they want until you show it to

them. A modern police force can do so much more than simply catch criminals.'

Brady walked past a row of houses. He was certain that if he went and knocked on the doors everyone who answered would be perfectly happy if the police did nothing *but* catch criminals.

And so would 90% of the coppers, sir...

Brady said 'good morning' to a man in his 30s who looked a lot fitter than his Labrador. Glanced at his directions again. *Continue along the bridleway to the first farm.*

This was a road, not a bridleway. But then the road bent to the left. The leaping salmon sign of the Esk Valley Walk pointed straight on. And Brady was very firmly on a bridleway.

Two male pheasants strolled across the track in front of him. Two more. The field to his right was full of them.

If I was younger and fitter I could catch Christmas dinner...

The river was to his right. He could see the row of trees that clearly marked it. Was there a walk down there? There was only one way to find out. A track to his right led down the side of a field to a five-barred gate. A hundred yards, maybe.

Brady looked around. He was alone except for the pheasants. He set off down the track.

The sign on the gate was uncompromising. *Stop, Look. Listen. Close and secure gates after use. Maximum penalty for not doing so £1,000.*

He slid the bolt back on the gate. Closed it behind him. And found himself standing on a railway line.

*The North York Moors Railway? Or the Whitby –
Middlesbrough line? Or is Grosmont on both?*

There was another gate between him and the river.
This time the bolt refused to move. Brady sighed and
started to climb over it. In his experience nothing good
came from climbing over gates that wouldn't open. But he
needed to see if there was a path by the river.

There was. Of sorts. But it was overgrown. Looked like
it ended in 50 yards. And you didn't walk your dog on a
path that could only be reached by climbing over a gate.

The river was to his right. But it was at the bottom of a
steep bank, heavily planted with fir trees. And protected
by a fence. Wooden stakes every four yards. Half a dozen
strands of barbed wire very firmly between him and
the Esk.

Wherever Gina had walked, it wasn't here. Brady
climbed over the gate, walked back up to the bridleway
and looked at the directions again.

*Go through the farmyard and follow the bridleway to the
next farm.*

There were no signs. Was this Ian Foster's farm?
There was no way of telling. But right now it didn't
matter. He was just someone out for an early morning
walk. Getting to know the area. Seeing where Gina might
have walked.

Brady glanced at his watch. Thirty-five minutes gone:
25 more and he probably needed to turn round.

There was an open barn on the left, what looked like
a woodshed to his right. A pile of logs, an axe waiting
expectantly on top of them. A washing line with a pair of

jeans and two towels on it ran from the end of the shed. A white pickup truck was parked at the far side of the yard.

And Brady was through the farmyard, starting to walk uphill now. He could see the second farm in front of him. But the path led away to the left, only wide enough now for one person. He went through a small gate. The path became old, worn stone steps, wet and slippery with the autumn leaves. Brady carried on up the hill, finally came to another field. Even more pheasants than the previous one, a stunning view across the valley.

But very clearly, *not* where Gina Foster had walked her dog.

He was going further and further away from the river.

Brady ate one of the bananas he'd brought and started to retrace his steps, slipping more than once as he went back down the steps.

He walked through the farmyard and back towards the bridleway. A wasted trip. He'd learned that his new walking boots were waterproof, but that was it.

There was another track off to his left, a field to one side of it, a row of trees on the other. Just wide enough for a tractor, bending slightly to the left and disappearing out of sight. Brady couldn't see a gate.

Does that mean the railway line has crossed the river? Can I walk down and have a look?

No, he couldn't. There was someone – a farm labourer maybe – in front of the farmhouse.

I could go back and ask. Pretend to be a walker who doesn't know the area...

He'd no sooner thought it than he dismissed it.

Supposing it's someone I have to question? 'We've already

met haven't we? Except I thought you were someone who didn't know the area?'

And he needed to get back for Ash. Three years and she could learn to drive. It couldn't come soon enough.

He walked back past the row of houses. Back over the bridge. The river was running quickly, swollen by the rain.

I need to come back. I need to see where that track leads. But first things first. Let's see what Frankie has to say...

5

Brady was there early. But not before Dave.

"Blimey, Dave, even on a Sunday morning at the end of September?"

"Aye, it's not just tourists. You've been here long enough now. Lads going out for a day's fishing. They need a bacon sandwich or two."

Brady looked past the kiosk and out to sea. "Looking a bit choppy," he said. "Rough out there today."

Dave looked at him sceptically. "Is that your way of trying to get out of our fishing trip?"

Brady laughed. "The North Sea. Barely light. Freezing cold. Seasick. Would I do that to you, Dave?"

"Aye, I'm beginning to think you might. End of October remember. An' a bit of swell is part of the fun."

Brady bought a bacon sandwich and a coffee. "And take the money for Frankie as well, will you? She should be here in five minutes."

"How's she doing?" Dave asked.

"You're talking about her mum now?"

Dave nodded. "Yeah. When the wife's mother was going downhill she was round there every day. Awake half the night worrying..."

"I suspect Frankie is much the same. It's – "

He broke off. Frankie had arrived. "What's this?" Brady said. "The official start of winter?"

The leather jacket was gone. She was wearing a charcoal grey winter coat, a grey beanie hat pulled over her ears. A black scarf. "As you're undoubtedly going to suggest we sit by the bandstand, yes. Loyalty to Dave is all very well," she said, giving Dave an exaggerated wink. "But making a member of your team – sorry, a building block – freeze to death is entirely another."

"The sun's trying to come out," Brady protested.

"And the wind's howling off the North Sea..."

Frankie collected her sandwich and coffee from Dave and they walked the 50 yards to the seats by the bandstand.

"He's unbelievable isn't he?"

"Dave?" Brady replied. "That and indestructible." He paused. Looked out towards the end of the pier. "I tell you, Frankie, there are very few people in this world I admire, but Dave is one of them. I went to see him. Did I tell you? He's sitting in his lounge. Three, maybe four days after he's come out of hospital. I ask him when he's going to put the business up for sale. He tells me to – well, you know Dave. You can imagine what he said."

"I'm guessing he was fairly blunt."

Brady laughed. "You could say."

"Put it up for sale? What the fuck do I want to put it up for sale for?"

"I just thought – "

"Yeah, so did the wife. So did every other bugger I talked to. But if I put it up for sale he's beaten me, hasn't he? Jimmy Gorse has frightened me off."

Dave reached forward. Defiantly ate half a slice of his wife's carrot cake in one mouthful. "It's not what happens to you in life, Mike. It's how you react to what happens. And if I sell the business because I'm going to see those steps every day then what's it mean? It means I can't walk down by the harbour any more. And if I can't do that then I can't go fishing. And if I can't go fishing then we might as well leave Whitby. Move to Spain and drink gin for my breakfast." Dave shook his head. "I'm not having that. I've talked to the doctor. Three weeks he says."

"What does Maureen say?"

"Three months. Three months somewhere warm in the winter instead of two. I can live with that. We've made a deal."

"The guy's a hero," Brady said. "In every sense of the word."

"From one hero to another," Frankie said. "How did you get on with Kershaw's speech?"

"Do you want the truth or do you want me to pay due deference to a senior officer?"

"As it's Sunday you probably ought to tell the truth..."

"In that case it was 3,600 words of management buzz-words and bullshit. I just hope no poor sod paid for a ticket."

Brady finished his bacon sandwich. Screwed the paper bag into a ball. "Sorry," he said. "I have to do this. I know it's childish. But Patrick did it the first time – the only time – we sat here." The rubbish bin was five yards away. He took aim. The bag arced gracefully towards the bin. And fell a yard short.

"You didn't allow for the wind off the sea, boss."

"You're right. The trick's obviously to wait for a day with no wind."

"Some time next April, then..."

"So tell me how you got on with Foster," Brady said. "Was Sally any use?"

"She didn't come," Frankie said.

"What? Kershaw specifically told me to take her."

"I'm sorry, boss. I did my best. I was ready to go. I went to tell her. She wasn't there."

"So where the hell was she?"

"On the train to Edinburgh, apparently."

"With Kershaw?"

Frankie nodded. "Phil Sharpe said Kershaw had changed his mind at the last minute. Decided he needed a female officer with him. Wanted to 'tick the diversity box.'"

Brady shook his head. "So who did you take?"

"I grabbed Jake Cartwright. My first thought was to take Dan Keillor, But then – with him pulling her out of the river – I thought it might be too much for Foster."

"Tell me the story then. We've ticked the 'writing speeches' box and the 'diversity' box. Just on the off-chance we need to tick the 'solving crimes' box."

"Can I get a refill, boss?" Frankie held her empty cup up. "Dave's coffee has moved up a notch. He said he had a new supplier. You want some more?"

"No, I'm fine thanks."

Frankie went for a refill. Brady looked across the harbour.

Five months since I sat here with Patrick. Five months since he told me about his new wife. A few weeks later I'm telling Frankie how I'm planning to catch his murderer...

Brady looked to his left. Couldn't see the hill where he'd scattered his wife's ashes because of the buildings.

I'm sorry. I've not been up to see you for a while. This week. I'll find time, I promise.

"Where do you want me to start?" Frankie said.

"Take it from when you arrive. But tell me which farm it is first. I walked through one yesterday morning."

"Barn on the left? White pickup truck?"

"Thanks," Brady said. "That's the one. So any detail, Frankie. However small."

"OK. So I got a nice, warm welcome," Frankie said. "I climb out of the car and his Border Collie – he's called Max – starts barking. I like to think I'm good with dogs, but this one decides to growl at me. Then Ian Foster turns up – "

"What's he like?"

"Black and white. Broad white stripe between his eyes..."

Brady forced himself not to laugh. "I understand there's a vacancy for a filing clerk in Arbroath, Detective Sergeant Thomson..."

"Sorry, boss. Open goal. I couldn't resist. Physically, Foster's tall. Broad. Dark hair that's receding. Hands the size of coal shovels. But right now he looks like a little boy lost. Rudderless. If that's not mixing my metaphors."

"Has he got anyone with him?"

"Says he's got a cousin. Says she's coming over in a few days."

"What about the daughter?"

"Maria?" Frankie shook her head. "She's away at school. Boarding school. Scarborough College."

"That's odd," Brady said. "What's she doing at a boarding school 20 miles down the road?"

"I asked him that. Said it was Gina's decision. He said Gina had decided there was 'too much interference' in the state sector. And she'd said they could afford it. He said that two or three times – how much he disliked paperwork. How he left all that side of things – all the books – to Gina."

"OK. Backtrack a bit. He takes you into the house..."

"Yeah. Dining kitchen. In what's very clearly a new extension. Lovely room – a big picture window looking out over the fields and across the valley."

"Gina again?"

"Emphatically. I asked him that. He said it was still a stable when Gina moved in."

"Did he make you a cup of tea?"

"No. Not because he was rude. I just don't think it occurred to him. Almost like he was looking round for Gina to prompt him."

"OK, so nice kitchen. Daughter's at boarding school. And he's lost without Gina. How did he meet her?"

"She was working at the solicitor's. He went in to sort out his mother's estate. There she was. Six months later they're married and she's moved in."

"What is he? Nine, ten years older than her?"

"Nine."

"So the daughter's not his?"

"No. Definitely not. She was two when he met Gina."

"Did you ask him about her background?"

Frankie nodded. "And this is where it starts to get interesting. Ian Foster says she's from Birmingham. He said he used to tease her about her Birmingham accent. Said he called her his 'little Peaky Blinder.'"

There was a fishing boat coming into the harbour. Brady saw the exact moment the harbour walls wrapped themselves around it. The moment the boat stopped fighting the swell and could relax...

"You think he loved her?" he said.

"I'd go further than that, boss. I'd say she's the only woman he's *ever* loved. Probably had a crush on someone at school. But she turned him down and he never plucked up the courage to ask anyone else out. He's one of those men that are just... awkward around women."

"So if she's from Birmingham, what's she doing in Whitby? People from Birmingham go to Rhyl. Weston-Super-Mare. Up the M6 to the Lakes."

"He said she wanted a fresh start. Somewhere new for her and the baby. And she'd seen Whitby on *Countryfile*."

Brady pulled his coat around him. "Presumably they weren't filming when the wind was coming off the sea. Just go back to when they got married. Did she stay at the solicitor's?"

"Sorry, boss. I didn't ask him that. But my impression was 'no.' That she started doing the books straightaway. More or less took control of everything."

Brady nodded. "It's working out well for Ian Foster isn't it? He gets a wife, a bookkeeper..."

"Someone to take over from his mother," Frankie said. "Stew and dumplings on the table when he comes in..."

"What's he say about Tuesday morning?"

"He says he feels guilty. Says he only kissed her once. He usually kisses her twice, he said. He was going to plough one of the fields, she was taking Max for a walk. She made him a flask of tea and a sandwich, said she'd see him at lunchtime."

"So then he gets back and she's not there?"

"He said at first he thought she'd gone to Sainsbury's. But then he saw the car was still there. So he thought she'd gone for a walk."

"Where's Max in all this?"

Frankie shook her head. "Foster said he was there when he came back. And that Gina sometimes went for a walk without him. He said she suffered from headaches. Said she had tablets but walking helped her when she felt a bad one coming on. But she didn't take Max because he always wanted to chase the pheasants. Fair point. There were hundreds of them in the fields."

"I've seen. Must be a poacher's paradise. So he finally phones at what? Four o'clock?"

"Just after. And we put two and two together and identify Gina Foster."

Brady was silent.

Someone else who's lost his wife. You'd better start liking paperwork, Mr Foster. Because doing the paperwork was the only thing that kept me sane at three in the morning...

"What's your gut feeling?" Brady said. "Is he telling us the truth?"

"Yes," Frankie said. "That is..."

"What?"

"He's telling us the truth as he believes it, boss. I'm certain of that. But whether the truth and what Ian Foster *thinks* is the truth are one and the same might be a different matter."

"So the obvious question. Was she murdered?"

Frankie stood up. Walked over and put her coffee cup in the bin. Came back and sat down. "We rule out suicide. Statistically she didn't commit suicide."

"Right. Farmers commit suicide, not their wives."

"Yes. And like we said the other night, you don't commit suicide in front of your dog."

"So you think it was an accident?"

"No, " Frankie said. "I don't. It's like I said to you about Mum. I swear to God she never talked about 'nearly falling in the river.' So I'm struggling with the idea of an accident."

The fishing boat was almost level with them now. A blue hull, orange cabin.

Has it been out overnight? Freezing cold and seasick is one thing. But freezing cold and seasick in the dark...

Judging by the number of seagulls it had been a successful trip. Whenever they'd gone out.

"We need to find where she went in the Esk," Brady said.

"There's a lot of river between Grosmont and Ruswarp," Frankie said. "And it won't all be Foster's land.

Not by a long chalk. That's a lot of walking, boss. Or a lot of search warrants."

"Good job I've got a plan then," Brady said.

Frankie looked doubtful. "You had a plan for Jimmy Gorse. That didn't quite work out..."

Brady smiled at her. "Don't worry. There's only me in this one," he said.

"What are you going to do?"

"Check the train timetable," Brady said. "And do what I should have done on Saturday morning."

6

'What I should have done on Saturday morning.'

Michael Brady opened a battered Ordnance Survey map. *Landranger 94. Whitby & Esk Dale.* A picture of a sunny Robin Hood's Bay on the front, the hill stretching out behind the village. A sheer drop from the cliffs into the North Sea.

The map was old. A sticker on the back said £3.25. Brady suspected OS maps cost a lot more now. But the river wouldn't have moved. Neither would the railway line.

That dotted line was the track he'd been on yesterday. Through the farmyard and into the woods, taking him away from the river and the black line that was the railway.

Brady's plan was simple. He was going to spend Sunday afternoon on the railway line. Technically, trespassing. And trespassing as far as Sleights if that was what it took.

The Whitby to Middlesbrough line criss-crossed the

river between Grosmont and Sleights. Never straying far from it. One, two, three... six bridges between the villages. The first one was far too close to the village. Five that he needed to worry about...

Trains were few and far between on a Sunday. There was one leaving Whitby at 12:50. Arriving in Middlesbrough at 14:28. One left Middlesbrough at 13:48 and got into Whitby at 15:22.

Let's allow 20 minutes for the train to travel between Whitby and Grosmont. Twenty-five to be on the safe side.

Brady didn't have a timetable for the North York Moors Railway – and the website was down.

Pickering to Whitby. So it goes through Grosmont. I'll have to risk it. A steam train will make plenty of noise. So a 90 minute window. Probably slightly longer. Not long enough to walk from Grosmont to Sleights and back. But unless Gina Foster strayed a long way from home on her dog walks, I've got long enough. And I don't think I'll need to cross all the bridges...

"ASH," he shouted upstairs, "How are you doing?"

"Two minutes," she called back. "I can't find my phone."

Brady was tempted to shout back and ask if she needed counselling. He bit his tongue at the last minute. Some days, 'It was a joke, love' was accepted as an explanation. Some days she simply looked at him. 'Dad, you're too old to make jokes. Middle aged men with grey hair are not funny.'

A year ago, even six months ago, he'd still seen traces

of his little girl. The one who sprinted down the hall and jumped into his arms as he came through the door. Now there was a young woman walking down the stairs.

Dark hair, a shade or two lighter than her mother's. The green in her eyes more pronounced. Only three or four inches shorter than him. Sassy, argumentative, confident.

And sarcastic. Brady loved that. Not that he told her...

"All set?" he said.

She nodded.

"Here." He handed her a bottle of red wine.

"What's that for?"

"To give to Fiona. To thank her for feeding you. I'm sure you and Bean will manage a glass..."

"Give it her yourself, Dad. I'm not matchmaking for you."

"I'm not asking you to 'matchmake,' Ash. It's to say thank you for roast beef and Yorkshire puddings, that's all."

"And trifle, Dad. Fi makes awesome trifle. And it's time you asked her out. I've told you before, Bean and I think it's a good idea. If you don't, someone else will."

"Shall we get in the car, sweetheart? You can give me dating advice as we drive to Bean's."

HE'D GIVEN Fiona the wine, stayed for as little time as was polite and promised to collect Ash by nine. He hadn't asked Fiona out.

Sunday afternoon and Grosmont was crowded. Tourists and walkers making the most of the late

September sun. Brady nosed into the last space in the car park, paid the council £2.50 for two hours and laced up his walking boots for the second time in two days.

He passed the houses again, said 'good afternoon' to assorted walkers coming in the opposite direction and was back on the bridleway.

Not for long. The path down to the railway line was on his right. Brady opened the gate. The fine for failing to close it was still £1,000.

Wonder what it is for trespassing...

Brady reached into the pocket of his bodywarmer. Found his disguise. Put it on. One of the best pieces of advice he'd ever received from a murderer...

'Just one question, Ray. Professional curiosity. How come no-one saw you?'

'Everyone saw me, Brady. But put a Hi-Vis on and no-one questions what you're doing. You want to kill someone in a hospital? Put a white coat on. You want to kill someone on a building site? Wear a Hi-Vis. Makes sense doesn't it?'

It did make sense. Brady fastened his bright yellow jacket and started walking down the railway line towards Sleights, the parallel lines of the tracks running in front of him.

Like the parallel planks on Whitby pier. Except this time there won't be Jimmy Gorse waiting for me...

How far had he walked? Half a mile?

Not even that.

Brady fought down the feeling of anti-climax.

It had been easy.

But that was real-life. You didn't always defuse the bomb with three seconds to go. Sometimes it really was easy. Some-

times it was done and dusted and you were in the pub well before the timer ticked down to zero.

Brady stood in the middle of the bridge. Old, pale green, criss-cross railings between him and the river. The latest health and safety edict had added a newer, pale blue row on top. He looked down. The Esk was wider than he'd expected. Twenty yards? Thirty? It was hard to judge from the bridge.

This was the place. It *had* to be the right place. To Brady's left a bank – framed by two large trees – sloped gently down to the brown water of the river. What were the trees? Beech? Sycamore? He'd always seen nature walks at school as a pointless distraction from cricket and football.

He reached for his phone and started to take photos. Leaned as far over the railings as he could. Was that the track he'd seen on Saturday? He forced himself to lean even further out. Took more photos. Stepped back and checked his watch. Still well within his 'no trains' window.

The river was swollen by the recent rain. Brady bent down and picked up the largest stone he could find. Tossed it into the middle of the river. The water fountained up. The river was deep. Flowing quickly.

He could see two lots of farm buildings. Ian Foster's must be the closest one. He'd find out soon enough...

He looked at the map again. The river went north, away from the railway line. Then turned back to it. Brady carried on walking towards Sleights. He had time to check the second bridge. But the bank went down to the river at a 45 degree angle. Perfect if you wanted to push someone in. Not so good if you wanted to guarantee they'd drown.

He turned and started walking back towards Grosmont. Looked at the gently sloping bank a second time. Took more photos.

And knew he'd found the place where Gina Foster went into the river.

Brady walked back to the gate. Was starting to take the Hi-Vis off when he heard a noise. A steam train. He quickly opened the gate. Twenty, thirty seconds. The noise – unmistakeable – grew louder. A dark green locomotive hurtled past, *Southern* written on the tender. No. 825. It was pulling three carriages. Brady saw the passengers, two or three of them looking at him. Just a railway worker in a Hi-Vis...

He remembered to close the gate behind him. Walked back up the track to the bridleway, looking like another late-summer tourist out for a walk. Not a man who'd just found a murder site.

He stopped and pulled the map out of his pocket. Counted the bridges again. The body would have floated under four of them as the river meandered its way to Sleights. *Could* that account for the marks on her cheek?

Then the river straightened out. Straight down to Ruswarp.

She'd have floated past the cottage where Carl's nan lived. Before she finally reached Ruswarp and Dan Keillor.

The body would have needed some... Brady didn't want to use the word 'luck.' But there were bends in the river. Some small islands in mid-stream. On another day she'd have snagged on a branch. Drifted into the bank and stayed there.

But it was academic. It didn't matter how she'd gone into the river. Or who'd been involved. Or whether the body had been 'lucky.' How Gina Foster had ended her journey down the Esk was now a simple matter of record.

BRADY WALKED BACK to the car park. He sat in his car and looked at all the photos on his phone. He needed to talk to Frankie. He needed to talk to Geoff Oldroyd. But it was Sunday afternoon. Frankie would be with her boyfriend. Geoff Oldroyd would be with his wife. Maybe even his grandchildren.

Detective Chief Inspector Michael Brady went home to an empty house. Made himself a fish finger sandwich. Gave half of that to his dog.

7

Monday was slow and painful. Frankie wasn't in. "She phoned in, boss. A day's compassionate leave. Her mother's had a fall."

Geoff Oldroyd was busy all day, Sally Brown didn't offer an apology or an explanation. Worst of all Kershaw's speech had gone well. 'Smug' was nowhere near adequate.

Ash had been late at school. Brady was waiting for her. And Geoff Oldroyd finally answered his phone.

"Detective Chief Inspector. What can I do for you?"

"I need to pick your brains, Geoff. Ten minutes, maybe 15. No more."

"No problem, Mike. And ten minutes sounds like a pint, not a teaspoon of Nescafé in the office."

"What time do you finish?"

"I'll be done by six. Some paperwork to wade through if you're alright with that."

"Perfect. I'll give Ash a lift home, organise some dinner for her and meet you. Where do you want to go?"

"Black Horse?"

"That's the one in Church Street? I'll be there as close to six as I can. I'll have a pint waiting for you."

BRADY PASSED Geoff a pint of Doom Bar. "What do you need to know, Mike? A pint of Doom buys you a fair amount of information."

"I'd like to talk about Gina Foster, Geoff. And how she died. But not in front of Frankie."

Geoff nodded. "Yep, I can see that."

"You're absolutely sure it's not suicide?"

Geoff shook his head. "It's not suicide, Mike. You've got to *work* at suicide. Drown yourself? You need weight and you need deep water. You want a text book example of how to do it... Well, that's why we're not talking about it in front of Frankie..."

Geoff reached for his drink. "Christ. What a fucking New Year's Day that was. And now the poor lass has got her mother going downhill at a rate of knots."

"So what would you do, Geoff? If you wanted to kill someone?"

"Around here? If I wanted to kill someone close to me I'd nudge 'em off the edge of a cliff. Have you been on the Cleveland Way lately? Couple of places where you're plenty close enough to the edge. Choose your time of day. It's deserted. No bugger can prove it wasn't an accident."

"Not drowning then?"

"Drowning's a bloody stupid way to kill someone, Mike. It's messy, it's unpredictable and, above all, it's time consuming."

"I thought you could drown someone in 30 seconds?"

"Of course you can. And you can drown someone in two minutes as well. But then you've got to be sure."

"So how long..."

"How long to drown our girl?"

Brady nodded.

"Alright, whoever's killed her has met her there."

Brady looked up, surprised.

"You're not the only one who can do detective work, Mike. I was curious. I had a drive out there last night. Just walked along the bridleway. You're not close to the river. I can't believe it's a chance meeting. He's met her there."

Brady picked his phone up. Tapped his code in. Opened *Photos*.

"Here, for example?"

Geoff took Brady's phone. Put his reading glasses on.

"Where's that?"

"At the side of a railway bridge. I walked along the railway line yesterday afternoon."

Geoff nodded. "Looks perfect. Looks better than perfect. If I had to drown someone that'd be as good a place as any. No paths near it?"

"Maybe one that I could see from the bridge. And I think there's a clearing just up from the bank."

"Like I said, my money's on meeting her there. Then he's dragged her down to the edge."

"There's no marks of that, though..."

"No. And there wasn't a lot of mud on her boots or her clothes either. A few hours in the river's taken care of that. But I stand by what I said, Mike. It's a bloody daft way to kill someone."

"Explain it to me..."

"Look at it from the killer's point of view. He has to force her under. Hold her there. He's not just got to drown her. He's got to watch her. The Esk is cold but it's not *really* cold. This isn't falling into the Arctic. There's three or four minutes watching her float off down the river."

"To make sure she's not faking?"

"Yep. Throw in meeting her and he's not going to get much change out of nine or ten minutes."

"And most of that time he's at the side of a railway bridge."

"Did you check the times of the trains?"

"Yes," Brady said. "Weekdays, early morning there's a 6:31 from Whitby. 6:55 from Middlesbrough. I don't know what time the North York Moors Railway starts – "

Geoff laughed. "It's not going to be half-six in the morning. But he's taking a risk with the other two."

"Yeah. The one from Whitby it's going to be dark – well, certainly not light – when it goes through Grosmont. And most people will get on the train and fall asleep."

"But the other one works," Geoff said. "The one from Middlesbrough."

"It does. And it's human nature. You're going over a river, you look out of the window."

"So he could be seen?"

Brady nodded. "It's unlikely. A witness would have to be on the right side. The angle might be wrong. I don't know. It can't take any time at all to cross the bridge. But it *could* happen."

"What happened to the old days, Mike? When a public spirited chap in a trilby pulled the communication cord and reported something suspicious?"

"You know as well as I do, Geoff. These days the public spirited chap's busy filming it. Wondering if it'll go viral."

"Shall we have another, Mike? The wife's at her sister's."

Brady couldn't say no. Geoff's refreshing bluntness always cheered him up.

"We've looked at it from the killer's point of view," Brady said when Geoff came back with the drinks. "What about from Gina's?"

"You're a ray of sunshine, I'll grant you that. Alright, drowning is a crap way to kill someone and it's an even crapper way to die. All this 'painless' and 'peaceful' stuff is – in the vast majority of cases – bollocks."

"Gina's being held down..."

"Right. She's face down in the water. Someone bigger, stronger than her. Either that or she's incapacitated in some way."

"But we've found no sign of that?"

Geoff shook his head. "None at all. She's not been tied up. Nothing like that."

"Maybe he's clever enough to cover it up..."

"But if he's that clever he's not going to choose the river. He's not going to drown her. I suppose that's why I phoned you the other day, Mike. It doesn't make any sense."

"How much pain would Gina have been in?" Brady said.

"A lot. That's what I meant. Don't believe this 'pain-less' nonsense. I remember talking to someone at a conference. He was in the sea, on holiday in Greece. Got caught by a current. Rescued in the nick of time. Said it was like someone pouring hot lava into his lungs. Anyone who thinks drowning is painless and peaceful needs to ask themselves why waterboarding is such an effective torture."

Brady finished his beer. Didn't say anything. Tried to push the image of Gina's final moments out of his head.

"Another thing," Geoff said. "Gina's in the river. She's breathed in. She can't help it. But she's at the edge so there's mud stirred up. That's what she's taken in. It's going to hurt like hell. It's a bloody awful way to die."

"So she knew she was dying?"

"Almost certainly. I'd say that was her last thought."

"What about the scuff marks on her face?"

Geoff nodded. "I've been thinking about those. Two options. One is he's holding her down. She's struggling. That would account for it. Or..."

"Go on..."

"Well, this sounds a bit more fanciful. Maybe she did it deliberately. Maybe *that* was her last thought."

"Send us a message you mean? 'I'm being murdered?'"

"*What was the expression on her face, Dan?*"

"*She looked resigned, boss. Like she accepted it. But – this sounds stupid –*"

"*No, Dan. Nothing ever 'sounds stupid.'*"

"*In that case, boss, she looked defiant as well. I don't know,*" *the two sound contradictory. But that's how she looked. 'I'm not going down without a fight.'"*

Geoff finished his pint. "Maybe," he said. "Maybe."

"Thanks, Geoff, I appreciate all that. The opinions as much as the details. You want another beer? Maybe talk about something lighter?"

Geoff shook his head. "Two's enough for me. Two's one too many for me. But I'm going to leave my body to science. Might as well give the pathology students something to talk about."

8

Three weeks and it would be dark at this time. "Come on, Archie. Let's go for a walk while there's still some light."

Archie wagged his tail, Brady reached for his lead. And his mobile rang.

Kate. His sister.

"Are you busy, Mike?"

"I'm never too busy for you. What's the matter?"

"Can I talk to you?"

"Sure. What's up?"

"No, talk to your face."

"This sounds serious, Kate. You don't want to give me a clue?"

"Can you come round, Mike?"

"I can, but I'll have to walk. I've had a drink with Geoff Oldroyd. The pathologist. So 15 minutes if that's OK? And can I bring Archie? He needs a walk."

Fifteen minutes was OK. Yes, of course he could bring Archie. Maddie was in. She'd take care of him while they talked.

"Ash? I'm going round to see Kate." Brady briefly wondered why 50% of his conversations with his daughter now involved him shouting upstairs. "I'm taking Archie. Maybe an hour? I'll lock the door."

He reached for Archie's lead a second time. Archie dutifully wagged his tail again. Brady wondered what Kate needed to tell him face to face.

HE RANG KATE'S DOORBELL. Five months ago he'd rung the same doorbell on Bill's 50th birthday. Ended the evening by coming face to face with Patrick.

He hugged his sister. Then held her at arm's length and looked at her. "You look tired, Kate. And you've lost weight. But before I commiserate with you I'd better say hello to Bill. Lounge or bedroom?"

Kate shook her head. "Neither," she said. "James Cook."

"Right. That's what you want to talk about."

Kate nodded. "And I haven't said anything to the girls. Give me a minute."

Brady walked into the kitchen. Archie followed him expectantly. "Maybe not, mate," Brady said. "I think you're going round the block..."

Maddie bounced into the kitchen. Just turned 18. Long brown hair falling past her shoulders, an open, enthusiastic face, her teenage freckles disappearing. Brady hugged her. The girl he'd brought back from Scarborough and her drug-dealer boyfriend.

What else are uncles for?

"How are you doing?" he said.

"Yep," she smiled. "I'm good. Except..."

"What?"

"What do you think, Mike?" Brady was secretly glad she'd dropped the 'uncle.' It made him feel old. "York or Lincoln?"

"Are we talking universities here?"

Maddie nodded. "Surrey first choice. York or Lincoln for back-up."

"Still forensics?"

"Chemistry with Forensic Investigation," Maddie said.

"I don't know. Depends how far away you want to be. Then again Guildford's far enough. York's Russell Group though isn't it?"

"Yeah. But they'll want higher grades than Lincoln."

"Have you been to see them both?"

"York, yes. Lincoln no. It's..."

"Difficult," Kate finished for her.

Bill had been diagnosed with bladder cancer five months ago. A course of chemo had rapidly followed. Brady had watched his brother-in-law struggle through the summer. A session of chemo, three weeks of recovery. He'd not been a happy patient.

"Lost my bloody hair. Lost my appetite. A week wandering round the bowels of hell. Don't ever get it, Mike. Chemo's bloody brutal. They try and kill everything without killing you. And all these bullshit quotes people keep spouting to try and make you feel positive. The bastard that said 'what doesn't kill you makes you stronger' never had chemo."

Brady had sat on Bill's bed. Told him how it was going

at work. Kept him up to date on the office gossip. Well, most of it...

And now he was back in James Cook Hospital at Middlesbrough.

"Maddie, will you take Archie round the block for me? I think my big sister wants to talk to me."

"Sure. Do I need any bags?"

Brady rummaged in his pocket. Gave her a handful of dog biscuits and three black bags. "Two's usually his limit," he said. "An extra one for luck. You should be alright."

"Kitchen table or lounge?" he asked after Maddie had gone.

Kate shrugged. "It doesn't make much difference. Do you want a drink? Another beer?"

Brady shook his head. "I'm fine. Two's enough for one night."

Kate sat down at the kitchen table. Sighed. Looked at Brady. "You know what I'm going to say, don't you?"

"Not exactly. But you clearly haven't won the lottery."

"They think the cancer's spread."

And judging by his sister's face, they thought it had spread a long way.

"How far?"

Kate shook her head. "They don't know. Or they won't say. They're doing some more tests."

Brady had consciously resisted asking Google about Bill's likely prognosis. He wanted to be positive for Kate. Didn't know a lot: but enough to know 'the cancer's spread' wasn't the phrase you wanted to hear.

"We've a meeting with the consultant in a couple of

weeks," Kate said. "They're doing some tests now. Blood count. White blood cells. All that."

"So..." Brady didn't know how to say it.

Kate said it for him. "Is my husband going to die? Yes. When is he going to die? I don't know. Presumably we'll have a better idea when we've spoken to the consultant. But you know what it's like. They told Marjorie – two doors down – her husband had three months. He lasted two years. Then they tell someone else a year and they're gone in a month."

Brady reached across the kitchen table and took her hands. "So you've some tough decisions to make."

Kate nodded. "Telling the girls. Maddie's got her A-levels. Work. That's an easy decision. I'm going to leave."

"You don't think... Just two days a week might be good for you?"

"I do think that. But what the hell do I do? You know our marriage hasn't been a bed of roses, Mike. But what do I say to him? 'You stay here throwing up, love and I'll be back at tea time?' I can't do it. However long he's got left – two months or two years – however much of a prick he's been, 'in sickness and in health' has to mean something."

"Shouldn't you wait until you've spoken to the consultant?"

Kate sighed. "You can tell, Mike. They do some tests, they look at the charts. Then they say, 'You're seeing Mr Hill?' And you say, 'Yes' and you both know what Mr Hill is going to say.

Brady nodded. He knew only too well.

. . .

HE LAY AWAKE, staring at the ceiling. Looked at the bedside clock. 03:14.

Brady sighed and swung his legs out of bed.

He'd always slept through the night. Whatever the pressures of the job – as long as he'd had Grace next to him he'd slept through the night.

But then three in the morning became an old friend.

He'd been worrying about Grace. Then coming to terms with her death. Worrying about Ash. Worrying about Patrick. Gina Foster. And now Kate... Two, three, four in the morning. Sooner or later he'd be staring at the ceiling, trying to read his book, or downstairs talking to Archie.

03:24 now – and it was the last one.

"Here," he said, tossing Archie a biscuit. "Come and sit next to me. Let's see if we can make sense of it."

Brady carried his tea – Earl Grey in the middle of the night – through to the lounge. He stretched out on the sofa, pulled the throw over him.

What have you bought that for, Dad? That's not the sort of thing you buy.

I saw it, Ash. Thought it would be nice for you and Bean if you were watching a film together.

Oh. OK. Cool.

It was an easy explanation. Easier than saying, 'Because I spend two nights a week on the sofa.'

Archie lay down on the floor. Brady reached a hand out and ruffled his head. "I'm going to go through it. Tell me if I get anything wrong, mate. There are three possibilities..."

But all Michael Brady needed was a physical presence. A body next to his. He reached down again. Felt Archie breathing peacefully. Pulled the throw round himself. Closed his eyes. Slept soundly until 'Presto' on his iPhone told him it was 6:30.

"YOU ALRIGHT, DAD?" Ash asked two hours later as he pulled up outside the school. "That's the third time in five minutes you've rubbed your neck."

"Yeah. Sorry. I must have slept awkwardly."

"You need to take care at your age, Dad. Beds can be dangerous things. Lots of people die in them. Especially old people..."

Brady smiled at her. "Stop being sarcastic. Or I'll get out of the car and hug you in front of your friends. I'll see you at..."

"Six," Ash said. "We're playing hockey at Pocklington. Bellatrix says – "

"Bellatrix?"

"Miss Gibson. When she has a bad hair day she looks like Bellatrix Lestrange. Anyway, she says we'll be back for six."

She opened the door, said, "Bye, Love you" and was gone before he had time to wish her luck.

Brady opened his contacts. Pressed *Frankie*. "All OK this morning?" he said.

"Yeah. Good. Well, good-ish. Louise is on duty today."

"Anything in your diary for this morning?"

"Nothing that can't be moved."

"OK. My office at nine. You, me, Dan Keillor and Gina Foster. Let's get this one nailed."

"No Dan?" Frankie said at one minute to nine.

"I've sent him out for some coffees. I swear to God my immune system won't survive that vending machine."

Brady hesitated. Decided to ask in person. "You said, 'good-ish' on the phone. How's she doing?"

Frankie shook her head. "I don't know. Good days, bad days. But the bad days are worse and the good days are what used to be bad days. How's the other patient?" she said. "Have you seen Bill lately?"

Should he say anything? No, it was Kate's decision how much she let people know. "Last week," he said. "Complaining about England's performance in the cricket and wishing he was on the golf course."

Dan was back with the coffees. "Flat white, boss? Frankie..."

"I want to make some progress," Brady said. "We *need* to make some progress. Kershaw seems happy to let this case drift... Sorry. Bad choice of words. He seems happy to have the case closed with the words 'accidental death' stamped on the file."

"And we have our doubts," Frankie said.

"We do. So let's go through the options. Frankie, I know you and I have covered some of these points, but only unofficially. I want to go through the whole process. Let Dan see our thinking. Feel free to interrupt me."

Frankie and Dan Keillor nodded. Brady poured a sachet of sugar into his coffee, mentally accepted he'd reached the age where he was never going to give up, and started talking.

"Gina Foster didn't die of old age so we have three options. Murder, accident, suicide. She had to die in one of those three ways. Suicide is statistically unlikely. And I've talked to Geoff Oldroyd... Frankie, I'm sorry to be discussing this in front of you – "

"It's alright, boss. We're all grown-ups."

"Even so, I'm sorry. I've talked to Geoff Oldroyd and suicide doesn't seem an option. Frankie there was nothing in your conversation with Foster to suggest she was unhappy?"

Frankie shook her head. "No. Foster didn't say anything like that. As far as he was concerned everything was fine. Except..."

"Except that?"

"Except he mentioned she used to go for walks on her own. Didn't even take the dog with her. That seems an unusual thing to do."

"Dan? Thoughts on that?"

"Maybe she was meeting someone, boss? Maybe she was seeing someone else? He's older than her."

Brady nodded. "Maybe. I've got to say that if she walked where I walked it's a bloody muddy place to have an affair. But maybe. Let's not rule it out. OK. Accident?"

"That's one I do rule out," Frankie said. "Like I said to you, boss. I'm certain she'd have gone on the same walk every day. My mum used to say that was one of the joys of doing the same walk. 'You see the seasons change.' I can hear her saying it."

"But we drive the same route into work," Dan said. "One day we have a crash."

"Right," Brady said. "But there's someone else involved. We don't suddenly drive into a wall."

"Unless we've been drinking. Or we're not paying attention. Or we're distracted. Or there's ice on the road," Frankie said.

"OK. I accept that..."

Am I arguing for it to be murder? Am I trying to persuade my junior officers? Do I need it to be murder that badly?

"...But do you think it was an accident?"

"No," Frankie said. "I'm not saying she couldn't slip and fall. You've got a dog, boss. How many times does Archie suddenly change direction and come close to tripping you up?"

Brady laughed. "Plenty. Especially if there's food involved."

"But," Frankie said. "There's a big difference between slipping and falling and slipping and falling into the river and drowning yourself."

Brady reached into his pocket. "Here," he said, handing Frankie his phone. "I did some scouting on Sunday afternoon."

Frankie stared at the picture. "You think that's the place she went in?"

"Scroll through," Brady said, "I took about 20. As many different angles as I could."

"What were you doing, boss? Standing on the railway line?"

"Yeah. The path I took on Saturday morning – the Esk Valley walk – goes further away from the river."

Frankie passed the phone to Dan. "It's ideal," she said. "Gently sloping bank. Shielded by the trees. Nice place for a picnic as well."

"Would there be footprints?" Dan said.

Brady nodded. "There might well be. But we can't just wander on to someone's land and start taking plaster casts until we've got just cause. Which is why we're talking now."

"Accident is more likely than suicide," Frankie said.

Brady nodded. "I grant you that. But we've still got a fit, relatively young woman with no significant trace of alcohol in her blood – no drugs, no medical evidence – having a bad enough fall to knock herself out and fall into the water."

"Geoff didn't say anything about a blow to the head."

"No. Because there wasn't one. So if it's an accident she's gone into the water conscious."

"Could she swim?" Dan said.

"Frankie? Did you ask Foster that?"

"Shit. No. I'm sorry, boss."

Brady shook his head. "No matter. We'll find out in time."

He paused. Asked himself the question again.

How badly do I need to prove myself in this new job? Supposing it's not murder?

"Murder," Brady said. "Let's consider the possibility that Gina was murdered. And the questions that go with it. Why? How? Who by?"

"The last two seem straightforward, boss," Frankie said. "Right now Foster is the only suspect. And given how she died, he held her in the water."

"Why would he do that though?" Dan asked. "I know nothing about farming but there must be 101 ways for a farmer to kill his wife before he needs to drown her."

"That's the problem for me," Brady said. "I asked Geoff Oldroyd how he'd kill someone. He said he'd push them off the cliff edge. You admit you were there. But there's no conclusive proof. It has to be the same for a farmer, surely? 'She was behind the combine. I started reversing. I didn't see her, officer...'"

"Unless that's how he wants us to think," Frankie said.

Brady shook his head. "I've only had one coffee. It's too early in the day for bluff and double-bluff. But murder's the only logical explanation for how she died."

"What about marks?" Dan said. "Where she was held down?"

"OK, she's got scuff marks on her face. Old bruises – as though someone has grabbed her – on her left arm. But marks where she was held down? There weren't any."

He stood up. Walked round behind Dan Keillor. Spread his hand out and put it between Dan's shoulder blades. "I press down now I'm going to leave a mark. You struggle, I press down harder, there's going to be a bruise.

But you're only wearing a shirt. Gina's wearing a t-shirt, sweatshirt and body warmer."

"Maybe he even uses his clothes, boss? Takes his jacket off?"

"I don't know, " Brady said. "I keep coming back to what Geoff said. Drowning is a bloody silly way to kill someone. Yes, sure, a rational person might use their own jacket as well. But drowning's an *irrational* way to kill someone."

"What about the marks on her face?" Dan asked.

"Three options," Brady said. "One, she scrapes her face on a bridge as she floats downstream. Frankie has spent a fun evening trying that in one of Whitby's alleyways. She says it's unlikely."

"Unlikely verging on impossible, Dan. Take my word for it."

"Two," Brady continued. "She's struggling. Logic says that's the most likely one. Three... She did it deliberately. What did you say, Dan? 'She looked defiant.' Maybe that was a last act of defiance. Sending us a message."

"There's a fourth possibility," Frankie said. "It happened at home. Again unlikely. But not impossible."

Brady finished his coffee. Made a decision.

The marks on her face. It can't be suicide. It wasn't an accident...

"Gina Foster was murdered," he said. "So we only have two more questions to answer. Who by? And why?"

Frankie smiled, "Who and why are our job, boss."

"Hopefully," Brady said. "Assuming I can convince Kershaw. Dan? Can you give us a minute? There's something I need to discuss with DS Thomson."

Dan Keillor stood up. "Can I ask one question, boss?"

"Of course you can."

"Boss... If she went into the water where you say she did. She's maybe three miles from where she ended up. I don't know how fast the Esk flows but..."

"But you think the body should have got to Ruswarp faster?"

Dan nodded. "Just simple maths, boss."

"Yeah, I've been thinking about that. I suspect the truth is that she got snagged somewhere for a while. Then she floated free again. There's plenty of bends. Little islands. That's probably the reason. Sometimes, Dan, we just have to deal with the facts we have. She took her dog for a walk. She met someone. Who held her under the water until she drowned. And later that morning you fished her out of the Esk."

10

"I'm sorry," Brady said when Dan had closed the door. "Some of that was going back over old ground. I wanted to do it for Dan's benefit. Thank you for being patient."

"No problem. Well, apart from the obvious one."

"Persuading Kershaw you mean?"

"What else? If he opens a murder investigation he has to find the killer. *We* have to find the killer. Kershaw's not going to want an unsolved murder on his record."

Frankie hesitated. "Can I speak freely, boss?"

"Yes, of course. You know that. You don't have to ask."

"Well. It's high risk for you as well. The first murder case since..."

"Since I arrived with my big-city reputation?" Brady shrugged. "You're right. And there'll be plenty of people who want me to fail. But what can I do? What can we do? If Gina Foster's been murdered it's our job to find out who did it. And my reputation doesn't matter. I'll go and see Kershaw now."

Frankie didn't speak. Simply raised her eyes to the ceiling and slowly shook her head.

"Oh for Christ's sake. Another bloody conference? Well if he's using my speech a second time he can pay me royalties."

FINALLY...

Kershaw had added another brick to his ego wall. Last week's conference by the look of it. 'Initiatives in Modern Policing' writ large on the wall behind him.

He's done well to get it framed so quickly...

"What can I do for you, Mike?"

So we're on first name terms this morning. He must need another favour...

"I want to talk to you about Gina Foster, sir."

"I thought that one was done and dusted? Accidental death. I told you not to waste your time on it. What did Thomson come up with?"

How am I going to play this one? Nothing concrete is the answer. But enough to make her uneasy.

"Enough to make me think it warrants further investigation, sir."

"What specifically?"

"Inconsistencies in Gina Foster's background. She was born in Birmingham. What's she doing in Whitby?"

Kershaw looked out of the window towards the Abbey. Slowly turned his attention back to Brady. "It's not a criminal offence to move from Birmingham to Whitby. Many would consider it a sensible decision. Which she clearly did. And then she had an accident."

"Maybe..."

"Maybe? What does 'maybe' mean, Brady?"

Brady took a deep breath. "It means, sir, that both DS Thomson and I think it may not have been an accident."

"On what evidence?"

"Right now there's no evidence, sir. But we don't slip and fall where we walk every day. And we don't commit suicide in front of our dog."

As soon as the last sentence was out of his mouth Brady knew it was a mistake. Kershaw laughed out loud. "I'm sorry? You want me to launch a murder investigation based on your psychological assessment – amateur psychological assessment – of dog-owners and their mental health?"

Bill Calvert had been the playground bully. Kershaw was much more. The sneering teacher who stood over you. Glanced down at your maths homework. Who told you with one look that you'd never amount to anything in life. And took pleasure in it.

Kershaw steepled his hands in front of him. "I tell you what I'll do, Brady," he said. "I've read your record. Your talent – for want of a better word – for not knowing when to see sense. So I'll give you a week. Come up with some incontrovertible evidence – preferably not relying on the psychology of dog owners – in seven days and I'll think about it. After that it's case closed. And that'll be an order."

Brady knew that he wouldn't get any more. He stood up. "Thank you, sir. At least we'll know. One way or the other."

Kershaw nodded. "We will. And Brady – one more thing."

"Yes sir?"

"No more trespassing on the railway line. I don't want one of my men getting hit by a train. It would make me look incompetent."

"I NEED to buy you a drink after work," Brady said.

"That sounds like an order, boss."

"Yes. Or as close to an order as 'I need to buy you a drink' can be."

"Gin," Frankie said and reached for her phone. "I'll tell Alex I'm going to be late."

BRADY PASSED HER A GLASS. "Whitby gin. Fever tree tonic, ice, slice of lime," he said.

"Thanks, boss. Perfect. Nearly. You need a heavier glass. Like fish and chips with your fingers. Whatever you drink it tastes better out of a really good glass."

"We've got a week," Brady said.

"A week to prove she was murdered?"

"A week to prove it wasn't an accident."

"It wasn't," Frankie said.

Brady nodded. "I agree with you. But we have to prove it. Or at least... create enough doubt in Kershaw's mind."

"There's something else," Brady said. And then he stopped. "You said you were going to paint your lounge. What were you thinking of? I like duck egg blue. Or a pale yellow..."

Frankie looked quizzically at him. And then understood. "Pale," she said. "A sort of blue/grey/green. We're just deciding between Turtledove Grey and Raw Cashmere."

"Raw Cashmere every time," Brady said. "Finish your gin and let's go for a walk."

"I'M SORRY ABOUT THAT," Brady said. "I don't want to sound like a 16 year old on his first date, but let's take the long way back to the car park."

Frankie didn't reply.

"I just felt... I suddenly didn't want to discuss it in the pub. I was speaking to Kershaw today," he said. "You know that. What you don't know – what I didn't want to say back there – was that he warned me not to go trespassing on the railway line."

Frankie stopped. Turned to look at him. "How did he know that?"

"There are only two ways. Either he saw me in my Hi-Vis jacket. Or someone told him."

"It certainly wasn't me. So Dan Keillor?"

"I doubt it. I doubt that Kershaw considers Dan Keillor worthy of his time. I think Dan told someone. 'Guess what the boss did on Sunday...'"

"And someone told Kershaw?"

"Yep. A useful lesson for Dan though. Learning early in his career that sometimes there's precious little difference between policing and office politics."

"...Which Kershaw has known all his career."

"Yes. I'm surprised he told me."

"Warning shot across the bows, boss. 'I know what's going on.'"

"And he doesn't care if we know."

They were back at the car park. Brady unlocked the Tiguan. "Just sit inside for a minute. I'm not sure I'm agile enough to get into your car." Brady turned the engine on. Turned the heater up. "We'll go and see Foster tomorrow."

"And are we going to tick the Family Liaison box?"

"You said you were a trained FLO That'll do for me, Frankie."

"You mean you don't trust Sally Brown."

"Maybe not. Someone told Kershaw. But she's not our main problem. We need to find something in the next week." Brady shook his head. "I don't understand Kershaw's motivation with this one. I can live with him wanting me to fall on my arse. I can't understand – not for the life of me – why he wants 'case closed' stamped on the file instead of 'case solved.'"

11

"You know where you're going, boss?"

"I was there on Saturday remember."

"Right. Trespassing. I'm trying to block it out of my mind."

They climbed into the Tiguan. Frankie sniffed suspiciously.

"Yeah, sorry," Brady said. "Autumn. Season of mists and mellow fruitfulness and very wet dogs."

"How's he doing?" Frankie asked.

"Archie? Absolutely fine. I sometimes think he limps a little bit at the end of a long walk. But given what happened, absolutely fine."

They drove out of Whitby. Brady turned left to Sleights and then right along Eskdaleside.

"I could live out here," he said. "The peace, the quiet, the countryside. The view across the valley. It'd do for me."

"Except you've got a teenage daughter."

Brady laughed. "Yep. Who'd see living out here as

some sort of punishment."

"And you'd be forever giving her lifts into town."

"Right. So I'm going to buy somewhere in town. Maybe somewhere that needs renovating. Where I can look out over the harbour."

"You wouldn't..." Frankie let the sentence trail away.

"What? Look out of my bedroom window and see the pier? Remember what happened? Bloody hell, Frankie, if Dave can go back to work, I can look at the pier. There –"

Brady broke off to point out of the window. "That house there. Perfect. Sit on that patio they've built, look over the valley and drink a beer."

"Write your book..."

"That's a bit below the belt, Detective Sergeant Thomson."

"How far did you get?"

"The book? Not far enough. But it's waiting for me in the drawer. Well, the virtual drawer. I'll finish it one day."

Brady slowed down behind a tractor. There was no chance of overtaking on the narrow country lane.

"The price you pay for the view," Frankie said.

HE STARTED down the hill into Grosmont. Went past the railway station where the train from Platform 9¾ had arrived at Hogwarts.

Carried on past the car park, gave way to a black Land Rover crossing the bridge. Another 50 yards and he turned right.

Brady drove onto the farm road, gravel scattered

across it, a strip of grass up the middle, puddles from the rain marking the potholes.

He steered the car carefully into the farmyard. The one he'd walked through. The barn on the left, the wood-shed on the right. The white pickup truck still parked at the far side of the yard.

"Still there," Frankie said.

"What?"

"The jeans and the towels on the washing line. Five pounds says Gina put them out the morning she died and they've been there ever since."

"Looks like we've got a reception committee," Brady said.

"Max?"

"Broad white stripe between his eyes? The suspect fits your description..."

Brady opened the car door as Ian Foster appeared.

Brady held his hand out. "Michael Brady. Detective Chief Inspector. And you've already met Detective Sergeant Thomson."

Some men try to crush your hand when they shake it. They've read an article. Some nonsense about alpha males...

And some men crushed your hand because – as Frankie had said – their hands were the size of coal shovels and they couldn't help it.

Brady looked into Foster's face. And he was back in his whites playing village cricket...

He looks like the opening bowler for the other team. Doesn't care how he sends you back to the pavilion but he'll buy you a pint after the game. But right now he looks like an opening bowler who's seen some willowy 16 year old in glasses stroll out and hit him all round the ground. He's got the ball in his hand and he doesn't know what to do. Ian Foster. His wife's dead and he doesn't know what to do next.

"You'd best come in. And I'm sorry about Max. He likes to get to know you."

They followed him round the corner of the house and in through the front door. Foster turned right, led the way into the dining kitchen.

Brady couldn't think of the last time he'd been in a farmhouse. He'd been expecting muddy boots, two damp spaniels, a bucket of potatoes that needed scrubbing. An Aga, obviously. A battered kitchen table that had been in the family for a hundred years.

One out of five. Just the Aga.

Frankie's description hadn't prepared him. A very modern, very stylish dining kitchen, the floor to ceiling window looking out across the valley. Two Velux windows letting in even more light. Foster gestured for them to sit down at the table.

Like Frankie had said, it would still have been a stable without Gina.

"Thank you for seeing us," Brady said. "And it goes without saying how sorry we are. We'll make this as brief as we possibly can."

Sally would have been useful. Someone to sit next to Foster. Balance the teams. Brady didn't want him to feel under pressure. "DS Thomson said your cousin was coming, Mr Foster?"

"Joanne? She's a few things to sort out first. Rings me twice a day though."

"...And your wife's daughter is away at school?"

"Maria. My daughter n' all. Since she were two."

"I'm sorry. She's in Scarborough?"

Foster nodded. "At the College. Went down to see her yesterday. Keep things normal, they told me. Seem to know what they're doing."

Brady wanted to go slowly. Tiptoe through the conversation.

"We just want to get some background, Mr Foster. Tie up all the loose ends. So..."

So that we know whether she was murdered or not. And I hope she wasn't. Because you look lost. Crushed. Not even sure how the Aga works...

"Have you always lived here, Mr Foster?" Brady asked.

"Always. My dad, my grandad before him." He paused. Looked as though he felt he was letting them down. "But I reckon it'll end wi' me. She's a bright girl is Maria. Organised, like her mother. But she's not a farmer's daughter."

Brady was looking at Foster's hands. Resting on the table. Hands that had spent a lifetime outdoors. That were rough and chipped and tanned.

They reminded him of Patrick's Chromebook. The laptop that had eventually led him to his best friend's killer. That had borne the bumps and scars of building sites. Ian Foster's hands bore the bumps and scars of the farmyard. The first finger of his left hand ended prematurely, an inch shorter than it should have been. He saw Brady looking. "Cutting a branch back," he said. "Power saw. My own fault. Anyway," he said, "You're not here to talk about farming accidents."

"No, we're not. As I said, Mr Foster. Just some background if it's alright with you. Help us build a picture. And I'm sorry if I cover the same ground as DS Thomson. We just want to wrap this up as quickly as we can."

"She fell in the river," Foster said.

Frankie leaned forward. "She did, Mr Foster. But she must have walked Max by the river any number of times. She – "

"Every day," Foster said.

"That's what we mean. She walked there every day. She must have known every inch of the path."

"How many branches have I cut back?" Foster said. "A thousand. One day I'm not concentrating an' I take my finger off. That's Gina. God knows why, God knows how. But that's what she did."

Don't let him dwell on her death. Take him back to happier times...

"How did you meet your wife, Mr Foster?" Brady asked.

"She was working at the solicitors. I went in to sort the estate out. After Mum had died. Some papers that needed signing. I'd been running the farm, but it was all in Mum's name. Gina was there. Doing some sort of admin job. She was just really bright. Really funny. I was depressed. No-one to turn to. Out of my depth with the paperwork."

"So you found an excuse to go into the solicitors the week after as well?"

Ian Foster smiled. Tight-lipped, but a smile. "Isn't that the way of it? I did. Found the courage to ask her out.

Stumbled over my words. But she said yes. Had to apologise for the mess the first time she came here."

"And you got married..."

"Just at the register office. Gina said she didn't want a big do, what with her having no family. And said we could spend the money better on the house."

"Did she stay at the solicitors?"

Foster shook his head. "No, pretty much as soon as we're married she started doing the books for me. Can't tell you what a relief it was. Me n' paperwork – like I told your partner – we've never seen eye to eye."

"So she's here. She's doing the books, looking after her daughter. Your daughter, I'm sorry. You didn't try for any more children?"

Foster stared at Brady. Was that a trace of anger? "Are you allowed to ask me that?"

"Sadly, Mr Foster, I'm a detective. I'm allowed to ask you more or less anything. But you're not compelled to reply."

"But if I don't reply you'll take it the wrong way."

Brady shook his head. "Not in the slightest. But it's like DS Thomson said, the more background we have, the better."

"Aye well, we did. I wanted a son, obviously. Still trying if you must know. Well, isn't going to happen now is it?" Ian Foster sniffed. If he was going to cry, it wouldn't be in front of strangers.

"DS Thomson said your wife was from Birmingham?"

Frankie stood up. "Would you excuse me, Mr Foster? I need to use your bathroom. Could I..."

"Course. Up the stairs. Second on the left." He turned his attention back to Brady. "Birmingham. That's right."

"Peaky Blinder country..."

Foster laughed.

An achievement in the circumstances...

"Aye. She told you did she? Gina had a way of looking at you that reminded me of Ada. Mind you, she'd have left me for Tommy Shelby. Watch it do you?"

"I saw the first series," Brady said. "I was deeply jealous of how little paperwork the police had to do."

"Same for all of us," Foster said. "God knows what I'll do now."

"I'm sorry," Brady said. "I know this is difficult for you. Just a couple more questions. Could your wife swim, Mr Foster?"

Why does he look surprised? Every man knows whether his wife can swim...

"A bit. I think so. Like most people I guess. But we never went on holiday. Difficult with a farm."

"And your daughter. Maria's what? Twelve now?"

"Thirteen."

"And you said she was at school in Scarborough?"

"The College. A few farmers send their children there. Started this term."

Brady had glanced at the website. Been impressed by the sports facilities and the drama. And then decided he couldn't afford it. And that he wanted Ash close to him as she grew up.

"Maria boards there? That must be expensive?"

"Gina said we could afford it. I took her word for it.

Where money was concerned I didn't pay much attention. Let Gina take care of it all."

BRADY HEARD the noise of Frankie coming back down the stairs. "We're nearly finished, Mr Foster. And thank you for your patience. Can I just ask one or two more questions about your wife's background? Her childhood, where she was brought up. Just a bit more detail?"

Foster hesitated. "She didn't... Didn't like to talk about it."

"Why not?"

"It wasn't happy. She'd said once she'd been abused. By an older man."

"That must have been traumatic for her... What about school? Where did she go to school?"

"She didn't talk about that either. I think it was one of the teachers that was... That tried to interfere with her. And she said everyone believed the teacher. She said he was black and they were frightened of being called racists."

Brady tried a different tack. "What about her family. Brothers, sisters, parents?"

Foster shook his head again. "She never knew her father. She was an only child. brought up by her mother. On a council estate. I don't think they had much money."

"But she must still be in touch with her mother? After all, she's got a granddaughter."

"She died. In a car accident. Around the time Gina had Maria. And I don't think they were speaking much by that time."

"So she didn't have anyone?"

"No. Just the life we had here. Just the two of us."

"What about Maria's father?" Frankie asked. "He must have wanted to see his daughter? And before she met you, Gina must have been entitled to child support?"

"She said it was nothing. Stupidity. She was only 20. And she wanted to stand on her own two feet. She said if she took any money he could interfere. Said she'd made a mistake. Had to learn from it."

Brady made one final attempt. "Why did she come to Whitby?"

"She wanted to live by the seaside. She loved the open air. She went for walks on the beach. But she liked solitude. Sometimes she drove into Whitby at night. Walked on the beach in the dark."

"But why Whitby? People from Birmingham go to Rhyl. Or Blackpool. Or Weston-Super-Mare. What made her choose Whitby?"

"She said she'd seen it on TV. She'd seen the Abbey. The harbour. She said it looked perfect."

Ian Foster looked at them defiantly. "And it was, for us."

12

Brady stood up. Allowed his hand to be crushed a second time. "Thank you, Mr Foster. I appreciate all your time. I can only say it again. We'll deal with this as quickly as we can."

"You're done wi' me then? I can go back to farming?"

"Yes," Brady said. "Yes, of course."

Yes. And you can go back to grieving. To going through a hundred different emotions. Lying awake and staring at the ceiling. Sleeping in the spare room because you can't stand being in the bed without her. Your cousin can't come soon enough, Mr Foster...

Brady hesitated. "There's just one more thing. I'd like to see everything if we can..."

"There's not much to see. The house. The yard. You've seen that."

"If you don't mind, we'd like to see where your wife walked. Just to get a feel for it."

Foster shrugged. "If that's what you want. You'll need your wellingtons though."

"I'm a farmer's daughter," Frankie said. "We've come prepared."

"You understand you'll have to go on your own? I can't... Not yet..."

"Of course," Brady said. "All you need to do is point us in the right direction..."

"Across the yard," Foster had said. "Along the track. You'll see another track on the left. Just where the hedge finishes."

They walked across the farmyard. Brady glanced to his left where a farm labourer – *Foster can't have many surely?* – was fixing a fence that marked the end of the front garden.

"I see what you mean," he said as soon as they were out of the farmyard.

"About Foster?"

"You're developing a worrying habit of reading my mind. But yes. You could see his whole life. An only child. Awkward, not sure of himself. Probably bullied at school. His best friends are the animals. Reaches 16, takes a year to pluck up the courage to ask Angela Miller out. She says no and that's it until Gina. I'm surprised he found the courage to ask *her* out."

"He reminds me of a dog," Frankie said. "He just wants to be loved. And fed..."

"Here," Brady said. "This is it, isn't it?"

The track was Land Rover wide. Muddier on the right where a stream ran down to the river. A row of small silver birch trees on the far side of the stream gave way to a line of bushes. An open field on the other side, the edge marked by wild grass and half a dozen small, staked trees.

"So where's this field Foster said he was ploughing?"

"Further up the hill?" Frankie suggested. "This looks too wet to me."

"You know what I'm looking for here?" Brady said.

"You want to put two and two together. You want this track to lead to the bank you saw from the bridge."

"I do. And I don't think we'll have to walk far."

"Just as well," Frankie said, skirting another puddle as drizzle started to fall.

The path curved round to the left. But Brady's eyes were fixed on a clearing. The one he'd seen from the bridge. Ten, maybe 12 yards wide. Dead ferns at the side of it, then a row of trees on the river bank.

The track continued round to the left.

That'll be where Gina walked the dog...

But Brady was focused on the bank. It sloped gently down to the river. Just like Frankie had said. On a sunny day it would have been perfect for a picnic. Bring the children. Eat your sandwiches and then walk back up to the clearing. Find a few flat stones, see if you could skim them across to the far bank.

But it was autumn. It was drizzling, the light was fading. It was a long way from picnic weather.

"This has to be the place," Brady said. "It just *has* to be."

He walked down between the sycamore trees he'd seen from the railway bridge.

The bridge was on the original stone supports. Brady had asked Google. The Whitby, Redcar and Middlesbrough Union Railway had opened in 1883. Those looked like the original supports. But there was a newer, brick support in the middle of the river, the brickwork stained by the water running down it. A dark green stain marked the high water line.

The river looked even wider, deeper from this angle. Frankie came down the bank behind him. "Careful," he said. "This might be the only evidence we find."

"Are we looking for evidence then, boss?"

"Always. See if you can find a convenient piece of Gina's bodywarmer fluttering from a thorn bush..."

"Bloodstained?"

"Obviously. And do the job properly, Frankie. A piece of her bodywarmer with two different bloodstains on it."

"Murderer AB negative?"

"Yes, please. The rarer the better."

Brady stood and watched the river, the water flowing downstream towards a small island. It looked shallower down there. 'Luck' was still the wrong word, but the body hadn't been certain to float downstream.

"Frankie," he said. "Come here."

She came and stood next to him. "What am I looking at?"

"The water," Brady said. "Watch it. Here at the side."

Brady walked across to one of the trees. Snapped two sticks off a dead branch. "Look," he said. He tossed the first stick into the river, two feet from the bank. The stick bobbed in the water, one current trying to carry it downstream, a second current pushing it into the bank.

"The water's lapping up against the bank," Brady said. "Now watch." He threw the second stick further out into the river. The current caught it, carried it downstream. "A yard further out," he said. "And it goes straight down the river."

"That's a stick though, boss. A stick isn't a dead body."

"Fair point."

Brady walked back to one of the trees. Looked in the tangled grass underneath it. Found what he was looking for.

A branch had fallen off. At least four feet long. Brady wrestled it free of the long grass, picked it up, needing both hands to carry it. Walked back down the bank to Frankie.

"Meet Gina," he said.

"Looks like she's had a rough night..."

"If I just throw her in at the edge she's not going anywhere."

Brady put the branch down on the wet grass. Took his coat off. Threw it over a bush. Picked the branch up and walked to the water's edge.

"Careful. It looks deep and cold."

"It *is* deep and cold. But she's got to go..."

Brady threw the branch as far out as he could. Six feet out into the river. A third of the way to the central support.

Far enough.

The current took hold of the branch, carried it instantly downstream. For a minute Brady thought it was going straight into the island. Then the current carried 'Gina' to the left of it, downstream and out of sight. Downstream to where Maisy saw her swimming...

"He pushed her out?" Frankie said.

"I'd say he did more than that. I'd say he waded out into the water. It's the only way he can be sure. The further out he takes her, the more certain he is."

"So we're looking for a footprint," Frankie said. "Half in the river, half on the bank."

"You start down there. I'll start under the tree. I'll meet you in the middle."

'Policing's like any job, Mike.' He could hear Jim Fitzpatrick saying it. 'You have good days, you have bad days. You do the same thing, the same routines, the same lines of enquiry. Some days you get lucky. Some days you don't. Like a footballer. Can't stop scoring. Then all of a sudden he can't hit a barn door from five yards. It's not about consistent results, Mike. It's about consistent effort.'

"Boss!" Frankie was pointing at the river bank.

Brady took a step away from the river, conscious of not wanting to disturb anything, to walk on any more potential evidence. Came and stood by Frankie, looked where she was pointing. "Jackpot," he said.

Half in, half out of the water. The outline of a boot. The edges blurred by the lapping of the water. But, very clearly, the outline of a boot. Brady reached for his phone. Took a dozen pictures. "What size do you think?" he said.

"I'm not an expert on men's shoes," Frankie said. "But it looks about average. Eight, nine, ten. What size are you, boss?"

Brady looked at the footprint again. "Nine, ten, depending on the fitting. About that," he said. "Pass me your phone will you?"

"What for?"

"Scale," Brady said. He took Frankie's phone. Placed it on the bank, as close to the print as he could. Took several more photos. "We know what size your phone is, so we can work out how big the print is."

"Plaster cast is going to be tricky," Frankie said.

"A plaster cast is going to be impossible unless I can convince Kershaw it's murder."

"You've convinced me," Frankie said. "I can't think of any other explanation for a footprint coming out of the river."

"Me neither," Brady said. "Fishing maybe. Your line gets snagged. But a fisherman would be wearing waders. They'd have a clear pattern on the sole, surely?"

"Factor in – how many days has it been? Nine? – of the water rubbing it away..."

Brady peered intently down into the water. "That's our lot isn't it? One footprint. I'll need more than that for Kershaw. Come on, let's go back to the car."

Brady walked back up the bank into the clearing. He stopped, turned back to Frankie. "We've only got his word for it, haven't we?"

"About what?"

"About that morning. Suppose he's working down here? He knows where she's going to be. 'Thought I'd surprise you, love.' Ten seconds later she's in the water."

"Except there are no signs of a struggle. And he seems hopelessly lost without her." Frankie paused. "Supposing he *is* guilty, boss? You're not worried about him running away?"

Brady shook his head. "No. Number one, I don't think he is guilty. Number two, where would he go? This is the only life he's known. You think he's lost without Gina? He'd be even more lost in Leeds."

They started walking back up the track to the farm. "Then there's the daughter," Brady said. "She's at a boarding school, 20 miles away. What's the point of that? Whitby must have a bus that goes to Scarborough College every day."

"And the cost," Frankie said.

"Twenty grand a year? But I'm guessing. Someone told me having a child at independent school costs as much as a racehorse."

Frankie laughed. "You'd better go and ask Enzo then."

"Don't worry, I'll be knocking on Enzo Barella's door sooner or later. You know what the Japanese say. Sit by the river long enough and the body of your enemy will float past. Enzo will make a mistake. And I'll be waiting. But right now Gina Foster is the priority."

13

"Pull over will you, boss?"

Brady had driven out of the farm. Through Grosmont and up the hill towards Sleights.

"You OK?"

"Yeah. There's something I need to tell you. Now we're away from the farm."

Brady slowed down, ran the car up on to the grass verge at the side of the road. "What is it?"

Frankie put her hand in the pocket of her jacket. Brought out some tissue paper. Toilet roll, Brady saw. Toilet roll that she'd folded. He watched her very carefully unfold it. She held her hand out, a small, pink tablet in her palm.

"What's that?" Brady asked.

"It's one of Gina Foster's headache tablets. Except it's not."

Brady looked at her. "What is it then?"

"It's the pill. The contraceptive pill."

"You're certain? One pink pill looks pretty much like the next."

Frankie shook her head. "It's the same one I take. Yes, I'm certain."

Brady was silent for a moment. "You had a look in the bathroom cabinet?"

"Yes. When I went to the loo. Do you want me to apologise?"

"You know me better than that."

"There was a small bottle," Frankie said. "The size you get aspirin in. No label. *Every* bottle in a bathroom cabinet has a label on it. So I had a look. I told you something didn't feel right."

"So Foster's downstairs saying 'we're still trying' and she's upstairs taking the pill every morning? In itself it doesn't prove anything."

"Except what I said before. The truth and what Ian Foster thinks is the truth might be very different things."

"You're *sure* this is the pill?"

"As sure as I can be. It will be easy enough to ask for her medical records."

Brady looked out of the car window, back across the valley. "This isn't going to end well, Frankie. We're starting to take Ian Foster's life apart." He turned to her and smiled. "And let's hope the poor bugger doesn't have a headache over the next few days..."

"This whole thing," Frankie said. "It doesn't make sense. You look at it from a woman's point of view. The story just doesn't make sense."

"Why not?"

"Because she's too young. It's too isolated. She's what? Twenty-two? Twenty-three, when she meets him? Working in a solicitors. OK, Whitby's not Leeds on a Saturday night but it's slightly closer to it than a farm outside Grosmont. She shuts herself away on the farm and does the books? Doesn't she have friends? Doesn't she want to go out?"

"She's got a child," Brady said. "Maria is three when she marries Foster? I seem to remember Ash needed a lot of attention at that age."

"Right. But you and Grace had the occasional night out, didn't you? You know, birthdays, anniversaries, date nights. A weekend in a hotel."

"Yeah, sure. Of course we did."

"But from what Foster's saying they didn't. Or he didn't give me that impression. And holidays. Did they never go on holiday? It's difficult with a farm but it's not impossible. You get someone in to look after the animals. We managed it. Gina was in her 20s. She must have wanted some sunshine. An excuse to get dressed up. Sit by the pool in her bikini."

"So what are you suggesting?"

"That any normal 24, 25 year old woman would have gone mad. Foster's hit the jackpot. Well, he's the father to someone else's child. But like we've said, he sure as hell didn't have a string of girlfriends before Gina. It's just wrong. Even if – I don't know... a young Jack Nicholson – had said to me, 'Frankie, I love you, come and live on a farm with me.' I'd have gone, but only for two weeks."

"OK, maybe she was agoraphobic. Maybe she was... I've gone blank. What's it called when you don't like other people?"

"Misanthropy. And going blank at your age is called worrying, boss."

Brady laughed. "Thanks. But whatever it is, it's all irrelevant if I can't persuade Kershaw."

Brady started the car engine. Frankie put her hand out to stop him putting the car in reverse. "Hang on, boss. There's one more thing."

"What now? Don't tell me you went through the laundry basket as well. What else did you find?"

"No. It's something I didn't find. I told you Foster seemed reluctant to talk about Gina's childhood."

"Yeah..."

"I walked through the house. Most of it. Through the lounge. Up the stairs. On the landing. There are photos of him. Photos of Maria. Only one of her. On their wedding day."

"What are you saying?"

"I'm saying that everyone has a photo of themselves when they were young. I've got a lampshade on my head, pretending to be a pop star..."

Brady felt compelled to reply. "On the beach," he said. "On a donkey. He was called Elvis."

"Right. I didn't see *any* photos of Gina. Nothing from her past. Nothing at all. It's like Gina Foster didn't exist before she married him."

14

A cold, crisp, sunny day at the beginning of autumn. In Brady's opinion, the very best the east coast had to offer. And Archie agreed...

He lifted the tailgate. Archie jumped out of the back of the car, desperate to be off.

Brady shook his head. Not much more than four months since he'd staggered back to the car. Tried to lift the tailgate to lay Archie in the boot. Knew he had to get to the vet. Looked up and seen Jimmy Gorse standing over him.

'*Here, move back slightly. I'll open the car for you.*' *Gorse had smiled down at him.* '*You can lay the pup in the boot. Get yoursel' away to the vet's.*'

Gorse had lifted the tailgate. Turned, smiled again. '*Aye, I did shoot your dog. I meant to kill him. But I see now this is better. Gives us chance for a wee chat.*'

Not that he'd told the police psychologist about it...

'*You're sure you're alright, Michael? No flashbacks? No*

nightmares? Coming on top of what's already happened to you?'

A different police psychologist, the same questions. 'I'm fine. The best thing for me is to start work.'

'You're absolutely certain? That incident must have been traumatic.'

'I'm fine. Really, I'm fine. I can't wait to get started.'

They walked down the Khyber Pass to the beach. "Let's go, Archie. We're going to work this one out, even if we have to walk to Sandsend."

But let's try and work it out without getting too introspective...

Brady looked up at the hill where he'd scattered his wife's ashes. "All good," he said out loud. "Well, good-ish. I'm going to start looking for a house. And Ash is fine. You'd be proud of her. And I miss you. It's going to be a lonely birthday without you."

Archie was slightly behind him, jumping up at the pocket of his bodywarmer. "No, Archie. No ball today. I need to think. Go and explore."

You inherit the family farm. You walk into the solicitors. Meet someone. She's younger than you, but she seems to like you. A week later you ask her out. Six months and you're married. She's doing the books, you're in the fields. Stew and dumplings when you come in. Life is perfect.

That's how it stays. But you want children. A son to follow you. It was your father's farm, your grandfather's. You think you're letting them down. But it doesn't happen. Well, now we know why it doesn't happen...

Then early one morning Gina walks down to the river. She's left her phone behind. Must have made a conscious deci-

sion to leave her phone. She slips and falls in? No, not with a footprint coming out of the water.

Archie had found another dog to play with. A whippet. They were chasing each other. "You're a bit optimistic, Archie," Brady shouted.

The Springer Spaniel raced across in front of Brady, almost tripping him. *'You've got a dog, boss. How many times does Archie suddenly change direction and come close to tripping you up?'*

Could Max have done that to Gina? No, not if I'm right about where she went in the water.

Brady carried on walking. He was halfway to Sandsend now. The sun was climbing higher in the sky. But the wind off the sea had other ideas. "Should have put a coat on," Brady muttered to himself.

If she's been murdered there's only one suspect. Another of Jim Fitzpatrick's pearls of wisdom. 'No-one knows what goes on in a relationship. Mike. Only the people in it.' Had Foster murdered his wife? Not unless he was a better actor than Jack Nicholson – was he the sort of man Frankie liked? – and Daniel Day-Lewis combined.

Maybe she was right. 'You look at it from a woman's point of view. The story just doesn't make sense. She's too young. It's too isolated. She shuts herself away on the farm and does the books? Doesn't she have friends? Doesn't she want to go out?'

But that just brought you back to Ian Foster...

He was almost at the breakwaters in front of the hotel now. Brady remembered the sniggers that had gone round the fourth-form classroom.

'Breakwaters? Who answered breakwaters? The correct name for them is groynes.'

Time to turn round. "Come on, Archie. Time to walk into the wind. Good practice for the winter."

Maybe he should look at it from the killer's point of view. How would he murder Gina Foster? Not by drowning her, that's for sure. 'Drowning's a bloody stupid way to kill someone, Mike. It's messy, it's unpredictable and, above all, it's time consuming.' Quickly, cleanly. Stab her. Shoot her. Ian Foster must have a shotgun on the farm. Maybe he'd hired someone? A hitman? Murder a farmer's wife in Whitby? Drowning was a long way down the list...

"Alright, Archie," Brady said. "I've done enough thinking for one morning. I'm getting stupid. Sorry, mate, I should have brought your ball."

Brady looked around the beach. Saw a piece of washed-up driftwood. Walked across and stamped on it. The driftwood broke in half. Two perfect sticks to chase. "Here you go, Archie. What more could a dog want?"

But supposing Foster did hire someone? That early in the morning. He must have stayed overnight. We need to check the hotels, B&Bs...

Brady reached for his phone. He needed to speak to Frankie. Then he stopped. He'd forgotten. She was on leave for two days. Painting the lounge.

Raw Cashmere wasn't it?

15

Two miles. Just under 18 minutes. Nine minutes a mile.

Not bad, considering it was the first run for a while. But nowhere near where I once was...

Brady stepped out of the shower and reached for a towel. Ash was staying at Bean's. He walked naked into the bedroom. Finished drying himself. Pulled on a pair of tracksuit bottoms and an old t-shirt. Went downstairs to watch football.

The phone woke him up. He'd fallen asleep. He looked at the score. Still 0-0. No wonder.

He glanced down at his mobile. Frankie.

What does she want? She's on leave. Painting her lounge.

"Michael Brady."

"I need to see you, boss."

"No problem. You're in on Friday morning. First thing is fine. What's the problem?"

"Gina Foster. And it won't wait. Are you in?"

"Yes, of course I'm in. You're sure it won't wait?"

"Can I come round?"

"What? Now?"

"I need to see you, boss."

There was real urgency in her voice.

BRADY WAS IN THE KITCHEN. Someone was coming round. Convention demanded that he made a token effort to tidy the house. He heard a knock on the front door. "I didn't want to ring the bell," Frankie said. "I thought Ash might be asleep. I didn't want to wake her up."

"You're fine," Brady said. "She's staying at Bean's. They were late at school. Fiona – Bean's mum – didn't seem to mind. So just me and Archie."

"I'm sorry about this," Frankie said. "It's just that... Like I said to you, I like order. I like things to make sense. And now they do."

"And it wouldn't wait?"

"No."

"You want to sit down and tell me?"

"Yes. And there's some stuff I need to show you."

"OK. But explain it to me first. You want a drink? Coffee? Beer? Wine? I've half a bottle of Shiraz left over from the weekend."

"Wine would be good. Thank you."

Brady reached for a glass. One of his best ones. Old fashioned, thick glass.

"What did you say? Like fish and chips with your fingers? I hope the glass is heavy enough for you."

He handed it to Frankie. "Thank you," she said. "I'm impressed."

She looked flushed. Excited.

"Come and sit down," Brady said. He saw she had a laptop bag with her. "Or do you want to sit at the table?"

She shook her head. "Maybe. Not now. Let me explain first. Interrupt me if you want. Feel free to throw me out. But I think I'm right. I know I'm right."

Brady sat on the settee. Frankie stood opposite him. She was wearing jeans. Ripped on the right knee. A black blouse under her leather jacket, the top two buttons undone. Hair still pinned up. Flat red shoes. No socks. "You mind if I take my jacket off?"

"Of course not."

She took her jacket off. Draped it over a chair. Put the laptop bag on the floor and sat down opposite him. "Am I going to like this?" Brady asked.

She looked across at him. "We're off duty? I'm in your house? I'm drinking your wine? I can say what I want?"

Brady nodded. "Like you said. You knew me before I was your boss. We're off duty. We're as off-duty as off-duty gets. Say anything you want."

She drank some of her wine. Leaned forward and put the glass on the floor. "Are you going to like it? Intellectually, yes. Professionally, no. Professionally you're going to wish this had never happened. You're going to wish I was at home with my paint brush. It's a can of worms. A bloody big can of worms. But it's the truth, and we both know that's what matters."

Brady held his hand up. "Have you eaten?"

Frankie shook her head. "No. I've been working on this. On what I'm going to show you."

He reached for his phone. "Pizza alright for you?"

She nodded.

"Anything else? And what type of pizza?"

"No. Pizza's fine. Thank you. And a bit of everything? Quattro Stagioni?"

Brady ordered the pizza. Turned his attention back to Frankie. "Fifteen minutes. Fire away."

FRANKIE KICKED HER SHOES OFF, brought her right leg up so her foot was under her left knee. "I started from two points," she said. "What Foster said to us. What he called her – "

"My little Peaky Blinder?"

"Yeah. So she's from Birmingham."

"Millions of people are from Birmingham."

"But why is she in Whitby?" Frankie asked.

"You want me to play Devil's advocate? Irritating defence lawyer? Why shouldn't she be in Whitby? That's what Kershaw said to me."

"Because like we said before. People from Birmingham don't come to Whitby. They go to Blackpool. Or Rhyl. Weston-Super-Mare. Straight up the M6 to the Lake District. Whitby is nearly 200 miles. Three and half hours. And then there's the lack of photos."

Brady nodded. "So you keep saying."

"I went round to see two of my friends," Frankie said. "I didn't. I went round to look at the photos in their houses. To prove my theory. Right both times. One on holiday in Spain. The other one playing under-14s netball."

"Not on a donkey called Elvis then? You want some more wine?" Brady said.

Frankie held her glass out. "It's really good. Alex always buys the cheapest he can. I mostly tip it into the stew."

"It's from a wine club. I should cancel the subscription. Seems a bit self-indulgent for one person. Is... It's no business of mine. Is Alex OK with this? You being round here?"

"He's away. Some sort of Outward Bound course. So he can spend every weekend yomping across the Moors with the sixth-formers. So that was the plan for my two days off. Paint the lounge and watch a single girl's lonely box set."

Brady laughed. "OK. So I wasn't painting the lounge. But I was watching a lonely bloke's football match. But down to business. Tell me where this is going."

"She's from Birmingham," Frankie said. "She's in the wrong place. She doesn't seem to have a past. She – "

Brady felt something. A feeling he recognised. Maybe only vaguely. But it was there.

It was her leg curled up under her. Her energy. Her excitement. "I'm sorry," he said. "Say that again, Frankie."

"She has no past. So I asked myself a question. Supposing she *does* have a past?"

"Everyone has a past," Brady said.

"Right. But supposing Gina Foster's past wasn't what we think it is? Supposing it wasn't the story Ian Foster told us?"

"Are you saying he lied to us?"

Brady's throat was dry. "I'm just going for another beer," he said. "Help yourself to the wine."

He felt her eyes on him as he walked to the kitchen, conscious he had nothing on under his tracksuit bottoms.

"No," Frankie said as he came back. "I'm saying she lied to him."

"So what is Gina Foster's past?" Brady said.

Frankie sipped her wine. Took her time replying. The second or third time she'd done that with him. Savoured what she was going to say.

Do I like that? Do I like her teasing me?

"Gina Foster is – was – Gina Kirk," Frankie said.

It took Brady ten or 15 seconds.

"Gina Kirk? Gina Kirk, the driver?"

"The chaperone," Frankie said. "The confidante. The one who went with the driver. Who told the children it was going to be alright."

Brady stood up and walked over to the window. Saw Frankie's car parked behind his. Looked across to the park. Saw the street lights reflected on the wet road. Rain running down the window.

"If that's true," he said. "And this is a bloody big 'if,' Frankie. If that's true it changes everything. Absolutely everything."

"It is true."

He turned round to face her. "Fuck, Frankie. If you're right – and I don't doubt you – if you're right this means Kershaw *must* have known. People above Kershaw must have known. She was murdered. Obviously she was murdered. The possibilities – "

"Yes," Frankie said, simply. "The possibilities of who killed her are endless."

Archie stood up and stretched. "I'm sorry, Archie,"

Brady said. "Come on. Two minutes, Frankie. However explosive this is I need to let Archie out. Come on, mate."

He came back in with Archie. Frankie was walking back from the front door with the pizza box.

"Have you paid? I need to give you the money."

She shook her head. Smiled at him. "Don't worry. I'm going to finish your wine."

Brady looked at the clock. 9:35. It didn't matter how long it took. Any trace of tiredness was gone. He went into the kitchen. Came back with two plates and some kitchen roll. "Eat as much as you want," he said. "Tell me the story."

"I'd spent the morning painting. But this is all I can think about. So I gave up. Went in the shower. Removed all trace of Raw Cashmere. Made a cup of tea. Typed 'major crimes in Birmingham' into Google. And an hour later there it is."

Brady shook his head. "She got about two years, didn't she?"

"Twenty-one months. She served eight. It was the Whitby thing. I couldn't understand why she was in Whitby. Then I stopped obsessing about 'where' and asked myself 'why?' Supposing Whitby wasn't her choice?"

"You're saying she was in witness protection? Witness protection put her in Whitby?"

Frankie nodded. "That was all I could think of. I read a book about a year ago. About the FBI programme. There was one woman's story. She was re-located from Brooklyn. They didn't give her a choice. Plonked her down right in the middle of Idaho or somewhere."

"And Gina's sent to Whitby? Found somewhere to live. Given enough money to live on until she finds a job."

"And to pay for childcare."

"Who looked after the daughter while she was inside?"

"Her mother."

Brady stood up and walked over to the window again. Tried to process what Frankie had told him. Tried to work out the implications. He turned round. Frankie was bending forward, reaching for her laptop, her shirt falling open. "You need to prove this to me," he said. "And you need to do it now. Because there's no way I'm going to sleep. Not knowing I've wasted two weeks. And that Kershaw has known all the time. And that…"

"That someone has to tell Ian Foster."

"Jesus. What did I say in the car? His life was unravelling. This is going to tear it apart."

Frankie stood up, her laptop in her hand.

"Come and sit at the table," Brady said. "Show me."

Frankie sat down. Opened her laptop. Opened a page she'd saved. Brady put the pizza box – three slices left – in the middle of the table.

"You can give someone a new name," Frankie said. "A new identity, a new face. Bloody hell, one woman in America got new boobs. But I don't think our witness protection gives someone a new voice."

"So she was always going to stand out…"

"So she went to hide on a farm. Shall I go through it from scratch?"

Brady nodded. "This is what you've been doing all afternoon?"

No wonder she wanted to come round...

"Gina is my age," Frankie said. "I'm in my last year at university. So I'm only dimly aware of the story. But it was there, somewhere in my memory. And once I found it online it all clicked into place."

"Why Whitby? Because the decision's been made for her."

"Well, maybe she has a choice of two or three places," Frankie said. "But it must depend on what safe house is available?"

"And she comes straight out of jail and goes into witness protection. Because she's informed – "

"And because she's had death threats from the public as well."

"Finish the pizza," Brady said. "Let me read the story."

Frankie reached for a slice of pizza. Turned to Brady. Her eyes were shining. "This is as good as it gets isn't it?"

Brady held her eyes. Nodded. Held her eyes for longer. "For you and me. Yes. You want some more wine? There's another bottle in the kitchen."

"Corkscrew?"

"Just open every drawer. Let me read this..."

"You want a glass?"

Brady nodded, his attention on the laptop. "Please. Just – "

Frankie laughed. "I know. Open every cupboard."

He clicked on the news report. There it was, from 2004.

Gina Kirk Released from Prison

Angry Mob Waits Outside Jail

Gina Kirk was released from HMP Foston Hall yesterday – the first person convicted in the high-profile child trafficking case to be released.

Kirk, 22, was sentenced to 21 months for her part in the case, but was released after serving just eight months.

It is believed that she will now enter the UK's witness protection scheme, a decision which has provoked fury in some quarters.

Emma Stacey, a prominent member of the Justice for Our Children campaign group said, "What she did was disgusting. She should never be released. The idea of spending hundreds of thousands of pounds of taxpayers' money giving her protection makes me sick."

It was Kirk's eventual decision to inform on the gang that led to the high-profile trial and the subsequent convictions.

There were three photographs. Gina coming out of prison, her face hidden by a blanket as she was confronted by about a dozen protesters.

Not quite a mob. But someone cocked-up there. The time of her release should have been kept a secret. Especially from the press.

Another one of Gina being driven to court.

She'd not been remanded then.

And the last one. Gina walking into the court on the day she was sentenced. A woman in her 40s – very clearly the solicitor – at her side. A man you wouldn't like to meet in a dark alley two steps behind her.

Gina was wearing a plain, demure business suit. She had short, dark hair.

A bob. Is that what it's called? Slightly punky. You could mistake her for the junior solicitor if you didn't know the story.

Frankie was back. She'd clearly found the corkscrew. "I'll need to take a taxi," she said. "I'll walk round for the car some time tomorrow."

"Make sure you drink plenty of coffee in the morning. Drunk in charge of a paintbrush is a serious offence."

Brady looked at the photograph again. "This doesn't prove it, Frankie. All we've got that links this woman to Gina Foster is what Geoff Oldroyd said."

"She wasn't a natural blonde."

"Right. But like he said, thousands of women aren't natural blondes."

"It fits though," Frankie said. "The story fits. It explains everything."

"Yes," Brady said, turning towards her. "It does. And it... It feels right. Every question we've asked, every inconsistency. It explains everything. And like you said." Brady looked into her eyes. "For you and me, this is as good as it gets."

FRANKIE PICKED up the last piece of pizza. "You want this?"

"Go ahead," Brady said.

"I'll share it with you."

He'd expected her to tear it in half. Instead she held it by the crust, offering it to him. Locked her eyes on his.

Brady leant forward, never breaking eye contact. Bit half the pizza.

Frankie reached her hand up. Touched his cheek. Still held his eyes.

He looked at her. Dark hair pinned up. Two stray strands escaping, coming down over her ears. Saw how smooth her neck was. A tiny pulse beating. The hollow formed by her collar bone...

"This is madness," he said.

She nodded. Moved her hand behind his head. Pulled him to her.

He breathed in. Drank in the scent of her perfume. The scent of her.

"Alien," she said, reading his mind.

Then she kissed him. Hesitantly at first. Then harder. Her tongue darting and dancing across his.

Broke off the kiss. Moved her hand from behind his head. Still held his eyes. Stood up. Reached out and took his hand. Pulled him to his feet. Slowly, deliberately, undid the buttons on her shirt. Let it fall open.

"Yes," she said. "It is madness."

"I haven't," Brady said. "Not since... It happened. Not with..."

She put her fingers to his lips. "I know," she said. "I know..."

THE SOUND of the key in the front door was unmistakable.

"Ash, is that you?"

"Unless you've been giving out keys to burglars, Dad."

Brady walked into the hall. Archie was jumping up at her. Ash was bending down to pet him. "What's happened?" Brady said.

"Bean started throwing up. Fiona said it was probably better if I came home. She phoned me a taxi. But I've no money. He's waiting outside. And someone's parked outside our house."

"Yes, sure, of course. Just let me get some money."

"Well you're not going to get it standing in the hall, Dad. Are you going to let me in?"

"Yes, sure. Sorry, Ash."

Brady turned round. Frankie was sitting at her laptop. She turned, smiled. Only one button on her blouse unfastened. "Hi, Ash. Sounds sensible. Is Bean OK?"

"Oh... Hi, Frankie. Yeah. No. There's this bug at school."

Brady had found some money. "We've just been going through some old cases," he said, thinking he had to say something.

"Yeah, we've just finished," Frankie said. "In fact, if that taxi's waiting..." She reached for her coat. "I've had a glass of wine," she said to Ash. "The down side of the job. You can't take any risks."

"Let me just pay him for Ash," Brady said.

He walked out into the rain, all too aware he was only wearing a t-shirt. Frankie followed him.

"Frankie," he said.

"Yes, boss?" she answered.

"Don't say anything. About Gina, I mean. We need to decide what to do. The implications of this..."

"Don't worry," she said. "I've got a lounge to finish. What else would I do?"

"I'll phone you tomorrow," Brady said.

She nodded. "I hope Ash is OK."

HE'D EXPECTED Ash to be in her room. Instead she was waiting for him. "Sorry, Ash," he said, clearing away the pizza box. "We were going through an old case."

"Was it Gina Foster?" his daughter asked.

"You know I can't talk about cases with you, Ash."

But she's 13. And she's not a fool...

"Then again," he said. "There haven't been that many people fished out of the river. Why do you ask?"

"Bean was talking about it," Ash said. "Maria used to be in her class."

"Did she?"

"She's the same age as us."

"She wasn't in your class? The first term you were there?"

Ash shook her head. "There's two classes in the year. She was in the other one."

"OK. Thank you. And say thank you to Bean. And tell her I hope she's alright."

WHAT HAD he said to Frankie? *You need to prove this to me. And you need to do it now. Because there's no way I'm going to sleep.*

The possibility of Gina Foster being Gina Kirk – and what it meant if Frankie was right – would have been enough to keep him awake. Staring at the ceiling into the small hours...

Then he saw Frankie's shirt falling open. Tried to push it out of his mind. Tried to focus on Gina Foster.

Failed.

Completely, hopelessly failed.

16

He needed to know if Frankie was right. He needed to know quickly. And he wasn't going to find out through the official channels.

So there was only one answer.

The lounge was as elegant as he'd remembered. Pale green wallpaper. The handmade desk. The bay window looking out over the sea. Classical music playing faintly in the background. "Thank you for seeing me at such short notice," Brady said.

Mozart still looked like someone who'd become a Maths professor at an impossibly young age. He raised his eyebrows. "You don't seem like a man who uses the word 'emergency' lightly, Michael. You don't mind if I call you, Michael? We're old friends now..."

Brady shook his head. Smiled. "Not at all," he said, "And 'emergency?' No, I'm not."

"So what can I do for you? Whose virtual filing cabinet are we rifling through this morning?"

Mozart had served him tea in the same art deco cups

he'd used last time. The bank of six computer screens was still elegant and impressive in equal measure. He'd added another picture to his art collection. So abstract Brady wasn't even sure what it was.

"I – we – have a theory. We're investigating a case – "

"Gina Foster, obviously."

"Yes." Why did Mozart always know what he wanted before he asked for it?

"And our theory is that Gina Foster is not – was not – Gina Foster. That she's Gina Kirk. From the Birmingham case, 12 years ago. I'm inclined to believe it..."

'It fits though. The story fits. It explains everything.'

'Yes. It does. And it feels right. Every question we've asked, every inconsistency...'

"That would be interesting," Mozart said. "More than interesting. But you'll need proof. Because there are implications. Consequences."

More implications and consequences than you can imagine. And a very long investigation...

"That's why I'm here."

Mozart nodded. "I can do that," he said. "You just want the confirmation?"

"Yes," Brady said. "Confirmation that Gina Kirk has spent the last ten years living on a farm outside Whitby. And if it's not too much trouble, I'd really appreciate as much background as you can."

Mozart nodded. "I know where to look. But it's going to take me a little time. Two hours maybe." He looked at his watch. "Maybe if you explore Saltburn, Michael. Drink coffee in Rapps. Or walk along the seafront."

"Thank you," Brady said. "I'm very grateful."

He started walking towards the door. Mozart held up a hand. "How does it feel?" he asked. "Being back here?"

"You mean now I'm back in the police?"

"Yes, I'm intrigued. I said to you before, you can learn a lot about a man from watching him stand still. You don't seem like someone given to rash impulses, Michael. Yet here you are. Technically putting your career at risk."

Not the only thing I've done which could put my career at risk...

"Yes. But as you say, there are implications. There are bound to be consequences. I've got to deal with them. And – "

Should I say this to him?

"– there's someone I need to protect."

BRADY WALKED across the road and down the hill. He needed to think. Needed to do a *lot* of thinking. But two hours should be long enough.

He walked down the slipway and onto the beach. Turned right, walked away from the pier. It was low tide, a sunny day. The wind chasing the clouds south towards Whitby. He looked up at the cliffs in the distance. 'Boulby,' someone had told him. 'The highest cliffs in England.' It looked a good place for a windswept walk with Archie.

Supposing Frankie is right? Someone is going to be handed a very short straw. A bloody difficult conversation. I'm sorry, Mr Foster. The woman you married wasn't who you thought you'd married. She was part of a gang that trafficked children. Yes, sex trafficking. She went with them. Told the children everything would be alright. She probably introduced them. To the 'clients.' I suppose that was the word they used. Anyway, how are things on the farm? And do you think you could break the news to your daughter?'

A young couple, laughing, joking, walking hand-in-hand, passed him. Brady felt envious.

Was there ever a time when life was that uncomplicated? If Mozart confirmed Frankie's suspicions then any number of people could have killed her. Gina had informed on a gang. Stopped a very lucrative racket dead in its tracks. Someone – any number of people – would have wanted revenge...

Brady shook his head. Hunting down a carbon copy of Jimmy Gorse was the last thing he needed. Or wanted...

Am I frightened? Physically afraid? Know I won't be that .lucky a second time?

He checked his watch. Still plenty of time. He turned round and started walking back towards the pier.

What had Mozart said? Implications and consequences? The biggest one was Kershaw. By a country mile. His immediate boss – and he must have known. Must have known that someone in the witness protection programme was living in Whitby. And he didn't tell me. Let us waste two weeks. No bloody wonder he wants it to be accidental death. The implications of someone in witness protection being murdered on his patch...

Brady kicked a pebble in anger. Must have caught it just right. Watched it skim across the sand, curve at the last minute.

Just inside the post. The keeper hopelessly beaten.

Brady saw the back of the net bulge. He tried it again.

Caught his foot on the sand. The pebble bobbled two yards in front of him.

And Frankie. It was his job, his responsibility to protect her. Tell Kershaw he'd worked it out. Make sure her career wasn't affected...

He was under the pier now. He looked up. Saw the sky through the wooden slats. The rust on the Victorian supports. Saw people walking overhead.

Saw Frankie. Saw her unbuttoning her shirt. Didn't push the image out of his mind. Re-ran the scene...

You need to think. Focus. Get serious.

And you can't spend the rest of your life avoiding piers. No-one is afraid of piers. There won't even be a fancy name for it. Pierophobia. Get over it. Go and walk on it.

He walked back to one of the kiosks and bought a flat white. The way onto the pier was round an amusement arcade. He walked to the left. Paused to read the plaque.

Opened in May 1869 the first Pier on Cleveland's coast was a great success. Within six months 50,000 visitors had paid at the twin octagonal entrance boxes to walk the 1,500 feet of timber decking and enjoy refreshments from the central booths.

There were no central booths now. Just a long walk out into the North Sea. 1,500 feet? Five hundred yards? It didn't look that long. But he walked steadily out to the end. The tide was a long way out. Less than a hundred yards to go. He'd only just reached the sea.

No lifebuoys, he noticed.

No ready-made rope for Jimmy Gorse to use on Carl...

And the planks ran across the pier, not lengthways.

The pier didn't curve round to the right. A gentler, more welcoming pier than Whitby.

You could walk down this pier holding a girl's hand...

He looked to his left. The beach stretched north to Redcar, the view dominated by 20, maybe 30 huge wind turbines in the sea. He could just make out the steelworks in the distance, the start of Middlesbrough.

He'd reached the end. The pier widened out. There was a solitary green bench, long enough for a family of four. Rusty white railings held in place by black supports. Nothing else. No spiked railings. No ladders going down. A pier where you sat in the sun with your family and watched the container ships heading for Teesport.

He sat down. Looked back up at the cliffs. Wondered if Grace had been watching him last night.

"I'm sorry," he said out loud. "I thought there would only ever be you. But..."

But I needed someone. I was lonely. I didn't realise how lonely. But I chose the wrong person.

That's not being fair to Frankie. But I work with her. She's my junior officer. Who I'm meeting tomorrow morning...

Sitting alone on the end of Saltburn pier it was a lot easier to think about who murdered Gina Foster. Or Gina Kirk...

She's hiding on a farm with her husband, her daughter. She's doing everything she can to keep a low profile. Is that why she didn't want another child? Then she sends her daughter away to school. Why? There's only one explanation. Someone found her. And she knew that someone had found her.

"You mind if I join you?"

Brady looked up. A man in his late 50s, maybe his early 60s. His head shaven, an almost white goatee beard. The frame of a big man, but shrunken inside.

"Not at all. Be my guest."

"Beautiful day," the man said. "What're you doing? Thinking?"

Brady laughed. "Yes, I was. Just running through a few options. Getting some thoughts in order."

"Don't waste too much time on it," the man said. "It's soon gone." He made a gesture with his right hand. The same 'look, it's gone' gesture a magician makes.

"That sounds very profound," Brady said.

"Live every day like it's your last. One day it will be. All too soon for me." He held his hand out. "Willie Carr."

"Michael Brady."

Like Dave, another person you instinctively liked.

"It sounds like a long story," Brady said.

Willie shook his head. "Not really. All my life in the steelworks." He gestured into the distance to his left, past the wind turbines. "Retire, take my pension, spend more time with the grandkids, buy myself a mountain bike. A month later the specialist is telling me it's stage four. No treatment, just manage the pain."

He pulled his coat tighter round him. "Wind's deceptive this morning."

"I'm sorry," Brady said.

"No," Willie answered. "Don't be. I can't do anything about it. So I can be angry or I can be grateful. My kids are settled. My wife won't be short of money. I've held my third grandchild. I'd like to see her on Christmas morning but they tell me it's touch and go."

"That's philosophical," Brady said. "A lot more than philosophical."

"I'm lucky," Willie said. "Someone loves me. I can still walk to the end of the pier. Hurts like fuck but I can still manage it. There's plenty a lot worse off than me."

"I'm sorry," Brady stood up. "You must excuse me. I'm really sorry but I've an appointment I need to keep. But... You take care, Willie. Give your granddaughter a hug from me."

They shook hands. Brady left him looking out to sea. Walked back down the pier. Back up the hill to what had once been the Zetland Hotel. Back to see what Mozart had to say.

He checked his watch. Still had ten minutes to wait. Almost long enough to walk back down the hill and up it again. If he let his fitness go now he'd never get it back.

He decided not to. Despite what Willie had said about the wind it was a warm day. Mozart's elegant lounge didn't seem the right setting for a thin film of sweat.

"You've sampled the delights of our fair town?"

"I've walked along the pier. Talked to someone. Come back up the hill."

"Yes," Mozart said dryly. "Even I do that. Sitting is the new smoking. Have you heard that phrase? I've ordered a standing desk. No doubt the police service already has them?"

Brady laughed. "You know I don't need to answer that."

"Quite," Mozart said. "You want answers, not my attempts at humour." Unlike Frankie, he didn't hesitate. Didn't savour the news before he delivered it. "Yes," he said simply. "Gina Foster was Gina Carmichael before she married. Gina Carmichael was the name given to her by witness protection."

"You're absolutely sure?"

"I'm absolutely positive. Do you want to have the proof in your possession? Or do you want to take my word for it?"

"If you don't mind..."

Mozart nodded. "I thought so." He passed Brady a white, A4 envelope. "I printed it all out for you. Gina Kirk was released from prison after serving eight months. Three months in a safe house just outside Telford. That's when she became Gina Carmichael. She went to Rhyl first of all. But she was recognised. Possibly there was a leak. Maybe a senior member of Her Majesty's Constabulary in North Wales decided life would be more peaceful if she wasn't on their patch. Who knows? But a concerned neighbour received an anonymous tip-off. Gina Carmichael ceased to be Rhyl's problem and became someone else's."

"So she ended up in Whitby? She and her daughter were shuttled round the country?"

Mozart nodded. "Yes – with the obvious worry that she might have to move again. You know what they say in America. 'The people in witness protection serve a life sentence. The people they informed on get parole after eight years.'"

"Thank you," Brady said. "I appreciate you doing this so quickly."

"What will you do now?" Mozart asked.

"Find the killer," Brady said. "But in the short term,

see my boss."

Mozart smiled. "Ah, the intrigues of the court. 'Yon Cassius has a lean and hungry look,' as Caesar said."

"Exactly. Yon Kershaw has an ambitious and well-fed look, but – "

"'Such men are dangerous.'" Mozart finished the quote for him. "You realise that if it goes wrong you'll get the blame?"

"Yes, I know. And I know that if it all goes right Kershaw will take the credit," Brady said. "But what do I do? I swore an oath to uphold the law, not to play politics."

Mozart nodded. "But you're here..."

The rest of the sentence didn't need saying. *You're here. Going outside the law. Outside the official channels. Because you're determined to solve it.*

"The sister should be informative," Mozart said.

Brady tried to hide his surprise. Had no more success than when he tried to push the image of Frankie away.

"Sister?"

Now Mozart looked surprised. "You didn't know? The details are in the envelope. Kenilworth in Warwickshire. But she's away on holiday for a week. Tenerife."

"Thank you," Brady said. "You've been incredibly helpful. As always." He stood up to leave. "You'll send me an invoice?"

"Of course. Did you remember to set up that Bitcoin account, Michael? I can see you haven't done it yet. Bitcoin is the way to pay me. And buy some shares in Apple. Bitcoin and Apple. They'll make your police pension look like loose change."

17

Brady sat in his car. There was a phone call he needed to make.

"Francesca Thomson, painter and decorator. How can I help you?"

"How are you doing with it?"

"One wall to go. But – "

"But I didn't ring to ask about your lounge? No, I didn't. Can you meet me tomorrow morning? Before we go in?"

"Breakfast?"

"Where else?"

"No problem. I'll be the one wearing the winter coat with streaks of Raw Cashmere in her hair..."

"Frankie. One more thing. She had a sister."

"What? Fuck. How have I missed that?"

"Probably because she wasn't in any of the reports."

"But you want me to see what I can find?"

"We're going to have to do it officially. But I'm not going to hold back on information. You got a pen?"

Brady gave her the name and address. "Am I allowed to ask where you found this, boss?"

"No, you're not. I'll see you in the morning."

HE SAW her walking down the hill towards Dave's, wrapped up against the wind off the sea, her leather jacket of spring and summer long gone.

...Asked himself the question he'd already asked himself a dozen times that morning.

What would have happened if Ash hadn't come home? Supposing Bean hadn't thrown up? Would I have ended up in bed with her?

Knew the answer was almost certainly 'yes.' Didn't know if he was pleased or disappointed.

"Poor lass looks frozen," Dave said. "You're a hard man dragging her down here for a meeting."

"There's a few things we need to talk about," Brady said.

"Is local woman's death murder? Police refuse to comment. Aye, I've read the papers."

"Local woman's death *might* be a very complicated murder, but that's between you and me."

"I'll read about it in Spain then. A few weeks an' I'm done for this year. After our fishing trip, obviously."

Brady pretended he hadn't heard the last sentence. "Your regulars are alright with it?"

Dave smiled. "Yeah, they understand. They read the papers n' all. Missed a trick though. Should've put my prices up now I'm a hero."

"How's your wife? She must be looking forward to it?"

"Three months in Spain? She's over the moon. She's learning Spanish now. Saying it slowly an' pointing always worked for me, but she's not havin' it. Says if we're there for three months we have to make an effort."

Brady laughed. "There's worse battles to lose, Dave. But don't spend too long over there. I don't want to come down one morning and find you've swapped bacon sandwiches for paella. Not that Archie would mind."

"My favourite man in the whole world."

Brady turned. "Sorry, boss," Frankie added. "I was talking about Dave. Especially on a morning like this."

"Obviously," Brady conceded. "And your breakfast's paid for."

HE MOVED AWAY while she ordered her breakfast: heard her commiserate with Dave about Newcastle United.

But five minutes was enough time. "Frankie," he said. "We need to talk."

She nodded. "Of course, boss."

"I'm not sure it's bandstand weather. Just walk up to the car with me will you? And until we're in the station this morning, forget the 'boss.'"

Brady put his cup on Dave's counter. "Thanks, Dave. I'll see you at the weekend with Archie. Saturday morning. *Sabado*. And keep warm."

"Aye, you n' all. And one step at a time. She's teaching me the numbers first. And I don't follow Spanish football. What team does Sabado play for?"

"Very good," Brady smiled. "See you at the weekend."

"You want to swap that mug for a take-out cup, Frankie?"

She did. They started walking up the Khyber Pass towards Brady's car.

"Is this about – " Frankie said.

"No. Absolutely not."

But you need to say something...

"No, it's not. But..."

"It can't happen again," Frankie said for him. "I know. You're 'boss' and I'm DS Thomson. And I'm in a relation-ship. One that's on life support – Ah, fuck. Sorry, boss. Not the most tactful way to start the day."

"You're fine. I can't dance around your sister. You can't dance around my wife." Brady looked at her. "And I'm sorry. I didn't know. You and Alex. I thought..."

"So did I," Frankie said. "At one point. But you didn't buy me breakfast to hear about that."

They'd reached the car. Brady pressed the remote to unlock it. "Jump in," he said. "I've a lot to tell you."

"Switch the engine on will you, boss? There's global warming and there's Whitby with the wind coming off the sea."

Frankie cradled her coffee. Brady started to talk. "I went to see someone yesterday," he said. "I'm not going to tell you who. The less you know the better."

"You went to check up on me?"

Brady shook his head. "No, not at all. But you must have known that if you were right – "

"You'd need to get it confirmed? Yeah, I worked that one out. Around the time I finished covering myself in paint."

"So I spoke to someone," Brady said. "And you're right. Completely right. A hundred per cent right."

"Which makes life complicated..."

"Which makes life bloody complicated. Gina Foster was Gina Kirk. And she had a sister."

"You found her?"

"Julie. Domestic bliss in Kenilworth. But not this week. She's in Tenerife. And you'll need to do it all again. Officially."

"Assuming you can square all this with Kershaw. Sorry, I'm going off at a tangent."

"This whole bloody case is going to be tangents, Frankie. Anyway, Gina Kirk comes out of prison and she becomes Gina Carmichael. She spent some time in a safe house and then started her new life in Rhyl. At which point someone found out her true identity – "

"Or was told."

"Or was almost certainly told," Brady said. "And she left Rhyl in a hurry and ended up in Whitby."

"Working in the solicitor's. Why didn't we check her maiden name?"

"Because it didn't matter. It was irrelevant. Carmichael wouldn't have meant anything to us."

"She asked *him* out," Frankie said. "She *wanted* to be hidden away. Didn't want to risk a repeat of Rhyl."

"Almost certainly. Or as near as makes no difference. Which begs the question – what else has Ian Foster told us that's not true? Although saying he asked her out... I think that's just insecurity."

"Not as insecure as he's going to be when you tell him the truth."

"You'd worked that out already had you? Yeah, that's going to be my job. Kershaw's going to say he's got an important meeting and our Family Liaison Officer is going to find an equally lame excuse."

Frankie looked along the North Promenade. "Kershaw lied to us," she said. "He lied to us and he watched while we wasted two weeks."

"No," Brady said. "He lied to me. I don't want you taking sides in this, Frankie. If Kershaw lied – and he did – then he lied to me. And you followed my orders. So you – and Dan Keillor – you're strictly neutral in this. And that means..."

Brady hesitated. Frankie finished the sentence for him. "That means you worked it out, not me."

"Yes. Because if Kershaw wants to blame someone – and he will – he can blame me. It's my job to protect you. And he'll believe that. My old boss worked on the original case for a while. When they were putting it together. I didn't know any details – I was a long way down the pecking order in those days – but he was away in Birmingham for about a month. So Kershaw will find it easy to believe it was me."

Frankie was silent. Took her time replying. "It was still a bloody good piece of detective work," she finally said. "I'm proud of that."

"It was. You should be. And I'll make sure you get the credit. But we need to find the killer first. And I need to deal with the politics."

"You want to walk up the road, boss? This is a lot to take in – sitting in a confined space."

"Yeah sure. You up to braving the wind off the sea?"

They walked across on to the promenade. Sat on one of the seats.

Fifty yards up from where I sat a few months ago. Where I tried to work out Patrick's death. Where I looked over to the left and saw the hill where I scattered my wife's ashes. Now I'm sitting here with someone else...

"What do you want first?" Brady said. "The killer or the office politics?"

"Save the best until last. Let's get the internal crap out of the way."

"So Kershaw knew. It's inconceivable that he didn't know. So for whatever reason he didn't tell me."

"What's your best guess on that?"

"You want my honest opinion? Prayer. Clearly someone gave an order that Gina Kirk's identity was to be on a need-to-know basis. That came as far down as Kershaw. He decided no-one else needed to know. Has he sent the news back up the food chain yet? Maybe not. As far as the rest of the world is concerned a farmer's wife is dead, not someone in witness protection."

"He wants it to be an accident," Frankie said.

"Desperately. And if he reluctantly concedes it's murder he wants Ian Foster to be guilty."

"So he's going to be pissed off."

"He's going to be more than pissed off. He's going to be as pissed off as only an unscrupulous, ambitious bastard who thinks his chance of promotion might be screwed can be pissed off."

Frankie turned and smiled at him. "You need to stop sitting on the fence, boss. Tell me what you *really* think."

Brady laughed. "Right. Sorry. You said you wanted the

politics. It just... well, pisses *me* off because Kershaw's going to tell me to break the news to Foster. I'm going to sit in his dining kitchen and... Whatever Ian Foster has left, whatever he's clinging on to, I'm going to take it away."

"So who killed her?" Frankie said.

"Bloody hell. Who didn't kill her? Right now my money would be on the gang – someone's just come out of jail. Or someone found out? Took the law into their own hands? If her identity has been leaked once it can be leaked again."

"But why now?"

"Right. Why now? What changed? Like I say, someone coming out of jail is the most likely reason."

"So that's where we start?"

"Hopefully. But where we start is with me seeing Kershaw. If I can't persuade him it's murder you and I are back on traffic duty. Or standing at the side of the harbour waiting for someone to land a crab that's two centimetres too small."

"But now we know..."

"No, Frankie. Now *I* know. You didn't discover anything, we didn't have this conversation. You've got a career to worry about."

"And you haven't?"

"I can always go back to writing."

"Very funny, boss. Shame I haven't got any coffee left. I could have snorted it down my nose."

"Come on," Brady said. "Time to get to work. I might as well see Kershaw first thing. Strike while the iron's hot. Or while it's only been cooling down for two weeks..."

They walked back to the car. Brady put the key in the ignition. "I've got some sympathy for her," Frankie said. "A lot of sympathy."

"Gina Kirk or Gina Foster?"

"Gina Foster, I suppose. Although we don't know enough about Gina Kirk."

"What do you need to know?" Brady said. "She sat with the kids. Told them it would be alright. Delivered them to the 'clients.' For want of a better word."

"She's what though, boss? Twenty? Twenty-one? What did you do when you were that age?"

"Right, Frankie. But there's a difference between getting drunk in the student union and child sex trafficking."

"Of course there is. But we don't know her story."

"Hopefully the sister can fill in a few blanks," Brady said.

"I was talking about living on the farm. It's a life sentence."

"Hell's teeth, Frankie. There are worse open prisons than a farm just outside Whitby."

"Yes. Sure. Think about the psychological pressure though. No contact with her family. Never. Her little girl never sees her grandmother. Gina's mother never sees her grandchild. How do you cope with that?"

"Maybe that's why she was determined not to have another baby."

"And what does she do when Maria leaves home?" Frankie said. "Five years and she's off to university."

What do I do when Ash leaves home...

"So why send her away to school?" Brady said. "There's only one answer."

"Someone found her."

"Right. And she didn't want to risk her daughter seeing what came next. We have to find out who found her. And we have to find out what other lies she told. That have been faithfully reported as the truth by Ian Foster."

"Maybe he found out," Frankie said. "Maybe she kept a diary. Maybe he found it. Realised she'd lied to him. Maybe Ian Foster did kill her..."

18

"Best of luck, boss," Frankie said. "I've just seen Kershaw getting a coffee. He's wearing his I-do-not-need-this-shit face this morning."

"Let's see how he copes with some more," Brady replied. "And let's see if we have a murder on our hands."

He tapped on Kershaw's door. "Come."

God, there must surely be a special place in hell for people who say that...

"Morning, sir. I wondered if I could have five minutes?"

Kershaw looked up from the file he was working on.

Best suit today. Clearly a meeting with the great and good. Another photo-op for the ego wall...

"What's it about?"

"Gina Foster."

"Good God haven't we put that one to bed yet? She slipped and fell in the river. If she was pushed it was the husband. Is that it, Brady? I've a meeting with the Chief

Constable and the local MPs. And the village idiot who fooled the voters into making him Crime Commissioner."

"I think she was murdered, sir."

Kershaw pushed the file to one side. Looked out of the window.

The Abbey's still there, sir. It's been there for 1,400 years. Come on...

Finally replied. "You think she was murdered?"

"Yes, sir. I think we should treat it as a murder enquiry."

Kershaw checked the Abbey again. Turned back to Brady. "On what evidence?"

"No evidence. Reasonable suspicion. We walk our dog in the same place every day. We don't slip and fall where we walk every day. And it's bloody difficult to fall in the Esk. At least where she went in. The husband can barely function without her – I've never seen a more unlikely murderer. And Geoff Oldroyd is suspicious about the marks on her face and arms."

"And on that flimsy basis I'm supposed to divert manpower and money into a murder investigation? With – if what you say is correct – no suspects and no proof she *was* murdered?"

"Yes, sir. I think... No, I believe that Gina Foster was murdered."

"And I don't." Kershaw screwed the lid back onto his Mont Blanc fountain pen. Very carefully closed the file he'd been working on. Placed it inside his Burberry brief-case. Emphatically clicked the briefcase shut. Finally turned his attention back to Brady. "You arrived here with some reputation, Brady. And at a convenient time. But..."

He paused, clearly looking for the right phrase. "I'm disappointed," Kershaw said. "You've promised much and delivered little. Actually, you've delivered fuck all. So bugger off and do something useful. I gave you a week. You've had it. So if you hadn't already guessed the answer is no. And it's staying no."

Kershaw reached forward and put his hand on his briefcase. A clear signal that the meeting was over.

Brady ignored the signal. He hadn't wanted to confront Kershaw. Twenty years' experience told him that direct confrontation almost never worked.

But sometimes there was no alternative.

He held his hand up. "One more thing, sir."

Brady stood up and looked out of the window. Not just the Abbey, the harbour. He liked the view from this office.

He turned round and faced Kershaw.

"It's not so much Gina Foster I think was murdered, sir. More Gina Kirk."

Brady replayed the scene a hundred times over the next few days. Found it impossible not to admire Kershaw.

The change of gear was almost instant.

The immediate acceptance of what he'd heard. The calculations. How it changed the dynamic between himself and Brady. The potential risks. What it meant for his career. A few minor changes in Kershaw's facial muscles was the only sign Brady had. Less than five seconds.

And the decision was made.

In the best interests of Alan Kershaw.

"Who told you?"

Remember. It's you and him. It's your job to protect her.

"No-one told me. I worked it out – "

"How?"

"My old boss worked on the case. And it didn't feel right. Not if you looked at it from Gina's point of view. So I put two and two together. And a few hours later I got four."

Kershaw steepled his fingers. "It hasn't been easy, you know. It's been a hard one to manage. Always the threat that someone would find out. And the sensitivity of the case..."

Where's he going with this? Clearly he wants me to say something. Let's disappoint him...

"I suppose I owe you an apology," Kershaw said, finally accepting that Brady wasn't going to answer him.

This isn't about getting an apology. It's not about getting angry. It's about getting what you want.

"Not me," Brady said. "DS Thomson. Dan Keillor. They've done a lot of work."

"You understand the sensitivity though, Mike? I said it to you before. Modern policing is about a lot more than – " Kershaw made the inverted commas gesture which always irritated Brady " – nicking villains."

"But you accept she was murdered?" Brady said.

"I accept two things, Mike. I accept that there's a mess we may need to clear up. When something like this happens on our patch – "

'My patch' when it's going well. 'Our patch' when the shit hits the fan...

"– It has implications. Repercussions. Complications.

It can impact all our careers. So I accept we have a situation we need to manage. And I accept that if she *was* murdered, Foster is still the most likely suspect. The only suspect."

Brady pursed his lips. "I'll concede that's possible."

"Foster would be the right result, Mike. Foster would be quick, simple, expedient. This case being settled quickly and simply would make a lot of people very happy. A lot of important people."

Brady looked past him at the ego wall. Shearer, Alex Ferguson, Kenny Dalgleish.

'Never trust a man who supports more than one football team.' He could hear his dad saying it now.

"Presumably those very important people would like the truth?" he said.

Kershaw sighed. "The truth? God save us from seekers after truth."

"How long have you known?" Brady asked.

"Long enough." Kershaw smiled. A 'we're in this together' smile. "To be honest, Mike. It's a relief to share the burden."

"Who else knows?"

"Below me? No-one. A child sex-trafficker next to you in the queue at Sainsbury's isn't what the good people of Whitby want to hear."

Brady hesitated for a moment. But only for a moment. "Or a story you'd want the local paper to report."

It was the same as before. The imperceptible change in expression. The instant calculation. No time at all. Just long enough for Brady to see that he'd made an enemy.

Kershaw looked at his Rolex. "I really must be going,

Mike. It never does to keep the Chief Constable waiting. The Crime Commissioner can barely tell the time but my Lord and Master is a stickler for punctuality. So..."

"So it's a murder enquiry?"

"It's a murder enquiry into the death of Gina Foster. Wife of a local farmer. Find her killer and you – we – will make some very important people very happy. Find Gina Kirk's killer and the consequences don't bear thinking about. For any of us."

"What about Ian Foster? He's entitled to know the truth."

Kershaw looked at him blankly. "Why? Once he knows he's going to demand answers. 'Why wasn't I told?' It's going to be all over Whitby in no time at all. I'll give you your murder enquiry, Mike. I won't give you carte blanche to tell all and sundry. You're looking for the killer of Gina Foster. And *only* Gina Foster."

And that's as good as I'm going to get.

Kershaw picked his briefcase up. "And take the FLO with you when you tell Foster. I know Thomson's qualified but take someone whose training is up to date." He reached for his car keys. "You probably know I'm away from tomorrow?"

"Yes, sir. That's why I wanted to talk to you today."

"Yes. We've a little place in Marbella. Always have two weeks at this time of year. Before the great unwashed arrive for half term."

Kershaw put his hand on the door. Then he paused. "One more thing."

"Sir?"

"You asked me who else knew. Let me ask you the

same question. Who have you told about this dramatic little piece of detective work you've done."

"No-one. No-one at all."

"Good. Make sure it stays that way." Kershaw paused. "Then again, you can't investigate a murder on your own. That would look slightly odd. Thomson. No-one else. And remind her what's at stake."

Her career. Don't worry, I know what's at stake. For both of us.

Kershaw smiled. "I'm glad we've had this chat, Mike. I can go away with a clear conscience knowing everything is in your hands. Make sure it's sorted by the time I'm back, won't you?"

He held out his hand. Brady shook it. Wondered how the hell he was going to 'manage the situation,' as Kershaw so delicately put it.

19

"Do you have a minute?" Brady said.

Frankie raised her eyebrows. Her question was obvious.

"Yes, I have spoken to him," Brady said.

She followed him into his office. "What did he say? Is it murder, boss?"

"Yes. And no. It's half a murder. My instructions are to investigate the murder of Gina Foster."

"What about Gina Kirk?"

"She doesn't exist. Not officially. And if we can clear up the murder of Gina Foster she'll never exist."

"Christ, boss. That's just bullshit. We can't – "

Brady held his hand up. "Those are Kershaw's orders, Frankie. And I've drawn the short straw. Obviously. It's my job to tell Foster his wife was murdered."

"And not tell him who his wife really was?"

"That's about it. And we need to take Sally Brown with us as well."

"Like I said before, we don't need to. I'm FLO trained."

Brady shook his head. "Kershaw's explicit instruction. 'Someone whose training is right up to date.'"

"Who'll report straight back to him."

"Of course. Why else would she be there? One other thing," Brady said.

"What's that?"

"More orders. The number of people who know about this has to be kept to an absolute minimum. So no Dan Keillor. It's just you and me."

Frankie looked at him. "Just the two of us? That's good enough odds for me."

"Yep," Brady said. "Me too." He reached for his phone. "Not much point turning up if Farmer Foster's gone to market."

"Mr Foster, it's Detective Chief Inspector Michael Brady. I'd like to chat to you again. It's important. I'd like to talk to you today if possible."

"I'm with the vet, Mr Brady. Bloody cows got out. One of the daft buggers got herself stuck on the fence. We'll be done by the afternoon one way or t'other."

"I swear to God the road didn't have this many potholes last week."

It was three in the afternoon, the autumn light already threatening to fade.

Sally Brown, Family Liaison Officer, late 30s, round face, hair cut square across her forehead, sat resolute, silent and unsmiling in the back seat.

Ash always hated travelling in the back. Said it made her feel sick. Let's see shall we...

Brady swerved late round one of the potholes, hoping it would provoke a reaction. It didn't. Sally Brown remained resolute, silent and unsmiling. Frankie shot him a 'you'll have to try harder' glance.

He was surprised to see another car parked outside the farmhouse. A very new, very white Audi.

"What's this then?" Frankie said, "Do you think Foster's spent the life cover already?"

"You'd hope he'd have her insured for more than the cost of a car. Besides, it doesn't look much good for towing a trailer."

"Or for staying clean in a farmyard..."

Brady parked as far away from the Audi as he could. Tried to avoid feeling guilty. Cleaning the Tiguan wasn't one of his strong points. And he was beginning to suspect that an air freshener might be a wise investment. The autumn tides were delivering a regular supply of dead fish for Archie to roll in...

He knocked on the farmhouse door. The wind was coming from a different direction this morning. Someone close by kept pigs.

The perks of living in the country...

"Afternoon, Chief Inspector." Ian Foster looked guarded, wary. "You'd best come in." He gestured towards the kitchen table.

A man stood up. Brady's age, maybe slightly older. An inch or two over six foot. Short grey hair, eyes that were half way between blue and brown, a tight lipped smile. A dark blue suit, pale blue open neck shirt. A man who'd been deeply sceptical when the *New Law Journal* told him a solicitor was 'more approachable' in an open-necked shirt.

"Stephen Curtiss," he said, holding out his hand.

A firm, decisive handshake. "Michael Brady. And Detective Sergeant Thomson. Detective Constable Brown, our Family Liaison Officer."

"Not sure I've enough chairs," Ian Foster said. "And this is my solicitor. I thought I should have someone with me. Seeing as this isn't a social call."

"No," Brady said, pulling out a chair and sitting down opposite Curtiss. "No, it's not a social call, Mr Foster – "

There's no point beating about the bush. This is a farmer. Who's seen his fair share of animals put down. Maybe even that cow this morning. Who's done it himself...

"Mr Foster, I'm here with bad news. There's no easy way to say this. I'm deeply sorry to tell you this, but we believe there's a strong possibility that your wife was murdered. We're now treating her death as a murder enquiry."

'Tell them the news. And watch, Mike. In those first few seconds, watch them.' More of Jim Fitzpatrick's wisdom. *'Those first few seconds will tell you more than an hour's questioning.'*

Foster shook his head. Not in denial. Incomprehension. 'Murder.' He was struggling to work out what the word meant. Why was someone saying it in his kitchen?

"You understand what I've said, Mr Foster?"

He nodded. Slowly, ponderously. "Someone pushed her in? Is that what you're saying? Is that – " Brady saw the possibility suddenly occur to him. "Is that why you've come? So many of you? Are you – "

Curtiss held his hand up and stopped him short. "Are we entitled to know why you think that, Mr Brady?" he smiled his tight-lipped smile. "And please forgive me not using your title. 'Detective Chief Inspector' is something of a mouthful."

"It's no problem to me. And right now, no, we're not at liberty to disclose any details. Our scene of crime officers will need access to some of your land, Mr Foster. Where –
"

'The incident.' What else are you going to say? 'Murder?'

"– where the incident may have occurred. The SOCO team are on their way."

"I'm a suspect," Foster said. "You think I did it. You're here to arrest me."

Brady's mind went back to Kara. Her husband had been murdered. But she'd been calm, held herself together. Bill Calvert had seen it as evidence of her guilt. Ian Foster was unravelling in front of him.

And that's before I tell him the rest of the story...

Brady shook his head. "No, Mr Foster. You're not a 'suspect.' And we're not here to arrest you. But you are the person with the most information. So I'd be grateful if we could work through it. And when we've done that DC Brown will explain how we can help you. And support you."

Stephen Curtiss reached for a yellow legal pad. "You don't mind if I make notes, Mr Brady?"

"Not in the slightest, Mr Curtiss."

"You first met your wife when she was working at your solicitor's office?"

Foster nodded. "You know I did. I've told you all this." He gestured at Frankie. "Told your partner."

"Would that be your firm, Mr Curtiss?"

The solicitor raised his eyebrows. "I'm not entirely sure I'm here to 'help with your enquiries,' Mr Brady. But in the spirit of goodwill, yes. At our Whitby office."

"And then you asked her out? Where did you go on your first date, Mr Foster?"

Let's see how good your memory is. Romano's Italian. Grace had salmon and pasta, I had meatballs.

"That's hardly relevant, Mr Brady."

"Humour me, Mr Curtiss."

"I took her to the Black Bull. At Ugthorpe. Knew the owner. Not now. It changed hands."

"Thank you. And... what? Six months later Gina moves in? And you were married..."

"In the summer. At the register office. Gina didn't have any family. So she didn't want any fuss."

"No family at all? No brothers? Sisters? No friends she wanted at the wedding?"

Foster shook his head. "No. Like I told you before. She moved up here from the Midlands."

"Where, exactly?"

"Birmingham? Somewhere just outside. She did tell me. I can't remember."

Brady paused. They clearly weren't going to be offered coffee. There was a red Gaggia on the worktop. Gina would have bought it.

It's just going to gather dust. He's already back on Nescafé.

"How old was your wife's daughter when you married?" Frankie asked.

"She was... let me work it out. Two. Nearly three."

"And she's 13 now?"

Foster nodded. "Just coming up to 14. Not going to have much of a birthday, poor lass..."

"She goes to school in Whitby?"

"Scarborough College," Foster said. "Just down the coast. Well, everyone knows where Scarborough is."

"She goes there every day?"

Foster shook his head again. "No. She boards."

"She boards? Through the week?"

"No. Through the term. It was Gina's idea. She wasn't much impressed by the schools in Whitby."

Brady didn't pursue it.

"OK," he said. "Take me back to that Tuesday morning. Gina's gone out for a walk really early?"

"You've been through all this, surely?"

Brady suppressed a sigh. Another solicitor who thought he wasn't earning his money if he didn't interrupt after every third question.

"We have," Brady said. "But clearly circumstances are different now."

Curtiss didn't suppress a sigh. "You'd better go through it again, Ian. Try and use simple words."

"I was up early. One of the cows had an infected udder. So I went to check on her. Then I was ploughing the top field. Takes me all morning. Gina made me a flask of coffee and fixed me a sandwich. We had some breakfast – "

"What did you have?"

"Really, Chief Inspector. Does what Mr Foster had for breakfast really matter? Or is he guilty of not having his five-a-day?"

I'm beginning to dislike you, Mr Curtiss. And while you

may like the sound of your own voice you're not doing your client any favours.

"Just a complete picture, Mr Curtiss…"

"Gina baked her own bread. Couple of slices of toast and I'm set for the morning."

"And Gina?"

Foster shrugged. "I went out. She doesn't usually have much."

"So you walk across the yard, get in your tractor and go up to the top field? Gina takes the dog out for a walk?"

"Pretty much."

"And that's the last you see of her until lunchtime? Or the last you expect to see?"

Foster nodded. "Yeah. Ploughing that field takes all morning. That's why Gina made me a sandwich. So yes. Thought I'd see her when I came back."

"But all you found was the dog?"

"Max. Yes. I just assumed Gina had gone to the supermarket. She usually leaves a note."

"But not this time?"

"No, I saw the car."

"So when did you start to get worried?"

Foster looked at his solicitor.

Is he worried about incriminating himself? It's a simple enough question.

"Maybe two. Two-thirty," he said. "I went back out. There was some work needed doing in the barn. Then I came back and she still wasn't here. That's when I started to worry."

"And you phoned us? When?"

"I don't know. Four o'clock maybe."

"The call was logged at 16:17," Frankie said.

"Did you phone anyone else?" Brady said. "Friends, anyone like that?"

He looked at the solicitor again. Curtiss nodded.

You might as well tell us. Because we're going to check the phone records. This isn't Bill Calvert in charge. Her phone isn't going to sit on my desk for a week.

"She's got a friend. Shirley. Mrs Lloyd. Lives at the Old Vicarage. Sometimes they go for a walk together."

"How did you know her number?" Frankie asked. "I don't know the numbers of my partner's friends. I don't have them in my phone."

Foster nodded towards the fridge. "There," he said. "Gina said Shirley had a new phone. She'd given her the number. So I rang it."

"And what did Mrs Lloyd say?" Brady asked.

"Said she was busy. Her mother wasn't well. Said she'd phone me back."

"And did she?"

"I don't know. By then I knew... The phone rang. I didn't answer it."

Brady nodded. Hoped he looked sympathetic. Let a few seconds pass.

"You must have some help on the farm, Mr Foster? You can't do it all yourself?"

"Gina does the paperwork. I told you."

Not the easiest interview I've ever had. Just Frankie and me and we'd have found out everything we needed. Throw in a solicitor and a waste of space FLO and we've got a bloody crowd scene. And a man who thinks he's on trial...

"Someone must come and help you with the manual side of things?"

"There's Jamie. Does three or four days a week most weeks. More when I'm busy."

"Thank you. Could you give me his number?"

Foster grudgingly scrolled through his contacts. Gave Brady a number. "Harkin," he added. "Jamie Harkin."

It was always the hardest question to ask. Always the question that brought them face to face with reality. Underlined what had happened.

"Can you think of anyone who might want to kill your wife, Mr Foster?"

Foster stared at him.

He still doesn't believe it's happened. He's been down to the morgue, identified the body, told his daughter, slept in an empty bed. And he still expects her to walk in through the door.

"No," Foster said. "No-one. No-one at all. I loved her. Everyone loved her. No-one would want to kill her."

He was right. There was no reason for anyone to kill Gina Foster.

"I'm ashamed of myself," Brady said. "Absolutely ashamed of myself. But what the hell can I do? Kershaw says don't tell him..."

"You can't tell him," Frankie finished.

"And supposing it wasn't Gina Foster that was murdered? Supposing it *was* Gina Kirk? Then I've got to tell him anyway. And he'll know I've lied to him."

Brady shook his head. "Come on. Let's go and see what Henry's up to. See if he's found anything."

"What did you tell him?"

"Look at the whole area. The grass bank and a good 30 yards either side. My guess is that Gina met someone. My second guess is they didn't walk very far."

"What are you looking for?"

"Everything. The footprint we found. Fibres. Anything and everything." Brady jumped across a puddle. "Christ, the track's even muddier than it was before."

He ducked under the blue and white incident tape.

Held it up for Frankie to follow him. Said 'hello' to one of the scene of crime guys. Walked towards the river bank. Wondered if Henry had found anything yet.

Stopped. Felt his heart sink...

On a sunny day it would have been perfect for a picnic.

The river bank – the 'crime scene' – was a sea of mud.

Henry Squire was in his late 30s. Thorough, intelligent, enthusiastic. A man who counted a day on his hands and knees at a murder scene as a day well spent.

Brady looked at the sea of mud again. "Tell me the worst, Henry."

"Useless, Mike. Absolutely bloody useless. Remember it pissed down a couple of days ago? The river's risen about a foot. If your footprint was half in and half out of the water before then there's no question where it is now."

"Floating down the river?"

"Somewhere in the North Sea, I'd say, given the amount of rain we've had."

"And then..." Brady looked around him. Gestured at the mud. "This never happened in Manchester."

Henry laughed. "Welcome to North Yorkshire. Someone's let the cows out. They've come down to the river to have a drink. Your crime scene is a precise 50/50 mixture."

Brady raised his eyebrows. "Of?"

"One part mud to one part cow shit. I'm sorry, Mike."

Brady stared at the river bank for a third time. What had once been the river bank. "Maybe 60/40 Henry but it's academic. You're a farmer's daughter, Frankie. How long do cows need to do this much damage? Not that they'd see it as damage."

"Not long, boss. Especially with the weather being like it is. You could see how wet it was just walking down the track."

"So it could have happened yesterday? When Foster said the cows got out?"

Frankie nodded. "Yesterday, or a week ago. There's no way of telling."

"What about the rest of the area, Henry? The bushes, the path, anything in the grass?"

"Nothing yet. But we'll keep looking. Well, tomorrow now. The light's just about gone."

"Thanks, Henry. Let me know if you find anything."

"Apart from cow shit?"

"It'd make the job easier... Come on, Frankie," Brady said. "Let's go." He turned and started walking back up the bank.

"Are you going to say anything to Foster?" Frankie asked, catching him up.

"No, I don't think so. I'd say he's had more than enough for one day wouldn't you. Me telling him his wife's been murdered. Sally Brown's useless platitudes about support. More than enough to keep him awake tonight."

"When he's alone in his bed?" Frankie said.

Yep. Alone in the bed. Staring up at the ceiling. Going to sleep in the spare room because you can't stand being in the bed without her...

"I've got a theory," Frankie said.

"About the murder?"

"No, about life."

"What's that then?"

"The really big moments in your life – good or bad – you're on your own."

Brady looked at her. "Yeah," he said. "You're right. That's how it was for me. One day the funeral's over. Everyone's gone home. You've done all the paperwork..."

"It works the other way as well though," Frankie said. "I had a friend at school. He was desperate to be a writer. He slogged away for years. Then there was a post on Facebook. Netflix had bought his book. So we all sent messages, saying how brilliant it was, how we remembered him from English. But we didn't have a clue. None of us had been through the years of rejection."

"Starving in a garret..."

"Not quite. He taught English. But then he sold his book. No-one else could share that moment. No-one else could know how he really felt."

"Except for the other night," Brady said.

Frankie turned her head. Held his gaze. "When I found Gina?"

"Like you said. 'This is as good as it gets for us.' I knew."

"Yes," she said. "You did."

21

"*Now* you've got house envy," Frankie said.

"The Old Vicarage. Vicars never lived in two-bed bungalows did they?"

Brady turned into the drive. He'd phoned the number on the fridge door. Broken the news about Gina. Arranged the meeting.

Shirley Lloyd was waiting at the door. Short blonde hair, no-nonsense glasses. A navy jacket over a red top. Every inch the chair of the local Women's Institute.

"Mrs Lloyd, thank you for seeing us. I'm Detective Chief Inspector Michael Brady. This is my colleague, Detective Sergeant Thomson."

They shook hands. Accepted the offer of a cup of tea. Followed her dutifully through to the conservatory. Admired the view across the valley.

Learned how she met Gina.

"We are all creatures of habit, Detective Chief Inspector. We all walk our dogs at the same time every day. And one day we just decided to walk together. And Roger and Max seemed happy enough."

"Roger's your dog?"

She looked at Brady over the top of her glasses. "He's not my husband, Inspector Brady. Although God knows it takes longer to train husbands."

Brady smiled. Suspected it wasn't the first time she'd used that joke. "That's very good, Mrs Lloyd. It's a long walk for you. Out to the Fosters' farm."

"I'm retired. I've plenty of time. And Roger needs the exercise. Husbands and Labradors, they both run to fat."

"So you'd meet each other quite often?"

"Three or four times a week. And gradually we accepted that we'd become friends. Gina – Mrs Foster – struck me as someone who needed a friend. I invited her to the WI a couple of times but she said she wasn't a meetings sort of person."

"You said you're retired, Mrs Lloyd. So a good bit older than Mrs Foster..."

"Significantly older. Old enough to be her mother, obviously."

"Did she confide in you?"

"I'm not sure what you mean. Do help yourself to some more tea. We talked as we walked the dogs. Nothing of any real consequence though."

"Did you ever go to the farm?"

Shirley Lloyd shook her head. "No, never. I got the impression that she and her husband kept themselves to themselves."

"Did Mrs Foster come here?"

"Just the once. One of those lovely days you get in April. When you can walk the dogs for miles. We ended up back here. We had a drink – and then she walked home."

An elderly Labrador – clearly just woken up from a sleep – padded into the conservatory and flopped down at Shirley Lloyd's feet. "Ah, Roger. Good boy. Come to corroborate my story."

Brady smiled at her. "I've a Springer at home, Mrs Lloyd. Only in exchange for a biscuit." He paused. Changed tack. "The news of Gina's death came as a complete shock to you?"

"More than a shock. I – well, I don't count myself a timid woman, Detective Inspector, but when you phoned me... Until you catch whoever is responsible Roger will have to settle for strolling round the village."

"Can I take you back to the morning of Gina's death, Mrs Lloyd?" Brady knew it was a longshot. "You didn't by any chance bump into her that morning?"

"No, I didn't. I was up early that morning – I'm a magistrate, I was due in court – so I was out early with Roger. But no, I didn't. Mainly because – there you are, I said we're all creatures of habit, now I'm contradicting myself – I wanted a change of scenery. So I went up the hill rather than along by the river."

"You didn't see anyone?"

"No, only the pheasants. You know your dog's getting old when he's not interested in a field full of pheasants."

Brady turned to Frankie. "Anything you'd like to ask, DS Thomson?"

"Just one question," Frankie said. "Did Gina ever talk about her marriage, Mrs Lloyd?"

Shirley Lloyd turned her head to look at Frankie. "Are you asking me if there was any trouble in the marriage?"

"I wasn't. But if there was it would help us to know about it. More generally, Mrs Lloyd, did she strike you as being happy?"

Shirley Lloyd stirred her tea. Took her time over the reply. "A perceptive question, Detective Sergeant. Men ask you what happened. Women ask you how someone felt about it. The detectives on TV never understand the difference. Content, I'd say, more than happy. Gina struck me as someone who'd made her bed. And accepted that her job was to lie on it."

"Is there anything else?" Frankie asked. "You seem a good judge of character."

Shirley Lloyd nodded. "I hope I am. I was a bank manager. The first female manager in the county. In the days when you made loans based on character and reputation, not credit score. Would you allow me to speculate?"

Brady smiled. *Not that I could stop her.*

"Be my guest, Mrs Lloyd. The more insight you can give us the better. Please, go ahead."

Shirley Lloyd finished her tea. "It's hard to put your finger on it. Sometimes, I felt... I've told you that she'd made her bed. Accepted she had to lie on it. Sometimes I felt that Gina Foster wanted reassurance. That she'd made the right decision in life."

Ten minutes later Michael Brady handed her his card. "Anything else you think of, Mrs Lloyd. Don't hesitate to ring me."

. . .

"SHE DIDN'T MENTION HER MOTHER," Frankie said as they climbed into Brady's car.

"No. And having said she was a creature of habit she changed her walk on the morning Gina died."

"No witnesses to where she went..."

Brady laughed. "There never are in the country. Unless you count pheasants. I could always send you undercover. Infiltrate the WI."

"I'm fine thanks, boss. The supermarket sells jam. And I'm not a fan of *Jerusalem*."

22

It was Carl's flat all over again. Maybe one or two rungs up the ladder. A slightly better area of Whitby. Slightly less clutter. No drawings on the wall. But all the signs of someone living on their own.

Eggs still in their cartons. Cans of beans lined up on the worktop like soldiers on parade. Monday, Tuesday, Wednesday...

Carl, now Jamie Harkin. He could see exactly the way they thought because it was exactly the way he'd thought.

'I'm going to eat them in the next three days so what's the point of putting them away?'

And then Grace sorted him out...

"Jamie, thanks for agreeing to talk to us. I'm Detective Chief Inspector Michael Brady. My colleague, Detective Sergeant Thomson."

He was tall, thin, wiry. Full of nervous energy. Three days growth of beard. Brown hair, brown eyes, a ring of barbed wire tattooed on the left hand side of his neck.

Yes, Ash, I know you're going to get a tattoo at some point. I accept it's inevitable. Just not on your neck, OK?

"Yeah. No problem. You want a coffee or anything? Just made one."

Brady looked at Frankie. She shook her head. "No, we're good thanks. Jamie – you don't mind me calling you Jamie?"

"No, it's my name isn't it? Call me Mr Harkin I'll think you want my dad."

"Thanks. We're just trying to get some background. But we're treating this as a murder enquiry now. So DS Thomson will take some notes."

Jamie shrugged. "Be as formal as you like. You want to sit at the table if you're writing?"

"Thanks."

The table was covered in a checked oilcloth. It reminded Brady of going to visit his grandmother. But without the cigarette burns, or the rings from her coffee mugs.

"Ian Foster told us you started work in the spring?"

Jamie nodded. "Late April, early May, some time like that."

"Where were you before?"

"In a field of potatoes. Fucking potatoes as far as you could see." He looked at Frankie. "Forgot my manners. Sorry."

"No problem," Frankie said. "I've arrested people on a Saturday night. But giving the field a slightly more precise location might help us, Mr Harkin."

"Driffield," Jamie said. "On the Wolds. A potato farm.

All those oven chips? That's where they come from. But I was bored. Didn't fancy another summer surrounded by spuds."

"So you came here?"

"Yeah. Fancied the sea air. I move around. Did a couple of days. Just casual. Then the bloke who did most of the work came off his bike. Smashed his pelvis Foster said. So that was me in for the summer."

"What do you do on the farm?"

"What don't I do, you mean? Feed 'em. Clean up the shit. In at one end, out at the other. Getting the harvest in, spreading more shit, repairing whatever needs repairing. All that for nine fucking quid an hour."

"So essentially there's just you and Mr Foster doing the work?"

Jamie nodded. "Pretty much. Like all farmers he'll get someone else in at harvest time. Gina – well, Mrs Foster – she did a bit but she was inside mostly."

Brady paused. "Have you always worked on farms, Jamie?"

"Yeah, pretty much. I'm dyslexic. I was dyslexic before it became fashionable. At least at the school I went to. So they decided I was stupid. Left as soon as I could. And animals don't really care if you can read that well."

"What did you make of Mr Foster?"

"You want my honest opinion? He's a lucky bugger. Inherits a farm. I'd like a farm one day. Smallholding maybe. Place of my own. Nice wife."

Does he mean he wants a nice wife? Or Gina was a nice wife?

Brady went with the second option. "You liked Mrs Foster?" he said.

"Yeah. Didn't see that much of her. But she brought me a cup of tea if she saw me."

"And Mr and Mrs Foster? Together?"

Jamie took his time replying. "Didn't see anything of them together. He was outside, she was inside. Maybe that's how being married works?"

"You didn't hear anything? No fights? Arguments?"

He curled his bottom lip back. Brought his front teeth over it in concentration. Shook his head. "Not that I can think of." He shrugged. "Besides, I'm not paid to hear anything am I? She left a gate open once or twice. Seemed a bit distracted. Some of the cows got out. Maybe that's what killed her."

"The cows?"

"Being distracted. Happens doesn't it?"

"What about that morning? The morning Mrs Foster died?"

"I was there. Went in for eight. Did all my normal jobs. Finished around dinner time."

"Did you see anyone?"

Jamie shook his head. "He was ploughing the top field. I knew he wouldn't be there."

"You didn't miss your cup of tea?" Frankie asked.

He shrugged. "Didn't think about it really. I was busy in the barn. Just left him a note of my hours and came home."

Brady looked around the flat. Jamie needed to open the window. It smelled of stale sweat. He stood up, held his hand out. "Thanks very much, Jamie. That's helpful. You'll still be here if we need you again?"

"Nowhere else to go, mate. And one farm's as good as the next. So long as it doesn't have potatoes. Besides, he's going to need someone now isn't he?"

Jamie stood up from the table. Winced as he put his weight on his right leg. Saw Brady looking at him. "Cow," he said. "Fucking cow kicked me. You ever been kicked by a cow? No? Keep it that way."

"What did you make of that?" Brady said as they sat in the car.

"He's right. My dad was kicked by a cow once. Had to use a crutch for about a week."

"Apart from that?"

"It all sounded plausible. Who wouldn't get fed up of potatoes? And farm labourers are always moving around."

"That all seems plausible to you? He turns up, does his work, goes home?"

Frankie nodded. "We had a guy like that. A lot like Jamie. Happier with animals than he was with people."

"Insights into their marriage?"

"Pretty much what we were saying. Foster's punching above his weight. He's older than her. But at least we know why she married him."

Brady tapped the steering wheel. "You alright for ten minutes?" he said. "If I drive up on to West Cliff? I don't know what it is. I can think more clearly if I'm looking at the sea."

They were there in five minutes. Early October, the light fading, drizzle. It wasn't hard to find a parking space.

Brady turned the engine off. Turned it back on again. "Like you say. There's global warming and there's Whitby in the winter."

Frankie didn't reply. Knew Brady needed to put his thoughts into words.

"When I was in Manchester," he started. "There were a couple of guys on the team. I just used to talk. They'd listen. Sometimes I worked it out. Sometimes I talked bollocks. But sometimes I need to talk bollocks."

"That's what you say to us, isn't it? Nothing is off limits. So give yourself the same permission, boss."

Can I? Can I do that? I'm forcing her to take sides. And my job's to make sure she doesn't take sides. And she's sitting close to me. And I can smell her perfume. Alien. But I've no-one else to talk to...

"Number one then. I'm going to be honest, alright? If I'm talking like this there's no point me not being honest. And this is as off the record as off the record gets."

I want to touch her. I want to reach my hand out and put it on her thigh. I just want the physical contact. Brady shook his head. *Focus on the bloody case.*

"I wanted this to be a murder. That sounds an awful thing to say. But accident or murder, it isn't going to bring Gina Foster back. So professionally, I wanted this to be a murder. I wanted to prove myself. Does that make me a bad person?"

"No," Frankie said softly. "It makes you an honest person."

"But I'm not am I? I've lied to Ian Foster. I haven't told

him who his wife really was. I didn't tell him she had a sister."

"You can't, boss. Not yet."

"I know. That doesn't make me think it's right. I've lied to Shirley Lloyd and I've lied to Jamie. OK, maybe it's not as important with those two, but I'm still lying. God only knows what Ian Foster's going to do when he finds out the truth."

"OK, but it's not your decision is it? Kershaw told you: don't tell them."

"Right. And now you've been forced into taking sides. And I don't want you to take sides. I want you to come out of this clean. No sly little notes on your record. You know what, Frankie?" Brady said. "I thought I'd been really bloody clever. I thought I'd got exactly what I wanted from Kershaw. But I haven't. He's reeled me in. Hook, line and sinker. This has nothing to do with Gina Foster and everything to do with Gina Kirk. We're not going to solve Gina Foster's murder because there isn't a murder to solve. The only way we're going to find the killer is to look for Gina Kirk's killer – "

"And the only way we can do that is to tell people who Gina really was."

"And Kershaw knows I'll have to make the decision. He's sitting in Marbella drinking mojitos and I'm in Whitby twisting in the wind."

"With Sally Brown texting him updates."

"For sure. He'll have the report on the conversation with Foster by now. And if the shit hits the fan while he's away – "

"You're the one responsible."

"Yes. Because I'm the one that took the decision. Because I'm a copper not a politician. Because – unfashionable as the fucking view is – I think people who commit murder should be caught."

"So it's simple," she said. "We just need to wrap it all up by the time Kershaw gets back. Find the killer, present him with a fait accompli."

"And do it without destroying Ian Foster's life and without alerting Whitby to the fact that there's been a child sex trafficker living peacefully in the town for ten years..."

Frankie laughed. "I didn't say it was going to be easy. Shirley Lloyd then, boss. True or bluff?"

"True. What reason has she got to lie? None at all. Although she seems a bit forgetful. What about Jamie?"

"True," Frankie said. "If only because the limp was so authentic. Trust me, that's one injury you do not want."

"So where do we go next?" Brady said. "Sorry, that's a rhetorical question. I know where I'm going next."

"Am I allowed to ask?"

"Barley Green."

"We're in the middle of a murder, boss. That sounds like a children's TV character."

"It's a village. At the bottom of Pendle Hill in Lancashire."

"Where the witches lived?"

"Yep. And where my ex-boss lives. I told you he worked on the case for a while. I'm going to see him. Find out what we're up against. See how far it went. If we're going into the ring, Frankie, we need to know who we're fighting."

Brady turned the ignition on. "I'll give you a lift home," he said. "And thank you."

She reached her hand out. Briefly squeezed Brady's hand on the steering wheel. "You're welcome, boss."

23

Another night staring at the ceiling. Another night when he ended up on the sofa. When Brady realised all he was doing was training Archie. "That's it isn't it, pal? That's all I'm doing. Training you to expect a biscuit at three in the morning..."

His phone rang at one minute past seven.

"Michael Brady." A number he recognised. 9-5-9-5 at the end.

Where have I seen that? Pinned on Ian Foster's fridge.

"Mr Brady, it's Shirley Lloyd."

"Good morning. I recognised your number."

"Mr Brady, is this a convenient time? You said I should phone you if I thought of something. I have."

"It's fine. I'm away today. I've a long drive. But yes, it is. And thank you for phoning."

"I told you I went out early that morning – the morning it happened."

"Yes. You went up the hill instead of along by the river."

"I did. And I was pre-occupied. I told you I was a magistrate. I was thinking about a long day in court. Looking at the pheasants in the fields. I saw a tractor, Mr Brady. I only realised in bed last night. You see a tractor ploughing a field and you don't see it, if you know what I mean, Mr Brady."

I do, like a man in a Hi-Vis walking down a railway line.

"I do. Thank you, Mrs Lloyd. Could I ask what colour it was?"

"Red. Not brand-new red. A well-worn red."

"And whereabouts?"

"Going up to the top of the hill."

What Ian Foster called the top field. Well, it would be easy enough to check. A well-worn red tractor. Not the sort of thing that was easily hidden.

"Thank you very much, Mrs Lloyd. That's helpful. If you think of anything else give me a ring. And thank you again."

Brady put his phone down.

What time is it? 7:05. I need to set off. One call first though...

"Boss? This is early, even for you."

"I've just had Shirley Lloyd on the phone. She told me she'd remembered something."

"Something significant?"

"Yeah, potentially – "

"Dad?" Ash walked into the room. "I thought you were going early."

Brady nodded at his daughter. Mouthed, 'I am.'

"Frankie, can I call you back in two minutes? I just need to sort Ash out."

"No problem."

"I am, Ash. It'll take three, maybe 3½ hours to get there. And I'm aiming to leave by two so I can collect you from school."

"Okay. Sounds cool. Who are you going to see?"

"My old boss. But he lives in the wilds of Lancashire. Surrounded by witches."

"Sounds even cooler." Ash ran a hand through her hair. Promised she'd let Archie out before she went to school. "Fiona's picking you up?" Ash nodded. "You need any money?" She didn't. "OK, I'll see you tonight. Love you."

"Love you too, Dad. And drive carefully. Remember your reactions slow down as you get older..."

"FRANKIE, I'm sorry. I needed to get Ash sorted out."

Not that she needs me to sort her out. I need to take her for a meal. Spend some time with her.

"You'll need to speak up, boss. I can hardly hear you."

"Yeah, sorry. I've just gone through Sleights. I'm driving up Blue Bank. Like I was saying, Shirley Lloyd phoned me. She went out for a walk that morning – "

"I remember her saying."

"Hang on. I'm at the top now. Give me a second..."

Two sheep had strayed on to the road. Brady slowed

down. Honked his horn, trying to frighten them back to safety.

"...Sorry, I'm back with you. No bloody signal, sheep wandering onto the road. Only in North Yorkshire. Shirley Lloyd. That morning she takes the high road, not the low road. Up past Ian Foster's top field. And she saw a tractor."

"Ian Foster's tractor?"

"A red one."

"Yeah, that's right. I mean he's obviously not the only farmer with a red tractor, but it was in the yard the day I went. Why didn't she tell us before?"

"Your guess is as good as mine. Said she had a busy day in court."

He could hear the scepticism in Frankie's voice. "Her friend's been murdered? She as good as tells us she doesn't feel safe going out for a walk?"

Brady pulled the sun visor down as he went round a bend. Late September and the sun was low in the sky. "I think we have to give her the benefit of the doubt," he said. "So I want you to spend the day on Plan B. Not that we ever believed in Kershaw's Plan A."

"What do you want me to do?"

"Go through the old records. Gina's court case. See who's inside. Who's just been released. And see what you can find on the children. See if there are any likely suspects."

"It could be a long list. I think there were about 40 mentioned in the trial..."

"That'll only be the tip of the iceberg. But see what

you can find. I'm going to see Jim Fitzpatrick now – and tomorrow morning I'm going to tell Foster the truth."

"Kershaw's not going to like that."

"Right. So if I'm going to war with him there's only one way I'm going to win."

"Find the killer."

"Exactly. It doesn't matter how long your list is. As long as the person who murdered Gina Kirk is somewhere on it."

24
___

It was the lounge he'd always imagined. Photos of their children and grandchildren. Graduations, weddings, christenings. Jim and Val on their wedding day. Jim being presented with his bravery medal. Val graduating from the Open University.

A couple who'd been through life together. Exactly what he'd imagined.

Except the pictures are Grace and me. Ash graduating. Ash getting married. Grace holding her first grandchild...

A picture window opened out onto the garden, and the Pennines beyond. Jim saw where Brady was looking. "You know what they say," he said. "If you can see the Pennines it's going to rain. If you can't see them it *is* raining."

Brady smiled. "So not much cricket this summer then?"

"Old Trafford? That was the plan when I retired. Leave Val in peace doing her family history – I'm Swedish by the way. Can you believe it? She did my DNA. I'm 22%

Swedish. She's got me convinced I'm a direct descendant of Eric Bloodaxe. Sorry, I've started to ramble. The pleasures of old age. Where was I? Thought I'd go and watch Lancashire. You know what? I can't be bothered driving into Manchester. Two miles up the road and I can watch Burnley in the Lancashire League. Sit in the sun, a pint of Bowland Gold to keep me company and I'm home in ten minutes."

They reminisced. Talked about old cases. Brady told Jim about Whitby. Brought him up to date on Ash. Val bustled in with the tea. Jim jokingly told her off for the scones. "Every scone I eat means I have to walk an extra mile up Pendle Hill."

Val winked at Brady. "He doesn't realise it. I'm fattening him up for the witches."

Brady smiled at her.

This was how I'd pictured it. Retired but still fit and healthy. Long walks in the country. The two of us at the top of Pen y Ghent, gazing out over the Dales. Grace still as beautiful as ever...

"He never saw the big picture, Val. Always pretended he did..."

Val walked over and kissed her husband. "I assume you boys want a serious conversation. I'll be in the garden if you need me."

"Do you, Mike? Want a serious conversation?"

Brady smiled at his old boss. "Val's scones are exceptional. But Whitby to Barley is a fair old trek."

"Good," Jim said. "I'm pleased. I need to keep my brain active. Sorry, I'm being selfish." He paused. "Let me ask you something before you dive in. Have you made the right decision?"

"Going back? I've made the only decision, Jim. It's who I am."

"Supposing that business hadn't happened? And you don't need to fill me in. The old coppers' network is as reliable as it's always been."

"Then... I don't know. I'd have written a bad book, I suppose. And taken about three years to do it."

"So..." Jim paused. "I won't use the word 'lucky.' But maybe some of the cards fell the right way?"

"At a high price for Patrick."

Jim spread his hands wide. "It's our line of work, Mike. There's always some poor bugger paying a high price. Keeps us in a job. Or a pension, in my case. But it's the life we chose. Fire away..."

"Gina Foster," Brady said. "Or Gina Kirk as I should learn to call her. You worked on the case, boss."

Jim smiled at what he'd been called. Brady laughed. "Sorry, old habits die hard. But they did call you in."

Jim nodded. "They did. For about a month. A month in the Birmingham Hilton. Then out of nowhere I get a call and I'm told to go back to Manchester. Case closed. Or gone as far as it's going."

"We fished her out of the River Esk," Brady said. "Three weeks ago. Late summer tourists ready to go on the boats. Then Gina floats past. At first we think it's accidental – "

"What made you suspicious?"

"There are old bruises on her arm. Scuff marks on her face. You know, like when you were a kid and you scuffed your knees? That and – I've got a really good DS, Jim. You remember Tessa? A lot like her. She sees it from a woman's point of view. And she was convinced it wasn't right from the word go."

"And she was the one that worked out your girl was really Gina Kirk?"

Can I tell him? I'm sitting in his lounge. Eating his wife's scones. My old boss. My friend. Who'll know if I lie to him...

"No, I spent a night with the laptop. She was absolutely certain. Came round to the house. Said she'd spent all day thinking about it. Convinced me to do some digging."

Jim let him off lightly. "Yes. I learned not to ignore Tessa when she was convinced of something."

Brady nodded. "So that was it. We'd spent three weeks thinking we'd pulled a farmer's wife out of the river – "

"And you'd pulled a sex trafficker out."

"Yes."

"And the chances of someone convicted of child sex trafficking in Birmingham accidently falling into the River Esk in North Yorkshire are pretty slim?"

"Exactly."

"What does Kershaw say?" Jim asked. "And I know him of old so you can be honest with me."

Ouch...

"Find Gina Foster's killer. And don't go any further."

"And can you do that?"

"Right now?" Brady shook his head. "As far as I can see no-one had any reason to kill Gina Foster. Whereas 101 people had a reason to kill Gina Kirk."

Jim nodded. "You're probably underestimating. But you're in the right area."

Brady leaned forward and poured some more tea, "Boss?"

Jim shook his head. "Not unless I want to get up for a pee at midnight. *Not* one of the pleasures of old age."

"He's hung you out to dry," Jim said.

"Yep. I can fail to find the killer – "

"In which case you're a laughing stock..."

"I can arrest the wrong person. Or – "

"Or you can open the can of worms." Jim leaned forward and helped himself to another scone. He took a contemplative bite. "You know what, Mike? We've been married 45 years next year. I still don't think I'm getting it right. Val does some baking. There's a golden rule. I have to eat enough to show that I appreciate it – but not so much that I'm greedy. Or that I'm getting fat. Married life, Mike, it's a minefield..."

The sentence trailed away into an awkward silence. "I'm sorry," Jim said. "She was a bloody wonderful woman. How are you doing?"

"Not bad. And it's fine. You can't dance around the subject. I'm doing OK."

"There's no-one else?"

Brady shook his head.

Jim looked at him. "You take care, Mike. Tread carefully. These are deep waters. If you *can* tread carefully in deep water. But you know what I mean."

"Kershaw's covered his back?"

"Always. A leopard doesn't change its spots. Or a hyena its stripes. But you knew that already. Let me warm this tea up in the microwave and see if Val's alright. And then tell me what you want me to do. Or need to know. And – " He raised a warning finger. "Not a word of this to Val. If she finds out she'll lace my bloody scones with weedkiller."

BRADY WALKED over to the window. The top of Pendle Hill was blanketed in mist.

It must be spectacular on a sunny day. And comforting. Sit at the top of the hill, eat your sandwich and know your wife is waiting in the garden when you get home.

Jim was back. "Go on then…"

"Two things, boss. Tell me the story as you saw it. And then speculate. How far you think it went."

Jim nodded. "Alright. There were plenty of rumours about what was going on in Birmingham. Nods and winks. You know how it is. And a few names mentioned. All a bit Jimmy Savile."

"Not him though?"

"No, no. But there's no better defence than being pals with royalty. So plenty of stories. But no evidence. Or no-one willing to provide evidence. And it was easier – and politically expedient – to look the other way. Then one of the kids turns up dead and another's found wandering by the side of the motorway. Even then it might have been kept quiet. A few lurid headlines maybe, but the fuss would have died down."

"Except Gina turns up."

"She does that. Walks into Solihull police station and blows it wide open. And there's no brushing it under the carpet because she's already told her story to one of the papers."

"Told or sold?"

"Who knows? But once she's walked into Solihull there's not a fan been built that can cope with the amount of shit that's going to hit it."

"Which is when you're brought in?"

Jim nodded. "Yeah. Me and Doug Taylor from the Met. Not sure that we did any good – there was a lot of political in-fighting. And a lot of interference. From serious places."

"And Gina ended up with 21 months?"

"That's right. Gina got 21 months. The notional ring-leader – a guy called Aleks Savićević – got 15 years. A sliding scale for the others."

"You said 'notional ringleader…'"

"Yeah. Doug and I were convinced there was someone else. It all fell into place too neatly. I remember sitting in the hotel bar talking to him about it. And then the next morning he's hauled back to the Met and I'm told to drive 90 miles back up the M6."

"So who do you think it was? That was behind it all?"

Jim was silent for a moment. "I'm not trying to avoid the question, Mike. I just don't think I can answer you. Not without speaking to Doug. We worked on the case together. I just don't think the knowledge – the guess-work, really – is 100% mine."

Is he frightened? I've never seen Jim Fitzpatrick frightened…

Brady nodded. "I understand that, boss. But if you could speak to Doug… I just want to know as much as I can. Know what I might be up against. Did you ever meet Gina?" he asked.

"Once," Jim replied. "I sat in on an interview. Maybe 20 minutes."

"What did you think?"

"Much the same as everyone else. I couldn't understand how she'd done what she'd done – with the children. So on the one hand I'm disgusted but on the other I'm full of admiration for her. The courage she needed to do what she did. She must have guessed at what it meant."

He sipped his tea. "Bloody hell, cold again. You'd think when you're retired you'd have time to drink a cup of tea before it went cold. I put 'em all in the microwave. Bugger peeing in the middle of the night. I'll make a fresh pot."

He was back ten minutes later. "Another scone, boss?" Brady said. "That'll be twice up Pendle Hill."

Jim laughed. "What did I say to you before? I reckon I've eaten just enough to show my appreciation. Another scone and she'll be threatening me with a mixed leaf salad. More seriously," he said. "What are you going to do about it? You've got her computer, obviously."

Brady nodded. "Yes. But I'm not holding out much hope. So I'll make a list. Work through it as quickly as I can. Work out who's only told me half a story."

"Who've you got on it so far?"

"If I'm following orders, Ian Foster, the husband."

"So it's not going to take you long." Jim paused. "Have you told him?"

"That the woman he married wasn't the woman he thought he'd married. No."

"Why not?"

"Kershaw."

Jim nodded. "Yep, that'd be par for the course. It's a bloody awful thing to do, but it's Kershaw. Then again..."

"Then again it may not come as such a shock?"

"It's a bloody long time for anyone to keep a secret, Mike. Are you sure he doesn't know?"

"As sure as I can be. And that's..." Brady nodded. "Yes, I'm sure."

"So you've got a decision to make."

"I have. Do I want to find the killer or do I want to follow orders?"

"The decision's going to have consequences. Either way. So when are you going to cross the Rubicon?"

"I've already crossed it, boss. About seven-thirty this morning."

Jim gave Brady a long, appraising look. "I remember the Sarah Cooke case," he said. "You took a big risk. Bloody nearly ended your career before it had started."

"But we caught the killer..."

"That we did. So who's on your list now?"

"One of the victims? They'd be ten or 12 when it happened. Early 20s now. But my money's on one of the gang members."

"If it's one of the gang members, Mike, why wait this long?"

"You'd guess because they've only just found out where she is."

"Or someone's told them where she is?"

Brady nodded. "Yes. But like you say, why wait?"

"Anyone else?"

"Given where it happened," Brady said, "An outraged member of the public. Someone recognised her in Sainsbury's."

"Someone whose child was abused?"

"Maybe. But it's a longshot. The chance of them ending up in Whitby is remote."

"You're missing one," Jim Fitzpatrick said.

I'm not, boss. But I want you to confirm it for me...

"One of the customers," Jim said. He looked at Brady shrewdly. "But you wanted me to say that didn't you?"

Brady laughed. "Am I that easy to read?"

"I've known you since you were in uniform. But you could see it. Short of money for some reason. She knows all the names..."

"I don't think she was short of money, boss. She sent her daughter away to school."

Jim nodded. "Maybe not, then. But don't rule it out. Don't underestimate the possibility that she might have been bored. Boredom's an undervalued motive."

"Did she strike you as the type for that?"

"When I talked to her? I tell you what she did strike me as, Mike. She struck me as calculating. There was a chip of ice in her. She knew she was going to jail. She must have known she'd be going into witness protection. But she'd made the decision. I could see her with a piece of paper with pros on one side and cons on the other."

"So she was a lot more than just a farmer's wife..."

Jim laughed. "Bloody hell, Mike, even I know you can't say that these days. Eat another of Val's scones.

You've a long drive ahead of you. And tell me what you want me to do."

"Talk to Doug, boss. I want to know how high up the food chain it went. Maybe how high it *still* goes. Drugs, gambling, whatever else you're into. You don't stop because the supply's been turned off."

"You're right. You find another supplier. I'll talk to Doug for you. And see if I can do a bit of digging. Talk to a few old friends. See if retirement has made them more talkative."

Brady stood up. "Thank you. I really appreciate it. Whatever Gina did in the past, wherever she's come from, it's my river she's ended up in. But I need to know what I'm up against."

Jim Fitzpatrick, coming up to 70, a few months away from his 45th wedding anniversary, the man who'd shaped Michael Brady's career, held his hand out. "Just remember what I said. You're fishing in deep water, Mike. Be careful what you catch."

25

"So what have you got?" Brady said.

Frankie looked up from her desk. "Overtime," she said. "Not enough hours in the day. Not enough manpower. And half a dozen people to look at."

"What time did you finish?"

"You want the honest answer? Nine o'clock. And that was only because I couldn't see straight any longer."

"Grab a coffee," Brady said. "Give me ten minutes will you?"

He looked around. No sign of Dan Keillor. Brady turned his mobile on and pressed the number. "Dan? Where are you?"

"Boss? I'm outside. Just padlocking my bike."

"Come straight into my office will you? Don't bother getting changed."

"How far?" Brady said two minutes later.

Dan Keillor walked into Brady's office wearing a yellow cycling top and black shorts. "Twenty miles, boss.

Just up on to the Moors, across and then back along the coast road."

"Did you come down Lythe Bank? That must have been a bit hairy."

"Is that the one coming down into Sandsend? I'd rather come down it than cycle up it."

"OK, Dan, I've got a question to ask you. Don't answer me immediately. Hear me out. Go and have your shower. Get some breakfast if you need some and then give me an answer. OK?"

"OK, boss. Should I be worried about this?"

"No, you shouldn't. Right, Dan, I want you to listen to what I have to say. What I'm going to tell you... This is a sensitive case, Dan. You can't discuss it with anyone except me and DS Thomson. You understand that?"

Keillor nodded. "Are we talking about Gina Foster, boss?"

"Yes. You remember just after you fished her out I asked if you'd be willing to help? If the case developed?"

"Just tell me what you need me to do, boss."

Brady held his hand up. "Not so fast, Dan. It gets complicated. And then it gets more complicated. Like I said, hear me out."

There was a knock on the door. Frankie opened it. "Sorry, boss. You want me to come back?"

Brady shook his head. "No, you're fine, Frankie. Sit down. I'm just bringing Dan up to date."

He turned his attention back to Dan Keillor. "You fished Gina Foster, farmer's wife, out of the Esk, Dan. What you didn't know – what none of us knew then – was that Gina Foster used to be Gina Kirk."

"You mean before she was married, boss?"

"No. If only life was so straightforward. Gina Kirk was involved with a child sex trafficking gang in Birmingham. Her job was simple. She was – maybe 'nanny' is the right word. Confidante. She was the person who delivered the children. Who told them it would be alright."

"Who took them to the punters? Is that what you're saying? Like delivering a pizza?"

Brady nodded. "Yes. That's a pretty unpleasant analogy, Dan, but yes. Like delivering a pizza. We don't know why she did it. We're seeing her sister next week so we'll have a better idea then. But that's what she did. And then one day she informed on the gang. Walked into Solihull police station and told her story. Almost certainly saved a lot of children. Very definitely cost someone – more than one person, probably – a serious amount of money. She served eight months and when she came out she went straight into witness protection."

Dan Keillor took a deep breath. "This is what I signed up for, isn't it?"

Frankie answered the question. "It's what we all signed up for, Dan. Finding someone's murderer. Even though part of you sympathises with what they did. Welcome to the Twilight Zone."

"There's something else, Dan," Brady said. "I received a direct order to find Gina Foster's killer. *Not* to disturb Gina Kirk. Not to tell her husband." Dan started to speak. Brady stopped him. "Just wait. I'm going to disregard that order. The only way I can find Gina Foster's killer is to find Gina Kirk's killer. I'm going to have to tell Ian Foster the truth about his wife. That's another thing you signed up for, Dan. Delivering bad news. Devastating news. One day you'll sit in someone's kitchen, tell them what you've found – and their lives will never be the same again."

"You want me to help?" Dan said.

"I want you to go and think about it. You've got to trust me on your career. So think about it and then give me a decision. If you help us – and God knows Frankie and I need some help – then you're going to piss Kershaw off. But I'll make sure everyone knows I put pressure on you."

Dan Keillor stood up. "I've made my decision, boss."

Brady shook his head. "No, you haven't. Go and have a shower. Have a think. And then come back in here – or say 'no' and do whatever you were supposed to do today. And Dan, one more thing."

"Yes, boss?"

"Get changed. Bluntly Police Constable Keillor, those cycling shorts are so tight they constitute a public order offence."

"ONE OF THE JOYS OF YOUTH," Brady said after Dan had closed the door. "Certainty."

Frankie smiled. "Don't worry, boss. I've got the antidote."

"Two minutes," Brady said. "I'm feeling lucky, punk. I'm going to risk the coffee machine."

"OK," Frankie said as Brady tasted his coffee and winced. "When Gina Kirk was convicted six people were sent down with her. Three relatively small fry. One of them, God help us, for stealing tranquilisers to give to the poor little sods. Three more that maybe we're interested in. Them or their families."

"Go on," Brady said.

"Jonathan Leyland was the bookkeeper. Collected the money, kept the accounts. Knew all the names and addresses. Which he kept to himself. Would have got a lighter sentence – "

"Much lighter, probably," Brady said.

"If he'd divulged the names. But he didn't."

"Which means someone put a lot of pressure on him," Brady said. "There aren't many gallantry medals given to accountants. Is he still inside?"

Frankie nodded. "The next parole hearing is in three months' time."

"Where is he now?"

"Open prison. And working in the library."

"Family?"

"Wife. Now ex-wife. She re-married about five years after he went inside. Two children, who now go by the mother's maiden name."

"So basically they're trying to forget he was ever part of their lives?"

"Looks like it."

"OK, what's next."

"Nikola Petrić. He was the enforcer. Collected the debts. Kept the children in line. Discouraged any competitors."

"Tell me he's still inside. I don't want a re-run of Jimmy Gorse."

"He's been out for three years."

"And he's gone back to what he was doing before?"

"As far as I can tell. In and around Birmingham. West Midlands generally. But he seems to spend as much time in Spain as he does in the UK."

"Was he in the UK when Gina was murdered?"

"He was. But he's 56 now."

"That doesn't make him too old."

"Statistically it does. The average age for someone convicted of murder is around 30."

"I'm not convinced, Frankie. 'I couldn't have held her under the water because I've got a bad back?' But I'm assuming you've saved the best for last?"

Frankie nodded. "Aleks Savićević – "

There was a knock on the door. A showered and changed Dan Keillor walked into Brady's office.

Brady looked up and smiled. "Welcome to the dark side. Take a seat. Frankie's just running through some work she did yesterday. She'll fill you in on what you've missed. Carry on, Frankie."

"Aleks Savićević. The boss. Twenty-eight when he was convicted."

"You're sure he was the boss, Frankie? Jim Fitzpatrick thought there might be someone else. Someone above Savićević."

"I wondered that," Frankie said. "Twenty-eight seemed young to me. Drugs yes, sex trafficking... For some reason I thought it was an older man's game."

"But you've no evidence? Nothing you found?"

"Nothing at all."

"So tell me about Savićević."

"Sentenced to 20 years with a recommendation he serve at least 15."

"So we don't need to worry about him for a while?"

"We don't need to worry about him at all, boss."

"Why not?"

"He died six months ago. There was a fight in the jail. Someone punched him. He fell back and hit his head."

"And died just like that?"

"It happens, boss. The inquest said he had an abnormally thin skull. Just unlucky."

"So we've a question answered. Right there. Thank you, Frankie."

Brady turned to Dan Keillor.

"One of the questions we've been asking ourselves is 'why now?' Why did someone come after Gina now? After all this time. There's your answer. Or there's *an* answer. Savićević dies in jail. He's going to have family. Brothers. A father. Maybe they blame Gina for their son's death. Maybe they see doing time as an occupational hazard. But dying inside is a different matter."

"It's not Gina's fault he has a thin skull," Dan said. "What about the guy that punched him?"

"The guy that punched him isn't our concern," Brady said. "As for Gina, they're not going to see it like that. They're going to blame her for putting him inside."

"It still doesn't answer the question of how they found her," Frankie said.

"No," Brady said. "But whoever killed Gina had to find her. Let's sort out 'who' first. Then we'll worry about 'how.'"

Brady sighed. *You wanted it to be murder. You wanted it to be complicated. Here you are...*

"What about the children, Frankie?"

"OK," she said. "It's the same. The rule of three. I looked at around 40 kids. All day yesterday and – apart from nipping out for something to eat – until nine at night."

And then went home to a relationship that's 'on life support...' Like I said, welcome to the dark side, Dan...

"Forty children, all trafficked by the gang and – we have to assume – all abused by the 'customers.' For want of a better word. Forty might be more than the tip of the iceberg – but it's not all of it. Not by a long chalk. My guess is the true figure was around 100. Maybe more. But there were 40 kids on the record. And you can make that 38 because two of them have committed suicide."

Brady looked at her. If Frankie was thinking about her sister she didn't show it.

"The children are now between 19 and 30. The youngest was seven when he was abused, the eldest was nearly 18. Mostly they're still in and around Birmingham. Half a dozen have drifted off to London. Half a dozen – I'm sorry about this, boss – seem to have drifted off *any* official records. Four of them – and all bloody credit to them – are at university."

"So who've you got for us?" Brady said.

"If I had to choose right now, there are three."

Frankie glanced down at her notes again. "The first one is a girl. You're going to say that if Gina was held under the water then a man did it. Hear me out. The girl is called Rochelle Hunter. She lives in Leeds now. And she's done well for herself. She's a boxer. She's on the fringe of the Great Britain squad. But..."

"This sounds like a big 'but...'"

"Yeah. When she was 14 she was involved in some gang stuff. Someone very badly beaten up. Suspected but not enough evidence. Looks like it was a turf war and a revenge attack. Then when Hunter was 16 there was another attack. A girl that had beaten her in a fight. A disputed decision – we're only talking amateur level here when she was starting out – but the girl was badly beaten one night as she was walking home. Lost an eye and never fought again."

"So there's a pattern of taking revenge."

Frankie nodded. "I think so. She was never convicted. So there's a *possible* pattern of taking revenge. But enough to make the short list. And Leeds is only an hour and a half away."

"OK, who's next?"

"Anthony Marshall. He's 26 – "

"So he was what? Twelve? Fourteen when he was abused?" Brady turned to Dan Keillor. "You're going to go home tonight. Get in the shower. And when you come out you still won't be clean. That's why I told you to think about it. Sorry, Frankie. Carry on leading us through the shit."

"He works in Birmingham," Frankie said. "Works for a shopfitting company. One that fits out supermarkets. And you know what's coming..."

"He was in Whitby?"

Frankie nodded. "Three days that week he was working on a re-fit at Sainsbury's. Staying in a B&B..."

Brady raised his eyebrows. "So he's here. He's presumably got access to a van. And he's got time. He won't start at Sainsbury's until – what? Eight in the morning?"

Frankie shook her head. "Marshall and two others. They were doing the re-fit at night. Working through the night."

"The B&B would be able to tell you if they had breakfast," Dan said.

"Maybe. But if they're working through the night they might just come in and go to bed. Maybe they have some sort of deal with the B&B that they get a meal later in the day. OK, Frankie. One with an inclination towards revenge and one that was in Whitby. One to go..."

"And if I have to put my pound on one, it's this one," Frankie said. "Jordan Rooney. He's 24. He's drifted in and out of gangs most of his life. He's been inside – and he was in the same prison as Savićević."

"So he's in the same prison as the gang that were trafficking him? Walking round the exercise yard with the man responsible for him being abused?"

"Yeah. But you know it doesn't work like that, boss. If Stockholm Syndrome exists for kidnappers I bet there's an equivalent."

"So you think – given his history of gang membership – that he's recruited in jail. Someone says, 'it was only business. No hard feelings.'

"I don't know. We've no way of knowing that. But you look at the other two, and you say, 'how did they find her?' and 'why now? Why wait?' You look at Rooney, you factor in when Savićević died and it works. Someone offers him a job. 'It wasn't us, it was Gina. Go and take your revenge. For all she did to you. And you'll be well paid for it.'

"You're assuming someone gave him – gave the gang – the address then?"

Frankie nodded. "Right now we have to assume that."

"Was he out of jail when Gina was murdered?"

"Yes. And he's still out."

"Where's he live?"

"Loughborough now. Just on the outskirts."

"Come on then, Dan," Brady said. "Put yourself in the mind of the killer. He's more or less your age. You need to kill someone. It's a 3½ hour drive. How would you do it?"

Dan took his time replying.

Good. He's thinking it through. The longer he takes to reply the better...

"I'd drive up. Three or four days early. Sleep in my car. A different place every night so no-one sees the car more than once. But I need to see her one morning. At least one morning before I do it. And I need to be able to get away."

"So how would you kill her?" Brady asked.

Dan hesitated. "If I've a silencer I'd shoot her. My big worry isn't killing her. It's... It's getting away."

Brady nodded. "Yes it is. Killing someone is easy. Getting away with it is the hard part. So whatever you do needs to be quick. Quick and silent."

"Yes, boss. What you're saying is... What you're saying is I wouldn't drown her. Drowning her makes no sense."

"Right. Exactly what Frankie and I have been saying for three weeks."

26

Denial – anger – bargaining – depression – acceptance.

The five stages of grief.

He'd been through them all with Grace.

And then again with Patrick.

Now it was denial and anger. The first two. He watched them chase each other across Ian Foster's face. With the anger directed at him.

Brady had told a wife that her husband had been killed. He'd sat opposite a married couple. Told them that the body in the woods was their daughter. Seen the light go out of the wife's eyes. Glanced across at the husband. Known that he'd be arresting him in less than a week.

He'd never told a husband that his wife wasn't his wife. That the woman he'd married – that he'd lived with for more than ten years – was a different person.

He'd never even considered the possibility.

I'm very sorry, Mr Foster. You married someone with a criminal past. Someone who was splashed all over the papers. Who grew her hair and dyed it. Who married you not because she loved you, but because you were safe. Not because you swept her off her feet, not because she found you irresistible. But because you'd just inherited an isolated farm on the North Yorkshire Moors.

"You ready for this?" he said to Frankie.

She nodded. "Are *you* ready for it, boss?"

"Someone's got to do it. And it was never going to be Kershaw."

Brady wasn't surprised to see the white Audi waiting for them in the farmyard. "Maybe we should be thankful for small mercies. At least he'll have someone with him."

"Curtiss? He's the last person I'd choose if I wanted a shoulder to cry on. And *two* small mercies. We haven't got Kershaw's spy in the back seat."

"Right. Thank God for the school vomiting bug – and a husband on an oil rig."

Brady parked the car in the farmyard. "Give me a minute before we go in will you, Frankie? I've spent half the night rehearsing this. But I'm nowhere near ready."

"You're never going to be ready, boss."

"No. There's no subtle way to do it is there?" Brady said. "There's no gentle introduction. No gradual realisation. All I can do is tell him."

"And watch his reaction, boss. Whatever Shirley Lloyd has said, we're coppers first, grief counsellors second."

"You're right. Let's go."

BRADY KNOCKED on the farmhouse door. Ian Foster – the perennial check shirt but a check shirt that hadn't seen an iron – opened it. "Detective Inspector Brady. Sergeant Thomson." He sighed. "What do you want with me this time?"

Stephen Curtiss – inevitably – hovered in the background. "Mr Brady. You're becoming a regular visitor. Can my client count on you when he's harvesting? And Ms Thomson."

"Detective Sergeant Thomson," Frankie said, clearly irritated.

Brady gestured towards the kitchen table. "Could we sit down? There's something I need to tell you, Mr Foster."

Foster nodded. And, as people always do, they sat in the same four seats as last time.

"So what is it, Mr Brady? You've found the killer. You have someone securely under lock and key. Or are you still stumbling around in the dark? Continuing to play blind man's buff at the taxpayers' expense?"

Brady looked at the solicitor across the table. Kept his voice as calm as he could. "We're doing our best, Mr Curtiss. And you may need to worry about your client rather more than our investigation."

Ian Foster looked alarmed. "What does that mean? You've come to arrest me? I was ploughing a field."

Curtiss put his hand on Foster's arm. "If they'd come to arrest you, Ian, they'd have come in a patrol car. Not Mr Brady's rather shabby Volkswagen."

"No, Mr Foster. We're not here to arrest you. As I explained on the phone, Mrs Lloyd called me..."

"So you don't need me. You can look for someone else. So why are you here?"

Brady took a deep breath. "Mr Foster, I'm very sorry to have to tell you this. Truly sorry. In all my years in the police, there's been nothing to compare with this. All I can do is tell you the truth."

Another deep breath. Like you just said. All you can do is tell the truth.

"Your wife, Gina... Her real name was Gina Kirk. She – "

Foster shook his head. "No, you're wrong. You're wasting your time, Inspector. Carmichael, not Kirk. That's what she was when I met her. Gina Carmichael – working in Mr Curtiss' office. He'll tell you."

"That's correct," Curtiss said. "Carmichael. And we were sorry to lose her. She was efficient. Unlike your own efforts, Mr Brady."

Brady shook his head. "No. As I've said, I'm truly sorry to tell you this. Your wife's real name was Gina Kirk."

It's the next sentence.

You're going to say it.

Ian Foster may never recover from it.

"Carmichael was the name given to her when she entered the witness protection programme."

Foster looked at him. Uncomprehending. Shaking his head. "I don't understand what you're saying. Gina was Gina Carmichael. I asked her out. Then I proposed to her."

He's probably never heard of witness protection...

"Your wife came from Birmingham, Mr Foster. In 2002 she was convicted and sent to prison. She came out eight months later – "

Brady looked at the two men opposite him.

Two faces. One crumbling. One hardening.

"She was convicted of being involved – "

Curtiss cut him off.

And he very definitely has heard of witness protection...

"Are you telling me, Brady? That she was Gina Kirk? From Birmingham? The child sex-trafficker? That nobody told us? That my firm – a respectable law firm – employed scum like that?"

Brady saw Ian Foster's world collapse. Denial and anger chased each other across his face. Denial, anger and desperation.

He had no idea. There's zero chance he killed her.

"Mr Foster. Your wife was convicted in 2002 of being complicit in a child sex-trafficking case. She – "

"She got 21 months," Curtiss snapped. "She should have got longer. A lot longer."

"Please, Mr Curtiss," Brady said. "Please let us explain to Mr Foster. You're not the priority here."

Curtiss stared back at him. "You'll find we're very much the priority when we sue you, Brady. We let that woman near our clients. North Yorkshire Police won't have a pot to piss in when I've finished with you."

Brady met his eyes. "I won't lose any sleep, Mr Curtiss."

"Well you should. You bloody well should."

"Rest assured, Mr Curtiss. I'll always find somewhere to piss." Brady held the solicitor's gaze. "Or someone to piss on."

"Are you threatening me, Brady?"

Yes, I am. Now fuck off back to your nice, warm office. Never mind your client.

Brady smiled. "Not in the slightest, Mr Curtiss."

Curtiss stood up. Reached for his briefcase. "I have the reputation of my firm to protect. You'll be hearing from us."

"I don't doubt it," Brady said. He saw Frankie lean forward across the table. Take Foster's huge right hand in both of hers.

"Should you be touching my client, Miss Thomson?"

She never took her eyes off Foster. "Shouldn't you be acting like a human being, Mr Curtiss? And I doubt Mr Foster will be your client for much longer."

"Be that as it may, we'll see you in court." The farmhouse door slammed behind him.

"Ian," Frankie said. "Your wife was an incredibly brave woman. Yes, she was convicted. Yes, she went to prison."

"Why didn't she tell me? I would have understood. Tried to understand..."

"To begin with? Maybe she was ashamed. Maybe she was afraid of losing you. And then... Once you've kept something secret for so long... And she loved you. You loved her. And you loved her for what she *was*, not what she'd been. And she didn't want to risk losing that. And like I say, as time went on..."

"But all this time. All this time I've been married to a different person."

Frankie shook her head. "No. You weren't married to a different person. What does a name matter? You were married to someone who was brave. Braver than any of us. And strong. Who risked her life to save children – a lot of children – from abuse. From being trafficked."

"But if she was so brave why did she do it in the first place?"

"Right now, we don't know. But we'll find out. And when we do we'll find out who killed her. And we'll give you an explanation. You'll be able to look back on what you had together."

"And what am I going to tell Maria?" Foster said. "School's taking care of her now. But this... This is my job. And it's half-term coming up."

"You'll find the right words. And you're her father. The only father she's known."

"I adopted her." Ian Foster looked up at them. Clinging on to the life raft that Frankie had thrown to him. "I adopted her," he said again. "Gina did the paperwork. But I'm her father."

THERE WAS a knock on the door. Brady heard it opening. "Ian? Are you in?"

He turned round. A woman in her early 50s. Solid, comfortable. Short brown hair, square framed glasses. A suitcase in her hand. "This is my cousin, Joanne," Foster said. "She's come to stay with me for a few days."

Brady stood up, shook hands with Joanne. Introduced himself and Frankie. Explained they were just going.

"I'll walk to your car with you," Foster said.

"You don't have to, Mr Foster."

"No. It's alright. There's something I want to say."

They walked across the farmyard to Brady's car.

Curtiss was right. It's more than 'shabby.' I need to change it.

Brady turned. "You wanted to say something, Mr Foster?"

Ian Foster looked down at the ground. Back up at Brady. "You knew," he said. "When you came out to tell me she'd been murdered. You knew then didn't you?"

Brady looked back at him. Held his gaze, just as he had with Curtiss. "Yes, I did. I'm truly sorry."

Foster lowered his head again. Moved it slowly from side to side.

Like a bull ready to charge...

"I should punch you. I don't swear, Mr Brady, but I should fucking punch you."

Brady felt Frankie step forward next to him. Held his hand up to stop her. Never took his eyes off Foster. He nodded. "You probably should. I was doing what my boss told me to do. Obeying orders. But that's a coward's excuse. So yes, Mr Foster, you probably should punch me."

Foster looked down at his right hand. Slowly, deliberately, unclenched his fist.

"I'll not shake hands," he said. "Whoever I married, I loved her. Now she's gone. Just find out who did it. Find who did this to me."

"Don't worry," Brady said. "I will, Mr Foster. I know my words probably don't mean much to you right now..."

"No, they don't. Fine words butter no parsnips, Mr Brady. That's what my dad used to say."

"He was right. But I'll find your killer, Mr Foster. The

first case like this I was ever involved in, I made someone a promise – "

Sarah Cooke. When I walked into the house and found her. Lying on the floor. The picture of her daughter clutched in her hand...

" – And I'll make the same promise to you. Whatever it takes. Whatever it costs me. I'll find who killed your wife."

Foster looked at him. He wasn't convinced. "Like I said. I'll not shake hands. Not 'til I respect you."

BRADY TURNED off the main road and pulled into a lay-by. Turned the engine off. Looked through the windscreen. Saw the Moors falling away in front of him, a container ship out at sea.

"Fuck," he said. "I thought..."

"You thought for a minute he *was* going to punch you."

"Yeah, I did. And a fist that size... Like being hit by a bowling ball."

"Do you think he knows?" Frankie asked.

"About Grace you mean? He doesn't strike me as a man who researches people on Google."

"Maybe he should..."

"No," Brady said. "What I did – not telling him the full truth – was... like I said to you when we came out. I was ashamed of myself. Anyway, you were... Bloody hell, I don't know the right word again. You were magnificent in there. I don't want to say 'perfect.' But... You gave him something back. Something to hang on to."

"Thank you," Frankie said simply. "I hope he's alright."

"Me too. More than alright. I feel... I feel responsible for him somehow."

"Yeah, I know what you mean. He's just vulnerable."

Brady carried on staring out of the windscreen.

"I don't like to use the word," he said. "I hate the word. But it's the only one that describes Curtiss isn't it?"

Frankie laughed. "Yes. That word and several others. And both of them. Curtiss *and* Kershaw."

"What the hell is he doing in Whitby? Why isn't he in Leeds or Manchester making people miserable?"

"Like so many men in towns like this. Big fish, small pond. Think they've got a big cock because they're the only pinstripe suit in the sandwich shop."

Brady looked sideways at her and smiled. "The only pinstripe suit in the sandwich shop? Did you just come out with that?"

She met his gaze. "Not just Maths, boss. I did English as well. It's a quote from *Pride and Prejudice*. Everyone knows that..."

27

Brady guessed she was about 50. A sharp, intelligent face. Grey trouser suit, a navy blue open necked blouse. Blonde hair still long enough to reach her shoulders. Maroon-framed glasses.

She held out her hand. "Susanna Harrall."

"Michael Brady."

"You said you wanted to talk to me about children who've been abused, Mr Brady?"

Brady nodded. Looked around the office. A photograph of two giggling children on a patterned settee.

Susanna saw what he was looking at and laughed. "It was the only time they weren't fighting at that age."

"Slightly older now?"

"Slightly. Both at university. Neither of them following their mother into psychology. Do you have children, Mr Brady?"

"A daughter. Thirteen. She says she wants to be a vet."

"Ouch!" Susanna said. "What's that? Five? Six years' training? You'll be paying her rent for a good few years."

Brady smiled, "So she tells me. But she's an only child."

Susanna pushed a brown manilla file to one side. "But you wanted to talk to me about children who are a lot less fortunate than ours..."

Brady nodded. "We're investigating a murder. And that means we're looking at some adults who were involved with the victim when they were younger – "

"Gina Foster? Gina Kirk as was?"

Brady held his hands up. "Technically I probably shouldn't say."

"But when it's splashed across the local paper..."

Brady nodded. "Exactly. They seemed to be having a field day."

Susanna looked at him over the top of her glasses. "That must increase the pressure on you?"

Brady saw little point in lying to a psychologist. "The textbook answer is that a woman has been murdered. We're doing our job like we always do. But you can guess the real answer."

Susanna turned to her computer. Took her maroon glasses off, sighed and put a pair of blue ones on. "I should get varifocals," she said. "But I refuse to admit I'm getting old."

It was Brady's turn to laugh. "I need reading glasses," he said. "But when did you see a TV detective put reading glasses on?"

"Morse?" Susanna said. "Jane Tennison? Cagney and Lacey? Those two must be due for hip replacements by now."

The maroon glasses were back on. "Forgive me looking at my notes just then. I did some research. This isn't my exact area of expertise but I can give you a good overview. What would you like to know?"

A question Brady had asked himself as he'd driven over the Moors that morning. "Everything really. How the children would react to what happened. What they'd be like as adults. Can they form relationships? Depression? What sort of behaviour traits do they have? A general overview to begin with."

"You're not entirely sure what you're looking for?"

"In some respects, no. But I think I'll know it when I see it. I'd like to understand as much as I can. And I do have two specific questions if that's alright."

Susanna nodded. "OK. Stop me if I say anything you don't understand. Feel free to interrupt with questions."

"You mind if I make notes?" Brady said.

She shook her head. "I don't mind at all. Use your phone recorder and record the conversation if it helps."

Brady did both. Then gave up making notes after two minutes so he could simply listen.

"These children – some of these children – were abused over a long period of time. So the effects are going to stay with them for an equally long time. Longer. Well into adult life. PTSD, eating disorders, depression, anxiety, low self-esteem, learning disabilities, even physical illness. They're going to have any number of problems."

"Are they going to be angry?"

"Yes. Very often. And it's an underlying anger that will erupt in any number of ways."

"Will they feel guilty as well?"

"Yes. A lot of them will blame themselves for what happened. You've got to remember that they may well have been abused – casually, in their birth family – before this more systematic abuse started. So they're starting from a low base. They're probably already feeling guilty before this started."

"Anything else?"

"You mean if that's not enough? Yes. There's a good chance they'll suffer from disassociation. They – "

"You said I could interrupt..."

She smiled. "Yes, sorry. Disassociation. Different mental processes. Which can lead – in extreme cases – to multiple personality disorder."

"So they're likely to say, 'That abuse didn't happen to me. It happened to someone else?'"

"In layman's terms, yes. So sudden, impulsive behaviour. In some cases destructive behaviour. Self-harm and suicide attempts."

"Two of the children have already committed suicide."

Susanna nodded. "There'll be more, I should think. Sad, but true. Something else you might see is trance-like behaviour."

"Not knowing what they're doing?"

"Maybe. It's linked to triggers. Something that reminds them of being abused. That makes them relive the abusive experiences."

"Go through it again? I hadn't realised..."

"No. People don't. The mental scars last far longer than the physical ones." She paused. "'Scars' is probably the wrong word. The river runs much deeper than that. But you understand my meaning."

Brady nodded. "Do they ever recover? In time?"

"Some do," she said cautiously. "But they're not the majority. Very often they're ashamed of what's happened. That's a barrier to seeking help. And..." She hesitated.

"Go on..."

"Well, I'm speculating here. And professionally I shouldn't do that."

"Please," Brady said. "That's exactly what I want."

"Well... If some of the rumours about the original case are true... Then these children have... They've not just seen people in positions of power ignore their appeals for help. They've been abused by those people. You can imagine what that does. Distrust, anger, resentment..."

"That's the second or third time you mentioned anger," Brady said. "Can I ask two specific questions?"

"Of course."

"These children are going to be angry," Brady said.

"Some of them are," Susanna corrected.

Right. But we only need one...

"Would that anger – could it manifest itself in a desire for revenge?"

Susanna sucked her breath in. *A garage mechanic telling you it's serious...* "Again, I'm speculating. I think the answer is 'yes.' But, it's 'yes' with a caveat."

Brady nodded. "That's fine. Like I said, the more I understand the better."

"So revenge, yes. But in my view it's unlikely to be

planned revenge. They're unlikely to have sat in their bedroom and worked out a plan."

"Supposing someone else worked out the plan?"

"That's one possibility. Yes, that's feasible. The other option is spontaneity. A flashback. Something triggers a memory."

"But then they'd need to be – "

"Need to be with the victim. Yes."

"OK. The second question is slightly more complicated."

This is like being back in a tutorial group at uni. How stupid is my question going to sound?

"There's Stockholm Syndrome for people who've been kidnapped," Brady said. "Is there an equivalent for people who've been abused?"

"Do they come to sympathise with their abusers?"

"Yes, I think so."

"My gut feeling on that is no. It's a generally held belief that children who've been abused are more likely to be abusers themselves. I have to say I'm slightly sceptical on that one. But do abused children empathise or sympathise with their abusers? No, I don't think so. But..." She shrugged. Made a 'what do I know' gesture. "I've been a psychologist for more than half my life. And nothing surprises me any more."

"Just like the police then," Brady said, smiling. "Thank you. You've been really helpful. I appreciate it." He stood up and held his hand out.

"I hope so," Susanna said as they shook hands. "Albeit slightly depressing for a bright, crisp autumn morning. Just remember," she added. "These are damaged people,

Mr Brady. They'll struggle to form and keep relationships in later life. They don't fit in. The person you're looking for – if it is one of these children – is unlikely to be happily married. He or she won't be a member of the Parent Teacher Association."

28

"I'll collect you at seven," Brady had said. "Google maps says it's three and a half hours to Kenilworth. I've told Gina's sister we'll be there for eleven."

"So no time for a full English at Woodall Services?"

"Sadly, no. Maybe a bacon sandwich while I'm driving. And then Anthony Marshall afterwards. Let's see what our shopfitter can tell us."

He was there five minutes early. Which was fine: she'd been ready for 15 minutes. 'Morning,' he'd said. 'Morning, boss,' she'd replied. 'Is Louise on duty today?' he'd asked. She'd nodded. Said, 'Yes, although she'll probably call her Frankie.' Told him they'd found a carer to go in three days a week which was helping.

He could smell the perfume. Looked across at her. Thought about saying something. Changed his mind.

"I saw a psychologist yesterday morning," Brady said instead.

"I'll resist making the obvious joke."

It was a dull, wet morning. The sort of morning when driving down the M1 meant two hours of staring into endless spray from an endless procession of lorries.

"What did he say?"

"It was a she. Someone in Scarborough. I was asking her about the children. What effect the abuse would have had. How they'd be likely to react."

"Would they be likely to murder Gina Foster?"

"Essentially, yes. And the essential answer seems to be 'no.' They're going to be angry, resentful. They're going to have low self-esteem. But they're not going to plan a murder. They might act spontaneously – "

"You mean if something triggers their behaviour?"

"Yes. But my psychologist seemed to think that planning – and God knows this needed some planning – wasn't likely."

"Supposing someone planned for them?"

"I asked that question. 'Yes' was the short answer. She said it was possible."

"You mean, 'here's the woman that did this to you. This is what you need to do?'"

"Yeah. But I'm not convinced. If someone is doing that, why use one of the children as your weapon?"

"Why not reach for Jimmy Gorse mark 2?"

Brady nodded. "A professional – or an unreliable amateur? Which would you choose?"

"Which brings us back to Aleks Savićević."

"Yes, it does," Brady said. "Just let me concentrate on the road for five minutes and you can tell me his story."

The Moors road dropped down to a small bridge over

a beck. Brady changed gear and started up the other side. Up towards the Hole of Horcum.

Where Jimmy Gorse shot my dog.

"Start telling me about Savićević, Frankie. Give me something to think about as I drive along here."

"He came to this country when he was seven," Frankie said. "Mother, aunt and a twin sister."

"No father?"

"No. He was killed in the fighting."

"Yugoslavian civil war?"

"Yes. The details are murky. The fog of war and all that. But the blame seems to rest with the Bosnian army."

"So mum decided that losing her husband was enough? She wasn't going to take any more risks?"

"Yes. And she came to Birmingham. Shepherd's Bush, Notting Hill, Birmingham – there are a handful of size-able Serb communities in England. And Halifax," she added.

"Halifax?"

"Since the Second World War, apparently. Monarchist refugees after Tito's revolution. For some reason they chose West Yorkshire."

"So young Aleks arrives in England?"

"Yes. And he's a bright boy. Learns English quickly, does well at school. But..."

"But there's a dark side to him?"

"When is there not, boss? By the time he's 16 he's left school. I guess he saw himself as the man of the family. His job to provide for his mother and sister."

"What happened to her? The twin sister?"

"She didn't need providing for. Or she doesn't now. She's a doctor. Consultant paediatrician."

"Slightly ironic given what her brother did. So while she's at medical school he's heading in the opposite direction?"

"Right. He's had a couple of brushes with the law – conviction for car theft but just community service – and then he discovers massage parlours."

"And it's a short step to realising that some punters might have more specialised tastes."

"You could say. Very specialised and very profitable."

"Presumably he'll be making videos of all this? While it's happening?"

"You'd be surprised if he wasn't. I'd guess that's where the real money came from."

"Do you think they realised?" Brady said. They'd reached Pickering. Brady drove across the roundabout by the Forest and Vale and on towards Malton.

"You've lost me, boss."

"A few nerdy scientists. When they invented the internet. When they thought, 'Oh, this is a cool way to share information.' That 30 years down the line it would be used for watching ten year old children getting fucked by middle-aged men?"

"Probably not. But that always happens doesn't it? Unintended consequences. And the wrong people getting rich."

Brady shook his head. "You know what, Frankie? I bloody hate this. I'll say it to you because there's no-one else I can say it to. But somewhere in this country there's two people like us driving to a meeting. They're talking

about work but they're having a normal, healthy conversation. Whether the graphic designers can get the
website done in time. Whether the nerds can get the
shopping cart working. They're not talking about how
much money you can make shooting videos of... Ah, fuck
it. There's a lay-by and a caravan up here. I'll buy you a
bacon sandwich."

29

They were ten minutes early. Brady pulled up outside the house. A town house opposite a parade of shops. A One Stop convenience store, 'A Cut Above' unisex hairdressers, a bread shop, 'Rest in Peace' funeral directors.

"Pretty much everything you need in life," Frankie said.

"You all set?" he said.

"Sure," she replied. "Let's go and deliver some more bad news. This one is taking its toll."

Julie Mason had the door open before they'd knocked. They shook hands, introduced themselves. Were shown into the lounge. Pale cream walls. The standard photos of two children getting steadily older. First day at school, then the obligatory gap-toothed smile. The daughter has a growth spurt, her little brother catches her up and overtakes her...

She made coffee. Laid out a plate of ginger nuts and Kit-Kats.

"Mrs Mason," Brady started.

"Jules, please. Everyone calls me Jules. Even my daughter when she's feeling feisty."

"How old is she?" Frankie asked.

"She's 14. A year to the day older than Gina's daughter." She hesitated. "Maybe some good will come out of this. Maybe we can be a family again."

Brady was prepared to take as long as it needed. "Mrs Mason. Jules," he said. "We'd like to understand more about your sister's childhood. What happened. What led to her involvement with... To what happened. But we appreciate that she's your sister. That you'll have some questions for us. As far as we're permitted to by the investigation, we'll tell you whatever you need to know."

Jules blinked away the tears that we're already forming and looked up. "Everything really," she said. "Just everything. I knew. I mean – we kept in touch. I know we shouldn't. I know I'll probably get into trouble – "

"No," Brady said. "No, you won't. There's no question of that."

"It's just... It's so unfair. Those that went to prison are out. Those that didn't are still driving around in their blacked-out Range Rovers. And Gina lost her whole family. Mum lost her daughter. Never saw her granddaughter again. I lost my sister." She shook her head. "You have to ask. Who are the ones that really got punished?"

Frankie stood up and walked into the kitchen.

"Is that your mum?" Brady said, nodding at a photograph on the mantelpiece.

"Yes. Gina looked a lot like her."

"I hope you don't mind me asking. Is she still alive?"

Jules shook her head. "She got cancer. It was one of those quick, aggressive ones. She was in the hospice. Just a few days. Then..."

Frankie was back with some kitchen roll. "I'm sorry, Jules," she said. "I couldn't see any tissues."

"Thank you," Jules blinked. "You're kind."

Frankie turned her head. Looked at Brady out of the corner of her eye. He understood what she meant. Let her take over.

"Jules," Frankie said. "Let me come and sit with you. I'll tell you what we know."

She sat on the sofa with Jules. Took her hand. Looked her in the eye. "Some of this isn't going to be very pleasant, Jules. But I'm sensing you want the truth, even if it's painful."

"More than anything. Yes. Please."

Frankie went through everything. Finding the body. Thinking it was an accident. Why they had doubts.

Jules looked up and smiled. "That's why you're a detective then."

Brady's walk by the river. The confirmation. The conversations with Ian Foster. Discovering Gina's true identity. What that meant for the case.

"So she was brave," Jules said when Frankie had finished. "That thing she did – at the end – so you'd know."

"Yes," Frankie said. "Very brave. You should be proud. Really proud."

Jules nodded her head. Frankie let go of her hand.

"And now," she said. "I'm going to send Detective Chief Inspector Brady into your kitchen, Jules. He's only a man, but he can make us another cup of tea."

Jules laughed. The tension was broken. Brady did as he was told. Opened all the cupboards until he found the tea bags. Came back with three mugs of tea. Left Jules sitting with Frankie on the sofa and reached for his notebook.

"What do you want to know?" Jules asked.

"Honestly, Jules, the simple answer is everything. The more you can tell us the better. The more we know the better chance we have of catching whoever did this. Of working out why it happened. Of giving you some closure. Like you said – so you can be a family again."

Jules took a deep breath. "I've never been asked before," she said. "Not the whole story. When I talked to the police last time, no-one seemed much interested. Like they wanted to get it over and done with. You know, wrap it all up and move on."

"Tell us about your childhood. Your parents," Brady said as gently as he could. "Ian has told us some of the story. But..."

But I'm guessing you're going to tell us a very different one...

"We were just normal. Dad worked for an insurance company. Mum worked part-time. Secretarial mostly. There were the four of us. Gina was a bit wild. And they spoiled her. But then you always spoil the youngest, I suppose."

"And you lived in Birmingham?"

"Just outside. Sutton Coldfield. And went to the primary school, and then to the comprehensive. Gina was clever. I mean, really clever. She would have gone to university. She wanted to do psychology. Or be a doctor."

"But she didn't?"

Jules shook her head. "No. She met this boy. And it just went downhill. Mum and Dad didn't know what to do. Dad had started going to church – this evangelical church – and there were fights and... And eventually she moved out. She didn't finish her A-levels, didn't go to university."

"Did you stay in touch with her?"

"Sort of. You know, text messages and things. But she was living in Birmingham. In a flat and she'd got a car. God knows how she was affording it. And I was working for NatWest and I'd met Bob. So for a couple of years we didn't have a lot in common."

"And then something happened?"

"I got a text one morning. I remember, I was on the bus, on the way in to work. Just a few words. 'I'm pregnant. Can we meet?'"

"And you did meet her?"

Jules nodded. "For a coffee. After work. And she'd changed. Her hair was short and – you could see, really expensively cut – and her clothes."

"But she wasn't working?"

"No. I think... Honestly I think she was someone's girlfriend. I sort of got the impression he was older."

"And was he the father?"

"I think so. There was no mention of a boyfriend. And

the one that had caused all the trouble in the first place.
He was long gone."

"So she kept the baby?"

"Yes. I said that to her. I said, 'Are you going to keep it'
and she said, 'I daren't do anything else.'"

"I don't suppose you've a photo by any chance, have
you?" Brady asked.

"Of Gina? Yes, I have," Jules said. She stood up,
walked into the hall and came back with her handbag.
Opened her purse and handed Brady a photo. "I keep it
in my purse. I know I shouldn't. Just…"

She handed Brady the photo. Two girls, maybe nine
and seven, matching red swimsuits, on the beach.

"I can understand that," Brady said. "Do you have any
others? Maybe of Gina and the baby?"

"I do. Just one. It's upstairs."

She left the room again. Brady looked across at
Frankie. She raised her eyebrows in a 'let's see, shall we'
expression.

Jules was back, holding out a photo in a small frame.
"I keep it on the shelf in the bedroom," she said.

There was a girl in her early 20s. Sitting on a picnic
blanket in a park. Wearing a red summer dress. She was
looking down at a baby. Maybe six months old, Brady
guessed. The baby had dark, curly hair. Brown eyes
looking straight at the camera. She was laughing. It was a
picture from an advert. A picture of a perfect mother and
baby.

"She's a lovely baby," Brady said.

"She was. I dare say she still is. Gina said she took

after the father. Big brown eyes and the most beautiful olive skin. I don't think he was English."

Brady reached for his phone. "Do you mind if I take a photo, Jules? A photo of the photo?"

Julie Mason shook her head. "Whatever you need to do."

"Gina *never* told you who the father was?" Brady said.

"No. Never. Said it was better if we didn't know. And then... Well you know what happened. The court case, the publicity. It was awful. People standing outside Mum and Dad's shouting things. Someone threw a brick through the window."

"And your mum looked after the baby?"

"Yes. I didn't see much of her because I had Claire and she wasn't well when she was young. A problem with her heart. She was in and out of hospital. Then she needed two operations. So I didn't see Maria. My niece..." Jules stopped. More tears rolled down her cheeks.

"And then Gina got released. And they were gone. Just like that. We never said goodbye. It broke Mum's heart. She'd had Maria for eight months and then she never saw her again."

"But Gina got in touch with you?"

"Yes. Two years later. And I'd got Ollie by then as well. And I suppose I was just getting used to the idea of not having a sister. And a letter came. Just an envelope with a piece of torn off paper. You know, out of a notebook."

"Have you still got it?"

Jules looked guilty. "No. I lost it when we moved. A box went missing. It was in there."

"Can you remember anything about it? The postmark?"

Jules shook her head. "It was smudged. I tried to make it out. To see where she was. But I couldn't."

"And what did it say on the paper?"

"It said, 'I'm safe.' And a phone number."

"So you rang it?"

"I didn't dare. I'd got two young children. I remembered what the gang had done. And I'd read about witness protection – I looked it up online – and why Gina had done what she'd done."

"Did you tell your husband? Bob?"

"No. I didn't dare do that either. I knew what he'd say. I lay awake at night. Night after night. Sometimes I'd get up and go downstairs. Three in the morning and I'm making a cup of tea and crying. And in the end it got the better of me. I couldn't stand it any longer."

Frankie reached her hand out. Took Jules' hand again. Squeezed it.

"Christmas Eve," Jules said. "I sent a text. 'Happy Christmas,' I put. 'I miss you.' And maybe ten minutes later she phoned me. All I can remember is I could hardly hear her."

She must have told Ian she was going for a walk. A bad signal in the woods...

"And did you keep in regular contact after that?"

"No. Just Christmas and birthdays. She said I had to buy a special phone. A pay-as-you-go. So her number wasn't on my bill. I used to count the days," Julie said. "Count the days away. Just to hear her voice. To know she was still safe. You can't imagine what it's like. To lose someone and then find them again. Even if it's just a phone call. And then she missed my birthday. And I knew. I knew something had happened."

The dam broke. And this time Brady didn't need a gesture from Frankie. He stood up, collected the cups. Disappeared into the kitchen for another five minutes.

30

"Let's see what Anthony Marshall has to say for himself then."

"Motive. Opportunity," Frankie said. "The bed and breakfast said he came straight in and went to bed. On the face of it he ticks some significant boxes."

"My money is still on Savićević. He *has* to be Maria's father. His family – looking for revenge. But let's tidy up the loose ends. Get this over and done with. I want to go home."

"You and me both, boss."

Brady opened the car door. Walked up the path of one of the neatest front gardens he'd ever seen. Heard Frankie mutter, "OCD planting" behind him.

Marshall answered the door. A round face, pale blue eyes. Short, brown hair that made Brady think of a choirboy. An older, more suspicious, more cautious choirboy. Jeans, a round-neck jumper. Mustard? Old gold? Brady had never been sure where one ended and the other began.

"Michael Brady."

Anthony Marshall's handshake was nervous, reluctant. The absolute minimum of contact.

"We won't keep you long. Mr Marshall. I know this will be painful for you. As I explained on the phone, we're looking into the murder of Gina Foster. Gina Kirk as you would have known her."

Brady had expected a reaction. Marshall simply sat down in his chair, nervously rubbing his hands together, washing them without soap and water.

"Gina Kirk – " Brady started.

"She's dead? You said she was dead. How?"

"She was murdered, Mr Marshall. Drowned. Someone held her under water. In a river."

For the second time Brady was surprised at the lack of reaction. Just a nod. A 'that seems fair enough' nod.

"And you were in Whitby that day, Mr Marshall..."

But Brady already knew it was simply coincidence. Maybe a hundred children abused, one of them in Whitby on the day Gina was murdered. Long odds. Very long odds. But not impossible odds.

"Sainsbury's," Marshall said. "Working through the night. Then we went to the B&B and straight to bed."

"All of you?"

Marshall nodded. "All of us in the van. Straight back. You can check with the other two if you want."

I will. But I know I don't need to.

"Mr Marshall, I'm sorry to ask you this. But could you tell us what role Gina Kirk played in all this? In what happened to you?"

Anthony Marshall's hand-washing got faster.

'You know what, Frankie? I bloody hate this. Somewhere in this country there's two people like us driving to a meeting. They're talking about whether the graphic designers can get the website done in time. They're not talking about how much money you can make shooting videos of...'

And they're not asking the people in those videos to describe what happened to them. Watching them wash their hands without soap and water.

"Like I say, I'm really sorry to ask, Mr Marshall. But it would help us to understand."

"She chose us," Marshall said. "Six of us. Ten of us. All lined up. She came with a man. Tall. Dark. An eagle tattooed on his neck. It was the only bird I knew. 'You,' she said. 'And you. We're going on an adventure.' And then they sent us off to have a wash – 'Go and clean your hands and face' – and then she sat with us in the car."

"Where did you go?" Frankie asked gently.

"Up in a lift," Marshall said. "That's what I remember most. Up in a lift. I'd never been in a lift before. Up to someone's flat. Penthouse I suppose you'd call it. New. Looking right out over Birmingham. Then... Then it happened."

"Thank you," Brady said. "I can't imagine what that must have been like."

Anthony Marshall stopped washing his hands for a moment and looked at Brady. Looked straight through him. "It never leaves you," he said. "The sense of being powerless. Just fucking useless. Like they can do anything to you."

Brady nodded. Knew that whatever he said would be inadequate.

"You know what I do now, Mr Brady? I go to work. And I get through the day. And then I come home. Here. To Tracey. And I'm safe. Do you want to know what I used to do?"

'Something else you might see is trance-like behaviour. Something reminds them of being abused. That makes them relive the abusive experiences.'

Something like a policeman asking questions...

"If you want to tell us," Brady said as gently as he could.

"You know what I used to do? I used to write my name. T – O – N – Y. I used to write my name on walls. I'd climb up on bannisters. Stairs. Ladders. Anywhere in the children's home I could. 'Cos I thought the higher up the wall I can write my name the less chance there is of someone rubbing it out. They beat me. Sometimes they took me places. Said, 'This boy's been bad. Can you punish him for us?' But I carried on writing my name. Because if I can see T – O – N – Y then I know I exist. And you know what that's done to me?"

"No, I don't. I can't imagine," Brady said.

"I can't sign my fucking name. That's what it's done to me. Here I am a grown man with a job and I can't sign my fucking name. Because if I do I'm a kid again climbing up a ladder to write T – O – N – Y and prove I exist. And no, you can't imagine. Not unless some fat bastard in a suit has bent you over a desk and unzipped himself and spat on your arse because he thinks it's enough lubrication and pushed himself inside you."

Anthony Marshall stopped speaking. Brady couldn't

remember a time when he'd felt more uncomfortable in an interview.

But I owe it to him to listen. I owe it to all of them to listen.

"Let me tell you something else," Marshall said. "Whatever you think the figures are, they're wrong. They're way too low. Every kid in that home – virtually every bloody kid – had been fucked. And fucked over for the rest of his life."

"I'm not going to say I understand how you feel. I'm sorry. Whatever I say sounds trite. Pointless."

"Yeah. It is. No-one has any fucking idea how I feel. How any of us feel. And I'll tell you something else shall I?"

Brady nodded. "Yes. Tell us anything you want."

"This. If a drug. Or a video game. Or even a Big fucking Mac. If any of them did half – one fucking tenth – the damage child abuse does the bloody politicians would be all over it like a rash. But they don't do anything about child abuse. And you know why, Mr Brady?"

"No, I don't," Brady said. "Why?"

"Because them – them and their friends – they're the fat, sweaty bastards in the penthouse. They're the ones unzipping themselves and spitting on your arse."

31

"What did you make of that?" Brady said.

"Are we talking Anthony or Gina's sister?"

"Anthony, for now."

"What I made of it is that I need a gin. And then another gin."

"We'll talk about it in the morning. What did we say to Dan Keillor? 'Welcome to the dark side?' I feel like telling him to find a new job. Get out before the dirt gets ingrained."

"It wasn't TV was it?" Frankie said. "It wasn't chasing the villains down an alley. Jumping over walls and flying rugby tackles."

"I've had my 'good TV' moment," Brady said. "Jimmy Gorse on the end of the pier will last me a lifetime."

Brady started the car and drove back towards the M69 and the M1. Turned left onto the motorway slip road. Accelerated to get ahead of a DHL lorry that was swaying ominously in the cross wind.

"Anthony Marshall washing his hands," he said.

"That's another image I'm going to see at three in the morning... You want to stop and have something to eat? Maybe talk about something lighter?"

Frankie shook her head. "Yes I do. But I can't. If you're alright with it, boss, let's just get back. I'm going to have to check in with Louise. See how many wheels have fallen off today."

"No problem. I'll stop at the next services. Get some coffee and a sandwich for us."

The lorry's horn blared. Headlights flashed, flooding the car with light. Brady yanked the steering wheel. Pulled the Tiguan back into the inside lane. "Christ, sorry," he said. "I'm so busy thinking about this bloody case. Sorry, I wasn't concentrating."

"And not sleeping much..."

No. Because half the time I try and go to sleep I see an image of your shirt falling open...

"The next service station's only six miles, boss. Let's get some coffee. Do you want me to drive?"

"No, I'll be fine. I was up too early this morning. Had to walk Archie before I came for you."

"You should take some time off when this one's over. Whitby in December. A perfect place for a holiday."

"December? Bloody hell, Frankie, Kershaw's back in a week or so. If we haven't got this one wrapped up by then I'll be looking for a job in December."

"There's always Father Christmas, boss. But for now just steer the sleigh into the services."

. . .

A FLAT WHITE and a sandwich later and they were back on the M1. "Just over two hours?" Brady said. "Is that going to work for you?"

"Yeah. I rang Louise while you were in the loo. She says Mum's having one of her good days."

Two hours. Plenty of time to talk...

"We've got to go back to the farmhouse," Brady said.

"Yeah. We need to find the phone."

"Did you get the number?" Brady asked.

"While you were in the kitchen. In between the tears."

"It won't do us any good," Brady said. "There'll only be Julie's number on it. But..."

"If she kept a phone hidden what else did she keep hidden?"

"A diary in a perfect world..."

"Dream on, boss. But there might be photos."

"What would *you* take, Frankie?" Brady said. "Supposing you were going into witness protection? Supposing someone turned up and said, 'You're leaving in ten minutes?' What would you take?"

"I don't know. Photos? My leather jacket for sure. Memories. Something that reminded me of my family. What about you?"

"I don't think I could do it," Brady said. "Gina has to leave her sister, her mother, her friends. I don't think I could do that. If you said to me, 'the only way to save your life is to never see Ash again...' Then I know what my reply would be."

"I'll take my chances?"

"Something like that. Maybe slightly less polite."

"The more you think about it the worse it is," Frankie

said. "Look at all the info we turned up. Yet half the gang didn't get prosecuted. Those that did are out or nearly out."

"Except for the one who died in jail."

"Granted. But Gina was serving a life sentence. So was her mother. Jules – who is completely innocent in this, who doesn't even know what's going on – has her life changed for ever."

"There has to be photos," Brady said. "Somewhere there *has* to be photos. We're talking 12 years ago. Maybe more. The millennium. Not like now – "

"Where every photo you've ever taken is on your phone?"

"Exactly. Proper photos. Taken on an Instamatic and developed by Boots. They're in the farmhouse, Frankie. And we have to find them."

32

Brady had just turned off the A64 when his phone rang. He glanced down at the car display. One word.

"The only person in your phone book without a Christian name?" Frankie said.

"Yes. And I'm tempted to let it ring. Tell him there was no signal. But..."

He pressed the green button. "Michael Brady."

"Brady? It's Alan Kershaw."

So my phone told me...

"I'm phoning for a progress report."

You're phoning because you already know what I've done. Because Sally Brown has sent you a text. 'He's told Foster the truth. It's all over Whitby.' Or words to that effect...

There was nothing Brady could do except spell it out. "OK, sir. The progress report is this. We made no progress in finding Gina Foster's killer. Ian Foster had an alibi. But we've made plenty of progress finding Gina Kirk's killer."

There was a moment of silence. Brady wasn't sure

whether it was the signal making its way to Spain, or Kershaw deciding between anger and sarcasm.

The latter.

"And in all this fucking 'progress,' Brady, you've found time to read the local paper have you?"

Child Sex Trafficker found dead in Esk. Local groups demand answers. Yes, he'd seen the headlines. He hadn't bothered reading the report.

"Yes, I've seen the paper, sir. But my focus – "

"Your focus? Your fucking focus, Brady? Your focus has been on making me – making North Yorkshire Police – look like fucking idiots. Christ, Brady, I thought you were overrated, but not by this much. I should have left that other self-proclaimed genius Thomson in charge."

Brady took his eyes off the road for a second. Turned. Smiled at Frankie. Raised his eyebrows.

"Detective Sergeant Thomson is sitting next to me, sir."

"Is she?"

The line went quiet. Brady could faintly hear music playing. Even more faintly he thought he heard Kershaw say, "Fuck."

Fifteen seconds to gather his thoughts. "Bring me up to date then, Brady. Let's see if we can salvage this mess."

"We're just coming back from the Midlands. We've spoken to Gina Kirk's sister and to one of the abused children we thought might be a suspect. But we've ruled him out."

"So who have you got in the frame?"

"My gut feeling is one of the gang members. Revenge

maybe. The ring leader died in jail. That's what we're working on."

"Bloody hell, Brady, they were all Albanians weren't they?"

"The ring leader – the apparent ring leader – was a Serb."

"Same part of the world. And a bloody fearsome reputation. I'd give them a wide berth if I were you."

"We have to find the killer," Brady said. "Irrespective of who's involved. Or what's happened."

There was another pause at the other end of the phone. "Well, I'm back next week. We need it cleared up by then. Otherwise we'll look like pricks. And the Chief Constable isn't going to stand for that. Neither is the Crime Commissioner. So it's in your hands, Brady."

And on my head. You don't need to spell it out.

"Like I said, we're making progress. Do you want me to keep you updated, sir?"

...Or shall I leave that to Sally Brown?

"No, I want to enjoy my holiday. We're flying at the weekend, so I'll see you first thing Monday morning. You can tell me it's case closed. And I don't want any more dead bodies either."

"I'll do my best. I'd better ring off, sir. I'm just coming into Pickering. Probably going to lose the signal as we go up onto the Moors."

"Right. Just get it sorted out, Brady. And Brady. One more thing."

"Sir?"

"Apologise to Thomson for me will you?"

Brady drove into Pickering. Turned his head and

smiled at Frankie. "He's sorry. You're probably still a self-proclaimed genius but he's sorry."

"So I heard. But I don't know if it means much coming from someone who's overrated."

"Vastly overrated, apparently..."

They were on the road to Whitby now, driving across the Moors. The rain had stopped, it was a clear night.

"We should pull over," Brady said. "Stop and look at the stars. Not much light pollution out here."

"Yeah, we should," Frankie said. "But another night, boss. I need to get back. And right now we're too busy wading through the shit to look up and see the stars."

33

"Why do you think she did it?" Frankie said.

"You're talking about Gina?"

"Boss, we don't talk about anything else."

"Fair point. It's like getting into the office earlier and earlier. Why do we do most things? We drift into them. Wake up one morning and it's normal life."

"Like living with the wrong guy."

"No, I didn't mean that."

"I know you didn't," Frankie said. "But it's a parallel isn't it? Gina's involved with someone – "

"Yeah. Remember what Jules said? Gina's clearly got money."

"So maybe it's Aleks. Maybe Aleks is the second boyfriend after she leaves home."

"First or second, Aleks is the one where it all changed," Brady said.

Frankie nodded. Drank some water out of her bottle. "Do you manage it?" Brady said. "Two litres a day?"

"No. It's like Dry January. I get bored. I try it every year. I'm bored by the first week in January."

"Gina..." Brady said.

"Yep. Like you said, she drifted into it. She's in love with Aleks. He says, 'the regular person hasn't turned up. This is all you have to do.'"

"And a fortnight later it's a full time job. So why did she stop?"

"Maria was growing up. Suddenly she can see her daughter at the same age as the youngest children?"

"Or one of the kids really gets to her..."

Brady looked across the desk at her. "It's not easy, is it? We're trying to find the murderer of a woman who was involved in child sex trafficking." He stood up and looked out of the window. "You walk out of here, go into Whitby, ask ten people in a fish and chip queue and nine of them will say, 'Good. Give whoever did it a medal.'"

"Except she was married. And she had a daughter."

"And she walked into Solihull police station and gave evidence. And maybe saved more kids than she harmed. Life, Frankie. It's never black and white. Good people do bad things. Bad people do good things. And half the time you can't tell the difference."

"And it's our job."

"Right. And it's a job we have to do quickly. Unless the Spanish air traffic controllers want to go on strike and keep Kershaw out there for another fortnight."

"Does it matter what her motives were?" Frankie said.

"Maybe not. We're dealing with what happened in Whitby, not what happened in Birmingham. But the more we understand Birmingham the more chance we've got of solving Whitby."

"So she walks into the police station..."

"Spur of the moment do you think? Or had she been thinking about it?"

"The second one. Jim Fitzpatrick said he sat in on an interview. Only 20 minutes he said. But she struck him as cool, calculating."

"So she's been thinking about it for a while. And then something pushes her over the edge. Makes the decision for her."

"Two children, Jim said. One found floating in the canal. One wandering by the side of the motorway. Once that had happened – and Gina had told her story – they couldn't keep it quiet."

"Were the kids – the one in the canal, the one by the motorway – were they at the same time?"

"That's a good question. And I'm sure we can find out. My guess is that they're a week, ten days apart. Something's happened. Maybe Gina tries to help one of the kids escape. Maybe she's fallen out with Aleks. Either way she gets to a stage where Solihull police station is the only option."

"We'll never know will we?"

Brady shook his head. "No. Gina's dead. Aleks is dead. No, we'll never know the full story."

"Like you say, boss. Bad people do good things."

"She took a hell of a risk," Brady said. "She walks into that police station and she knows her life is changed for ever. She's almost certainly going to jail. She has no idea what sort of deal she'll be able to do – "

"Unless she's already talked to someone..."

Brady nodded. "That's possible. Jim didn't say anything about that."

"And she's trading her daughter's life for her family. Even then she's not sure. The gang *must* come after her. She's got to think that."

"Her heart must have stopped in Rhyl. She thinks she's finally safe. Can finally relax. And then someone gives her away."

"Do you think that happened here?" Frankie said.

"No, I don't. I think Kershaw – and everyone above him – wanted a quiet life. Forget she was on their patch."

"Your patch, boss," Frankie said, smiling at him. "We're playing by Kershaw's rules. If it all goes wrong it'll be *your* patch."

THE OFFICE DOOR OPENED. Dan Keillor stood there, a tray with three coffee cups in his left hand, a paper bag under his arm and an envelope between his teeth.

Brady looked at him. "Frankie, make a note in this man's personnel file. Exemplary initiative and an uncanny ability to read the mind of senior officers. How much do I owe you, Dan?"

Keillor shook his head. "I thought it was probably my round. And this was in the post for you, boss."

He gave Brady the envelope. "It looks like a card," Frankie said.

Brady opened it. "Yeah," he smiled. "It is. Birthday card from some of the team back in Manchester."

"Hey, happy birthday, boss," Frankie said.

"Thank you. But it was yesterday."

"Yesterday? When we were driving down to Birmingham? Why didn't you say?"

Why didn't I tell her? I don't know...

"We were working. Time enough when this is over. And here..." He reached in his pocket and gave Keillor a ten pound note. "Save your cash. Save it for the Black Horse when we've cracked this. Does that bag have Danish pastries in it?" Keillor nodded. "Brilliant. You'll go a long way in the police, Dan..."

"We're in Gina's shoes – or in her head," Brady said as he stirred his coffee. "Trying to see it from her point of view."

"And it's complicated," Frankie said. "A long way from black and white."

"She thinks she's been recognised," Brady said. "She thinks someone might be coming for her."

"So she has two choices," Frankie said. "Run away or stay and fight."

"Three choices," Brady said. "Run away on her own. Run away with her husband and daughter. Or like you say, stay and fight."

Frankie was silent. Turning the choices over and over. "That's not a life sentence. That's a death sentence. Whatever she chooses."

"Yeah. Run away and leave your husband and daughter behind. Give up your life for the second time. Or take them with you. Tear your daughter away from the only life she's ever known. Tell your husband he has to leave the farm that was his father's and grandfather's."

"Or wait for someone to come for you."

"We know what she chose," Brady said.

"Do we?" Frankie said. "Can we be sure she decided to stay? Sacrifice herself for Ian and Maria?"

"What do you mean?"

"Maybe she hadn't decided. It sure as hell isn't a decision I'd take quickly."

Brady nodded. "You're right," he said. "No-one would take that decision quickly. No wonder she went for so many long walks. But it's like her motives when she first got involved. It doesn't change anything. Not as far as we're concerned. Whatever decision she'd made, someone forced her into the Esk and held her under."

"It doesn't affect us," Frankie said. "But it *does* affect her husband. And her daughter. If she knew she'd been discovered... Then she risked her own life to save theirs. We can give them that."

Brady was silent for a moment. He looked at Frankie. Nodded. "Yes," he said. "We can give them that. But let's give them the killer as well."

34

Brady started to stand up. "Boss?"

"What's up, Dan?"

"Can I ask a question?"

Brady sat back down. "Yes, of course you can. You know that. What do you want to know?"

Dan Keillor hesitated. "I suppose it's Maths really. What I can't get my head round... I can't work out how much money was involved in all this. In the original crime, the one they all went to jail for."

Brady nodded. "OK, I can see that. You want to know if it was worth it? Why didn't they just open another massage parlour?"

"I guess so..."

"I asked Frankie to do some figures. Not detailed research, but not back of a fag packet either. Frankie?"

"Sure. They're not pretty. But they're impressive..."

"Thank you." Brady turned back to Dan Keillor. "Let me give you some advice, Dan. Do your own Maths. Never trust the official figures. They'll be too high or too low. Someone *always* has an agenda. You want accurate figures? Do them yourself. Or ask someone who used to be a Maths teacher. All yours, Frankie."

"OK," Frankie said. "I'm going to do this in round numbers. Not to insult your intelligence, Dan, just to show you it doesn't need to be complicated."

Dan nodded. "Do I need to take notes?"

"No," Frankie said. "Because you won't forget the figures." She paused...

I know what she's thinking. The same as me. 'Crime doesn't pay.' It's complete crap. Crime pays remarkably well. Ridiculously well. Drugs, girls, children. There's always a demand...

"Mr Average has sex with a prostitute," Frankie said. "What does he pay?"

Dan Keillor shook his head. "I don't know."

"Of course you don't know. An hour in her flat? A hundred quid. But Mr Average isn't average. He has other tastes – that a child sex trafficking gang can satisfy. So he's going to pay a lot more than a hundred quid."

"I thought there weren't that many paedophiles? People like that?"

"Bear with me, Dan. I need to go stats-nerd on you. The population of the UK is around 65 million. The population of the West Midlands is around six. So a little under ten per cent. It was generally thought that there were around 20,000 people in the UK with a sexual interest in children – "

"So if the maths works out around 2,000 in the West Midlands?"

Frankie shook her head. "No. Because it's becoming

more and more recognised that the 20,000 figure is wrong. There's more evidence – especially from the dark web – that it's probably closer to 140,000."

"Evenly spread across the UK?" Brady said.

"No. Being blunt, boss, if you're interested in fishing you go where the fish are. If you're interested in sex with children..."

"You don't go and live in the Scottish highlands," Brady finished for her. "So the numbers could be even higher?"

"Yes. But let's settle on 10% of 140,000. Fourteen thousand. That's a hell of a customer base."

Dan Keillor looked embarrassed. "Can I ask another question?"

"Sure."

"Is this like sex with your wife or girlfriend? Or is it the same pattern as a serial killer?"

"Good question," Brady said. "Does a paedophile need to build up to it?"

"Right," Frankie said. "All the literature says that's how it is for a serial killer. He kills someone, he's satisfied. Then the urge builds up again. Let's say it's that way for a paedophile."

"So how often?" Brady said.

Frankie spread her hands. "Who knows? Once every four weeks is 3,500 potential customers a week. Once every seven weeks is 2,000 a week. Maybe only – again it's a guess – 25% of them are active. That's still 500 customers."

"So 500 a week at a hundred quid..."

"A lot more than a hundred quid, Dan. And probably people who can well afford it."

"What did Anthony Marshall say? A penthouse looking out over Birmingham?"

"Exactly," Frankie said. "Then you've got to add in the videos as well. A proper business empire. Does that answer your question, Dan?"

Dan Keillor nodded. "I see now..."

"Think what that income could buy," Brady said. "Power, influence, protection."

What had Julie said? 'When I talked to the police last time, no-one seem much interested. Like they wanted to get it over and done with. You know, wrap it all up and move on.' It was easy to understand why...

"Thank you," Brady said when Dan Keillor had gone. "That was... I was going to say 'helpful.' Eye-opening for Dan, I think."

"Thanks, boss." Frankie paused. "Miss Marple didn't have this shit, did she? Nice, normal people committing nice, normal murders. Maybe we joined the wrong police force."

"Maybe we did... Gina disrupted a lucrative business."

"A *very* lucrative business. And like I said, I think the figures could be under-estimates."

"It's like drugs. You can do your best to control the supply – "

"But you can't do anything about the demand," Frankie finished.

"It still doesn't answer the question. Why now? I can

see any number of reasons why someone wanted to kill Gina. What I can't see is why *now*. I need a long walk with Archie to work it out."

"And then a shower," Frankie said. "I stood in the shower the other night. I didn't know if I was trying to wash Raw Cashmere off me or the job I do."

Brady sighed. "Someone's got to stem the tide, Frankie. Some poor bastard has to clean the stables. And God chose you and me."

"He did," Frankie said. She paused. Looked straight at Brady. "You always say nothing's off limits. We can say anything."

"Yeah, that's right. You know that."

"In that case, Detective Chief Inspector Brady, I'm pissed off with you."

"Why? What have I done?"

"Your birthday. You should have told me."

Frankie Thomson stood up and walked out of Brady's office.

What the hell did I do wrong?

35

"Put yourself in Gina's head," Brady said.

"Bloody hell, boss, I spent all night in Gina's head."

Brady laughed. "Yeah. Me too. Surprised we didn't see each other."

Assuming you've forgiven me...

"So come on, she's hidden a phone. I think that's going to be easy to find. Whatever else she packed in the ten minutes she was allowed... Maybe not."

"Especially as we don't know what we're looking for."

Brady swerved round a new pothole in the farm track. Glanced in the rear view mirror. Detective Constable Sally Brown sat in the back seat, silent and unsmiling as ever.

"Somewhere in plain sight," Brady said. "Ian Foster doesn't strike me as an inquisitive man. Maybe I'm wrong. I don't think so."

What was this? The fourth time? Brady drove into the farmyard. Parked the Tiguan.

"No sign of a white Audi," he said.

"What's that then?" Frankie was pointing across the yard. There was a grey metallic Golf parked by the barn. A grey, metallic Golf that had parked outside Brady's house countless times.

"Shit," he said.

"What's wrong?"

"The Golf. It belongs to the mother of Ash's best friend. Fiona Gilroy. She's a solicitor. It never occurred to me that she might be Foster's new solicitor. Bloody hell, I nearly fell asleep on her sofa the other week. Ash keeps telling me I should ask her out."

"Foster must have said he wanted someone else," Frankie said.

"I can't blame him for that. But this is going to be bloody awkward."

Frankie raised her eyebrows. "All you can be is professional. That's what she'll be."

"Let's hope so. I have to stand next to her at a hockey match on Saturday."

"Maybe you could ask her out afterwards, boss..."

And what's that supposed to mean?

BRADY SHOOK HANDS WITH FIONA. She smiled at him. "Detective Chief Inspector Brady. And Detective Sergeant Thomson, I assume?"

"And Detective Constable Brown," Brady said. "She's our Family Liaison Officer, and she'll be our logger."

Fiona turned to Ian Foster. "Not in the lumberjack

sense, Ian. Detective Constable Brown will record any items that are taken away."

"What should I call you?" Brady said to Fiona. "Mrs Gilroy? Ms Gilroy?"

"The former. And as you can see, I've taken over advising Mr Foster from my colleague. We thought it was better all round."

"That's obviously between you and your client." Brady thought he ought to be diplomatic.

"How long do you think this will take?" Fiona asked. "Mr Foster still has work to do on the farm."

Brady decided to lay his cards on the table. "Honestly Mrs Gilroy? I have no idea. We're looking for a mobile phone – and something else. But we don't know what that something else is."

"But you'll know it when you find it?"

"Yes," Brady said. "I think so." He turned to Ian Foster. "Mr Foster, let me be honest with you. We know what happened to your wife. And I'm truly sorry for that. You probably know what happened to my wife. So I can empathise with you. But I – we – have a job of work to do. We have to find out who's responsible for your wife's death. And we're at the stage where we need your help."

Fiona looked at him. "I think for the record, Detective Chief Inspector – "

"Please Fi – . I'm sorry. Mrs Gilroy. I know we both need to be formal. But call me Mr Brady. Just Brady if it's easier. If you call me Detective Chief Inspector we'll be here until milking time."

Fiona smiled. Brady felt the tension ease.

"So what can my client do for you?"

Brady leaned forward. "We know Gina was in contact with her sister. We need to find the phone she used. We know that she left her previous life in a hurry. But she was only human. She must have brought something with her. Mementoes. Keepsakes. Something that might give us an insight into her previous life. Mr Foster, is there anything like that?"

Foster shook his head. "Not that I know. Not that she ever showed me. But then she wouldn't, would she?"

"So where do you propose to look?" Fiona said.

"To begin with, in the office and in the bedroom. And we propose to do it with as little intrusion into your life as we can, Mr Foster. But if we're going to catch who's done this... I'm sorry, we have to do it."

"Can't say I'm happy." Foster said. "Seems to me I've lost my wife and now you're poking around in her private life. Trampling on her memory."

Brady nodded. "I wish we didn't have to do it, Mr Foster. But it's the only way. We'll be as quick and as thorough as we can. Mrs Gilroy, if Mr Foster agrees, I'll do the office and Detective Sergeant Thomson will start in the bedroom. That seems more..."

"Appropriate," Fiona finished for him.

Brady stood up. "Are you alright if we make a start, Mr Foster?"

Fiona held her hand up. "One thing, Mr Brady. If you find anything you're obviously going to take it away with you."

Brady nodded. "Yes, you know that."

"My client has committed no crime. He's volunteering his help. Whatever you find, Mr Brady, I do not expect him to become the subject of gossip or ridicule. Police stations don't have a reputation for being the most tight-lipped places in the world."

Brady nodded again. Stared at Sally Brown. "You have my word," he said.

36

"You're sure you know what you're looking for, Mr Brady?"

Brady looked up. Foster stood in the office doorway, seemingly wanting reassurance rather than an answer to his question. "Yes, I do. Like I said, I'm looking for a phone. And anything else. But primarily, a mobile phone."

Brady searched in silence. Not the first drawer. Cheque books. Pens. A couple of spare pads. What everyone keeps in the top drawer of their desk.

"How did you cope?" Foster suddenly asked. "When your wife died. How did you cope?"

Should I talk about this with him? According to procedure, no I shouldn't. According to being a decent human being...

"How much of the story do you know?"

"I read it. Joanne found it for me – online."

He said 'online' in the same way he might have said 'witchcraft.'

"If you don't mind me asking. How did you cope?"

Brady wanted to search the desk.

But he's entitled to an explanation. And if he can find some comfort in it...

"I went through a range of emotions, Mr Foster – "

"Ian. If I'm not a suspect you'd best call me Ian."

Brady nodded. "I went through a range of emotions. A psychologist would be better at explaining them than I am. But I suppose I was lucky. I had my daughter. Like you do."

Foster didn't say anything. Brady felt compelled to continue. "The hard part for me was the waiting. Grace was on life support for six months. But looking back, I knew all the time. That there'd only be one outcome."

"So I've been lucky as well? No waiting?"

"You can't say that, Ian. But you've got the farm. And you've got Maria. And I promise you we'll get to the bottom of this. We'll find out what happened. And who's responsible."

I should come and talk to him when we've found the killer. Have a beer with him. But if we don't find anything we're not going to find the killer...

Brady opened the second drawer. Files full of receipts. He flipped through them. Standard farm receipts. Two A4 Pukka Pads underneath them. Gina had been a woman who liked her stationery. Brady picked them up and looked inside. Did what he always did and turned to the back page. Predictably, disappointingly blank.

The third drawer. One of those drawers arranged to take hanging files. Brady flicked through them. First file, second file... And there it was. Brady felt the weight as he moved the third file.

He gently picked the phone out. A Nokia. Three years old? Four? From around the time they'd finally cracked under the pressure and told Ash she could have a phone for her birthday.

"Have you ever seen this before, Mr Foster? Ian?"

Foster looked down at the floor and slowly shook his head. As though he hadn't believed the story. Had somehow thought that Brady had made it up. But here was the proof. A well-worn Nokia.

"No. Never." He shook his head again. "Never seen it."

Brady pressed the on button. But it was out of charge. He looked back in the drawer. Pushed the hanging files to one side. Found the charger. Put it in the evidence bag with the phone.

And now for the photographs. Or whatever Gina brought with her.

But Brady drew a blank. The office was functional. Gina had done the farm accounts. Nothing more, nothing less.

There were no personal notes. No pictures. No drawings by a four year old daughter taped to the wall.

Brady admitted defeat. "We're done in here, Ian," he said. "Let's see what's been happening upstairs."

FRANKIE WALKED INTO THE KITCHEN. Looked at Brady. Shook her head. "Nothing, boss."

"Nothing?"

"Exactly what you'd expect in a bedroom. Nothing that we were looking for."

Fiona had followed her in. "But you clearly found what you wanted, Mr Brady?"

Brady was still holding the evidence bag containing the phone.

"Yes. We'll check the calls. See what numbers she called."

And there'll be one. Her sister...

"So are we done for today? Or are we done for good? Clearly you can't call back on a daily basis. My client's goodwill only extends so far."

It has to be here. There has to be something. No-one walks away from their life and leaves everything behind.

"Could you give us ten minutes, Mrs Gilroy?"

Fiona looked at her watch. "We both have children, Mr Brady. And I'm sure Detective Sergeant Thomson has commitments."

Brady nodded. "We do, you're right. And yes she does. But we have to find out who killed Mr Foster's wife. Would you just give us ten minutes?"

"Ten minutes more searching?"

"Ten minutes thinking, Mrs Gilroy."

Brady walked out to the car. Frankie followed him. He unlocked the car and climbed in.

"Did she give you any grief?" Brady asked.

"Fiona? No, she stood in the doorway. We didn't make girly small talk as I went through Gina's knicker drawer. But..."

"But what?"

"She seems to like you. She asked what you were like to work with."

"I won't ask what you said. Tell me what you found in the bedroom."

"Exactly what you'd expect to find. Socks in her sock drawer, knickers in her knicker drawer. A vibrator at the back of it that will give Ian Foster a serious inferiority complex when he finds it. Not many dresses and skirts. Plenty of pairs of jeans."

"Did you go right through the wardrobe?"

Frankie nodded. "Coats, shoes. Again, exactly what you'd expect to find."

"Neat? Organised?"

"Yes. Everything arranged by colours. In comparison I'm a failure as a woman. My guess is she wore jeans nearly all the time."

"All new?"

"You mean anything from 12 years ago? Women aren't like men, boss. They don't become emotionally attached to a pair of shorts long after they've fallen apart."

"What about his wardrobe?"

"The same. What you'd expect to find. T-shirts, a lot of checked shirts. A dark suit. Probably last worn at his mother's funeral."

"What else was in the bedroom?

"Double bed. King size. An old chaise-longue by the window that I suspect Gina used to read on and Ian Foster will now throw his clothes on."

"Books?"

"Plenty at her side. And a good selection as well. *Jane Eyre, Girl on the Train, Bridget Jones, Pride and Prejudice.*"

"What about him?"

"What you'd expect probably. James Patterson. Lee Child. *Farming Monthly*."

"Plenty of nights when he fell asleep and she was reading."

"That would be my guess. So you can file it under 'normal marriage,' boss."

"OK. Leave their marriage to one side. Where the hell would she hide something? Something she really valued?"

"But wanted access to," Frankie said. "So not outside."

"Right. You heard what Foster said. 'I'm in charge of everything that happens outside. She's in charge of everything that happens inside.' So it's in the house. Think it through, Frankie. If you were hiding something from Alex, where would you hide it?"

"The middle of the lounge carpet would be fine. He's moved out."

"Oh... I'm sorry. I..."

"Don't be. I've got the place to myself. He left me eight cans of Pale Ale. Life is good."

Brady didn't know how to respond. Frankie did it for him.

"Let me ask you the same question, boss. If Grace had been hiding something from you, where would she have hidden it?"

"Given how long it took me to do any DIY in the tool box probably."

"Does Foster strike you as a man who cooks?" Frankie said.

"No. And definitely not now Joanne has arrived. What are you thinking? Biscuit tin?"

"Something like that. Cake tin? Baking cupboard?"

"Maybe. He doesn't strike me as a man who cooks but he does strike me as a man with a sweet tooth."

"Freezer," Frankie said. "Alex cooks – cooked – but nothing that meant he had to think ahead. I'm not sure he knew how to de-frost a chicken breast."

"Laundry cupboard?" Brady said.

"No. He'll want his favourite shirt one day. He'll go poking around for it."

"Let's say we're looking for a tin. Something like a tin of Quality Street. You know, like the ones your Gran had at Christmas. Every family has a tin like that."

"So it's got to be somewhere you'd expect to find a tin."

"Yeah. Hidden in plain sight."

"So we're back to the baking cupboard."

"Or a medicine chest."

"What about a set of instructions?" Frankie said. "Everyone's got a file where they keep guarantees and instruction books and all that crap. Supposing she'd brought photos and letters? You could easily store those among the instructions."

"Supposing he wants to fix the central heating?"

"She's thought of that. Anything he might want is in a separate file. By the boiler."

Brady looked at his watch. "Two minutes," he said. "We need to sort this out today. And we don't have time to turn the house upside down. Kershaw's clock is ticking."

"So you want to search the baking cupboard, the freezer and the instructions for the washing machine?"

"It's a start," Brady said. "Let's go. They'll have had enough of DC Brown's wit and repartee by now."

He put his hand on the door handle. "And the sewing cupboard," he said. "I knew where to find a needle and thread but I had no idea about the rest of it. Grace did – is it called cross-stitch? She did that occasionally. Said it helped her unwind. She kept all that in old biscuit tins. Ian Foster might not look like a man who cooks. He looks even less like a man who knows how to thread a needle. Come on."

37

Fiona Gilroy was sceptical. So sceptical the formalities were back. "You want to empty my client's freezer, Detective Chief Inspector?"

"Yes. And while I'm doing that DS Thomson would like to go through the baking cupboard. Which one is it, Mr Foster?"

Foster found it with some difficultly. It took Frankie less than five minutes to go through it and find exactly what you'd expect to find in a baking cupboard.

The freezer was the same. Well stocked with meat. McCain's oven chips. Frozen peas. A plastic freezer bag with 'Chilli Sept 7th' written on it. Something in the bottom drawer so encrusted with perma-frost it was impossible to tell what it was.

Except that it wasn't mementoes of Gina's previous life.

Fiona took a very pointed glance at her watch. Brady could feel the pressure.

She might be Bean's mum, I might have thought of her as

a friend. Still think of her as a friend. But Curtiss is going to ask her what happened. And it won't be long before the story makes its way back to Kershaw. 'I understand you and DS Thomson carried out a raid on Foster's freezer, Brady. I must have missed that new initiative in policing. Still, at least you managed it without a SWAT team...'

Brady looked at Foster. "Where do you keep all the instructions, Mr Foster? You know, for things like the boiler, the washing machine, all the kitchen appliances?"

"Gina kept a file," he said helplessly. "It might have been red."

Fiona stood up and walked over to a corner of the kitchen. There were a couple of cookbooks on top of the microwave. And neatly between the microwave and the wall, a red lever-arch file. She handed it to Brady. Smiled at him. "It's where everyone keeps it, Mr Brady. There or under the boiler."

It took even less time to check than the cupboard. A very neatly ordered file with instructions, guarantees and warranties. Nothing that was of the slightest use to them.

Brady played his last card.

"Did your wife do anything like needlework, Mr Foster? My wife used to do cross-stitch. She said it helped her relax..."

Foster smiled. Almost for the first time that afternoon. "Aye, she did. Except she knitted. I told her she was too young to knit. Told her it was an old woman's hobby. But she said I didn't understand."

"Where did she keep it all?"

Foster pointed across the living area. "In the sideboard. She'd get it out on an evening."

"Do you mind if I take a look?"

"Go ahead, Mr Brady. You've looked everywhere else."

Brady walked across to the sideboard. Opened the door Foster had pointed out. Found a ball of wool with two knitting needles through it. What looked like the beginnings of a scarf. Light blue and dark blue. Several more balls of wool. And three tins.

He opened the first one. Odd scraps of material Gina must have saved. A smaller tin full of pins.

Reached for the last tin. A defiant stag on the front of it. Snow-capped mountains behind him. A tartan border. *M&S All Butter Scottish Shortbread Biscuits.*

He opened the tin. And saw Gina Kirk's life.

"Have you ever seen this tin before, Mr Foster?"

Foster looked confused. "I don't know. A tin of shortbread? I might have done. I don't know."

"Or this picture?"

Brady already knew the answer. Knew he'd only need to show Foster one of the pictures.

He passed it across. Almost the same picture Jules had shown him. The two girls in their matching red swimsuits. Julie and Gina, arms round each other on the beach.

Foster shook his head. "Is that Gina?" he said. "My wife?"

A tear rolled down his cheek.

"Thank you," Brady said. "I'm sorry we had to do this, Mr Foster. Truly sorry. We'll leave you alone now."

38

"Happy, boss?"

Brady looked across at Frankie. "Very happy," he said. "The only thing that'd make me happier is Ian Foster fixing these potholes."

"Your friend the solicitor was impressed. I saw her looking at you when you found the shortbread tin."

Brady laughed. "I doubt it. She's seen the worst of me. She's always turning up at the house when I've failed to do something for Ash."

He turned out of the farm drive, drove through Grosmont and started up the hill towards Sleights. Turned right into a development of new houses. Dropped Sally Brown off. "Thanks for your help, Sally. See you in the morning."

"It's gone six," he said to Frankie. "Do you want me to drop you at home? At your mum's? Or is your car in the car park?"

"I walked," Frankie said. "And none of the above. I want to look at old photographs."

"We should book them in at the station."

"Right. And you're going to do that? Or do you have two pairs of plastic gloves at home?"

Brady didn't even bother replying.

He pressed *phone* on the car's display. Ash answered on the third ring.

"Hi, sweetheart. How are you doing?"

"Hi, Dad. I'm good. I've fed Archie for you."

"Thank you. I don't deserve you. Have you eaten?"

"I've had a sandwich. Why?"

"Because I'm on my way home. There's some work stuff I need to look at. I was going to get pizza."

"I'm good. But if you're getting pizza I'll eat some. And so will Archie."

"OK. Fifteen minutes. Love you."

"Pizza again..." Frankie said.

"You're fine. We're both fine. There's a chaperone."

"Not that we need one, boss."

"No, Detective Sergeant. Not that we need one."

BRADY PUT his key in the front door. Wasn't sure whether Archie was more excited by him, Frankie or the pizza.

"Ash?" he shouted upstairs.

"Hi," floated back down the stairs.

Brady put the pizza boxes down on the table. "You alright to eat out of the box?"

Frankie nodded.

Brady walked into the kitchen for some napkins. Felt his mouth go dry again. Said a small prayer of thanks for Ash being at home.

"You want a drink, Frankie?"

"Mineral water seeing as we're working, I guess. If you've got some."

"Peroni mineral water or Brewdog?"

"Tough one. Brewdog, I think."

Brady fetched two beers from the fridge. Consciously sat on the opposite side of the table. Heard his daughter coming downstairs.

"Hi Ash, you remember Frankie? Detective Sergeant Thomson – from the other night?

Ash nodded, said 'Hi.' Casually announced that Bean had been dumped by her boyfriend – "By text, the loser" – and that her counselling services were urgently needed.

"You want a lift?" Brady asked. "Two minutes. There's no point walking."

"You've just got pizza," Ash said. "Two pizzas. Sorry."

"It's no problem," Frankie said. "Your dad can give you a lift. I'll put them in the oven."

"Come on then," Brady said. "Jump in the car. You want me to come for you later? Say, nine o'clock?"

Ash shook her head. "Fiona will bring me back. I'm sure she will."

"I'm sorry, Frankie," Brady said. "I'll only be ten minutes. Will you be OK?"

Frankie laughed. "Of course. Archie and I are old mates now."

Brady threw his coat on and reached for his car keys. Opened the passenger door for his daughter.

"Unusually chivalrous tonight, Dad. Is that because of – " Ash made exaggerated inverted commas with her fingers "– Detective Sergeant Thomson?"

"Frankie Thomson is a work colleague, Ash. Nothing more, nothing less. We need to go through some photographs. And that's all I can say."

"Of course, Dad. I understand. She looks hot with her hair pinned up, doesn't she…"

39

It took 20 minutes. He'd felt morally obliged to speak to Fiona. She'd laughed about the formalities. Promised to bring Ash back. Said it was easier in their day when you couldn't be dumped by text.

"I'm sorry," he said to Frankie. "The dark nights. I don't like her walking. Ah – that's tactless of me. I didn't mean to – "

"Remind me about Katie? Just being in October does that. Come on, eat some pizza. I've spent the last ten minutes telling Archie he'll have to be patient."

"Thanks for keeping it warm."

"No problem. Ovens aren't difficult..."

They ate in silence for two minutes.

"You know what I can't understand?" Frankie said.

"How she kept the tin hidden for so long? I think that's easy. I wouldn't have gone near Grace's cross-stitch in a thousand years."

Frankie shook her head.

Is she going to let her hair down? I like it pinned up...

"No, you're right. I understand that. What I don't understand is... How can anyone like pineapple on a pizza? I've worried about it for years. It just seems fundamentally wrong."

Brady laughed. Realised he liked that in her. The sudden veering off at a tangent. Never being completely sure what she'd say next. The mental challenge.

"This is good," Frankie said.

"What is?"

"Eating pizza."

"Is this leading somewhere?"

"We're eating pizza. There's a tin on the table. We're *desperate* to look inside it. But we're delaying the pleasure while we eat pizza. It's a sign we're not psychopaths."

"Did you consider that we might be hungry?"

"Did you never have a relationship with a psychologist? Phil Parker, my first year at university. It's the only thing I can remember – apart from the disappointing sex. If a child can't learn to delay pleasure – eat the chocolate later – it's a potential sign of psychopathy in later life. Delayed gratification, to use the technical term. Or – if you want to vanish completely up your own arse – the marshmallow principle."

"So being hungry has nothing to do with it?"

"Obviously not. Just like not wanting to contaminate the evidence with mozzarella and pepperoni has nothing to do with it."

Brady reached forward. Picked up the last slice of meat feast. Made an 'am I OK to eat this' gesture. Just as he'd done with the last three slices, made sure he left the crust. Walked into the kitchen. Gave Archie what he'd been whimpering for.

Put the pizza boxes in the bin. Washed his hands. Waited for Frankie to come down from the bathroom.

"It's like an old-fashioned quiz show," Frankie said. "Opening the mystery box."

"Opening the mystery tin of shortbreads. Let's see..."

Brady stood up and walked round to Frankie's side of the table. Sat next to her. Took the lid off the tin.

Photographs. Not as many as he'd expected. A folded piece of paper. An envelope at the bottom.

Brady unfolded the piece of paper. "Maria's birth certificate," he said. He scanned rapidly across to 'father's name.' Looked at it twice.

Looked at the blank space twice.

"So who's decision was that?" he said. "Gina not wanting to name the father – "

"We're assuming she knew who the father was then?"

"I think so. But maybe he didn't want to be named on the birth certificate?"

Brady picked the photographs up. Gina and her sister on the beach. The photograph he'd shown Ian Foster.

Gina and her mother. Gina was 11 or 12, her mother in her mid-forties. "There's something about the pose," Brady said. "A hint of rebellion. You can see the teenager lurking in the shadows."

"Maybe it was the last photo she ever had with her mum?"

"Maybe. You're probably right..."

Gina in the delivery room. A navy blue gown, the hospital name tag round her wrist. The exhausted/ecstatic/relieved/I've done it look that all new mothers have. Maria cradled in her arms. Eyes shut, already asleep.

"Who do you think took that one?"

"The father? One of the nurses?"

"You think the father cared enough to be at the birth?"

Then Gina and her baby in the park. "She's about a year old there," Frankie said. "Just starting to walk."

Gina was holding a flower out, smiling as Maria reached out to take it.

The last photo. Gina and Maria in the same park, maybe even the same day. But with a man. An older man, his hair just starting to turn grey. A dark blue shirt, a grey sweater draped over his shoulders, loosely tied at the front.

"*That's* the father," Brady said. "That has to be the father."

"I thought you said Savićević was the father."

"Look at the way he's standing. I've photos of the three of us. He's looking at Maria the way I looked at Ash..."

Protective. Standing the way I stood. Protecting my family.

"He's a lot older," Frankie said. "At least twice her age."

"But it fits with what Jules said about an older man, doesn't it? That's the father, Frankie."

"So who is it?"

Brady looked at the picture again. He was standing protectively over Gina and Maria.

But there's something else. Something in his body language. 'This is mine.' Threaten it at your peril.

"Who is it?" Brady said. "Like everything else in this bloody case – I have no idea. Absolutely no idea."

40

Brady opened the envelope. Slid out two folded sheets of A4. Unfolded them. Laid the two sheets on the table. Felt Frankie lean closer to him as they read together.

Maria, my darling

I hope – with all my heart – that you never read this letter.

I pray that one day I can tell you all this. Face to face. Holding your hand – and hoping that you understand.

But, if you're reading these words then it means I never got that chance. It means that what follows must be my voice. My explanation. So that if others tell you stories about me, then you can come back here, to this letter, and hear me talking to you.

I did bad things in my life. Dreadful things. I was sent to prison but that was nothing. I carried my own guilt every day. Remember I once read Christmas Carol to you? Do you remember the Ghost of Jacob Marley? 'I carry the chains I forged in life.' That was me.

Why did I do those things? Because I was young. Because

I was in love. And because the man I was in love with – although he was handsome and ambitious, funny and charming – also had a dark side to him. A dreadful dark side that I saw, and that terrified me. And I had you. And – as you'll know yourself one day when you hold a baby in your arms – there is nothing a mother will not do to protect her child.

That man – Aleks Savićević – is your real father. He's dead now. He died in jail. And he was in jail because finally I found the courage to tell the police about him. Finally I found the courage to be an informer.

My name then was Gina Kirk. And one day you will see the newspaper headlines: 'Gina Kirk. How could she do it?'

Putting both sides of the argument doesn't make headlines, doesn't sell newspapers. I can only say it again. I did bad things. But I was young, I was in love and I had you to protect.

I knew the price I would pay. I would never see my own mother, or my sister, again. I would go to jail. I would live the rest of my life in hiding. Never trusting anyone, wary of every stranger.

But it was a small price to pay to protect you. To keep you safe. To give you, for want of a better phrase, a 'normal' mum.

And so I ended up in Whitby, on the farm. Married to a good man.

And Ian – your dad, the only dad you have known – is a good man. He married me, he gave me a home. Somewhere I could watch you grow, keep both of us safe. I never told him the truth. I wish I had. But sometimes you have lived the lie for so long it becomes the truth.

Your dad loves you. With all his heart. He will always be

there for you, even if I cannot be. Even if, one day, my past catches up with me.

I love you more than you will ever know. Well, one day you will know. You will hold your own child in your arms. You will be astonished – unable to understand – just how much you love him, or her, the grandchild I will never see. That is how much I love you. So do not think ill of me.

Your real father told me once that his great-great-grandfather was a prince. So maybe you are a princess. That was what I called you. 'Sleep tight, my little princess' I said every night.

I look at my letter now and see there are one or two tearstains on it. I will leave them. As I re-read it I can hardly see the paper for the tears. But those tears are for you, my darling.

Everything I did, I did for you.

And there, written in Gina's round, open handwriting:

With all the love in my heart

Gina, your mum

Brady exhaled. Stayed silent. "How many times did she write and re-write that?" he finally said.

"Five?" Frankie said. "Ten. A hundred? She must have been writing it in her head for years."

"We need to give it to Ian Foster. It's his job. His responsibility to decide when to give it to Maria."

"Not now, boss. It's evidence."

"It's all evidence isn't it?"

Frankie put her hand on his. "Evidence of a mother loving her daughter. That's all."

"And evidence of the father," Brady said. "Maybe I was wrong about the photo?"

"Why would Gina lie to her daughter?"

Brady shook his head. "I don't know," he said. "Right now I can't think of a reason."

HE'D DROPPED FRANKIE OFF. "Hope your mum's had a good day."

"We'll see," she'd said.

He'd phoned Fiona. Told her he'd come and collect Ash. "How's Bean?" he asked as Ash climbed into the car.

"I convinced her she was better off without him."

"So she's alright now?"

His daughter sighed theatrically. "No, Dad, she's not alright. Don't ask. You're too old to understand relationships."

Ten minutes later and Ash announced she was going to bed. "Don't spend all night counselling Bean by text."

"Maybe... Night, Dad."

"Night, sweetheart. Sleep well."

Brady opened the back door for Archie. Told him for the third time that there was no pizza left. Wondered if it was too late to have another beer. Never made a decision because his phone rang...

"Jim, it's late. Is everything OK?"

"Yeah, sorry, Mike. I meant to ring you earlier but Val filled me full of Chicken Pie. I must have dropped off..."

Brady walked over to the table. He'd need to make notes. "You've spoken to Doug Taylor, boss?"

"I have. Sorry it's taken a while. He was away on holiday. Spain."

"What is it with Spain at this time of year? It must be full of English coppers."

Jim laughed. "Catching up with the ones that got away, Mike. But you don't want to talk about that, or how good my wife's pie was. Have you got a pen?"

"I'm sitting at the dining room table. Fire away."

"I spoke to Doug," Jim said. "Like I said." Brady could hear the tension in his old boss's voice. "This is one where any sane, rational man would let sleeping dogs lie. Murdered but not enough evidence. Reflect on your pension and close the case. But..."

"But what, boss?"

"I know you of old, Mike. I'm not saying you're not sane and rational. I am saying you should take care."

"Who is it?"

"Doug and I thought the man who was really pulling the strings – who was behind it all – was a guy called Marko Vrukić. V – R – U – K – I – C. He's Serbian. Accent on the C. Not that you'll need it. Lived in the UK for a while now. But he's made plenty of visits over the years. Very well connected. And not a man to be trifled with, Mike."

The name vaguely – very vaguely – rang a bell. But Brady couldn't place it. "Who is he, boss?"

More than a hundred miles between them and he could almost see Jim shaking his head. "Just the name, Mike. I promised Doug. But you won't have any trouble doing your research. Marko Vrukić has his own page on Wikipedia."

. . .

Brady turned his laptop on. Tapped his passcode in. Opened Chrome. Typed in *Marko Vrukić Wiki.* Clicked the link.

Read a very short, clearly very edited biography. Looked at the photo in the top right. Looked at it again. Reached forward and took Gina's photographs out of the tin. Looked at the last one. A smiling, paternal figure with a mother and her baby.

Supposing he is the father? Supposing Gina felt she had to protect Maria from knowing who her father really was?

He looked at the picture on Wiki for a third time. Slightly older. But definitely the same man.

A man who very clearly frightened his old boss. Who *must* hold the key to her murder. Who could be Maria's father.

'This is one where any sane, rational man would let sleeping dogs lie. Murdered but not enough evidence. Reflect on your pension and close the case.'

Michael Brady looked at the two photographs again. Reached down and patted his dog. "This is it, Archie," he said. "Where I stop being sane and rational..."

41

"Frankie?"

"Morning, boss. You sleep well?"

Brady laughed. "What do you think? Awake half the night seeing those photos in front of me."

And awake the other half of the night wondering what I'd say to Ash if I had to write a letter...

"I'm going to be out this morning. Should be back around lunchtime. I'll bring you and Dan up to date then."

"Anywhere exciting?"

"Don't ask."

"Is that the same 'don't ask' as before?"

Brady smiled at her. "Don't ask. Can you book the evidence in for me?"

"Statement to the press as well, boss? DCI Michael Brady said that a tin of shortbread biscuits was helping the police with their enquiries..."

"Obviously. And make sure it's on Sky News so Kershaw sees it in Spain."

. . .

"Sit down, Michael. Have a cup of tea. I count you as a friend. I hold you in high esteem. So let me be honest. I am frightened for you."

"You think I've bitten off more than I can chew?"

Mozart laughed. "Marko Vrukić? You may have just won the Understatement of the Year Award, Michael. But never let it be said that you lack courage."

"Give me the background. Forewarned is forearmed."

"Michael, the sensible reaction to 'forewarned' about Vrukić is a one way ticket to Argentina. But I've read the report on…"

"You can say it. On the case that killed Grace. You know I'm stupid. You know I won't let go."

Mozart nodded. "Well, 'stupid' isn't the word I'd have chosen. But this is about more than 'not letting go.' Listen to what I have to say. Then make your decision."

Brady nodded. Sipped his Earl Grey. "Before you start," he said. "Do you have a photo?"

"Of course." Mozart turned one of his computer screens on. Opened a file. A picture came up. "What do you think?" Mozart said. "A young Paul Newman? Slightly darker. He's in his early 20s there. And then…" He closed the file. Opened another. A commander in front of a tank, surrounded by cheering men. In his early 40s. Army uniform and a beard. A machine gun in his left hand, a bottle of champagne in his right. Toasting victory.

Brady reached into his pocket. Brought out the photo.

Gina and Maria in the park. An older man, his hair just starting to turn grey. A dark blue shirt, a grey sweater draped over his shoulders, loosely tied at the front. Looking at Maria the way I looked at Ash.

He handed the photo to Mozart. "What do you think?"

Mozart glanced at it. Looked at the picture on his screen. "Different worlds," he said. "Very different worlds. But the same man."

"That's what I was afraid of," Brady said. "You'd better tell me the full story."

Mozart smiled. "The full report then. The one that reaches the parts Wikipedia clearly hasn't been allowed to reach. Marko Gaćinović was born in 1950, in a small village in what is now Serbia and what was then part of Yugoslavia. It was a mountain village, cut off in the winter – and with a fierce, tribal culture dating back to the 13th or 14th Century. Unusually, a matriarchal culture. His father had been a pilot in the Second World War. Ended the war close to Tito so the family – father, mother, three sisters and the young Marko moved to Belgrade."

"Marko? I thought that was Roman? From Mars?"

"His father's name, obviously. And there was a Serbian Prince Marko in the 14th Century. He's a national hero – defended his people against the Turks. But yes, from Mars, the god of war."

"So he's in Belgrade, the son of a well-connected war hero?"

"...Who abused his children, apparently. Not sexually. Physically. Marko's reported as saying his father didn't so much hit him as body slam him to the ground. Then – when he's 14 or 15 – the father ups and leaves. Abandons the family, takes up with a younger woman. A year later he's found with his throat cut."

"Marko is responsible?"

Mozart shrugged. "No-one knows. The woman's husband? Her father? The secret police? Maybe Gaćinović Senior is a security risk by this point. But if you offered me ten-to-one on his son I might invest a pound or two."

"So he's 15 and he might have killed his father?"

Mozart nodded. "By now his uncle has taken him under his wing. Filip Vrukić. His mother's brother – who's head of the State Security Administration, the UBDA."

"The secret police?"

"One and the same. And he takes his uncle's name."

"Out of respect?"

"Out of convenience, I suspect. Saying it when he's been arrested is a sure-fire way to get released. By this time Marko is a petty criminal – thief, pickpocket and almost certainly part-time hit man for his uncle."

"That doesn't sound very petty…"

"Wait for the rest of it. By the time he's 20 he's a fully-fledged armed robber. Paris, Stockholm, Berlin. He's also married – to a woman five years older than him. Two children, now living with their mother in America – and using their mother's name. Those are the first of eight children from three marriages. Plus God knows how many more. His bastards must be all over the Balkans."

"What are we up to now? 1970? Thereabouts?"

"Yes. The 70s are spent running round Europe, holding up banks, gambling away the proceeds, fathering children and ending up on the wanted list of every police force there is. Then in the early 80s he's back in Belgrade running a nightclub and casino. And finally behind bars. A fight in the casino and he breaks someone's arms. Unfortunately for Vrukić it's the President's brother."

"How long did he get?"

"Six months sabbatical in Belgrade Central Prison. Meanwhile Tito has died and Yugoslavia is gradually descending into civil war. Vrukić goes through marriages two and three, the last one to Dina Vajda, who at the time was Yugoslavia's answer to – sorry, popular culture isn't my area – Britney Spears? Kylie Minogue? You get my drift."

"And then the war broke out?" Brady said.

"Yes. From Vrukić's point of view the best thing that ever happened to him."

"So what happened? How did he transition from nightclub owner to warlord?"

"Not just warlord," Mozart said. "By the end of it he's so strong, so powerful and so rich that he can act with impunity. Murder people in front of witnesses. Who subsequently have no memory of what they've seen. Anyway, let me go through it for you. I've pieced this together as best I can."

"From..."

Mozart smiled. "Various sources. Some in the public domain. Some less so."

"Thank you," Brady said. "I appreciate this."

Ten times more efficient than going through the police bureaucracy. And a hundred times quicker...

"It all started with football hooliganism," Mozart said. "Vrukić is the leader of the *Delije* – supporters of Red Star

Belgrade. The word roughly translates as 'heroes.' Maybe even 'studs.' They more or less have a pitched battle with the supporters of Dinamo Zagreb."

"From Croatia?"

"Yes. So you've got the simmering Serb-Croat war right there on the football pitch. A week later Vrukić creates a paramilitary force – the Volunteer Guard. He starts to talk to other Serbian groups. Gets arrested by the Croats for allegedly straying into their territory. The Serbian government reportedly pay a million dollar ransom for his release. He's increasingly being seen as a hero. A defender of Serb nationalism. There are stories of him and his men training at a remote monastery in the mountains. And then war breaks out."

"And he's got blood on his hands?"

"Blood on his hands? He's turned the shower onto max and stood under it. The Volunteer Guard is now called the Dragons. It's led by Vrukić and Uroš Gaćinović, his second-in-command. A hard core of maybe 200 men. Between 500 and 1,000 at its peak. Men who'd follow him to the gates of Hell. And expect to win the battle. The Dragons are active from 1991 to around 1995 and they massacre thousands – maybe tens of thousands – in Croatia and Bosnia-Herzegovina."

"Who's supplying them?"

"The rumours suggest the Serbian police. And, of course, the weapons they capture. But they're involved in everything. Ethnic cleansing, burning villages. And Vrukić led nearly all the operations. He – and his closest allies – are starting to become seriously wealthy from looting. There are rumours of links with the Camorra in

Italy. Arms smuggling, people smuggling. You name it, Vrukić is involved in it."

"So what happens when the war ends?"

"When the war ends he's a hero. A hero in Serbia. In Croatia he's the bogeyman. Mothers tell their children to behave or Vrukić will come for them. Then gradually he returns to family life and business. He buys a football team. They play in the second division. A few years later they've won the Yugoslavian League. It's generally acknowledged that scoring against them is not a sensible career move."

"But then it started to go wrong?"

"Then it all gets very murky. That's the point where there's information I can access but only with time. And – I'll be honest with you, Michael – only at some considerable risk. By now the NATO bombings have started. Vrukić is accused of war crimes. He's not so much breached the Geneva Convention as trampled it underfoot. At first the accusations are only from journalists – and the first one to say anything is found floating in the Danube – but then it becomes more widespread. There's the latest assassination attempt. There are rumours he's hiding in the Chinese embassy. And then suddenly he's not in Belgrade, he's in Brize Norton. And shortly after that in a hundred acres of prime English countryside just outside Birmingham." Mozart shook his head. "It's all a long way from Saltburn. What are you going to do?

Brady stood up. Walked over to the window. Looked out to sea. A container ship heading to Teesport, a dark cloud behind it.

"Do the only thing I can do," Brady said. "Go and see him."

"...And that's why I said I was frightened for you. You make an enemy of this man..."

"Even in the English countryside?"

Mozart nodded. "He's clearly done some sort of deal. Traded information for being allowed to live here. Used some of the proceeds of looting to make a sizeable donation to the right politicians. I don't know. But tread carefully. Very carefully."

Mozart, Jim Fitzpatrick. Both saying the same thing. But what's the alternative? I need to know what happened. And I need to know quickly.

"Do you have his phone number?"

Mozart handed him a slip of paper. Plain, exercise book paper. The sort you could buy in any corner shop. Untraceable. A mobile phone number written in biro.

"Do not underestimate this man, Michael. He speaks half a dozen languages. And he's lived by his wits for more than 50 years. He's survived four or five assassination attempts. He'll be 65 now. That doesn't make him any less dangerous."

"Give me some background. What does he do now?"

"Supports Aston Villa. Raises money for charity. Lives relatively modestly. Well, lavishly for you and me. Modestly for a retired warlord. When are you going to see him?"

"On the off-chance he'll answer his phone to a number he won't recognise... As soon as I can."

"I'll be thinking of you." Mozart hesitated. "There is one other thing I should tell you. This sounds stupid. But

Vrukić has a moral code. His word is his bond. It goes right back to the village of his childhood. He was fiercely loyal to his men: they returned the loyalty. He's responsible for the death of thousands. Tens of thousands, probably. He's beyond ruthless. But – here in the UK – he's almost singlehandedly funded a new children's wing for the local hospital."

Brady stood up. He needed to be back in Whitby. "Bad people do good things," he said.

"Bad people do bad things as well, Michael. This is a man you definitely don't want as your enemy."

Brady smiled as they shook hands. "Or as a friend? Thank you. As always."

"Take care," Mozart said, "And remember the old saying."

"Which one is that?"

"'He who sups with the Devil must use a long spoon.' He who sups with Marko Vrukić must use a *very* long spoon, Michael. Attached to the end of a very long stick."

42

Brady drove slowly back down the coast road. Stopped and stared at the sea. Went over everything Mozart had told him. Went over it a second time.

'His bastards must be all over the Balkans.'

It makes sense. Vrukić comes to the UK. Meets Gina, gets her pregnant. How can she tell Maria that her father is a mass murderer? Aleks Savićević, maybe. Marko Vrukić ... How could Maria live with that?

Brady reached for his phone.

HE'D REHEARSED his message as he'd been driving. Hadn't expected the call to be answered. *'My name is Michael Brady. I'm a Detective Chief Inspector with North Yorkshire police. I'm investigating the murder of Gina Kirk and I'd like to ask Mr Vrukić some questions. You can ring me on this number to arrange a meeting...'*

He was betting on not needing to explain who Gina Kirk was. And on Vrukić being cooperative.

Snug and warm in the Warwickshire countryside? Cooperation must be part of the deal.

What he hadn't been betting on was someone answering on the third ring.

"Mr Vrukić's phone."

Brady was taken by surprise. A woman's voice, only a trace of an accent, maybe in her late 20s.

"My name is Michael Brady."

"How did you get this number? Whatever you are selling, we don't want it."

"I'm not selling anything. My name is Brady, and I'm a Detective Chief Inspector in the police. I'd like to talk to Mr Vrukić about a murder."

He could see her shrug from 200 miles away. "You'll need to be more specific, Mr... Brady was it?"

"I want to speak to him about the murder of Gina Kirk."

All she has to say is, 'Who? Mr Vrukić has never heard the name.' She says that and you're back to square one. Square zero with Kershaw back on Monday.

She didn't.

"One moment."

Brady looked at his watch. 'One moment' was 67 seconds.

She's clearly had to walk somewhere. So a short conversation.

He heard what sounded like heels clicking on a stone floor. "Mr Vrukić will see you on Monday morning at 10am. Whoever gave you the phone number obviously gave you the address as well."

"Thank – "

"We will have coffee waiting, Mr Brady."

The line went dead.

Monday at ten. Kershaw's back on Monday. A Serbian warlord – or a tanned, smug and sarcastic Kershaw?

It wasn't a difficult decision to make.

"COME IN AND SIT DOWN," Brady said. "Dan, I've saved you the trouble. I've been to the coffee shop myself."

Brady passed Frankie and Dan Keillor their coffees. "You've given up on the office machine then, boss?"

"It's the office coffee or my liver, Frankie."

She shook her head. "Coffee's supposed to be good for your liver, boss. Supposed to lower the risk of cirrhosis."

"Really? So I can drink a bottle of vodka as long as I have a skinny hazelnut latte after it?"

"Good luck finding a skinny hazelnut latte in Whitby..."

"Today's Friday," Brady said. "Kershaw's back on Monday. He'll be expecting to see me. I won't be here."

"Where are you going, boss?"

"I'm going to spend a day in the English countryside, Frankie. I'm going to see a man called Marko Vrukić . Jim Fitzpatrick thinks he holds the key to all this. And he's the man in the photo."

"The one looking at Gina and the baby? The one you think is the father?"

"Maybe," Brady said.

"But if he's the father, why does Gina tell her daughter it's Aleks Savićević?"

"Because Marko Vrukić was a Serbian warlord. One of the most prominent figures in the civil war. A mass murderer. A man who's committed war crimes. Look at his Wiki entry and you'll see a fine, upstanding citizen raising money for charity. It's a lie."

"But," Dan said. "If he's committed war crimes what is he doing here? In the UK?"

"I don't know," Brady said. "But you want the answer in one word? Politics. Whatever bargaining chip Vrukić had was clearly big enough to do a deal with the British Government."

"But your old boss is convinced?" Frankie said.

Brady nodded. "He says he came to the UK three or four times a year. Maybe he'd been setting it up for a few years. Building up a business – for want of a better word – over here."

"And you think on one of these visits – maybe more than one – he has a relationship with Gina?" Frankie said.

"Yes. Maybe."

Frankie leaned back in her chair. Took a deep breath. "Can I speak freely, boss?"

I'm surprised she needs to ask after the other day...

"You know you can."

"You're overthinking it. You're making it more complicated than it needs to be."

"Are you going all Occam's Razor on me, DS Thomson?"

She nodded. "If you'll let me, boss."

Maybe she's right. Maybe I am overthinking it. But I need to solve this case. And it's getting to me...

"Go ahead. And you're right. The simplest solution is usually the right one."

"This is how I see it," Frankie said. "Gina's brought up in a good home. But she's not the first teenage girl to go off the rails. Falls out with her father, moves out of the family home. She's in 'full rebellion' mode and she meets a man she's attracted to. He's older – not that much, maybe five years – and he's attractive for all the wrong reasons."

"You're talking about Aleks Savićević now?" Brady said.

"Yes. He's maybe in his mid-20s. Building up his business – "

"His crime business."

"Yes. But he's exciting. He's got money. He takes risks. He's everything Gina's father wasn't. And he likes her. He moves her into a flat. My guess is that Savićević is building up his brothels business and Gina is doing the books."

"What is she?" Dan said. "Twenty? Isn't that a bit young – "

"To be involved in that business?" Brady said. "Jim Fitzpatrick said she struck him as calculating. 'A chip of ice' was the phrase he used. I think she could cope."

"So she's working for Savićević," Frankie said. "Probably living with him as well. She's got money – remember what her sister said, boss – and then she gets pregnant with Maria. Let's say she takes a year off – maybe that's when Savićević brings the other bookkeeper in, the one that's still in jail – and when she comes back the business has changed."

"And Savićević says, 'I've got a new job for you?'"

"Yeah. If Savićević is trafficking girls for the brothels it's a short step to trafficking children. And finding some local ones. No-one from the children's homes was ever prosecuted."

Brady spread his arms in a gesture of frustration. "What can we do? A lot of people were never prosecuted. The gang was the easiest target. Back to Gina, Frankie."

"Savićević says 'I've got a new job for you.' What can she do? Nothing. He's the father of her child. She's worked for him. She's seen what happened to people who crossed him. And she's got Maria to protect."

"So she's trapped."

"Completely trapped."

"So what changes?" Brady said. "Why does Gina walk into Solihull police station and blow it wide open? She must know she'll go into witness protection. She must know the risks she's running."

"If what Jim says – about her being calculating – is true, then yes. She must have worked it out. Like we've said, maybe one of the children gets to her. Maybe she doesn't have the chip of ice any more. Maybe being a mother has changed her. Maybe she's putting Maria to bed one night and realises someone has to stop it. And the only person who's going to do that is her."

"We'll never know will we?" Dan said.

Brady shook his head. "No, we won't. And you're right, Frankie. I have been overthinking it. Thank you."

"So what now, boss?"

"Frankie, I want you to go over to Leeds. See Rochelle Hunter. Rule her in or rule her out. Dan, go through everything again. The children, the people in jail, anyone mentioned in the newspaper reports. Make sure there's no-one we've missed."

"And you're going to spend a day in the country, boss?"

"Warwickshire. Vrukić. If anyone knows the full story – anyone who's left alive – he does. So let's find out what it is. And then I'm going to see one of the children on the way back."

"Jordan Rooney? The one that's been in and out of jail?"

"Yes. He lives somewhere near Loughborough now. So it's on the way."

"Kershaw's not going to like it," Frankie said. "You not being here when he gets back."

"No, he's not," Brady said. "But you know what, Frankie? Fuck Kershaw."

43

It had been a long day. Brady reached for his mouse one last time.

Power. Shut down.

If only... Shut down. Come back on Monday morning and start again. Leave it all behind for the weekend. But I'm seeing Vrukić on Monday morning...

"Come on, mate," he said to Archie 15 minutes later. "Let's take you out. See if Maddie'll walk you round the block while I talk to Kate."

Brady let Archie out of the Tiguan – "Wag your tail, Archie. Look pleased to see people. Don't go straight to the fridge" – and rang the bell.

"How's he doing?" he'd always ask he gave his sister a hug.

For the last few weeks the answer had been 'much the same.' There'd been a temporary pause in the chemo so Bill could recover. He spent most of his time watching sport or pottering in the garden until he was too tired.

'You should have written that book, Mike,' he'd said. 'I'd have had time to read it.'

Brady and Bill would gossip about sport or how policing wasn't what it was. Bill was watching *Peaky Blinders*. 'Golden age of coppering, Mike. You never see Sergeant Moss buried under a mountain of paperwork...'

Kate was doing a lot of baking. 'Bill always wants home-made pork pie. Don't ask me why. He can't finish it.'

Kate opened the door.

...And Brady knew it had changed.

Knew just by looking at his sister's face what the news was. Sat at her kitchen table with his hands cradling a Middlesbrough FC mug while she told him.

"It's spread. Stage four. It's in his bones. In his lymph nodes. It's everywhere."

Brady let go of the mug. Reached across the table. Took Kate's hands in his. "What are they going to do?"

"Pain relief. Palliative care. There's a Macmillan nurse coming round tomorrow." She brushed a tear away. "You think... I went to a Macmillan coffee morning last year. You think... that's nice. What a great charity. You never think they'll be knocking on your door."

Brady didn't know what to say. "Is Bill upstairs?"

Kate nodded. "He's asleep."

"It's... I'm sorry, Kate, I don't know how to phrase it. 'Definite' I suppose..."

His sister nodded a second time. "Yes. They've said it's reached the stage where any more treatment is just going to cause him more pain. More suffering."

"Did they say how long?"

"The consultant was very nice. He said he didn't want to give us false hope. He said he's seen cases like this go on for a year and he's seen them take a month. But he wouldn't look at us when he said it."

Brady saw Bill marching into Kara's kitchen.

There to arrest her. Nostrils flaring, scenting victory. Certain he was right. Self-important, impulsive, making a big mistake.

But full of life. Full of energy. Now he's asleep upstairs. Waiting for his turn.

"How's he taken it?" he asked.

Kate smiled. Shrugged her shoulders. "Far better than I thought he'd take it. Maybe it hasn't sunk in. Maybe he's just being defiant. He's told me to order a normal sized turkey for Christmas."

"What about the girls?"

"Maddie's trying to lose herself in her work. Lucy is watching *Friends*. I don't think it's real for them. Or maybe it is real and they're doing a better job of blocking it out than I am."

"Is there anything I can do?"

Kate shook her head. "Keep coming round. Keep bringing Archie. He cheers me up. And seeing as I'm coping with it by making pork pies..."

"Archie's happy enough. You tell me though," Brady said. "Anything I can do. anything at all."

Kate stood up. Brady walked round the table and hugged her. "Tell him I came round. Shall I bring him a bottle of whisky next time?"

"There's no point. He's lost his sense of taste. That's probably what's depressed him the most. He's come to terms with dying. He'd just like to taste a single malt before he goes."

"How are you feeling? Am I allowed to ask?"

"How am I feeling about being a widow you mean? To be honest, Mike, I have no idea. I'm taking it one day at time. He has good days, he has bad days. So do I. Presumably... sooner or later... Well, you know what I'm saying. But..." Kate hesitated.

"But what?"

"I can tell you this. You're the only person I can tell. I was thinking about leaving him. I'd got it all planned. The day after Lucy went away to uni. I wouldn't quite be 50. I could start again. I'd given him the best years of my life but it wasn't too late. Now... Why is life so fucking perverse, Michael? Now he's dying he's a much nicer person. And he's the girls' dad. I remember when we were trying for Maddie. I was checking my temperature. I phoned him at the station. 'Come home. We need to have sex.' He turned up in a patrol car. Blue light flashing. You've never seen a copper get his uniform off so fast. I'm going to miss him."

Brady parked the car outside Bean's. The curtain twitched back and ten seconds later Ash was opening the front door.

"Hi sweetheart. How's things?"

"Yeah, good. I'm hungry though. Fiona was out so we only had a sandwich."

"You and Bean can cook. She's bound to work late some nights."

"No, she was going out. She had a date. Someone was taking her to the theatre in Scarborough. He turned up in a white car. A really nice one. Bean and I were looking out of the window."

"Respecting her privacy..."

"I said you should have asked her out, Dad. Looks like you've missed your chance."

44

'You have reached your destination.'

"Maybe not," Michael Brady said out loud. He pulled over onto the side of the road and looked at the text on his phone again. The woman with only a trace of an accent had taken pity on him. A text had arrived five minutes after she'd said 'Monday at ten.'

The lane bends sharply to the right. Keep straight on.

The bend was 200 yards in front of him. But there was what looked like a forest road. Gravelled, leading into the trees. Nothing else. No sign.

Brady followed the instructions, driving through the trees.

Is this the drive to Ian Foster's farm again? Half a mile of potholes before I find the house?

It wasn't. Five hundred yards – long enough to convince someone they'd taken the wrong turning – and the gravel gave way to tarmac. The road bent round to the left, the trees finished, the ground fell away to his right and there was the house.

A stately home. Alright, a small stately home. But still...

The road curved round in front of the house. Two cars parked outside: a black Range Rover, a red Porsche.

Maybe I should leave the Tiguan in the servants' quarters...

A small hedge protected an immaculate lawn. The house was framed by more trees. The unmistakable call of a peacock drifted across to him.

Brady locked the car. Walked up the stone steps onto the terrace in front of the house. He turned round and saw the carriages arriving for the summer ball. The butlers, the footmen, the eligible daughters of the local gentry. The gallant young officers of the Royal Warwickshires – confident that 'one last big push' at the Somme would mean they'd be home for Christmas. Back in the arms of their sweethearts...

"One of your dukes built it. A hunting lodge."

The accent was hard to place. Southern Europe – and 70s American TV series.

Maybe that's what he did between bank robberies. Learned English from Starsky and Hutch...

Brady turned. Mozart's 'young Paul Newman' was long gone. Marko Vrukić's hair had turned grey, almost white. Cut close to his head. The beard was neatly trimmed, equally grey. A pair of reading glasses hung on a chain round his neck. A dark blue roll neck jumper. A camel coloured sports jacket. The retired CEO of a hedge fund.

"Michael Brady."

"You do not need to introduce yourself, Mr Brady. Rest assured that only the people we expect get this far."

Vrukić took a step towards him. Held out his hand. Brady shook it. A firm, decisive grip.

Twenty years in the police and the first time I meet a mass murderer it's at a stately home in the Warwickshire countryside...

"Come inside, Mr Brady. We have some coffee waiting. You have had a long drive. You found us easily enough?"

"Thanks to the text message I was sent. And yes, coffee would be good."

Vrukić led the way into the house, noticeably limping. "You cannot live the life I have lived and not have some bruises to show for it," he said over his shoulder, reading Brady's mind for the second time.

Brady stood in the entrance hall. Looked around him. The oak panelling, the wide, elegant stairs in front of him.

'Hall' is the wrong word. It's three times the size of my lounge...

"As I said, one of your dukes. A hunting lodge. Somewhere to entertain his friends. A place to keep his mistress."

Vrukić led the way into a lounge. It was the residents' lounge in a country house hotel. Maroon walls, leather sofas, bookcases, pictures of 18th Century grooms holding their Lordships' horses. The lounge Vrukić used for visitors.

It's the hotel Grace took me to for my 41st birthday. Before I spent the next one sitting on her bed...

Vrukić gestured at one of the sofas. There was a large

cafetiere on the coffee table in front of it. Two coffee cups. A tray of biscuits.

"Let me pour you some coffee, Mr Brady. And let me also wish you happy birthday for last week."

Which is a not very subtle way of saying, 'I've read your file.' Why am I not surprised?

"Thank you," Brady said. "Although my birthdays of late – "

Vrukić nodded. "Have not been happy ones. My sympathy to you. We have all lost people we love. I hope you and your daughter are coping?"

"As best we can," Brady said. "You obviously know the story."

"I've read the reports," Vrukić said. "But then you would expect me to do my homework." He leaned forward and poured the coffee. "Just as you, no doubt, are aware that my Wikipedia entry is largely a work of fiction."

He's got his own version of Mozart. Don't give anything away.

"I've read one or two stories online. There are a lot of gaps..."

"And you came to see me because your old boss told you I would be able to help. Because even though I only made occasional visits to this country he saw my hand behind the events in your second city."

Christ. Sixty seconds of conversation and he's skewered me, my daughter and Jim Fitzpatrick.

Brady tasted his coffee. Possibly the best coffee he'd ever tasted. Decided there was little sense in lying. He'd driven 200 miles to find out the truth. There was no point dancing round the subject.

"I'm investigating a murder, Mr Vrukić – "

"Gina."

He said her name simply. But with affection.

"Yes," Brady said. "Gina Kirk. Gina Foster when she was in Whitby."

"And you think she was murdered because someone found out where she was. Someone with a score to settle?"

"Yes. That's the only explanation I can come to."

"And so you thought you'd come to me. You thought, 'I can spend a year investigating this and not get anywhere.' And Jim Fitzpatrick tells you, 'Vrukić was responsible.' You are impatient. And you are under pressure. So you think 'fuck this. I will go and see him.' You are impetuous. And brave..."

Vrukić finished his coffee. Leaned back in his chair and crossed his legs, his left ankle resting on his right knee. Made an expansive gesture with his right hand. "Why am I here, Mr Brady?"

Brady had assumed he'd get 20 minutes. Maybe half an hour at the most. But clearly Vrukić wanted to talk. He smiled. "There's a limit to how much I could find out online, Mr Vrukić – "

"There is a limit to how much the person you asked could find out, you mean. But don't worry. I am told he has covered his tracks."

Have I put Mozart in danger as well?

Brady conceded defeat. "In that case, yes. So I assume you are here for your own safety. Because there are always people who are not welcome in their own country."

Vrukić nodded. "I was a hero. But I became an inconvenient hero. When the government decides that you know too much you have no option other than to leave. So here I am. I have exchanged Belgrade for Warwickshire. Beautiful summers and cold winters for endless rain. A bullet in the back of my head for boredom."

Brady smiled. "Red Star Belgrade for Aston Villa?"

"Ah. I love my football. You should come to a game with me, Mr Brady. But it is not the same. The – what do you call it? The executive box. Men in suits with no passion. You should watch a game with the real fans – "

"The *delije*..."

Vrukić laughed. "Exactly. But those days are behind me. Besides – " He spread his hands wide. A gesture which said, 'How has this happened? I am only a simple man.'

"Exactly. But then I would not watch the game with Prince William. Did you know? He supports my team." Vrukić stared at him across the coffee table. "It is always good to be well connected, Mr Brady. There is no better insurance policy than the next king."

"Next but one."

"Maybe. We shall see." Someone had appeared in the doorway. Had Vrukić signalled him in some way? Brady hadn't noticed. "Luka. Some more coffee if you would."

Luka walked noiselessly across the room. Brady glanced up at the man who was very clearly Vrukić's bodyguard. The two of them exchanged a few words in what Brady assumed was Serbian. He caught what sounded like café – which was obvious – and a word like 'chevvy.'

"Chevvy?" Brady asked.

"*Šefe*. It means chief. Boss. Luka has been with me a long time."

'You thought, 'I can spend a year investigating this and not get anywhere.' And Jim Fitzpatrick says Vrukić was responsible. So fuck this. I will go and see him.' Yes, Marko. That's exactly what I thought. And so far all I've done is discuss football and coffee.

"Can I talk about Gina Kirk?" Brady said.

"Of course. That is what you are here for."

Brady was beginning to wonder if he was there to talk about anything *but* Gina Kirk. "I need to know who killed her," he said.

"So your reasoning is this," Vrukić said. "She has died. Been murdered. Obviously it is connected to her previous life. She was responsible for members of a Serbian gang going to jail. One of them has died in jail. So someone wants revenge. You come to me. At that time I came to England two, maybe three times a year. But you are given my name. And like I said, you are impatient, you are under pressure. So your bet is worth placing. One day against a year's work. Maybe I can clear the case up for you. Maybe I can't. So you make your bet. But there is also something else..."

Brady forced himself not to show emotion.

"Once your friend has told you my story," Vrukić said, "You want to meet me."

Yes. I did.

"You have dealt with murderers. You have arrested

them. You have even – alright, indirectly – killed one. But you have never met a mass murderer. Someone – "

Vrukić leaned forward. His eyes went flat. Brady could feel the intensity – the electricity – crackling off the man.

What had Mozart said? 'His men would follow him to the gates of Hell.' And they'd expect to win the battle as well.

"Someone who has done what I have done." Vrukić leaned back. Now he was having an everyday conversation. Someone with a friend round for coffee. Talking about the new car, the holiday in Spain.

"It was a spring morning, Mr Brady. A beautiful, clear spring morning. I rounded up a hundred Bosnians. I needed information that would protect my people. Save many lives. I had to shoot seven before I got what I needed." Vrukić made a dismissive gesture. A man brushing away a fly.

"We had to do that sometimes. My men used to gamble on how many I would have to shoot. So yes, I am a monster. When mothers said to their children, 'Behave, or Vrukić will come for you...' When they said that they were right. But then I crossed the border into Serbia and I was a hero. And if my country needed me to do the same again... If I needed to shoot the other 93 on my beautiful English lawn... I would not hesitate."

Vrukić paused. "You are thinking I committed war crimes. I know that. Let me tell you, Mr Brady. When you are fighting for your people, your family, there is no such thing as a 'war crime.' It is a fiction for hypocrites, politicians and lawyers."

Brady thought he'd been frightened of Jimmy Gorse. He hadn't understood what fear was. But now, sitting in an elegant lounge in an English stately home, drinking the best coffee he'd ever tasted, talking to Marko Vrukić. Now he was terrified.

"What does this have to do with Gina?" he forced himself to say.

"This," Vrukić said. "I am loyal. Fiercely loyal. Loyal to my country, loyal to its people. And below that, loyal to my village. To my family. But you must understand this, Mr Brady, in the part of Serbia that I am from, the village *is* your family. Wherever you are in the world."

"So you are saying..."

Vrukić nodded. "You are beginning to understand. Why am I in England? I like this country. I speak the language. But I am here for two reasons. I had a bargaining chip I could exchange for a hundred acres of your countryside. And I had family here."

"Who was your family?"

"Aleks Savićević was my nephew."

Brady was silent. *Had anyone checked? No. Because no-one had needed to check. Because the names were different. Because small details were overlooked. Because people wanted the case closed.*

"He is my cousin's son."

"Technically – "

Vrukić waved his hand. The dismissive gesture again. "I know what you are going to say. In England your cousin's son is not your nephew. In my village he is. My family moved to Belgrade. My mother's sister stayed behind. Her daughter is my cousin. She is Aleks' mother. Aleks was my nephew."

'A fierce, tribal culture dating back to the 13th or 14th

Century. Unusually, a matriarchal culture...'

"And in your village – your region – the mother is important."

Vrukić nodded. "So you see now why I – why my family – had nothing at all to do with Gina's death?"

"So Aleks is Maria's father?"

For once he'd caught Vrukić by surprise. "Of course. Who else would it be?"

"I thought – we found a photograph – I thought *you* might be the father. Given your reputation."

Vrukić laughed out loud. Struggled to stop himself laughing. "You flatter me, Mr Brady. And you dishonour me. But we are friends now, so I will let it pass. When I arrived in England Aleks was already with Gina. I cared for her – but as a father cares for his daughter. Besides – " Vrukić smiled. "Gina was attractive. But..."

He seemed to be able to summon people at will. A woman appeared. Late 20s or early 30s. Poised, beautiful. Several degrees beyond beautiful. Long black hair, almond eyes that held Brady's gaze. "Jelena," Vrukić said. "My companion."

He spoke to her in Serbian. Jelena laughed. Turned and looked at Brady. Ran her eyes up and down his body. Laughed again and answered Vrukić. "Gina was 20 when she had the baby. Jelena says I should only fuck a 20 year old if I wish to commit suicide. She thinks you may still have a chance. But she says you should not waste time."

Jelena spoke again, gestured at the coffee. "Of course," Vrukić said. "Sit down. Stay with us. You are good for me."

"So when you arrived in England," Brady said. "The

business – for want of a better word – is established. Aleks is with Gina?"

"At that time I am only visiting," Vrukić said. "Making my arrangements. But one day I land at the airport – the same day Gina gives birth to a baby girl. We are a super-stitious people, Mr Brady. Aleks names his daughter after me. Marko. Maria. As close as he can get in English."

"So as Aleks is your nephew..."

"Correct. Maria is my niece. Given her age, maybe my granddaughter. But part of my family. My blood is her blood."

Vrukić paused, finished his coffee. "You think I haven't known where Gina has been all these years? You think I have not kept watch on her? If I had wanted her dead I would not have waited 12 years. I did not kill Gina. No-one in my family killed Gina. And be certain that no-one connected to Aleks killed Gina. Because if they did, they would have me to answer to." Vrukić smiled. "Well, I am an old man now. They would answer to Luka. But I give you my word. The word of someone from my village. The death of Aleks Savićević had nothing to do with the death of Gina Kirk."

"Not Nikola Petrić? Someone acting alone?"

Vrukić laughed. "Nikola? You have done your home-work. I admire that. Nikola was with me in the old days. A true warrior. Especially after a bottle of *rakija*. But no, not Nikola. He is a loyal soldier. That and the bullet he took. He will be in a wheelchair soon."

Brady stood up. "I'm sorry, Mr Vrukić – "

"Marko. I told you. We are friends now. So you call me Marko. And I know. You need to walk out into the garden because you need to make a phone call. And you need to make sense of what I have told you."

Brady smiled. "Bluntly, yes."

"Take as much time as you like, Michael. Mihailo in my country. I will call you Mihailo."

BRADY WALKED out onto the terrace. It was starting to rain.

'I exchanged beautiful summers for endless rain.' So you did, Marko...

He looked at the lawn. Didn't see the carriages and the gallant young officers of the Royal Warwickshires. Saw 93 men shivering with fear. Saw them lined up as Marko Vrukić walked towards them. As his men placed their bets...

It was her answerphone.

"Frankie? It's Brady. I'm at Vrukić's house. Mansion. Look, Frankie, he says the gang had nothing to do with Gina's death. I'll tell you why when I see you. But I believe him. We're back to square one. Unless you've found something with Rochelle. Or I get lucky with Rooney. I'll get back as soon as I can. Thanks, Frankie. See you tomorrow."

THE COFFEE HAD DISAPPEARED when he walked back inside, replaced by a tray of cold meat and cheese. "I thought you might like something before you drove back," Vrukić said.

"Thank you."

"So Mihailo, you are happy with what I told you?"

Vrukić asked.

Brady met his gaze. "Happy? No. It means we've wasted a lot of time. And effort. But do I think what you've told me is the truth? Yes."

"So now you must look at the children? And maybe someone local. Help yourself," Vrukić said, gesturing at the food. "I have it flown in from Belgrade."

"Yes." Brady had lost his appetite. But knew he would offend Vrukić if he didn't eat something. "Yes, we have a lot of work to do."

Vrukić nodded. "You will get there. Which is good. Because I need to know that the killer of Maria's mother has been found. You do not improve a girl's life by killing her mother. So you will find the person who killed Gina. And I will be in your debt. You will find I can be a good friend, Mihailo."

And a very bad enemy. You don't need to spell it out, Marko.

THEY TALKED for another ten minutes, mostly about football. Finally Brady stood up to leave.

"I have given you much to think about, Mihailo."

"You have sent me back to square one. Back to the beginning. But..."

"But maybe on a shorter journey? I hope so."

They stood on the terrace. The rain had stopped, the sun was trying to break through the clouds.

'So you will find the person who killed Maria's mother. And I will be in your debt. You will find I can be a good friend, Mihailo.'

'Maybe I can clear the case up for you. Maybe I can't. So you make your bet.'

Michael Brady decided to make one more bet.

"You said we were friends, Marko."

Vrukić nodded. "We are. And now you want something from me, Mihailo..."

Do I want to be in this man's debt? Dare I be in this man's debt? But I have to know...

"Please. Ask me," Vrukić said.

"Do you know who killed my wife?"

The Serbian warlord living in the Warwickshire countryside held his gaze. "Who killed her, Mihailo? Or who gave the order?"

"Both."

Vrukić weighed up his options. "No. But you think I could find out?"

Brady nodded.

"You are right. I could. So we have a deal. Find who killed Gina and I will be in your debt. But do not be impatient, Mihailo. There is a saying in my country. 'Impatience has cost many crowns.' There will be a time for you to take revenge. And when that time comes, take it. You will have no peace until you do."

Marko Vrukić held out his hand.

'He who sups with the Devil must use a long spoon. He who sups with Marko Vrukić must use a very long spoon. Attached to the end of a very long stick.'

Detective Chief Inspector Michael Brady threw away the stick.

Then he threw away the spoon.

And shook hands with the Devil.

45

From the sublime to the ridiculous. From a country estate to a flat on the outskirts of Loughborough. They were all the same, Brady thought. A front door that didn't close properly. A pile of post in the hall. The faint smell of damp. The certainty that you weren't going to find what you wanted.

At least he's had the good manners to live on the ground floor. Save me seeing the evidence of the weekend as I walk upstairs...

Brady knocked on Jordan Rooney's door. "Give me a minute." A girl's voice.

The door finally opened. She had blonde hair. A hairstyle that convinced Brady he was getting old. Shaved on one side, long and spikey on the other. A stud above her top lip, a matching one below her bottom lip. A dozen studs in the ear he could see. Three stars tattooed above her right eye.

"Detective Chief Inspector Michael Brady. I'm here to see Jordan."

"You'd better come in. He sure as fuck can't come to the door."

Brady walked through into the lounge. Or bedroom, he wasn't sure which. Jordan Rooney was lying on a bed settee. Long brown hair pulled back into a bun. Pale blue eyes, a belligerent face. A black hoodie, red shorts with the Liverpool badge on them.

Two crutches by the side of the bed settee. Jordan with his right leg in plaster to just below his knee.

"Detective Chief Inspector Michael Brady."

"I heard." The voice was lighter than he'd expected. At odds with the face. Willing to cooperate.

"Like I said on the phone, I'm investigating a murder. Gina Foster. Gina – "

"Pen, go out will you? This is private. Give us five minutes."

"Can't I stay?"

"No, you can't," Jordan said. "Go out. Five minutes. That's all. I'll tell you later."

Pen walked out of the room, making only a token effort to look upset.

"She doesn't know the story?" Brady said.

Jordan shook his head. "No. I'd rather keep it that way."

"She wouldn't think any less of you."

"You think so? It's not a risk I want to take. Not a risk any normal bloke would take."

Brady nodded. Said, "Yes, I can understand that." Knew that he couldn't begin to understand it.

"What happened?" Brady said, nodding at the plaster cast.

"Football. Five-a-side. Well, four-a-side about two minutes in."

"What've you done?"

"Tib and fib, they call it. Both bones, just above my ankle."

"When?"

"Six weeks ago."

So the last thing you were doing was walking along the banks of the River Esk.

The medical records would be easy enough to check but Brady knew he wouldn't need to. "How much longer?" he said.

"Another month or so. Long time before I can play football though."

Brady nodded. Stood up and walked over to the bed settee. Held his hand out. "Best of luck with it. I hope you're back playing soon."

Jordan nodded. "You and me both. And other things."

Brady laughed. "I'm sure you've found a way…"

"Can I ask a question?" Jordan said.

"Sure. If I can answer it."

"How did she die? Slowly, I hope."

"It depends on your definition of slowly," Brady said, "She drowned. Someone held her under the River Esk."

Jordan Rooney nodded. "Yeah," he said. "That seems about right."

46

Brady pulled into the car park at Donington Services.

Two and a half hours to get home to an empty house. Let's hope Beth's remembered to let Archie out. Thank God for next door neighbours...

He opened the car door. Skirted the puddles, dodged the rain, made it into the services building without getting too wet. If Hell existed it was almost certainly a motorway service station. On the Saturday of a bank holiday weekend. When Liverpool and Manchester United were playing away and you were on the same motorway as the travelling fans.

But in late afternoon on a wet Monday in October Donington Services was almost deserted.

He was walking towards M&S Simply Food when his phone rang.

"Frankie, how are you doing?"

"I'm not. I'm stuck in a traffic jam trying to get out of Leeds. I'll never complain about being behind a tractor again."

"What about Rochelle?"

There was five seconds of silence. "I'm sorry, boss. She's not our girl."

Fuck. One who can't get out of bed, one who's going to be in a wheelchair – and now this. When was the last time I lost three suspects in a single day?

"Why not?" he said.

"She was at the gym."

"That simple? You're certain?"

"I went down there myself. Checked the records. Spoke to two people who train with her. On the fringe of the GB team... She's a minor celebrity so they all know her. Ninety minutes every morning. Thirty minutes of cardio, an hour of weights and stretches."

"Bugger."

"How did your day go, boss?"

"Badly. The only bright spot was I drank some really good coffee. But I crossed Petrić and Jordan Rooney off the list. And got a cast-iron guarantee from a mass murderer that the gang had nothing to do with it."

"You said."

"Yeah. Sorry. I forgot we spoke at lunchtime. I'll bring you up to date in the morning, Frankie. It's pissing down here and I want to get home."

Brady went into M&S. Picked up a sandwich and a small bottle of orange juice to go with it and walked towards the checkout.

"It's Mike, isn't it? Michael Brady?"

He looked up. A man about his own age. Receding hair, round glasses, smiling broadly, one front tooth overlapping the other. His son at his side. Seven or eight, glasses like his dad, wearing a Sheffield Wednesday goalkeeper top.

He looked vaguely familiar. Brady knew he should recognise him. Three, four seconds of embarrassed silence while he rummaged around in his memory.

At last. "Kevin? Good to see you. How are you?"

"Yeah, I'm good. Fancy seeing you in a motorway services. After all these years. What are the chances of that?" He glanced down. "This is my boy, Tim. Wants to be a goalie like his dad, don't you?"

Tim grinned sheepishly. Brady's memory finally clicked into gear.

"Hey, he was good was your dad," he told Tim. "School team goalie until he was about 14. Where did you move to, Kev? I can't remember…"

"Sheffield. That's where we are now. Just been down to Leicester though. There's a specialist down there. Tim's got a problem with one of his eyes."

"Nothing serious I hope…"

They stood in the middle of Marks and Spencer's – Brady still cradling a BLT and a bottle of orange juice – and had that conversation you have with someone you haven't seen for 30 years and will never see again.

"What brings you down this way, anyway?"

Brady laughed. Tried to make a joke of it. "I'm in the police – "

"Yeah, I heard that. Someone put it on Facebook."

"Just been down to Warwickshire to interview some-one. You know, 'helping with enquiries.'"

"Long drive for you though," Kevin said. "Talking of which, we need to get back. Got to collect the wife from work. Her car's in the garage."

Brady put his sandwich down. They shook hands. Promised to keep in touch. "I'll send you a friend request on Facebook," Kevin said. Brady wished Tim luck with his goalkeeping. Promised to look out for his name in Wednesday's team in a few years.

"We should all get together," Kevin said. "A big class reunion. You know, when we're all 50 or something."

Brady said that sounded like a great idea. For some reason they shook hands a second time. Kevin and Tim headed for their car. Brady finally made it to the checkout.

HE WALKED BACK across the car park. The rain was heavier now. He unlocked the car and threw the drink and the sandwich onto the passenger seat. Turned and looked at the reflections on the wet tarmac.

It was getting dark. A long drive home, with only the spray from the lorry in front of him for company.

And a conversation with Marko Vrukić on constant replay...

He climbed into the car and reached for the sand-wich. Hit play for the first time.

'I give you my word, Mr Brady. The death of Aleks had nothing to do with the death of Gina. You think I haven't

known where Gina has been all these years? You think that if I wanted her dead I would have waited 12 years?'

Brady finished the sandwich and the orange juice. Opened the car door and walked across to a rubbish bin. He wanted to stand in the East Midlands rain. Wanted it to wash away the implications of his deal with Marko Vrukić.

'So we have a deal. Find who killed Gina and I will be in your debt. But do not be impatient, Mihailo. There will be a time for you to take revenge...'

...Knew that no amount of rain would wash it away.

Brady walked back to the car. Climbed in and sat there. Listened to the rain hammering against the roof. Watched the lights of the services blur as the water ran down the windscreen. Knew he was back to square one.

If the gang didn't kill her then who did? Should I believe Vrukić? What reason does he have to lie? Which leaves me with the children. Or a vigilante resident. Maybe 100 children. Me, Frankie and Dan Keillor. And Kershaw wanting answers in the morning. I'll have to ask him for more time. Suffer the humiliation...

He was finally back on the M1. Switched the wipers onto fast. Eighty miles until he turned off onto the A64. It couldn't come soon enough. Brady fought against tiredness as the adrenalin of the meeting with Vrukić wore off. Fought against the hypnotic swish of the wipers.

What had Jim said?

'Once Gina's walked into Solihull police station there's not a fan been built that can cope with the amount of shit that's going to hit it.'

Forget Solihull. Insert Whitby. If he didn't have something for Kershaw soon then it wouldn't just be shit hitting the fan. It would be his career.

Focus on something else. You need to go and see Bill. Drive straight there. Maybe he'll still be awake.

He turned the phone display on. Dialled Kate's number.

"Good morning," Brady said. "Kate said it was OK to call on my way into the station. I was going to come last night, but..."

Bill was propped up in bed. Navy blue pyjama jacket, his grey dressing gown spread out on top of him. "But I was asleep," he said. "Yeah. Morning's my best time of day. I get so bloody cold," he added, gesturing at the dressing gown. "No fat left to keep me warm."

"How are you doing?" Brady said. "Apart from being bloody cold?"

Bill shrugged. "Fuck knows," he said. "I know what they tell me at the hospital. One day I think it's bollocks, I feel fine. The next day I think it's bollocks, I feel shit. Beyond shit. Some days I don't think I'll make it to the afternoon."

Bill started to cough. Tried to sit up more . Brady passed him his water. He sipped it as best he could, sank back on the pillows. "I tell you one thing," he said.

"What's that?"

"I'm not dying in the afternoon. The last thing you see in this life is Cash in the fucking Attic? No thanks."

Brady laughed despite everything. Made a can-I-sit-down gesture. Bill nodded. "Help yourself, Mike. Help yourself."

"You want to talk shop?" Brady said.

"If you want."

"I'm still trying to find Gina Foster's killer. I'm seeing Kershaw at ten. I need more time."

"Good luck with that. The man's a prick. The stories – " Bill had another coughing spasm. Brady passed him the water for a second time.

"I thought..."

"You thought we were friends? Necessary evil, Mike. It's the only advantage of dying. Lets you tell the truth."

Bill took a deep breath. Hauled the air into his lungs.

Almost making a deliberate effort to breathe. Does he need oxygen?

"You want me to get you anything else? Make you a cup of tea? Toast?"

Bill shook his head. "No. Can't taste anything. What's the bloody point? My auntie wrote to me. Mum's sister. Said she'd read that living on carrots was the cure."

Brady laughed again.

What's that line in Macbeth? 'Nothing in his life became him like the leaving it.' Kate's right. Bill's a nicer person now he's...

"Steve Jobs did it," Brady said. "Lived on carrot juice for a week. Apparently he turned orange."

"Fuck that. I'm not dying looking like a bloody Martian."

"I think technically, Bill, Martians are green..."

Bill smiled. Brady watched him make a conscious effort to gather his strength. To focus.

"Look, Mike. You're here. I want to say something to you. While I still can. Before they wheel me into the bloody hospice and fill me full of morphine."

Bill reached out and took Brady's hand. Gripped it with surprising force. "Kate," he said. "I've been a shit husband, but I love her. She's your sister, so I know you'll keep an eye on her. The girls as well. Don't let either of them marry a dickhead."

"So no-one in the police?"

Bill started to laugh but it turned into another coughing fit. "No. No-one in the police. No-one with a bloody neck tattoo."

"You know I will, Bill. Your girls... They're like Ash. They'll know their own mind. But I'll do my best."

"I know. Thanks." He let go off Brady's hand. "Fuck. I need to go back to sleep. Bloody hell. It just hits you."

Brady stood up. "I'll see you at the weekend."

Bill nodded. "Yeah. Assuming I survive *Cash in the Attic*..."

Brady put his hand on Bill's shoulder. Felt how much weight he'd lost. "You take care, Bill."

"Yeah. You as well, Mike."

Brady walked across the bedroom. Reached for the door handle.

"Mike."

He turned back. "You want some more water?"

"No. What happened to you. Grace. It was shit. But it wasn't as shit as this. Don't let it define the rest of your life, Mike."

48

'I'm seeing Kershaw at ten.'

Famous last words...

Kershaw was tanned. More tanned than anyone in a cold and dark North Yorkshire had a right to look. And casually dressed...

"You're looking very... relaxed, sir."

"Is that sarcasm, Brady?"

So it's 'Brady.' And no doubt it'll be 'our patch...'

"I've been at a conference. That's why I couldn't see you this morning. 'Social media and its Role in Modern Policing.' Facebook, Instagram, Twitter. Very informative. And very useful."

"I'm sure it was, sir."

Almost as informative and useful as catching a murderer...

"Do you have a Twitter account, Brady?"

"I'm not sure I even know what Twitter is, sir."

Kershaw shook his head. "That's why you'll never rise any higher, Brady. You're stuck in the past. Still think policing's about catching criminals. Take my advice. Get yourself a Twitter account. Absolutely key tool in getting our message across. Interacting with the public. You'll thank me, one day."

He has an infinite capacity for bullshit. Bullshit and knowing which way the wind's blowing. The sad thing is, he's probably right...

"I'll do that, sir. I'll ask my daughter for help. Could I just concentrate on the here and now for a minute?"

"You're talking about Gina Foster, obviously. I'm disappointed, Brady. I'd hoped it would be settled by the time I got back. Sadly not."

"We're making progress, sir."

"Not from what I hear. I left you in charge. All you've produced is a lot of negative headlines in the press. You've lost control, Brady. Ruled plenty of people out and no-one in. How long is it since she died?"

"Six weeks, sir."

"Six weeks is long enough, Brady."

Not with you wasting the first two weeks by not telling us the truth.

"The first inquest was adjourned wasn't it?" Kershaw said. "Let's get this over and done with. Death by misadventure. Then we can all get back to work and the fucking journalists can find another bone to chew on."

"We need more time, sir."

Kershaw shook his head. "I'm sorry, Brady. I've made a decision. I'm closing the investigation. Time to cut our losses."

"You can't do that."

"Are you questioning my authority, Brady? I repeat,

you've lost control. Clearly I'm going to have to clean up the shit."

Ian Foster. Maria. Julie. Even Marko Vrukić. They're entitled to the truth.

"No," Brady said. "You're not."

"What did you say?"

Brady smiled. Saw Bill propped up in bed.

'I'm still trying to find Gina Foster's killer. I'm seeing Kershaw at ten. I need more time.'

'Good luck with that. The man's a prick. The stories – '

"You know Bill Calvert's my brother-in-law, sir. You obviously know he's not well..."

Kershaw looked at him. "Obviously I know that. I was just about to ring his wife and see how he's doing."

"I'll save you the trouble. Badly is the answer. But Bill and I have talked a lot. He's told me some stories about the old days. About your career. I think he wanted to... Maybe 'come clean' is the best expression, sir."

Kershaw steepled his hands in front of him. What Brady now knew was his negotiating pose. "We're playing poker are we, Brady? And for quite high stakes seeing as it's your career on the line... Alright then. I'll see your 'stories about the old days.' And I'll raise you three more days. Find me the killer by Friday. Or you can go back to that book you were promising to write."

Brady nodded. "Three days? That's fine, sir."

He stood up, walked towards the door, turned and looked back at Kershaw. "And who knows? If we manage to do anything so outdated as find the murderer... You could post it on Twitter, couldn't you, sir?"

49

Where was the torch?

In the cupboard under the stairs. Brady went upstairs and put his waterproof trousers on. Came down and reached for his winter coat. Archie wagged his tail expectantly. "I'm sorry, mate," Brady said. "This is something I have to do on my own."

He opened the back door. Archie looked at the rain. Looked up at him. An expression that very clearly said, 'I'm fine, thanks...'

"I'm going out for a walk, Ash."

"I guessed. I can see you've put your incontinence pants on – "

"They're waterproof walking trousers, Ash."

"They're incontinence pants, Dad. And only a madman would go out tonight. It's pouring down. There's a hurricane blowing."

"I need some fresh air."

Ash sighed. Shook her head. "How long are you going to be?"

"An hour, no more."

Five minutes to drive to Sandsend. Ten minutes to walk up to the cliff. Time to talk to her. Make up for lost time. Home within the hour.

"Dad..."

"What, love?"

"Why have you got the torch sticking out of your pocket?"

"I..."

"Don't do anything silly, Dad. Not on a night like this."

"I'm not going to do anything silly."

"Are you sure? You've got your this-isn't-sensible-but-I'm-going-to-do-it-anyway expression again."

BRADY DROVE into the car park at Sandsend.

'Don't do anything silly, Dad.'

He wouldn't. Walking up to the cliff top in the pitch black, picking his way by torchlight as the wind howled off the sea and the rain drove into his eyes...

It wasn't silly. He needed to talk to her. He needed her strength.

'We're playing poker are we, Brady? And for quite high stakes seeing as it's your career on the line... Alright then. I'll see your 'stories about the old days.' And I'll raise you three days. Find me the killer by Friday. Or you can go back to that book you were promising to write.'

There weren't any stories about the old days. No doubt Bill could have told him plenty. Maybe he should have asked before. Talked to him earlier. Almost too late now...

We are playing poker. And right now Kershaw has two aces and I've got the three of diamonds and the six of clubs.

Brady shone his torch ahead of him. Walked slowly up the steps to the path along the cliff top. The Cleveland Way. Whitby to Sandsend. There wouldn't be any walkers out tonight...

He reached the top, splashed through a puddle. Almost came to a stop as the full force of the wind hit him.

This could have been beautiful. A clear night. A full moon. Just enough frost to make the ground hard but not slippery. The lights of the ships out at sea...

There were trees on one side of the path, bushes on the other. But no protection from the wind and rain.

Brady came to the top of a rise. The bushes had ended now. He could just make out Grace's hill. A hundred yards in front of him. He needed to leave the path. Walk across... What had Ash said?

'It looks more like the surface of the moon every time we come.'

A wet, muddy, slippery surface of the moon. A gust of wind hit him, forced him to take a step backwards. Brady wiped the rain out of his eyes. Looked down at the North Sea below him. Low tide, but still driven against the cliffs by the gale...

"Don't do anything silly, Dad. Not on a night like this."

"I'm sorry, Grace," he said out loud. "I can't. Not tonight. I'll walk down to the beach."

Picking his way back down the uneven steps was harder than walking up them. He finally made it back to the car park.

"Bloody madness," a voice said.

Brady looked up. A man was opening the tailgate of his Discovery. A very wet Labrador jumped into the back. "Absolute bloody madness," he said again.

"They need their walks," Brady said, almost shouting to make himself heard against the wind.

"Madness," the man said for the third time. "Should be at home in front of the fire. Bloody madness."

Brady resisted the temptation to get into his car. He owed it to Grace to walk down onto the beach. At least look up at her...

Sea level. The wind was even stronger on the beach. Spray mixed with the rain. Brady tasted the salt on his lips. Stood with his hands in his pockets and faced out to sea. Felt the wind crash into him, the spray sting his eyes.

I've let them all down. Frankie, Dan. Ian Foster and Maria. Gina and her sister. Ash. Six weeks and I'm nowhere near finding the killer. And I've got until Friday...

He shook his head. Wondered what the hell it was about Kershaw that provoked him so much. That made him so desperate to prove himself.

'Playing for quite high stakes seeing as it's your career on the line...'

Brady turned and started walking towards Whitby. Realised he hadn't looked up at Grace.

I'll do it on the way back...

An image of Marko Vrukić floated into his head. *'So you have not found Gina's killer. Maria is still at risk. Maybe we are not friends after all, Mihailo...'*

Another image. Kershaw taunting him. *'Bloody useless,*

Brady. Absolutely bloody useless. Maybe I should go and talk to Bill Calvert. He'd do a better job from his bed.'

Brady turned round. His hour must be nearly up. Time to go home.

'Maybe I should go and talk to Bill Calvert. He'd do a better job from his bed.'

Bill... In his bed. What did he say this morning?

'Look, Mike. You're here. I want to say something to you. While I still can. Before they wheel me into the bloody hospice and fill me full of morphine.'

'Before they wheel me into the bloody hospice and fill me full of morphine.'

The hospice...

Brady stood on the beach, felt the spray on his face and knew the most important conversation he'd had yesterday hadn't been with a Serbian warlord. It had been with a 40-something ex-goalkeeper.

What are the chances of seeing you in a motorway services?

Thank you, Kevin. The chance of seeing you in a motorway service station is about the same as someone seeing Gina in a Midlands hospice...

Brady ran back to his car. Ran his fingers through his wet hair. Wiped the spray out of his eyes. Reached for his phone. Dialled her number.

That was how it happened. That had to be how it happened.

"Jules? It's Michael Brady. The detective. I came to see you..."

People don't need reminding. Especially when the conversation was about their dead sister...

"Jules, I need to ask you a question. I need you to answer me honestly."

"I... I'll do my best." Brady could hear the worry in her voice.

"Whatever the answer is, you're not in any trouble. You understand that?"

"Yes. I think so."

"Jules. Did you phone Gina? Did you tell her your mum was dying? Did you see her in the hospice?"

The dam burst for a second time.

"I'm sorry. I didn't dare tell you. I thought I'd broken the law. But I had to tell her. Just had to. After what Mum had done, looking after Maria for her."

"And she came down?"

"Yes. I didn't recognise her. Long blonde hair. I was sitting by Mum's bed. In the hospice... Near the end... You can stay there all night. It was maybe ten o'clock. Wednesday. Two days before the end. This stranger walked in. I didn't even recognise her at first. 'Hello, Jules,' she said."

"When was that, Jules?" Brady said as gently as he could.

"Just after Easter. Wednesday, I think. Mum died on Friday night."

"Thank you, Jules. That's all I wanted to know. Thank you for telling me. And trust me. I'll find Gina's killer for you."

Brady rang off. Instantly dialled another number. "Frankie? Tomorrow morning. As early as you like. It's one of the children. Gina went to the hospice. Someone must have recognised her. We need their records. Whoever was working that night."

Brady laughed. "Yeah. Sorry. I won't sleep tonight either."

HE TURNED the car engine on.

Home, make some notes, think it through again, try and sleep. Get in the office for seven in the morning...

His phone made the Robin-Hood-in-Sherwood-Forest noise that told him he had a text message.

He glanced down. Made out *Kara. Attachment. 1 image.* Couldn't tell what the image was in the dark. Switched on the overhead light. Opened the image.

It was exactly the same expression.

Exactly the same exhausted/ecstatic/relieved/I've done it look that he'd seen on Gina's face in the picture with Maria. Exactly how Grace had looked as she'd held Ash. The look that all new mothers have.

Kara, smiling, tired, happy, with a baby boy cradled in her arms. And three lines of text underneath.

Patrick Michael – 7lbs 13oz – 20th October

Talk soon. Love from both of us, Godfather

xxx

He'd known she was going to call him Patrick. 'Michael' was a complete surprise. A total surprise.

Life. Bloody life. Turned on its head in 15 minutes.

Brady looked at his godson again. His best friend's son. "Welcome to the word, Patrick," he said out loud. It was a long time since he'd felt so happy.

He drove out of the car park.
Or so determined...

"I could make this complicated," Brady said. "I could give you a lengthy explanation. I won't bother. I fucked up. Kershaw made us waste two weeks working on Ian Foster. I've wasted the rest of the time obsessing about the gang. It's not the gang. It's one of the children."

"You're certain?" Frankie said.

"Yes, I am. Gina's mother – Gina and Julie's mother – was dying. Julie thought Gina would want to see her. Felt she had to give her the chance at least. So she phoned her. Told her. And Gina went to the hospice – "

"Where someone recognised her?"

"Yes."

"That's a hell of a longshot, boss."

Brady shook his head. "I was driving back home on Monday. I stopped for a sandwich at a motorway service station. Bumped into someone I was at school with. Yes, it's a longshot. But think of all the times you *don't* bump into someone. Sooner or later it's going to happen. And I think it happened to Gina when she went to the hospice."

"Someone recognised her?" Dan said. "Or someone read the visitors book? And how did they find her?"

"Recognised," Brady said. "My guess is she signed in as Gina Foster. That's the name she's been using for ten years. She wouldn't suddenly write Gina Kirk without being conscious of it. But what else do you write in a visitors book, Dan?"

"Name. Time in. Who you're seeing."

"Come on, think about the last time you stayed in a hotel."

The light dawned. "Car reg number."

Brady nodded. "Car reg number. I'm betting one of the hospice staff recognised her, got her reg number from the visitors book and somehow had it traced. Maybe he or she's sleeping with a copper. We'll soon see."

"We're ruling out someone in Whitby?" Frankie said.

Brady nodded. "We've two days, Frankie. Bluntly, we don't have time to rule them in. Kershaw told me we were playing poker. We are. And we're all in. All in on the children. I want you to ring the hospice for me. Ask them to scan the visitors book for the night Gina was there. And let us have a list of all the staff that were on duty. Say, a week before Lizzie Simpson died. That should cover it."

FRANKIE WAS BACK. And shaking her head. "They won't co-operate, boss. They're saying it contravenes data protection."

"Oh for God's sake. Who were you talking to?"

"Mrs Hope? General manager."

"Give me the number, Frankie."

Brady dialled the number. Absolutely certain he was right. "Good morning, my name is Michael Brady. I'm a Detective Chief Inspector in North Yorkshire police. I need to speak to Mrs Hope ... yes, it is urgent ... no, it's probably best if I speak to Mrs Hope."

"Supposing..." Frankie said.

Brady put his hand across the phone. "Supposing we're talking to the person who recognised her? Gina went at night. I don't think managers work at night. But it's a risk we have to take. I – Mrs Hope, good morning, my name is Michael Brady. Detective Chief Inspector Michael Brady. You've just been talking to my Detective Sergeant..."

It took less than five minutes. Brady was polite but insistent. The suggestion that the hospice might be employing a murderer seemed to concentrate Mrs Hope's mind.

Brady gave her his e-mail address. Promised all the necessary paperwork would be with her later in the day – "Sort it out will you, Dan?" – but he really did need the copy of the visitors book. And the list of staff that were working at ten at night. Yes, the first week in April. "Names and addresses. Maiden name if you have it. And in the next half hour would be wonderful. Thank you. And I'd appreciate you keeping this absolutely confidential, Mrs Hope. For obvious reasons we don't want to send a patrol car round. We don't want to distress your – " *Residents? Patients? Which one was it?* "Your patients. Thank you so much. I really do appreciate your help."

· · ·

MRS HOPE WAS as good as her word. Ten A4 scans. An e-mail with a note of apology. A promise of confidentiality.

The visitors book from early April.

More or less the time I drove over the Pennines with Ash. Ready to start a new life. Ready to write a book. Ready to be a good dad to my teenage daughter. When Patrick was still alive. When I had no intention of going back into the police...

Half a dozen neat columns.

Date – Name – Visiting – Time in – Time out – Car reg. no

And there she was. Gina Foster.

Tuesday April 7th.

Jules had made a mistake. She'd been a day out. But it didn't matter. Tuesday or Wednesday, it was all the same.

Visiting: Mrs E Simpson – Time in: 10pm – Time out: 10:45.

And her car registration number. Brady read it out to Frankie. She checked her notebook. Nodded. "The same, boss. It matches. So who was working?"

Brady looked at Mrs Hope's list. "Two receptionists," he said. "Five different nurses. Someone in the kitchen who doesn't need a day off."

"Someone in the kitchen?"

"Dying is a 24/7 business, Dan. Most hospices will make you a cup of tea and a sandwich in the middle of the night."

"So one of the nurses..." Frankie said.

"Or a receptionist."

Brady handed Frankie the printouts. "You do the honours, Frankie. Every breakthrough we've had in this case has come from you. Eight names. Check them against the list of kids. Find Gina's killer."

Frankie took them from him. "My pleasure, boss. Ten minutes."

She walked over to her desk. Brady looked out of the window at the entrance to Whitby Hospital. Didn't see it. Saw Kershaw's face instead. Smiled to himself. *'We've made an arrest, sir. Perhaps you'd like to put it on Twitter...'*

FRANKIE WASN'T BACK in ten minutes.

Twenty.

And not looking happy. "Nothing, boss. No matches. Nothing at all."

Brady didn't say, 'You're sure?' If Frankie said none of the names matched...

"Shit," he said instead. "I knew it was too easy. Have you got everyone's maiden name?"

"All but one. One of the nurses."

"Give our new best friend Mrs Hope another call will you? See if the nurse is on duty. Or if her best mate is on duty. Someone who knows her maiden name."

"On it, boss."

Brady stared into space.

Think this through. What did the psychologist say? 'These children were abused over a long period of time. The effects are going to stay with them. Well into adult life. PTSD, eating disorders, depression, anxiety, low self-esteem. They're going to have any number of problems. These are damaged people, Mr Brady. They'll struggle to form and keep relationships in later life. They don't fit in.'

Does that sound like a nurse? No, it doesn't.

Brady reached for his mobile.

"Jules? It's Michael Brady again. One more question. I'm sorry."

If she can't remember, we're done. It's over.

"Jules, that night when you were in the hospice with your mum. The night Gina turned up. Do you remember seeing anyone else?"

There was silence. Jules trying to think back. "The nurse I suppose. They always came to check on mum last thing. There was a tablet she needed to take."

"No-one else? It's important."

Another silence. Brady didn't dare look out of the window. Didn't want to see Kershaw smiling back at him.

"A cleaner came in," Julie said. "She said she wanted to check the flowers had some water. I remember because Gina spoke to her. Said she thought they were alright. The cleaner said it was no bother."

"Thank you, Jules. Thank you very much indeed."

"Mr Brady. I seem to have spent all morning on the phone to the police."

"It's our last question, Mrs Hope. You employ a cleaner. We need the one who was working on the nights in question. A woman..."

"Ah, there I can't help you, I'm afraid. Our cleaners come through a local employment agency. They'd have all the details."

"Do you have their number?"

Mrs Hope did. Brady phoned. Was transferred to the

owner. Went through the explanation a second time. Promised he'd e-mail any paperwork they wanted. Waited while the owner went away to check the records. They must have been downstairs. The owner was out of breath when she came back to the phone. "Thank you," Brady said. He asked one more question. Looked at the notes he'd made. Went and spoke to Frankie.

"Jennifer Ellis," he said.

Frankie looked up. "Who's Jennifer Ellis?"

"She's the cleaner at the hospice. That's the good news. I spoke to Julie. She said the cleaner came in to change the water in the flowers. Gina spoke to her. Check the list."

Frankie shook her head. "I don't need to. She's there. I've checked the list so many times I know it off by heart now... So what's the bad news?"

"She was working. I got her name from an employment agency. They checked the records. Whoever held Gina Foster under the Esk it wasn't Jennifer Ellis. She was 200 miles away, mopping floors."

"So she told someone."

Brady nodded. "Time to go and see Ms Ellis. I've got her phone number and address. And when Dan comes in turn him loose on the children's home records. There must be someone she's related to."

Brady dialled the number. "Yeah, it's Jen. I'm busy. Leave a message and all that shit."

And what's going to happen if I leave a message? She'll never return it. She might warn someone...

Brady pressed the red button on his phone. Phoned back ten minutes later. "Yeah, it's Jen..."

Third time lucky.

"Jennifer. Good morning – my name – "

"If you're selling something piss off. We don't want it."

"I'm not selling anything. My name is Michael Brady. I'm a police officer. I'd like – "

"Is this about tomorrow? I thought you weren't supposed to phone witnesses?"

"No, it's not about tomorrow. My name is Brady, I'm a detective with North Yorkshire police. We're investigating a murder – "

"So nothing to do with the accident?"

"No. I don't know anything about an accident."

"I'm a witness, aren't I? All fucking day hanging around a bloody court waiting to be called."

"Right. I didn't know that. So you're not available tomorrow?"

"I've just told you haven't I?"

"Friday morning then. We're driving down from York-shire. We'll be with you about 11. We're investigating the murder of a woman called Gina Foster."

Frankie had been listening. "You don't think we should have her picked up by West Midlands?"

Brady shook his head. "If she's going to warn someone she'll be doing it now. No. It's a risk we've got to take. Just give our pal at West Midlands a courtesy call will you? Tell her we're paying another visit."

Two days left. And one of them lost because Jennifer Ellis is spending it 'hanging round a bloody court.'

"What are you doing tomorrow?" Brady said.

"Seeing as we're not going to Birmingham, paperwork."

"No. I've got a psychologist friend I need to see again. Come with me. Time for some theory before we do the practical."

51

"Thank you for seeing me again. And at such short notice. This is my colleague, Detective Sergeant Thomson."

Susanna Harrall smiled. Shook hands with them both. "My pleasure. A blessed relief from NHS budgets. Are we in Sherlock Holmes territory, Mr Brady? Is the game afoot, as Watson used to say? Or am I not allowed to ask?"

Brady laughed. "I think the fact that we're talking for a second time..."

"Means I probably shouldn't ask. How can I help you?"

"Last time we talked I asked you about revenge."

"Yes, I said it was unlikely to be planned."

Brady nodded. "That's what I – we – want to get straight. Make sure we understand it properly. So revenge could be a spontaneous act?"

"Are we talking in general here? Or the unfortunate Mrs Foster?"

"Both," Brady said. "Like before, the more we understand…"

"The answer is possibly. Something triggers a memory. A flashback. They might act it out in later life."

"So a child who's been abused in a particular way might repeat that pattern of abuse as an adult?"

She smiled at him. "In simple terms, if someone's held my head in the toilet and flushed it when I was a child, am I likely to do that to someone else when I'm an adult? Or hold them under the River Esk?"

"Yes. Exactly."

"It's much more complicated than that," she said.

Brady sighed. "I thought it might be."

"Abuse isn't sex, it's power. So if I'm abusing you, it's not just the sex. It's because I can. 'I'm doing this because I'm more powerful than you and there's nothing you can do about it.'"

"If it's not the sex," Frankie said. "Do the abusers sometimes abuse simply because they can? To demonstrate that power? Almost… to amuse themselves?"

Susanna Harrall raised her eyebrows. "Do managers ever ask their staff to do pointless things? Army sergeant-majors? Yes, it happens in every hierarchy. Official or unofficial."

"So it's not as simple as 'this was done to me so I'll do it to someone else?'

"No, it's complex. The adult might try to re-create the situation and it could trigger the same feelings he or she had as a child. Helplessness, anxiety… It could end up triggering a full-blown anxiety attack. And I couldn't predict what would happen and neither could the child. The adult, sorry."

"But they're not to know that? They don't know what will happen until they try it?"

"Until they try to re-create the situation? Yes, that's right." She looked at him over the top of her glasses. "I suspect I haven't helped you very much, Mr Brady?"

Brady let out a long breath. "To be honest with you – and please call me Michael – this whole bloody case has been like that. As far away from traditional policing – "

"Cops and robbers? White hats and black hats?"

"Exactly. Everyone's wearing a grey hat."

"But that's life, Mr Brady. Michael. Everyone has two sides to their character. Good and bad. Yin and yang. And they're intertwined. Two sides of the same coin."

Brady looked across the desk. "That's about the truest thing I've ever heard." He stood up. Held his hand out. "Thank you," he said. "You've probably been more helpful than I realise right now."

"My pleasure. Come back to me if there is anything else I can help you with. But remember – we all wear grey hats, Mr Brady." She smiled. "Even police officers and psychologists."

52

"My third trip to the Midlands in two weeks. I've had my fill of the M1."

"Maybe you should buy a flat, boss."

"No, thanks," Brady said. "I'm going to have enough work to do in Whitby."

"Seriously?" Frankie said. "Have you found somewhere?"

"Yeah, I'm excited. Or as excited as a man of my age gets. It's a house in the old part of town. Three floors, looks out over the harbour. I can make a bedroom/lounge area for Ash on the top floor. Main bedroom and a study underneath. Kitchen, lounge. And five minutes, 30 seconds to the beach for Archie."

"It sounds ideal. I'm jealous."

"There's only one disadvantage," Brady said.

"What's that?"

"It needs gutting. And I have the DIY skills of a fridge magnet."

Frankie shook her head. "That's not a disadvantage.

That's brilliant. Besides, you said you wanted somewhere that needed renovating."

"Renovating, not rebuilding. It might be a grand design too far. But Ash is already making plans for her 'penthouse.' So I'm committed."

"It'll be fine. And you get the house exactly as you want it. You've got four or five months before your lease runs out, haven't you? They've accepted your offer?"

"Yep. It was an old lady's. Her husband had been a fisherman. She died, the daughter wanted a quick sale. We complete in a couple of weeks."

And what will I do? Stand in the middle of my bedroom? Look out over the harbour and wish Grace was there to share the view? It's time to stop...

"Raw Cashmere," Frankie said. "I recommend Raw Cashmere for the walls. Helps you think."

"We're here," Brady said. "Artillery Terrace. There's a politically incorrect name these days. I'm surprised the council hasn't changed it."

"Artillery Terrace that has become fashionable," Frankie said. "Ten minutes from the town centre? What more could you want?"

She was right. The road was a mix of terraced houses and semis. Half very clearly renovated, half very clearly waiting for the next owner. Number 27 was at the end of a terrace – and halfway through its transformation. Builders were working on the roof. Brady ducked under the scaffolding and rang the front doorbell.

"How are we going to play this?" Frankie had said half an hour earlier.

"She's one of the children on the list. She was working

at the hospice on the night Gina was there. I don't see any need for subtlety. And we haven't got time for it. Not with Kershaw scenting blood."

A woman in her mid-20s answered the door. Red V-neck jumper, a black skirt. Long black hair framing a weary face. Sleeves pulled up. A barbed wire tattoo round a thick left wrist.

"Jennifer Ellis? I'm Detective Chief Inspector Michael Brady. We spoke on the phone. This is Detective Sergeant Thomson."

She looked them up and down. "You got any ID?"

Brady and Frankie fished in their pockets. Pulled out their ID. Well-worn in Frankie's case, still new for Brady.

"You'd better come in then. And you'll have to cope with the noise. They're working on the roof."

No cup of tea. Not for the first time Brady wondered where police officers ranked in the cup of tea league. His theory was well below halfway. Obviously bailiffs were at the bottom. Funeral directors would be at the top. You couldn't discuss dad's hymns without a cup of tea...

They were shown into a crowded lounge. "Building work," Jennifer Ellis said. "Only been in two months. Other half wanted to get the work done straightaway. Absolute bloody nightmare. Damian wants to play on his PlayStation. He wants to watch football. Driving me to drink."

Brady and Frankie perched on the sofa in front of the TV. Clearly where the 'other half' watched his football.

"This won't take long will it?" she said. "I need to get to the supermarket."

"I hope not. Can I call you Jennifer?"

She shrugged. "Call me what you like, love. Doesn't mean I'm going to answer your questions."

Fair enough. Let's see shall we...

"As you know, Jennifer, we're investigating the murder of Gina Foster. Or Gina Kirk as she was previously known."

Anthony Marshall had shown no emotion. Jennifer Ellis was the exact opposite.

She looked up at Brady. Smiled. "You won't get any sympathy from me. She had it coming."

"She had a teenage daughter," Frankie said.

"Right. And how many teenage girls got fucked by middle-aged men because of her? Me for one. How many young boys? I'll not be shedding any tears for that one."

"We know you were one of the children involved, Jennifer. We don't need to go back over it. It's the present we're concerned with. And finding the killer."

Jennifer Ellis shook her head. Stuck her jaw out. "So what do you want with me?"

"You work as a cleaner at the hospice."

"Did. I've moved on. Last month. Like working the night shift in God's waiting room. And there's only so many pools of piss you can clean up before school dinners look like a better option."

"You were working there on the night of April 7th?"

"If you say so. If it was a week day I was working."

"It was a Tuesday. Did anything unusual happen that night, Jennifer?"

"Any visitors?" Frankie said. "Anyone you recognised?"

She sucked her lips in. Brought her top teeth over her bottom lip. A pretence – at least – of trying to remember.

"I haven't got a clue."

"You had a patient," Brady said. "Elizabeth – Lizzie – Simpson. She died a few days later."

"There were lots of patients. And they all died. That's what happens in hospices. People die. You don't go into a hospice to get well again. Especially that fucking plague pit."

"Lizzie Simpson used to be Lizzie – Elizabeth – Kirk."

No emotion...

"She was Gina Kirk's mother. The family had to change their name after the conviction."

Jennifer Ellis shrugged again. "Should I care? Like I said. Old people die."

"Gina Foster came to see her mother that night. She was desperate to see her. She hadn't seen her for 12 years. She wanted to get there before her mother died. She walked in and signed the visitors book. 'Gina Foster,' the name she'd been writing for more than ten years. But she was thinking about her mum. For once she let her guard down. She wrote her car registration number."

Another shrug. "I don't see what this has to do with me. I was working. Mopping up piss. So what?"

Frankie stood up. "Would you mind if I used your loo, Jennifer?"

Jennifer Ellis shook her head. "Top of the stairs. Don't blame me if the ceiling falls on you."

Brady didn't wait for Frankie to come back. "Did you see Gina Kirk that night, Jennifer?"

"No. Besides, I was 14 the last time I saw her. I

wouldn't recognise her would I? And that time of night –
I was probably cleaning one of the common rooms. I
didn't do bedrooms at night."

He heard Frankie coming back downstairs. "Jennifer
was just telling me she didn't see Gina Kirk, DS Thomson. And if she had seen her, she wouldn't have recognised her. But she didn't see her because she was
probably cleaning the common room at the time."

"That's alright then," Frankie said. "I'm glad we've
cleared it up."

"Let me ask you again," Brady said. "You're absolutely
certain you didn't see Gina Kirk?"

"Certain as I can be."

"You're sure you didn't recognise her? You didn't tell
someone you'd recognised her? Your partner, for
example?

"No." She looked at her watch. "I need to be going
out."

"Two more questions," Brady said. "What does your
partner do, Jennifer?"

"What's that got to do with it? He's a plasterer. Those
are his mates working on the roof. Supposed mates.
Cowboys if you ask me."

"And what does his brother do?"

She hesitated.

I already know. And you can tell. So don't lie to me.

"The same as you," she said. "He's a copper."

Brady nodded. "I know he is. West Midlands Police."
He paused, reached into his pocket. Handed her a business card as he stood up. "That's got my numbers on it.
We're going to be driving back up the M1. Maybe three

hours until we get back to Whitby. I'd forget the super-market if I were you, Ms Ellis. I'd sit down and think about what you've just told us. Perverting the Course of Justice is a common law offence that is tried before a jury in a Crown Court. It carries a maximum sentence of life imprisonment. A PlayStation in your lounge might soon be the least of your worries."

Jennifer Ellis stared back at Brady. "You've no fucking idea. None at all. Pretty boy like you. They'd have paid plenty for you. See yourself out, won't you?"

BRADY OPENED THE CAR DOOR. Sat in the driver's seat. Swore. Drove the heel of his right hand into the steering wheel.

"Fuck!" he said. "Just fuck. Two weeks of Kershaw pissing us about. My stupidity. And the bloody answer is there all the time."

"We weren't to know that, boss. And we couldn't do anything about Gina's sister being on holiday."

"I'm certain." Brady said. "I was certain before. I'm even more certain now. Something Gina did or said. Jennifer recognised her. Went and looked at the visitors book. Saw the car number. And found Gina's address."

Frankie nodded. "Yeah. I can believe that."

"When I was a young detective," Brady said. "The first case I worked on – Jim Fitzpatrick said to me... And I tell you, Frankie, this has never, *ever* let me down. He said, 'If you ask someone, 'did you steal the apples?' and they answer 'no' then you *might* have a suspect. If you ask someone 'did you steal the apples' and they say, 'I don't like apples and besides I don't have a ladder to climb over the orchard wall and even if I did I'm scared of heights so I wouldn't have done it anyway and I was walking the dog when the apples were stolen...' Then you've *definitely* got a suspect."

"What did she say?"

"Word for word? 'I was 14 the last time I saw her. I wouldn't recognise her. I was probably cleaning one of the common rooms at that time. I don't clean the bedrooms at night.' Almost exactly that."

"How did she know the time..."

"Right. So she's protecting someone. Which widens the bloody net even further. Her partner. Her partner's brother. It was West Midlands Police that checked the car registration?"

"Yes. I checked through the PNC. So it's the partner's brother. He's called Street. PC Duncan Street."

"Well, let's hope PC Duncan Street hasn't made any plans for Christmas."

"Do you think she'll phone you?" Frankie said.

"Jennifer? No. Not a bloody chance."

"You don't need to widen the net too far," Frankie said quietly.

"Why not?"

"I think we're looking for Jennifer's brother."

Brady looked across at her. "Why do you say that?"

"This." Frankie picked her phone up. Opened *Photos*. And showed Brady a picture of what was very clearly a brother and sister.

"When did you take that?"

"When I went to the loo. It's on the upstairs landing. I

was going to come down and say something corny – 'There's a lovely view from the landing' – hoping you'd get the hint. Then I thought a procession of incontinent coppers might make her suspicious. So I took a photo."

"It's Jennifer, isn't it?"

"Absolutely. She's what? Thirteen? But there's no mistaking her."

"In care?" Brady said. "About to get fucked by middle-aged men..."

"And if she was abused her brother was abused..."

"So it's come full circle. Not enough photos in Gina's house. One too many in Jennifer's."

Brady started the car engine. "Let's get back. I'll talk to Dan Keillor as we're driving."

"There's just one problem," Frankie said. "There weren't any brothers and sisters on the list. Two sisters. Two brothers. No brothers and sisters."

"Adoption?" Brady said. "Half-brother and sister? Different surnames."

"We can narrow it down," Frankie said. "Look at the photo. He's two years younger than her. Maybe three years."

"So we need the boys on the list who are two or three years younger than Jennifer Ellis."

Brady pressed *Phone* on the car display. Six spaces for pre-sets. Ash, Kate, Fiona, Frankie, Dan Keillor and an empty space. Brady pressed Dan Keillor.

"You need another friend," Frankie said as the phone rang.

"Hi. This is Dan Keillor. I can't answer my phone right now, leave a message and I'll get right back to you."

"Dan? It's Brady. Ring me the minute you get this message. Sooner if possible."

"What the hell is he doing?" Brady said. "One o'clock. Why the hell is his phone turned off?"

He pressed Dan Keillor a second time. "Hi. This is Dan Keillor. I can't answer my phone – "

"Fuck it. Ring the station will you, Frankie? Six – one – eight – "

"I know the number, boss. Although it's not one of my six friends…"

"Sorry. I'm tense. Bloody traffic. Who the hell wants to live in a city?"

"Jane? It's Frankie Thomson. DCI Brady needs to speak to Dan Keillor … it's urgent … well dig him out of the bloody meeting … Yes … Tell him to phone Brady as soon as he can … Sooner … Thanks. Yeah … driving back from Birmingham … you too."

"What the hell is he doing?"

Frankie was silent for a moment. "I'm not sure I dare tell you…"

"Tell me what?"

"Kershaw's called half a dozen of them in. He's giving a presentation. Social media and policing. Why they need Twitter accounts. Sorry, boss."

Brady shook his head. "No, you're fine. I admit it, Kershaw's right. I'm a dinosaur. Stuck in the past. I've got this notion that bad people do bad things and we arrest them. You know, protect society. Do you remember your oath, Frankie? 'I do solemnly and sincerely declare and affirm that I will well and truly serve the Queen in the office of Constable.' I must have learned the wrong one. I don't remember anything about Twitter..."

She laughed. "At least you've relaxed, boss. Just don't get nicked for speeding on the M1..."

It was half an hour before Dan Keillor rang. "I'm sorry, boss. Jane came in with the message. Kershaw said he was just finishing. Then he took questions..."

Would I have done it at his age? Walked out of one of Jim Fitzpatrick's meetings? No.

"No problem, Dan. But I need you to do some more work for me. Dull, boring checking. But you're going to find Gina Foster's killer. Adoption records, old files, every record you can find on the original case. One of the children in the report is called Jennifer Ellis. I need you to find her brother. He's going to be two or three years younger than her. And he'll have a different name."

"I'm on it, boss."

"Thanks, Dan. He won't be among the 40 kids in the court case. You'll need to dig deeper than that. Ring me the minute you find anything."

"When are you back, boss?"

"Couple of hours? The satnav says four o'clock."

"OK. Drive carefully. It's pretty foggy here."

Brady pressed the red button to end the call.

"There's something else," he said. "Something about her."

"You mean she was lying?"

"No," Brady said. "She *was* lying – and maybe what she's

lying about is so important she's prepared to go to jail. But no, not that. Something else. Something I can't put my finger on. Put some music on. Maybe if I stop thinking about it..."

"What music do you like?" Frankie said.

"Me? You have no idea how dull I am. *Test Match Special* if it's on."

"It's October, boss. What's your second choice?"

"Bowie. I like blues. I've a soft spot for Amy Winehouse. *Fairytale of New York* at Christmas."

"Agreed," Frankie said. "With a custodial sentence for anyone who plays that Paul McCartney dirge."

"*Wonderful Christmas* or whatever it's called? That's your problem, Frankie. You're too lenient..."

BRADY TURNED off the A1 and onto the A64. Bowie and Amy Winehouse had finished. Whatever was in the back of his mind was still in the back of his mind.

"An hour to get back," he said. "Let's see how Dan's doing."

"I've got all the records, boss. Nothing so far. Two sisters..."

"Yeah, we know about them. It's definitely a brother and sister we want."

"I'll get back to you, boss."

"Quick as you can, Dan. It's getting foggy. As soon as we're coming over the Moors we'll lose the signal."

Brady shook his head. "Play this through with me, Frankie. Whatever was in the back of my mind is even further out of reach. Role play it with me."

"OK, she's in the hospice. Christ this fog's thick. Where did this come from?"

Brady slowed down. They were passing Tadcaster and the visibility was falling all the time. "I hate driving in fog," he said. "Fog and snow. I hate the way snow swirls in your headlights. Almost like it's hypnotising you."

"You and me both. Pickering to Whitby is going to be fun."

"Jennifer Ellis is in the hospice," Brady said. "She's in the room for some reason. Maybe Lizzie needs something. Someone says, 'Take this will you, Jen? I'm busy.' Maybe she's in reception. Sees Gina walk in."

"*Would* she recognise her?" Frankie said. "Ten or 12 years on? Gina's grown her hair. It's a different colour. Jennifer was only just a teenager. Gina wasn't much more than 20."

"Maybe," Brady said. "I can't recognise an actor from one film to the next. Ash laughs at me. 'Dad, how can you not see that Legolas is Will Turner?' Grace was the same. She recognised everyone, even minor characters. But this is the girl that delivers the kids to the clients. That goes with them. They're not going to forget her."

"Maybe it's not the face," Frankie said. "Maybe it's the voice. Maybe it's a phrase she uses."

"Christ, that's a bit tenuous, Frankie. What's a phrase you say to your dying mother *and* to a child you're delivering to a Birmingham penthouse? I'm bloody sure I can't think of one."

There was five seconds of silence in the car. Ten seconds.

"Let me look at you."

Another ten seconds of silence while Brady played both scenes. "I apologise," he said. "Unreservedly. You're right. Absolutely right. 'Let me look at you, Mum.' 'Let me look at you, Jennifer.' Slightly different tone of voice, but – "

"But it doesn't matter. It's the words."

"So Jennifer goes out," Brady said. "Can't believe what she's seen. Goes back in again. 'I've forgotten to change the water in your flowers, Lizzie.' Has another look to make sure. Walks across to reception."

"And there it is," Brady said. "Gina Foster. It's a different surname but it doesn't matter. 'Gina' is enough. And the car registration. And Jennifer goes home that night, climbs into bed next to her boyfriend and says, 'You know your brother. Would he do me a favour...'"

"Two days later he comes back to her. Gina Foster. Just outside Whitby."

"And then the $64,000 question. Who does she tell?"

"She tells her brother," Frankie said. "The boy in the photo."

The cars in front of them were slowing down even more. "Don't tell me there's been an accident," Brady said.

53

There had been. Blue flashing lights. Two police cars, one ambulance. But they managed to limp along the York by-pass in single file.

"Still an hour," Brady said. "The satnav says half-four now. Assuming the fog doesn't get any worse. Straight to the station. See where Dan's up to."

"You think you'll get an extra day out of Kershaw?"

"I think an extra day is all we need. Arrest someone on Saturday, put our feet up on Sunday."

"Hopefully..." Frankie bent forward, picked up her handbag from by her feet.

"Polos?" Brady said.

"Lip salve," Frankie replied. "I went for a walk on the beach last night. The cold wind, the salt. My lips always get cracked and dry at this time of year."

Frankie unscrewed the top of a small tin. "Organic," she said. "From a little shop in Church Street. You can get it for men as well. You should get some if you're going to walk Archie on the beach all winter."

She rubbed the middle finger of her right hand in the tin. Brady turned his head slightly. Watched her smear the salve backwards and forwards across her lips. Move her mouth as though she'd put lipstick on.

He turned his attention back to the road. Slowed down, looked at Frankie again. Still touching her lips.

Michael Brady knew he'd found the killer.

"Jamie," he said.

Sitting in Jamie's flat. He curled his bottom lip back. Brought his front teeth over it in concentration. Shook his head.

And perched on Jennifer's sofa. She sucked her lips in. Brought her top teeth over her bottom lip. A pretence – at least – of trying to remember.

"Jamie," Brady said again. "Jamie Harkin. Thank God for your sore lips."

"You mean – "

"I mean the thing that was bothering me about Jennifer. That was at the back of my mind. When she was thinking... She sucked her bottom lip in. Brought her front teeth over the top of it. I knew I'd seen it before."

"Jamie?"

"Jamie. When we asked him about the relationship between Foster and Gina. Whether they'd argued. Family mannerisms, Frankie. Don't tell me you don't have unconscious mannerisms you share with your sisters."

"Yes. Twirling our hair when we're thinking. Or nervous. Katie was the worst. Put her finger against her neck. Twirled... Bloody hell, boss."

"Christ, Frankie."

Brown eyes, a ring of barbed wire tattooed on the left hand side of his neck.

Sleeves pulled up. A barbed wire tattoo round a thick left wrist.

"Shared tattoos. They must mean something?"

"Barbed wire? It means suffering, time in prison... And yeah, abuse." Frankie paused. "Do you think she'll warn him? Do you think she's already warned him?"

"No, I don't. Because she must realise... If she does that she's implicating her partner. Her partner's brother. I think she's hoping for the best. Pinning her faith on us being stupid."

"Six bloody weeks and the answer's on the farm all the time. We should have realised. I'm a farmer's daughter for God's sake."

"Yeah. He saw us walking down to the murder scene. You remember – we saw someone fixing the fence – "

"Jamie."

"Right. And a day later he lets the cows out."

"You want me to phone ahead. Get a patrol car round to his flat? Get him picked up?"

"No, I don't. Because I just know that fucking Kershaw will go with it. But we swore an oath to uphold the law, Frankie. Not to get our picture in the paper."

Brady handed her his phone. "Here. One more call. Just to be absolutely certain. Then we can let slip the dogs of war."

"Who do you want me to phone?"

"Jordan Rooney."

"How did she die? Slowly, I hope."

"It depends on your definition of slowly. She drowned. Someone held her under the River Esk."

"Yeah. That seems about right."

"The guy you saw the other day?"

"Yep. I've got one question to ask him."

JORDAN ANSWERED on the fourth ring. "Bloody hell, mate, where are you? The moon?"

"Heading up on to the North Yorkshire Moors. In the fog. How's the leg?"

"Yeah. Not bad. I saw the specialist. He seemed OK with it."

"Jordan, I've a question. About your time..."

There's no easy way to say it.

"...About what happened in the home."

"Have you found out who did it?"

Brady knew what was coming.

If I say 'yes' he'll clam up. 'No way. I'm not grassing anyone up for you. Sort it out yourself.'

"No. We haven't. This is a delicate enquiry, Jordan. Some of the people we're talking to – trying to help – have had some really bad experiences. We're working with counsellors. Doing our best to help them..."

I'm sorry, Jordan. The necessary lie...

"So what do you want to know?"

"I'm seeing someone tomorrow. Jamie Harkin. I'm just trying to get as much background as I can."

There was silence. Then, "Yeah, I remember him. Skinny kid. Nervous. Always in trouble at school 'cos he couldn't read or write. He had a sister. Big sister. Looked out for him. Then she got moved somewhere else."

"Thank you. That's really helpful. I really appreciate that, Jordan. Thanks again. And all the best for – "

"Hang on. There's more."

"What's that?"

"One day, we were all lined up. Me, Jamie, three or four others. Boys and girls. She sent him off to wash his hands and face. Like she always did. 'Let me look at you,' she says when he comes back. I can hear her saying it. He hadn't done it properly. She slapped him. Really hard. He's lying on the floor. This foreign bloke she's with comes over. Screams at him. Orders him to strip. There, right in front of us. Then they throw a bucket of cold water over him. 'Now you're fucking clean,' the bloke says. And they leave him there. Stark naked and soaking wet."

54

Brady sighed. "That's it then. Phone the station. Send the troops in."

"You sound like you don't want to, boss..."

"No. Not at all. I just... I can't imagine what a childhood like that would do to you, Frankie. But he murdered Gina Foster. Held her down until she drowned. So phone the station. Get them round to Jamie's flat."

"I can't," Frankie said thirty seconds later. "The fog. I can't get a signal."

"Try it again."

"Same result. Twice. The signal's never good on this road. But it's this fog."

"What are you on?" Brady said. "What network?"

"Three."

"Try it on mine. EE. See if that works..."

It didn't. "OK, so for now we're the troops," Brady said. "That's fine. We'll be there soon – "

Brady looked through the windscreen. Saw the fog. Saw nothing *but* the fog. Could barely make out where the road ended and the Moors began. Flicked his headlights onto 'full.' But all they did was reflect straight back at him.

"Slow down, boss. The last thing we need is to hit a sheep in this."

"Have you tried your phone again?"

"About eight times. It's like you said. It's you and me."

"I'm not even sure I know where we are," Brady said.

"The long straight bit," Frankie said. "Coming up to the Hole of Horcum."

"Then the bend down to the left..."

"You think it's worth stopping in Sleights? Bang on someone's front door and use their landline?"

Brady shook his head. "By the time we're in Sleights we're what? Ten minutes from Jamie's flat. Let's just get there... Hell's bells, I've never seen fog this thick. Remind me to avoid this road for the next six months."

The car park at the Hole of Horcum emerged from the fog. A hundred yards later the road bent down and round to the left.

"Slow down, boss. There are always a lot of sheep around here."

"Talk to me will you, Frankie? Help me relax. I'm going mad staring into this fog. On second thoughts just listen," Brady said. "Let me talk it through. Pick holes if you want... I'm Jamie. I've been abused as a child. God only knows what that's like. I have no idea. But like the psychologist said, I'm damaged. Badly damaged. Can't form relationships. Don't relate to other people. No idea of the future."

"You're sure you want to do this?"

"Yes. It helps. Really."

"OK. You do know you're ticking off the main traits of a psychopath there?"

"Yeah, I suppose so."

"Let me ask a question," Frankie said. "If you're Jamie. If you want revenge... Why don't you kill her as soon as you can? Presumably you're in touch with Jennifer. She's nagging you. Asking you why you haven't done it yet."

"Because she's recognised me," Brady said.

"How?"

"Like we said, how did Jennifer recognise Gina? Jamie's tall, wiry, full of nervous energy. Maybe it's the way he looks at her. But that's the only thing that makes sense. That's why he doesn't kill her."

"He's there," Frankie said. "On the farm. She knows her secret's blown. He sees her every day. Twisting in the wind."

"And she can't go to her husband. She knows that. I know that. This is *better* than killing her. I'm torturing her. Every single day. Well, not every day," Brady said. "Jamie doesn't work every day. But enough."

"No," Frankie said. "Every day is right. I had a friend. Her husband used to hit her. All the time. He went away on a conference. I remember saying to her, 'At least you've got a week off.' She said, 'No. I know what'll happen when he comes back. All he's done is give me a week to think about it.'"

"You think he wants anything else?" Frankie added. "Sex? Money?"

"I don't know. Where's a psychologist when you need

one? Sex? Probably not, given what she said about relationships. Money – "

"Remember what he said to us, boss? He wanted a place of his own. A smallholding. Maybe he was blackmailing her."

"Bloody hell, Frankie. This fog's getting even thicker. You think it'll be clear in Whitby?"

"Dan said – "

Brady stamped on the brakes as two red rear lights suddenly appeared in front of them. "Christ, have they never *heard* of fog lights? He can't be doing more than 10mph."

Frankie put her hand on his arm. "Calm down, boss. There's no way you can overtake. Jamie will be making his tea. He's at home. Listening to music. He's not going anywhere."

"Try your phone again will you?"

Frankie shook her head. "I just did."

Brady changed down a gear as he followed the red lights uphill. "Where were we?"

"Blackmail," Frankie said. "Was he blackmailing Gina?"

Brady changed down again. *I'm going to run out of gears at this rate...*

"My gut feeling is no. There's only so much money to go round. The farm can't be *that* profitable. However good Gina is with the books, she can't be paying school fees *and* money to Jamie."

"She's screwed," Frankie said. "Between a rock and a hard place. Whatever the farming equivalent of that is. Jamie can watch her suffer for as long as he wants."

Six months since I drove across here with Ash. If it had been this foggy she'd have made me turn round and go back to Manchester.

Ash. Who's the same age as Maria...

"I think we're in trouble," Brady said.

"The guy in front? It's not much further."

"No. Jamie. It wasn't Gina. It was Maria. It *is* Maria."

"What?"

"I just said it. 'She can't pay school fees and money to Jamie.' Why is she suddenly paying school fees?"

"Ian said she lost faith in the state system."

"Right – Come on! For Christ's sake, come on." Brady flashed his lights. Sounded his horn. Did everything common sense told him not to do.

"When did Gina send Maria to boarding school? Not at the start of secondary school. Year nine. Year ten. Whatever bloody year Ash is in now. Why would I send Ash away to school? I wouldn't. I looked at Scarborough College. But she's my only child. I wanted her with me. What's the *only* thing that would make me send her away to school?"

"Someone threatening her," Frankie said.

"*That's* why she was sent away to school. That's why Gina's dead. Jamie told her what he was planning. 'Your daughter's going to suffer like I suffered.' Gina's protected her all through the summer holidays. But knows she can't do it for ever. So she sends Maria away to school. Buys herself some time. Six weeks until half term..."

"And knows she has to kill Jamie," Brady continued. "That's the only way to protect her daughter. To protect Ian from the truth. It's kill Jamie or run away again. Run away with her daughter. Leave Ian. Uproot Maria from the only life she's ever known."

"So she arranges to meet him…"

"It's all she can do. 'I've got some money for you.' 'I want to make a deal.' Something like that. We should have counted the knives, Frankie. There'll be a kitchen knife missing."

"There are easier ways of killing someone than using your carving knife."

"In a farmyard? Yes. But not for Gina. She doesn't drive the tractor does she? She doesn't operate any machinery. So she says, 'Tomorrow morning, I'll be walking the dog. Meet me.'"

"*That's* why he was limping," Frankie said. "He didn't get kicked by a cow. Max bit him. Trying to save Gina."

"It's half-term, Frankie. Ash breaks up for half-term today. Scarborough College will be the same. Ian Foster will be collecting her. He'll be driving back to the farm. Jamie will be waiting. Try your phone again, Frankie, For God's sake get through to someone."

Frankie reached for her phone. Michael Brady floored the accelerator, wrenched the steering wheel to the right and pulled out into the fog.

55

"Bloody hell. You realise that was driving without due care and attention. Could have been – "

"Could have been any number of things. Yes. I'm sorry. But we're not going to save Maria's life in 2nd gear."

"Or Ian..."

"Or Ian. Shut your eyes. We're at the top of Blue Bank."

Whitby's down there. The Abbey on top of the hill. The beach. The sea. It's a beautiful view. We can't see any of it.

A blue traffic sign loomed up at the side of the road. Brady knew what it said. Knew what it said because he'd seen the photographs of the fatal crash. Barely a month ago.

Slow. Keep in low gear.

He pressed the accelerator.

AND THE FOG WAS GONE. Halfway down Blue Bank and the fog simply vanished. Like someone had lifted a curtain. Sleights, Whitby, the Abbey, the sea. Ships out at sea. Brady could see everything. The light fading slightly on an autumn afternoon. But otherwise a clear day.

"Here," Brady said, handing Frankie his phone. "Ian Foster first. Warn him. Then the station."

Brady heard Ian Foster's phone ringing. And ringing. No answer.

Heard Frankie speaking to the station. Heard her frustration. "There's been an incident in Robin Hood's Bay. A fight in the pub. Dan Keillor and Jake Cartwright have had to go."

"How long will it take them?"

"To get to the farm? Twenty minutes? Twenty-five?"

"No-one else?"

"It's Friday afternoon," she said simply.

"So it's you and me."

"Looks like it."

"That's enough," Brady said. He turned left along Eskdaleside. "Ten minutes, Frankie. No more."

"Unless we get stuck behind a tractor..."

THEY DIDN'T. They dropped down into Grosmont. Through the village, under the railway bridge, over the river and turned right.

Where I first came to look. Where I climbed over the gate onto the railway line. Where I saw the river bank...

"Any ideas?" he said.

"None at all," Frankie said. "Drive into the farmyard. Calmly and carefully arrest him."

"Shotgun? Pitchfork?"

"You worry too much, boss..."

FOR ONCE BRADY didn't notice the potholes. Didn't notice the pheasants.

Did notice the fading light. And the pickup. A dad back from collecting his daughter, the white pickup parked neatly by the house.

And a motorbike he'd never seen before.

Saw those. Couldn't help but see Max. Standing in the farmyard. Standing over something, barking furiously. Ian Foster lying on the ground.

But didn't see Maria.

Didn't see Jamie Harkin.

Brady slammed the brakes on. Was out of the car almost before it had stopped. But he wasn't as quick as Frankie.

"Is he – "

She shook her head. "He's fine. That is, he's not fine. He's been hit. But he's stunned, that's all." She touched her hand to the back of his head. "And bleeding. He needs an ambulance."

Brady bent down. "Ian? Can you hear me? It's Brady. Michael Brady."

Foster's eyes flickered. "Ian? We know who did this to you. Where is he? Where's Maria? Frankie, take Max inside will you? And where the hell is Joanne?"

"Shopping," Ian Foster whispered. "Food for the weekend."

"Ian. Where's Jamie? Where's Maria?"

Ian Foster – the man who'd found a wife and a

daughter in a solicitor's office. Who would have loved his wife even if she'd told him the truth: who finally knew who'd killed her – made an effort. Made an enormous effort to speak. "She's down at the river," he said. "Down at the river laying some flowers for her mum."

"Jamie. Where's Jamie?"

"The bugger's gone after her."

Ian Foster slumped back on the cold ground of the farmyard.

"Stay with him," Brady said. "Dan Keillor can't be far away. Get an ambulance for him."

"Boss – "

"What, Frankie? Wait for back-up? Wait for Dan Keillor? She's the same age as my daughter. What else can I do?"

56

The same track. The one he'd walked down with Frankie. The one that led to the clearing. Where the bank sloped gently down to the river. Where he'd imagined a family eating a picnic. Skimming stones across the river. Watching the train from Whitby to Pickering steaming over the bridge. Waving at the passengers...

Not today. Definitely not today.

The track was even wetter than it had been four weeks ago. Brady's feet were soaked. He didn't care. Mud, puddles, cow dung. None of it mattered.

Keep running. One job. Just one job. Get to Jamie before he reaches Maria.

"Jamie!" he yelled for the fourth or fifth time. "Jamie! Stop!"

'Something else you might see is trance-like behaviour. Not knowing what they're doing.'

"Jamie!"

There! What's he carrying? A long stick? It doesn't matter. One job. Just one job.

Brady felt his left hamstring starting to tighten as he ran.

The pain doesn't matter. Nothing matters...

He could see the track bending round to the left. Could see the clearing. The top of the river bank. Saw Jamie stop. Saw him stand and look down at the river. Saw what Jamie had been carrying.

Not a long stick.

An axe.

The axe he'd seen in Ian Foster's woodshed. The axe lying patiently on a pile of logs.

Jamie started to walk down the slope. Brady rushed forward. Saw Maria. Saw her kneeling at the side of the river. Still in her school uniform. Saw irrelevant, inconsequential details.

She's put some wellingtons on. Brought a groundsheet to kneel on...

Jamie walked towards her.

Brady half ran, half slipped down the bank, slithered through the mud.

"Jamie! Don't!"

Jamie turned to face him. Swung round. His right arm came up, his hand holding the axe.

Maria saw it. Screamed. Ran for the cover of the trees.

Brady did the only thing he could. Dived forward.

Crashed into Jamie.

Felt the momentum carry him forward. Felt the cold shock of the water hit him. Felt Jamie's weight on top of him. Felt the River Esk flowing into his lungs.

Let go of Jamie. Knew he *had* to let go of Jamie. Coughing, gasping for breath, struggling to his feet.

Up to his knees in water. Saw Jamie facing him, his brown hair matted, the barbed wire tattoo on his neck. Saw no sign of the axe.

Brady coughed again. Sucked a lungful of air in. Felt the weight of his wet clothes. Tried to speak. "Jamie Harkin, I am arresting you – "

"What are you doing?" Jamie looked distraught. Angry. Thwarted. "What are you doing, you bloody idiot?"

What the hell's happening here? He's not supposed to react like this.

Brady stepped forward. "Jamie Harkin, I am – "

Brady had forgotten how tall he was. Strong, wiry. "No! You fucking idiot. You're not arresting me. You've got it wrong. Wrong! All bloody wrong."

Jamie lunged at him. Pushed him in the chest. Brady tried to keep his balance. Slipped on the river bed. Fell back into the water. Felt the Esk close over him a second time. Forced himself back to the surface. Saw Jamie stumbling up the river bank.

Looked up. Saw Frankie running towards Jamie. "No, Frankie! Leave him! Get Maria! Make sure she's safe."

Jamie was running up the slope towards the railway bridge.

A gap in the fence. Wide enough to squeeze through.

Brady remembered it. Walking along the railway line. Looking for a murder site...

He struggled out of the water. Slipped, stumbled, clambered up the bank after Jamie. Stopped. Took his sodden jacket off. Threw it on the ground.

"Boss! Let me – "

"No, Frankie. No. Stay with Maria."

Brady was at the top of the bank.

Please, God. No. Don't do this, Jamie.

Black hoodie, denim jeans, water dripping off him, framed by the autumn trees... Jamie Harkin was standing in the middle of the railway line.

Brady held his hand out. Forced himself to be calm. "Jamie, we know what happened. We know what you've been through. We'll sort it out. Just come with me."

Jamie stared back at him. Shook his head. "You don't understand. No-one understands. Piss off. Leave here."

"You know I can't do that. Tell me what I don't understand."

"Maria."

The same sound he'd heard on that Saturday afternoon. The unmistakable sound of a steam engine. The vibration through his feet. The North York Moors Railway. The last train of the day.

"Jamie, there's a train coming. We're standing on the railway line."

"Maria. I knew you wouldn't understand."

"Just come off the bloody railway line. Then tell me what I don't understand."

"No. It's better this way."

"Jamie – " But now Brady was having to shout to make himself heard above the noise of the train. A long, loud blast on a whistle...

"I'm too old for this crap," Michael Brady said out loud.

He darted forward. Wrapped his arms round Jamie. Pulled him to the side of the track. Pressed them both into the green railings of the railway bridge. Watched locomotive no. 825 and three red and cream carriages thunder past.

"YOU ALRIGHT, BOSS?"

Brady pulled the blanket round him. He was sitting in the barn. On a large white sack.

Hay? Wool? It's soft. I'm sitting on a bale of wool...

He looked up at Frankie. She was holding out a mug of tea. "Joanne's back from Sainsbury's. Mugs of tea and real life drama. This is her moment."

Brady started to laugh. Ended up coughing. "Yeah, I'm alright. I'm bloody cold and it might take a while to get the Esk out of my lungs. But I'm alright. What's the rest of the damage?"

"Maria's inside. I've spoken to her. She's shaken but she'll be OK. She's a tough kid."

Marko Vrukić's blood in her veins...

"Ian's got a nasty gash. Bruise like an egg. But he's told the paramedics he's not going to hospital. Said he'd only go to hospital if the paramedics would milk the cows for him."

"What about Jamie?"

"He's in the patrol car. Dan Keillor and Cartwright are just going to take him in."

Brady shook his head. "Tell them to wait. I want to talk to him. Just let me drink this tea."

He struggled off the bale of wool. Limped across the

farmyard to the patrol car. Opened the back door. Slid in next to Jamie. "You as wet as I am, mate?"

Jamie nodded. "Reckon so."

"You alright?"

"Been better. I'm cold."

"Here, have another." Brady took his blanket off. Passed it to him. "Anyone offered you a cup of tea?"

Jamie held his cuffed hands out in front of him. "Bit difficult with these."

"You take sugar?"

"Are you for real? Yeah, one."

"Dan, go inside and find Joanne. Cup of tea, one sugar. Jake, come round here and unlock these handcuffs. Then make yourself scarce for five minutes."

"Fucking authority, eh?"

Brady laughed. "Yeah. Absolute power. Or maybe not." He stopped speaking while Jake Cartwright unlocked the handcuffs.

"Thanks, Jake. Now give me five minutes." He turned to Jamie. "Back there – in the water – you told me I'd got it all wrong. 'Fucking idiot' I think you said."

Jamie looked down. "You thought I was trying to kill her."

Brady nodded. "Yeah. The axe..."

Dan Keillor tapped on the car window. Brady opened the door and took the mug of tea. Passed it to Jamie.

"I was trying to save her," Jamie said.

"You don't save someone with an axe, Jamie."

"I don't know why I took it. Maybe thought Foster was coming after me. I don't know. I just wanted..." He turned to Brady. Tears were rolling down his face. "I just wanted to save her. Take her somewhere safe."

"Save her from what, Jamie?"

"Can't you see? From her. From Gina Kirk. She was starting again. Starting the business again."

What business? With the children? What's he talking about?

"Is that why you killed her? And drink your tea before it goes cold."

"I... I don't know why I killed her. She said she wanted to meet me. I came here and got a job. Because Jennifer told me to. She sent me. Told me what I had to do. And –"

"Gina knew who you were?"

"I don't know. I think so."

"So you met her down by the river?"

"She told me to meet her. And to begin with she was nice. Telling me there were things I could do. Places I could go. Then she started shouting at me. And then..."

"Then?"

"Then she slapped me. Like she did once before."

Jamie looked at Brady.

He's looking for help. Looking for answers...

"And I don't remember what happened after that. I sort of blacked out. Then Max bit me."

"But you told us you'd been kicked by a cow. And you let the cows out to churn up the river bank."

"Yeah. 'Cos Jennifer always told me – when we were young – 'Do what you have to. Don't get into trouble.' But all I wanted to do was get Maria safe. Just somewhere safe."

Frankie tapped on the window. Brady opened the door. "Dan says he needs to get Jamie in, boss. While there's still someone at the station."

"OK. One minute."

Brady turned back to Jamie. "Can I ask you one more question?"

Jamie shrugged. "I can't stop you."

"You said you wanted to save Maria. Because Gina had started the business again. What made you think that?"

"Because it was obvious. Because another one turned up."

"Another one. Another what?"

"A foreign bloke. She was always with a foreign bloke when she made us line up. Romanian. Greek. Something like that. One of them turned up here."

"Turned up here?"

Jamie nodded. "I saw him. Walking through the farmyard."

Brady nodded. Finally understood.

Saw Marko Vrukić finish his coffee.

'You think I haven't known where Gina has been all these years? You think I have not kept watch on her?'

He'd sent Luka. Not to speak to her. Just to walk through the farmyard. 'Maybe some photos, Luka. Tell me about it. Where she lives.'

And Jamie had seen Luka. 'A foreign bloke. Romanian. Greek. Something like that.' He'd seen Luka walking through the farmyard. And drawn the only conclusion he could.

Brady knocked on the car window. Mouthed 'let me out' at Dan Keillor. "Child locks," he said to Jamie.

"Doesn't matter what rank you are. Got to ask to be let out."

Dan opened the door for him. Brady climbed out. Then he bent down, spoke to Jamie one last time. "You'll be alright. I promise... Dan?"

"Yes, boss?"

"Make sure you take care of him."

57

Four days later. Ian Foster bent down and patted Max. "I suppose I've got him to thank, have I? If he hadn't bit the bugger..."

Brady laughed. "Among other things, yes. Max, a chance meeting in a motorway services, some bloody good detective work – none of it by me. We got there in the end. We'd have got there – "

Brady cut the sentence off.

We'd have got there sooner if Kershaw had told me the truth. If I hadn't decided it was the gang. Maybe we wouldn't have got there at all if I hadn't gone to see Marko Vrukić. Ifs, buts, maybes...

"You told me the truth," Ian Foster said. "It wasn't what I wanted to hear but you told me the truth. I've got to be grateful for that. I realise that now. Supposing I found out when I was 50? Sixty? That's my whole life gone." He paused. "I still wish she'd told me."

How do I reply to that? I don't...

"What will you do now?" Brady said.

"Same as I've always done. Plough fields. Make sure the animals are alright. Carry on being Maria's dad. At least for the next few years."

"You'll always be her dad."

Ian looked at him. "Will I? What about this new family she's found?"

Brady nodded. "She's going to want to get to know them, that's for sure."

You're probably on safe ground with Jules. Marko Vrukić might be a different matter.

"What's he like, this Vrukić?"

There's a simple question that needs a two hour answer. As different to you and me as it's possible to be. Except that he'll love Maria. And she'll find his life – the romance of it – hard to resist...

"What do you want, Ian? The truth or what it says on Wiki?"

"What you've always given me. The truth."

"He's complicated. He's a war hero or he's the Devil. It depends which side of the border you're standing. He's rich. He knows what he wants. He's given a lot of money to charity. He more or less funded the new children's ward at his local hospital. He's like all of us, Ian, a mixture of good and bad."

Just on a much wider scale than the rest of us...

"You think he'll come up here?"

Wouldn't that be something? The man who walked along a line of prisoners executing them one by one until he got the information he needed... Peacefully eating fish and chips on Whitby seafront.

"My guess is it's unlikely. But he'll keep an eye on

Maria. You know, the sort of interest a grandfather takes. That's probably the best way to think of him."

And the safest...

Ian Foster held his hand out. His huge, coal-shovel right hand. "There was a time I wouldn't shake your hand. I was wrong. I'm sorry."

Brady took it. Felt the pressure on his own hand. "I was wrong as well. Following orders. You deserved more than that."

"Come and have a cup of tea some time," Foster said. "We can talk about teenage daughters."

Brady laughed. "I'll do that. Not that either of them will cause us any problems..."

He walked across the farmyard and climbed into the Tiguan. The still unwashed, still shabby Tiguan. "All good?" Frankie said.

"Yeah, all good. He invited me to come out for a cup of tea."

"You should do it," Frankie said. "Just one word of advice from a farmer's daughter though."

"Yeah? What's that?"

"Give him a couple of weeks. Let him find a new farm labourer. You don't want to be asked to help out. I don't see you shovelling shit, boss."

"Thanks, Frankie. I'll resist the obvious reply..."

Brady started the car. Drove down the track out of the farm. "Just when I'd perfected slaloming through the potholes as well..."

"Don't worry, boss. There'll be another farm track before long. Or its equivalent."

"There will. But it can wait a while. I'm taking the rest of the week off. Spend some time with Ash. Drive down and see Kara and the baby. Take Archie for a few long walks before it gets too dark and cold."

Frankie looked across at him. "You want some company on one of those long walks?"

Brady tried to hide his surprise. "Sure. Absolutely. Yes. That would be lovely. Tomorrow morning?"

"Sounds good to me."

"Beach?" Brady said.

"Sure. The forecast's good. Where else would you go?"

"Sandsend and back then. Late breakfast at Dave's when we're done. I'll collect you at nine."

BRADY KICKED the ball into the distance. Archie scampered after it for the hundredth time.

"They never get tired do they?" Frankie said.

"He'll have a rest in a minute. He'll find a dead fish. You read the small print didn't you, Frankie? 'Pick you up at nine, buy you a bacon sandwich and you give Archie a wash if he rolls in a dead fish?' You read that part of the contract?"

Frankie laughed. "No, I trusted you. Don't tell me that was a mistake..."

They walked along the beach towards Sandsend. "Low tide," Brady said. "A bright, sunny morning in autumn. I love it."

"Pleased you came back then?"

"Yes, I am. It was the right decision..."

I was going to say, 'for Ash.' But it was the right decision. Full stop.

"You want to talk about it?" Frankie said. She was wearing jeans, a maroon parka, fur round the collar, hair loose for once.

A girl to walk on the beach with...

"Coming back to Whitby? Or Gina Foster?"

"Gina. We've not really talked about it."

"No..." Brady said. "I've been... I don't know. Trying to sort it all out. Thinking back to what the psychologist said. Black and white, good and bad. Thinking about everything. Anthony, Jordan, Jamie... We're cops, Frankie. Cops and robbers. It's supposed to be simple."

"Except it wasn't."

"No. It wasn't. Thank God for your lip salve."

Lip salve and a chance remark from Bill Calvert...

"Kershaw's spinning it as a 'triumph for methodical policing.'"

Brady shook his head. "No doubt he'll have the lecture tour lined up."

"You and I know the truth," Frankie said.

"It doesn't help me sleep," Brady said. "I was lying awake last night thinking about the trial. I feel like I could give evidence for the defence as much as the prosecution."

"You should have phoned. I was awake thinking about Julie. She's going to wake up one morning and think, 'If I hadn't told her that Mum was ill...' That's going to be tough to live with."

"You could say the same about Vrukić. If he hadn't

sent Luka... Jamie wouldn't have seen him. Drawn the only conclusion he *could* draw."

"Has he rung you?"

"Vrukić? No. I'm surprised. I'd expected a call by now."

"Are you going to tell him? About Luka?"

"That sending Luka might have led to Gina's death? No. What good would it do?"

I'll keep Luka to myself. Who knows when I might need a bargaining chip with Marko Vrukić?

"It would have boiled over sooner or later," Frankie said. "Gina and Jamie. He couldn't have worked on the farm indefinitely... You think he *ever* meant to kill her?"

"You want my opinion?"

Frankie stopped walking. Put her hand on his arm. Smiled. Looked up into his eyes. Spoke softly. "You're a man, boss. You're going to give me your opinion whether I want it or not..."

Brady laughed. "Ouch! Serves you right if Archie finds a dead fish."

"Go on then. Jamie..."

"He's stayed in touch with his sister. Life's taken them in different directions. Different children's homes. The sister stays in Birmingham. Jamie's adopted – "

"Someone loses the paperwork so we can't trace it."

"Right. And it won't be the last time that happens. But he drifts north. And they've got a bond. A shared resentment. A shared belief. Somehow they'll get even. And one day Jamie gets a phone call. 'You'll never guess who came into the hospice the other night.' And comes to Whitby. Gets a job with Foster."

"He can't guarantee that though."

"Maybe," Brady said. "Maybe not. What happened to the guy before him? Came off his bike? It's not impossible to make someone do that. Jamie gets chatting to him. They go for a drink one night. Or maybe Jamie just gets lucky."

Brady kicked Archie's ball hard across the sand. "That one looked like frustration, boss."

"Yeah. There's so much we have to guess at. What I wouldn't give to speak to Gina. But for what it's worth I think Jamie did what his sister told him to."

"But just being there..."

"The pressure on Gina must have been enormous. Seeing Jamie every day. Everything she thought was behind her. We think *we* can't sleep at night..."

"And so it finally explodes. She can't take it any more. Maria's away at school but Gina knows she'll be back in the holidays."

"You think Jamie threatened Maria?"

"No, I don't. I'm not saying Gina imagined it. Maybe she saw them talking? Hell's bells, Maria's 13. There must have been times she was lonely on that farm."

"Gina sees it, puts two and two together. Makes five."

"Yeah, maybe has a confrontation with Jamie."

"The marks on her arm?"

"Can you think of anything else?"

"No."

"Me neither... We've reached the breakwaters."

Was it only a week ago that I stood here? Barely able to stand up in the wind? Soaked by the rain and the spray?

"Time to turn round. Talk to me about something more cheerful, Frankie."

"Groynes, boss. The correct word is groynes."

"I know, I know. Groynes just sounds ridiculous."

They walked back towards Whitby, the sun rising higher in the sky, Archie still scampering after his ball. The pier in front of them, reaching out into the North Sea.

I didn't look up at Grace's hill when we were at the break-waters. The first time I haven't done it...

"Boss?" Frankie stopped walking again. Turned and faced him. "There's something I need to say."

"That's your serious face, Frankie. Is this why you wanted to come for a walk?"

She shook her head. "No. I wanted to come for a walk. Period. But there is something I want to tell you. Face to face. Before you hear it on the office grapevine."

"This sounds ominous."

Frankie shook her head. "No. It's not. I don't think so."

"But I'm not going to like it..."

"I hope not. Professionally, I mean..."

"So what is it?"

"I'm going to take some time off," Frankie said. "A sabbatical. Six months. Maybe a year."

Brady was silent. *I don't want her to take time off...*

"I don't need to ask why," he said. "Your mother?"

"Yes. Some days she knows who I am, some days she doesn't. That's not going to last much longer. I want to spend some time with her while she knows who I am. While she knows she has a daughter. And..." She hesitated.

"Something else?"

"Alex has gone. You know that. I'm on my own. I want some time to get used to it."

Brady started to speak. She stopped him. "No, don't. It has nothing to do with sharing a pizza. But he's gone and – with Mum, this case, everything – I need some time. I need to press control, alt, delete. Re-boot myself. No..." She reached out. Put her hand on his cheek. "It has nothing to do with sharing a pizza."

"So you're leaving me alone with Kershaw?"

Frankie smiled. "You can cope, boss."

"I'd better get myself on Twitter then."

"Obviously. It's the only way to save your career."

They'd reached the slipway at the end of the beach. "You want your bacon sandwich? Or an early lunch? Archie likes fish and chips even more than bacon."

"Bacon sandwich," Frankie said. "I'm going out for fish and chips tomorrow night."

"Anything special?"

"A few friends. That's all..."

58

His teenage daughter looked him up and down. "Maybe a different shirt, Dad. That one's a bit boring. But you've no time to change. You'll have to do. Come on, let's go."

Michael Brady – pale blue button down shirt, freshly pressed jeans as instructed, navy jacket – smiled to himself. Just like her mum...

"I didn't even know you liked fish and chips, Ash."

"It's Whitby, Dad. Everyone likes fish and chips. And I've booked a table."

"When did you ring them?"

"Dad, no-one rings anyone any more. I did it online. That's how you do everything now. Try and keep up, Dad."

Brady smiled at her. She'd done her hair differently. She looked older every day. "Your mum would be so proud, Ash."

She surprised him. Took a step forward, reached up and put her finger on his lips. "I hope so. But not tonight, Dad. Look forward, not back."

He parked the car opposite the harbour. They walked past the tall ship, past the seat where he'd eaten fish and chips with Frankie.

What was that? Five weeks ago? Six?

'You're ruling out an accident? So we're left with suicide. Or murder.'

The lights from Church Street – the pubs, the shops, the houses behind them climbing steadily to the Abbey – still sparkled and danced across the water.

I still need Carl here to do it justice...

They walked towards the swing bridge and then turned left towards Marine Parade and Pier Road. "This is lovely, Ash. We should do this more often. Just the two of us."

Because four years from now you'll be 18 and going to university. And Archie won't go online and book a table...

"There's a queue, Ash," Brady said as they reached the Magpie Café.

"There's always a queue, Dad. But we don't need to worry. Come on."

Ash put her arm in his and steered him up the steps to the front door. "Excuse me... thank you..."

"Hi, we've got a booking," Ash said. "Michael Brady?"

"Hi, yes," a waitress said. "You know where to go? Upstairs and straight through."

"They didn't ask what time," Brady said. "Are you sure you've booked?"

"You need to trust me, Dad. I hope you weren't this difficult when Mum took you out."

He followed his daughter upstairs. "This way, Dad. I booked a table looking out over the harbour."

"That's lovely, Ash. Maybe we can see the new house."

But she was ahead of him, walking through to the far end of the restaurant. "This isn't very busy," Brady said. "How come there are so many people queueing? This whole section is empty."

"He's not ower clivvor, Ash pet. It's a wonda he ivvor arrested any gadgie at aall."

A broad Geordie accent, exaggerated for his benefit.

Brady turned. "Dave! You bastard. What are you doing here?"

"Not just us. I browt wor lass alang n' all."

"Alright," Brady laughed, "You can stop talking like Alan Shearer and Jackie Milburn's lovechild."

He stepped forward and hugged Dave wife's. "Take him to Spain as quickly as you can, Maureen. I couldn't stand it if he spent all winter talking in that accent."

He turned back to Dave. "What are you doing here? Is this just coincidence – "

Ash coughed. Glanced towards the door. Brady looked. Kate, with Maddie and Lucy. Dan Keillor behind them, a beautiful blonde girl on his arm. Then Bean, waving furiously at Ash. Fiona just behind her. They walked towards him. Hugs, kisses. He turned to Ash. "Did you – "

"Did I set this up? Yes, I did. Happy birthday, Dad. Happy belated birthday."

She hugged him. Fiercely. Brady fought back the tears. Failed hopelessly.

"Thank you," he managed to say. "Thank you all."

"I had a co-conspirator," Ash said. And glanced towards the door a second time.

Brady turned. She was wearing a black top, cut low, a single black strap running across to her shoulder. Tight black jeans. Black boots. Her hair pinned up like the first time he'd seen her. Still looking like a warrior princess. The girl who strapped on armour in *Lord of the Rings*.

"Frankie," he said.

She walked over, kissed him on the cheek. A faint hint of Alien...

"Sorry, boss," she said. "I was under orders. Detective Chief Inspector? Easily outranked by a teenage daughter..." She turned to Ash, hugged her, broke off and high-fived her.

"Is that it?" Brady said. "I'm... I'm astonished. I'm honoured. I'm... Slightly worried that my daughter could outwit me so easily."

He sat down. Looked around him at the people who were part of his new life. Was only marginally more successful in fighting back the tears.

"There's an empty chair," he said. "Who's missing?"

Frankie leaned across. Put her hand on his. Looked into his eyes. "He's been delayed, boss. A photo-opportunity with the Queen. Said he couldn't disappoint her. But Kershaw will be here in five minutes."

"I warned you before DS Thomson. That vacancy in Arbroath is still open. Seriously, who's missing?"

Frankie shrugged and raised her eyebrows. "Ash," she said. "Someone's missing apparently. Any ideas?"

Ash shook her head. "Dad's the big-shot detective. He'll just have to work it out."

"You've beaten me," Brady said. "I'll try and work out what to eat instead."

But he couldn't concentrate on the menu. Dave was trying to persuade Dan Keillor's girlfriend to come fishing with him. Kate was deep in conversation with Fiona. Ash and Bean were in an urgent conference with Bean's mobile.

"I'm going to take a wild guess you're not ready to order yet?"

Brady looked up. "I'm sorry," he said to the waitress. "You might be able to force a drinks order out of us though."

"I might as well start with you then, sir."

"I'm driving," Brady said. "But I can risk a bottle of –"

He stopped speaking. Looked past the waitress.

He'd first seen him in a run-down flat in Whitby.

He was 18 or 19. Hair combed forward, cut straight across the middle of his forehead. An attempt at a beard outlining a round face. Brown eyes. A grey round-necked sweatshirt. He looked like a medieval squire.

The last time he'd seen him had been in a hospital bed. After Jimmy Gorse had casually, calmly, tossed him off the end of Whitby Pier into the North Sea.

Brady made no attempt to hold back the tears this time. Walked forward. Threw his arms round the bravest person he knew. "Carl. Thank you. I don't know what to say."

Carl Robinson – 20 now, longer hair, looking a lot less like a medieval squire and a lot more like an art student – hugged him back with some difficulty. He was carrying a canvas in his right hand. "Good to see you too. Thought – seeing as how you saved my life. And seeing as someone promised me free fish and chips – thought it was the least I could do."

Brady stepped back. Gestured at the canvas. "What's that?"

"That?" Carl said. "It's for your daughter. She's a hell of a negotiator. You wouldn't want to steal her parking space when she's older."

"Come and sit down," Brady said. "You know a few people. Dave, Frankie... This is my sister, Kate. Maybe you'd be better introducing yourself."

Ash had stood up. "He can do that in a minute, Dad." She bent down and picked up the canvas Carl had given her. Held it out to him. "Happy birthday, Dad. This is from all of us. For the new house."

Brady stood up. Took the picture. Folded back the cover. Saw Carl's distinctive pencil style. Shades of grey, the sea merging into the sky. Whitby Harbour. The pier beyond it curving out into the sea. An exhausted fishing boat coming home. The town's lights flickering across the water as night closed in.

"Carl," he said. "This is... I don't know what to say. It's stunning. It's – "

Brady's phone rang. He glanced across the table. Smiled at Dan Keillor's girlfriend. "I've already warned him, Zoe. You're never off duty."

He looked down at the display. Knew it was a call he had to take.

Marko Vrukić.

"Ash," he said. "I'm sorry, sweetheart. This is a call I need to take. Two minutes. No more."

He stood up, walked away from the table. "Michael Brady."

"Mihailo." The accent was just the same on his mobile. Southern Europe mixed with 70s American TV series. "You know who this is."

"I do, Marko. But I'm in a restaurant. I can hardly hear you. Give me one minute."

Brady walked down the stairs. Past the queue and onto Pier Road. Stood with his back to the old fish filleting sheds.

"Sorry, Marko. I was in a restaurant. I'm outside now."

Where is he? In the lounge where he met me? No. In a study. A private room. One even Jelena isn't allowed in...

"So, Mihailo. You have found the killer. The battle is won. You are celebrating with your men. Gina is at peace. Maria is safe. And she has found a family. Two families..."

Yes. And one day she might find one of them a lot more exciting than the other. I hope you don't tempt her Marko. I hope she doesn't break Ian's heart...

"...And I am a man of my word. So you would like to know who killed your wife. Who gave the order. Two days, I think. Maybe three."

Brady had been listening to Vrukić . Hadn't realised he'd been walking down Pier Road. Found himself outside Dave's kiosk. Looked across the road. Saw the steps. Saw Jimmy Gorse throw Carl to one side. Saw the knife flash down as Dave charged. Saw Dave lying on the steps. Felt the warmth of the blood on his hand.

He looked back up the road. There was still a queue outside the Magpie Café.

"Mihailo? Are you there? Three days, I think. At the most."

"Yes, Marko, I'm here."

"So we made a deal. You found Gina's killer..."

Brady was back on Saltburn Pier. Talking to Willie Carr.

'Touch and go whether I see Christmas. But I'm lucky. Someone loves me. I can still walk to the end of the pier. Hurts like fuck but I can still manage it. There's plenty worse off than me.'

Standing in Bill's bedroom, his brother-in-law propped up in bed.

'What happened to you. Grace. It was shit. But it wasn't as shit as this. Don't let it define the rest of your life, Mike.'

"Mihailo? Are you still there? Fuck. This country! We have better phone reception than this in the Balkans."

"Sorry, Marko. I'm still here. I was thinking."

"Good. You have found Gina's killer for me. I will find who ordered your wife's death. I will phone you in three days. No more. Then Mihailo... Then you can take your revenge."

Brady saw his daughter take a step towards him. Saw her raise her hand. Felt her finger on his lips. Heard her voice.

'I hope so. But not tonight, Dad. Look forward, not back.'

"No, Marko," Michael Brady said. "I don't want the name. One day maybe. But not today. Not in three days."

"But you asked me for the name. We have a deal."

"I did, Marko. And I respect your offer. I know you can deliver what I want. What I thought I wanted. But – "

Ash. Kate and the girls. Dan Keillor. And Frankie. I'm

responsible for them. I care about them. I want the name, Marko. But tell me who killed my wife and... I have to go after them.

Vrukić finished the sentence for him. "You have to take action. The name I give you... It cannot sit quietly on your desk."

"No, it can't."

Brady could almost hear Vrukić making the calculation. "I understand. But supposing I already know the name, Mihailo?"

"Then – as a man of honour – I would ask you not to tell me."

Vrukić chuckled. "A good answer, Mihailo. So we are in each other's debt it would seem."

Brady nodded. "So it would seem."

"We will speak again, Mihailo. Enjoy the celebration with your men."

Brady laughed. "Not quite 'my men,' Marko. But yes, I will."

He turned and walked back up Pier Road. Looked to his left across the harbour. Saw the house he'd bought. Remembered he needed to phone the joiner.

He said 'excuse me' to the people still queuing for the Magpie Café. Walked up the stairs.

To Kate and Maddie and Lucy. To Carl and Dave. To Dan Keillor and Frankie. To Ash.

Detective Chief Inspector Michael Brady smiled to himself.

And went back to his birthday party.

REVIEWS & FUTURE WRITING PLANS

Thank you for reading *The River Runs Deep*. I really hope you enjoyed it.

If you did, could I ask a favour? Would you please review the book on Amazon? The **link to do that is here:** https://www.amazon.co.uk/dp/B08ND3W4MD

Reviews are important to me for three reasons. First of all, good reviews help to sell the book. Secondly, there are some review and book promotion sites that will only look at a book if it has a certain number of reviews and/or a certain ratio of 5* reviews. And lastly, reviews are feedback. Some writers ignore their reviews: I don't.

So I'd appreciate you taking five minutes to leave a review and thank you in advance to anyone who does so.

What next?

This is the second book in the *Michael Brady* series. The third book – also available from Amazon – will be published in the early summer of 2021.

But before that I'm going to publish a Michael Brady novella – the story of Sarah Cooke, taking you back to his very first case as a detective. The book will be available by the end of March.

If you'd like to receive regular updates on my writing – and previews of these books – you can join my mailing list by clicking this link: https://www.subscribepage.com/markrichards

SALT IN THE WOUNDS

His best friend has been murdered, his daughter's in danger.

There's only one answer. Going back to his old life.

The one that cost him his wife...

'Salt in the Wounds' is the first book in the Michael Brady series. It's available on Amazon.

"Fabulous! Had me gripped from the start. Reminds me of Mark Billingham's detective, Tom Thorne."

"Loved the book from the first page. Straight into the story, very well-written. Roll on Brady 2."

"Loved everything about this book. A gripping plot with unexpected twists and turns. Believable characters that you feel you really know by the last page. I could smell the sea air in Whitby..."

ABOUT ME

Way back in 2003 I was at a meeting of Scarborough Writers' Circle.

At the time I had a business in financial services – clients, suits, stripy ties. But I also had a small voice inside me: 'Let me out,' it said. 'I'm a writer.'

The speaker that night was the editor of the local paper. "We'd quite like a humorous weekly column if anyone thinks they can write one," he said. That was the start of my writing career – a light-hearted look at family life from a dad's point of view, which ultimately became the 'Best Dad' books you can find on my Amazon page.

But writing was very much second-best to the day job, until – in 2009 – my brother died of cancer.

When Mike died it was one of those pivotal moments in life: a time when you realise that you either pursue your dream – do what you've always wanted to do – or you forget about it for good.

So I sold my business, sent my stripy ties to the charity shop and started writing. I've worked full-time as a writer since then. Starting from scratch I built a business as a freelance copywriter and content writer – something I still do for a small number of clients.

Then, in the spring of 2016, I had the latest in a long line of mid-life crises and invited Alex – my youngest son – to come for a walk with me. I wanted to do a physical challenge before I was too old for a physical challenge and – despite never having done any serious walking in my life – asked Alex if he wanted to walk 90 miles on the Pennine Way, one of the UK's toughest national trails.

The walk took us five days, and the result was *Father, Son and the Pennine Way* – the challenges we faced, the experiences we shared and what we learned about ourselves and each other. The book is also, sadly, the sorry tale of how I became the first person to walk a mile of the Pennine Way in his underpants...

Pennine Way now has more than 300 reviews on Amazon, the overwhelming majority of them at 5*. 'Brilliantly written, insightful, brutally honest and laugh out loud funny.' And my personal favourite among the reviews: 'I was laughing so hard at this book my husband went off to sleep in the spare room.'

The book is available on your Kindle for £2.99, or in paperback for £7.99. Here's the link to the Kindle version.

Father, Son and the Pennine Way was followed by *Father Son and Return to the Pennine Way* – picking up where the first book left off – in 2018 and *Father, Son and the Kerry Way* – 125 miles around South West Ireland – in 2019.

You can find all my books on my website, or on my Amazon author page.

JOIN THE TEAM

If you enjoy my writing, and you would like to be more actively involved, I have a Reader Group on Facebook. The people in this group act as my advance readers, giving me feedback and constructive criticism. Sometimes you need someone to say, 'that part of the story just doesn't work' or 'you need to develop that character more.'

In return for helping, the members of the group receive previews, updates and exclusive content and the chance to take part in the occasional competitions I run for them. If you'd like to help in that way, then look for 'Mark Richards: Writer' on Facebook and ask to join.

ACKNOWLEDGMENTS

As always, a number of people helped me with the book. Let me start by thanking the members of my Reader Group for their support, encouragement and constructive criticism. I'd especially like to thank those members of the Group who proof-read the book for me: I cannot tell you how much I appreciated your diligence and attention to detail.

I'd also like to thank the serving and retired police officers who helped with the book. The small details they corrected has, hopefully, produced a better book.

As usual I've worked with my regular team of professionals: Kevin Partner who converted my Word file into something that works on your Kindle, and Linnhe Harrison for her help with the website and the publicity. And my long-time collaborator, Paul Wilson, for a thoroughly wet, thoroughly enjoyable morning spent on the banks of the River Esk.

I'd also like to thank Grosmont Estates for allowing me access to the river bank I used as the murder scene.

But the main thanks must go to my wife, for her unfailing patience when I interrupted her to – yet again – discuss the plot. I'd like to claim the credit but I have to confess that most of the best plot lines were hers...

Mark Richards
January 2021